Kate Robb

KateRobbWrites.com

BY KATE ROBB

Kitty St. Clair's Last Dance
This Spells Love
Prime Time Romance

Kitty St. Clair's Last Dance

Kitty St. Clair's Last Dance

A Novel

Kate Robb

The Dial Press
New York

The Dial Press
An imprint of Random House
A division of Penguin Random House LLC
1745 Broadway, New York, NY 10019
randomhousebooks.com
penguinrandomhouse.com

A Dial Press Trade Paperback Original

Copyright © 2025 by Kate Robb
Dial Delights Extras copyright © 2025 by Penguin Random House LLC
Excerpt from *A Solar Eclipse of the Heart* by Kate Robb copyright © 2025 by Kate Robb

Penguin Random House values and supports copyright. Copyright fuels creativity, encourages diverse voices, promotes free speech, and creates a vibrant culture. Thank you for buying an authorized edition of this book and for complying with copyright laws by not reproducing, scanning, or distributing any part of it in any form without permission. You are supporting writers and allowing Penguin Random House to continue to publish books for every reader. Please note that no part of this book may be used or reproduced in any manner for the purpose of training artificial intelligence technologies or systems.

THE DIAL PRESS is a registered trademark and the colophon is a trademark of Penguin Random House LLC.
DIAL DELIGHTS and colophon are trademarks of Penguin Random House LLC.

This book contains an excerpt from the forthcoming book *A Solar Eclipse of the Heart* by Kate Robb. This excerpt has been set for this edition only and may not reflect the final content of the forthcoming edition.

ISBN 978-0-593-73412-4
Ebook ISBN 978-0-593-73413-1

Printed in the United States of America on acid-free paper

1st Printing

BOOK TEAM: Production editor: Cindy Berman • Managing editor: Rebecca Berlant • Production manager: Meghan O'Leary • Copy editor: Laura Dragonette

Book design by Erich Hobbing

The authorized representative in the EU for product safety and compliance is Penguin Random House Ireland, Morrison Chambers, 32 Nassau Street, Dublin D02 YH68, Ireland, https://eu-contact.penguin.ie.

For You

Kitty St. Clair's Last Dance

Prologue

"All right, babe, you're up."

Zoe hands me the empty bottle of Jose Cuervo with an exaggerated wink and giggles, making me suspect she's primarily responsible for its empty state.

I'm trapped. Our little party within a party has commandeered the entire dock to the left of the *Sharma*'s massive boathouse with our game. Now I'm wedged between Zoe's cousin with the perpetually sweaty hands and some summer tourist Zoe picked up at the beach today—both of whom you'd describe using words like *beefy* and *broad*. My back is to the lake, and although I have no desire to take a midnight dip, the idea is preferable to the tequila bottle in my hands and the rules that go along with it.

"I should probably go." I attempt to stand so I can head back to my tiny apartment above the pizzeria and, more important, my bed, but Beefy Tourist grabs my wrist and tugs me back down to the circle.

"Can't leave before it's your turn." He shoots me a grin that I'm certain he thinks is sexy. And although I'm three drinks past my usual one-drink limit, there is no doubt that I'll remember this entire exchange in the morning. He, however, either will not recognize me or will not acknowledge that he does when he stumbles into the coffee shop tomorrow at noon to order his double Americano.

"Come on, Jules." Zoe sticks her lower lip out in a pout. "One little spin. Live a little. It's just for fun."

I don't see how playing spin the bottle is fun. We're not in middle school. More important, we shouldn't be at this party. It wasn't like they were checking invites at the door, but we're townies, and there's an unspoken rule that we don't mix with the summers unless we're fucking with them. But I promised Zoe I would "be chill" tonight—my birthday gift to my best friend. However, kissing random summer boys is where I draw the line. If they won't let me off the hook, I'll have to get creative.

"Okay, fine. One spin." I place the bottle down in the center of the circle and give it a hard flick with as much strength as my five-foot-three frame can muster. The bottle skitters across the deck, but instead of falling over the edge toward Lake Huron below as planned, it hits Beefy Tourist's beer, spraying him as it ricochets back toward the boathouse. It rolls to a stop next to a guy sitting in a Muskoka chair, half-hidden in the shadows of the boathouse's roof. He picks up the bottle and tosses it into the air, where it flips at least twice before he catches it with the skill of someone who has clearly handled a few liquor bottles in his life.

He's got that quintessential summer resident look. Faded blue swim trunks with a wrinkled blue linen shirt rolled to the elbows. Expensive but not overt. I'd bet my meager barista paycheck he's a Toronto boy with money who, every Friday to Sunday, June through to the end of August, comes up here to *get away from it all*.

It isn't until he looks over and his brown eyes meet mine that I realize I'm staring. He smiles and holds up the thankfully still intact bottle as if to ask if it's mine.

I want to blame the tequila working its way through my bloodstream for my inability to look away, but I know I'd only be lying to myself.

He's so beautiful it's unfair.

Dark wavy hair that hits below his ears, day-three stubble on his cheeks, and skin like mine—a usually pale complexion brought to a deep bronze by many long days out under the summer sun.

I'd say I'm smitten if I were naive enough to believe a girl could fall in love with a single look. Or if I weren't the type of girl who would be perfectly fine if she never fell in love at all.

"Nicely done, Jules." At some point during my man ogling, Zoe made her way into Beefy Tourist's lap, and she's now poking me in the ribs with her bony elbow. "Go get 'em, tiger."

I'm grateful a wild dance party is happening on the other side of the dock because Zoe does not know how to use her indoor voice.

I make a second attempt to escape, and this time, when I stand, no one stops me. I move toward the stairs, sliding the screen of my phone open so I can use the flashlight to help me up the darkened path to the cottage, but before I reach them, someone calls out.

"You forgot something."

I turn at the sound of the strange male voice. Beautiful Summer Boy stares back at me, the empty tequila bottle dangling between his outstretched fingertips.

"Oh. That's not mine." I turn to leave again, but he gets to his feet, moving toward me.

"So you throw random bottles of tequila at strangers?"

My back straightens, an instinctual reaction as I steel myself for a fight until I realize he's smiling at me, full-blown dimple and all.

"I didn't throw it. I spun it. Hitting you was an accident." I grab for the bottle, but he lifts it high out of my reach.

"Why were you spinning it?"

I track my brain for any excuse less embarrassing than the truth and come back with nothing other than "A very stupid game."

He turns toward my friends, who have, in my absence, located a replacement bottle. Beefy Tourist appears to be up. He takes his spin and smiles when his bottle stops facing a girl I've known since the seventh grade. We watch as she climbs into his lap, and their tongues intertwine.

"Spin the bottle?" he asks like a question, and I don't bother denying what is clearly unfolding in front of us.

"Immature, I know. But it's my friend Zoe's birthday month—"

"Month?"

I resist the urge to roll my eyes. "It makes much more sense when you know her. She's persuasive, which is why I agreed to play in the first place."

"So this was your turn." He stares down at the bottle, which is now clasped between both our hands, and then raises a brow as if he's only now noticed we're both holding it.

"You're welcome to kiss me at any time."

I feel heat rush to my cheeks. "I'm not kissing you."

My stranger laughs.

"The look you're giving me says you think the experience would be painful. It's not, by the way. Or at least no one has ever complained."

"I don't think that's the accolade you think it is."

He shrugs. "Fair point. But I'm pretty confident it's a pleasant experience. There's a very easy way to find the answer." He flips the bottle in the air and catches it.

"I'm not kissing you," I say a second time.

His smile falls for the briefest of seconds before it flashes again like it never left in the first place. "Well, that's too bad. I was looking forward to being kissed. My all-boys school didn't lend itself to too many spin-the-bottle games. It's a rite of passage I missed out on. But if you're not into kissing me, can I offer an alternative?"

I should say *no* and *good night* and then leave because nothing good can come from listening to his suggestion. Still, I find myself nodding.

"What if I kissed you?" he offers.

I should have bolted when I had the chance. I could be halfway down the driveway by now, thinking about the crisp cotton sheets of my bed, not the way his brown eyes look almost black, as if they're tempting me. Luring me toward jagged rocks and what could only be an inevitable disaster if I give in to the very Zoe-like voice in my head telling me to live for once in my life.

"That's looking to me like a yes." His voice is low, a hint above a whisper. "I'm going for it."

He waits until I whisper back exactly what he wants to hear. "Yes." Then his hands are cupping my chin, and his lips are upon mine, feather-soft like he's testing the waters. His tongue parts my lips, and if I wasn't kissing him back before, I most definitely am now.

My heel pops, and my head swirls. All the things that were never supposed to happen to a girl with my common sense are happening. It's so perfect it almost feels clichéd and yet—

"Yeah! Ju-Ju! You get that dick," a voice that sounds awfully like the actual Zoe calls out. It's the cold bucket of water I needed to wake me from whatever trance this siren of a man has put me under. *Get ahold of yourself, Jules.*

"I've got to go." I step out of his embrace and back to reality.

"Already?"

He smells like summer. Campfire and pine with a hint of Canadian rye on his breath. A seductive cocktail if you're not careful. But summer here at the lake is fleeting. Just when it's lulled you in with its heat and endless nights—it's gone. Leaving you cold and bitter. I've lived here most of my life. I have watched, over and over, what happens when you fall for a summer boy.

"I've got to go," I repeat, but I don't actually move.

I do. I need to go. All of my instincts are telling me to cut and run. I shouldn't be here at this party. I shouldn't like the way his eyes never leave my face.

He takes a step closer. "But what if you hung out for a bit instead?" He nods back toward his chair and the one next to it. "I'd like to get to know the girl behind that kiss."

My heart flutters and I simultaneously snort. "You're pretty charming for a guy drinking alone in the dark."

He inclines his head up toward the cottage. "My younger brother is friends with Megh Sharma. I tagged along at the last minute. Forgot most of them are dicks."

Maybe it's the fact that he's crashing this party, too. A little on the outside. Someone else who doesn't quite fit. Although it goes against my better judgment, I follow him back to the chairs.

He stops just short of the closest one and extends his arm. "I'm Reeve, by the way."

I laugh as I take his hand, less at the sudden formality and more at the absurd order of tonight's events. "Jules."

He gestures at the two Muskoka chairs and waits. When I'm settled, he sits, then reaches over and pulls my chair closer so our armrests touch before leaning over and grabbing two beers from a cooler hidden by the shadows of the boathouse roof.

"It's not tequila," he says as he hands one to me.

"That is a good thing. I'm much more of a beer girl, anyway."

As I crack the tab, I hear a loud scream from the other end of the dock. We both turn in time to see Beefy Tourist scoop Zoe onto his shoulder and carry her toward the stairs.

"Is she okay?" Reeve asks, and I like that he looks ready to take on a stranger who easily has fifty pounds on him. But before I can tell him she's just fine, Zoe slaps the guy on the ass with a "Let's go, big boy," then lifts her head long enough to give me a wink and a "Don't wait up" before dropping her head back down.

"I'm guessing that's Zoe?" Reeve looks at me with that same expression most people have after encountering Zoe for the first time.

"The one and only."

He leans back in his seat. "You two been friends long?"

I nod at that understatement. "Since first grade."

"You're both from West Lake?"

I take a sip of beer. "Born and, for the most part, raised."

Reeve shifts his weight in his chair so that he's facing me. "For the most part?"

I hesitate, trying to figure out the best way to answer. "My mom and I moved away a few times but always managed to end up back here. The women in my family tend not to stray too far."

Reeve nods along. "What about you? Ever think of straying?"

I think about his comment. A month ago I would have immediately answered with a wholehearted *never,* but then I remember the application half filled out on my computer.

"I haven't really thought about it," I lie. "What about you? You're obviously from Toronto." I nudge his leather deck shoe with my sneaker.

He stretches out his leg and tries to look offended, but it lasts only a moment before he grins.

"Born and, for the most part, raised. I just finished grad school at Queens."

"Finance?" I guess, sensing the pattern.

He shakes his head. "Fine arts management, actually."

I don't expect that answer. It throws me off so much that I wait for him to grin and follow up with the punch line.

But he doesn't.

"I'm back in Toronto now, though," he continues. "I'm trying to get a job in a gallery, but there aren't a whole lot of entry-level openings at the moment. I'm probably going to volunteer at the film festival in the fall—hopefully that will help me get my foot in the door there, or I'll have to take an unpaid internship or two."

"Wow . . ." The word slips out as I realize how inaccurately I had him pegged.

He, however, shrugs it off.

"Yeah, my dad gave me that same look when I told him my plan, but I figure a few months on a tight budget will be worth it. I can't imagine myself being happy if I'm not doing something I love every day."

I know exactly how he feels. It's the same reason I spent every weekend last summer in MCAT prep courses, the same reason I took a night class to retake Statistics & Epidemiology so I could up my grade from an A– to an A.

"I'm applying to med school for next fall," I say, blurting out the secret I've kept from everyone. "At the University of Toronto."

His brows shoot up, but I get the impression it's more out of interest than surprise. "U of T? Really?"

I nod. "There are a lot of folks up here who can't even get a family doctor right now. . . . I'm trying not to get my hopes up, but my grades are good. I wrote a pretty decent MCAT, so I guess I'll see."

He holds my gaze for a beat and then two. Finally, he tips his beer can toward mine. "Maybe next year we do this in Toronto."

I almost laugh at the absurdity of that thought as I clink our cans together. "Maybe . . ."

We talk for three more hours—about school and art, his overachieving brothers and my underachieving mother, and the best place to get late-night Chinese on Spadina (Swatow) or butter tarts in West Lake (Lou's Groovy Grill). He tells me all the things I will love about living in Toronto. And he doesn't say *if*, but *when*.

Like med school is going to happen.

And I start to picture myself walking the campus and attending classes, admitting out loud this future I want so badly.

It isn't until the lonely wail of a loon cuts across the water that I realize the party is long over. We're completely alone and likely have been for some time.

He stands, groaning as he stretches the stiffness from his legs. He holds his hand out and helps me to my feet. "It's pretty late. We should probably head up."

My phone screen puts it at close to four. The pitch-black is so dark that even with our cell phones lighting the path, I still stumble and trip over tree roots.

He doesn't let go of my hand when we reach the lawn, lit up by the lights of the cottage, and sidestep the sleeping bodies curled up next to the plastic swimming pool filled with sticky orange liquid and a hundred drunk mosquitoes. He pauses at the side door, the porch light illuminating the tips of his long eyelashes as he steps toward me and leans in.

"I'm going to kiss you again." He brings his fingertips to my hip and waits. "My earlier effort was pretty solid, but I think I can do better."

I don't actually speak. But I think I nod because he slides his hand from my hip to just under my ribs, and I melt into him. His lips meet mine a second time—and yes, he was right. So much better.

As we separate to catch our breath, my eyes drift toward the driveway that leads to the road that will take me to town and then home. His gaze follows my path, and he clears his throat.

"You *could* come inside with me." He doesn't ask it like a question this time.

"And you'll be the perfect gentleman?" I counter, laughing off the flutters in my chest.

"No." He shakes his head; his fingers twist the hem of my shirt to tug me closer. "I have no intention of being that at all."

I awaken a few hours later on a twin-sized bottom bunk.

My naked body is engulfed in his big spoon.

The Ninja Turtles on the bedsheets seem to smirk at me, having witnessed how he touched and explored every inch of my body and how I let go, giving in to the need to be wanted so badly.

I gently lift his hand from my hip and wiggle out, using the light from the window to find my clothes puddled on the floor—grateful I'm not expected at the cafe this morning until eight.

He stirs as I slip my tank top over my head. "You're leaving?" He sleepily brushes a lock from his forehead, watching me dress.

"I have to head to work."

He sits up, realizing only at the last minute that he's on a bottom bunk, ducking just in time to avoid smacking his head. "When are you done?"

"Four," I answer, then remember I have the interview for the job at the Sunnyvale Retirement Home tonight. "Actually, six."

He nods, and for a moment, I worry that I read this all wrong and he just wants me gone. But then he leans over and picks up his phone from under the bed.

"I'll call you later." He holds it out to me. "I'm heading back to Southampton this afternoon, but it's not too far. . . ." He doesn't finish his thought.

Maybe because I'm already taking his phone and hastily plugging in my number, panicking a little that I won't have time for a shower before my shift and will have to show up for my interview later still looking like I spent the night being ravaged.

I toss his phone back to him. He looks down at the screen and smiles.

"I'll call you," he says again.

"Sure," I say, trying not to show just how much I want him to.

I close the door behind me.

As much as it is not in my nature, I find myself wondering if last night might have been the start of something really good.

I hate how wrong I am.

Chapter 1

Two years later

KITTY ST. CLAIR's casket is from Costco.

She bought it online six months ago when Dr. Shahid sat her down to tell her her lung cancer had progressed to stage IV, and Kitty decided she was done fighting it.

"Why waste good money on a box," she had said to Zoe and me as we wheeled her from her spacious one-bedroom suite down to the retirement home's dining hall later that night. "I'll be long gone by the time you bury me in the thing." She raised her eyes to the ceiling. "I'll be up there, drinking Veuve and dancing on the tables. Looking down at the two of you, every so often, to send you signs to live a little."

I have always been undecided about the existence of an afterlife. But at that moment, I had no doubts that if there were one, Kitty St. Clair would be there kicking off the after-party.

And that is the image I have in my head as we stand in the Sunnyvale Retirement Home's parking lot, watching Father Herold make the sign of the cross as Kitty's casket is loaded into the back of the elegant black hearse that will take her body south to Toronto.

The funeral plans Kitty laid out during the weeks following her prognosis were, for the most part, pragmatic and sensible—a small service with her three children back in Toronto, followed by a burial next to her late husband, Beau, in the Mount Pleasant Cemetery. A fitting end to the sophisticated and refined version of Kitty, who had her curls set at the beauty parlor every Tuesday and was never caught without her Chanel lipstick or pearls. But she left some unconventional instructions for West Lake, the town where she spent both her formative years and her final days.

Instructions that paid homage to the other side of Kitty: the side with a wild streak. We were not to mourn her, but instead were to gather at the Legion for a celebration to honor all ninety-four years of her extraordinary life.

"I've had my fill, girls," she had said. "Shed a tear or two if you must, but then send this old doll out with one they'll talk about for years, okay? I always loved a good party."

What Kitty St. Clair wants, Kitty St. Clair gets.

When I arrive, the party is already in full swing. I push open the doors to the Royal Canadian Legion Branch 587 and am hit with the familiar smells of sour beer and fish fry.

The Legion hall looks the same as I imagine it did seventy-five years ago when it made 34 St. Mary Street its official branch headquarters. The interior boasts white wainscoting, green paisley wallpaper, and an industrial carpet whose hideous shade of maroon is excellent at hiding spilled beer and the occasional hot wing stain. There's a dartboard on the far wall next to the broken pinball machine. The wallpaper around it is covered in tiny pinpricks from too many shots gone wild—most of them by the Senior Ladies League that coincides with the Tuesday night sixteen-dollar pitcher special.

The bar itself is simple oak and stretches the length of the entire back wall. Above it, smack in the center, is a taxidermied buck with glossy black eyes that give the illusion that they follow you as you move about the room. Legend has it that Bill Withers bought it at a garage sale down in Grand Bend sometime in the eighties, then lost it in a poker game to Donny, the bartender, along with his prized Ski-Doo.

The Legion is the hub of West Lake.

Half of the crowd tonight would be gathered here whether it was Kitty's unofficial funeral or just a regular old Wednesday.

Zoe and I have been coming here to drink since we were sixteen. Donny is her uncle, and although he was well aware that we were underage, he had a far stronger belief that the government should have zero say in who should or shouldn't be able to enjoy a cold beer.

I'm almost done with my PBR when Zoe slides into the empty barstool beside me and signals to Donny with a sharp whistle, holding up two fingers when he looks over.

"I have spotted your future husband." She clinks her glass with mine just as Donny sets two new beers in front of us.

"If you are trying to set me up with your cousin Clive again, I—"

"Clive is a catch in some circles," she interrupts. "But this guy isn't local. He came in about twenty minutes ago. The Anderson twins cornered him immediately, and I swear I keep catching him giving you come hither glances, and I really think you should."

"Should what?" I twist around in my seat to see the guy in question, but the crowd is too thick.

"Hither on over there," Zoe continues, walking her fingers along the bar. "Fall in love or at least get laid."

I snort. "We're at a funeral, Zo."

She leans back in her seat, holding up her hands. "Technically, it's not a funeral, and you and I both know the odds of a hot piece of ass stumbling in here between now and May are virtually zero.

I have snagged the only decent man in a fifty-kilometer radius, which means unless you change your tune about Clive, this is probably your only opportunity for hot sex until summer. I am just looking out for you."

She does make a point. It's almost October, which means the tourists and summer residents are long gone, except for the handful trying to stretch the season to Thanksgiving. Everyone who's left is either not worth doing or has been done back in high school.

"Listen," Zoe says, tucking a stray strand of hair behind my ear, then smoothing my right eyebrow with her thumb. "He's dodged the twins, and now he's coming this way." She glances at something over my shoulder. "Look like you're interested in tennis. I feel like that's probably his type."

"Jules?"

I don't expect the deep voice behind me.

The way it reverberates inside me like a plucked guitar string.

Or the way my body reacts. The blood whooshing from my head and dropping straight to my feet, leaving me woozy and unsure if I'm about to swoon or throw up as I turn, eerily slow—as if I know exactly what will happen.

"Hey," he says. "I thought that was you."

He looks the same. The grin. The eyes. His mathematically symmetrical features that instantly remind you that life is unfair.

Oh shit.

"Reeve?"

"Reeve, huh?" Zoe drags a finger down the seam of his perfectly pressed white dress shirt. "Yes, you *are* a Reeve." She winks at him before turning to me. "Who is this guy? And why do you know him and I don't?"

Her question is valid. In the Venn diagram of our lives, my social circle and Zoe's overlap completely. We do the same things.

We go to the same places. There are no secrets between us simply because there's nothing to keep.

Except for Reeve. I never told her about our night together.

At the time, I told myself it was because it meant nothing to me. But deep down, I know the opposite is true.

I made a mistake that night.

I cracked open the box of unspoken dreams I kept hidden in a corner of my heart. I let him see. And when he responded with unabashed optimism, I let myself think they were possible.

Then I made the bigger mistake of letting myself hope—and hope left in the wrong hands can get you hurt.

"He was at a party a few summers ago," I explain to Zoe. "You were birthday-drunk and making out with that guy who always kitesurfs. The one with the man bun."

Zoe shakes her head as if she doesn't recall any of it. "I mean, that sounds like me." She hitches her thumb at Reeve. "So this one. Good egg or rotten?"

I give a single, sharp turn of my head. Zoe—who once cheated on an entire multiple choice calculus exam by reading my facial expressions—interprets it perfectly.

"Too bad. I guess you're not having hot sex tonight, huh?"

I roll my eyes as Reeve's go wide. "Wait. Do I get to vote on this?"

"No," Zoe and I say in unison.

My mind quickly rewinds, realizing we've skipped over the most obvious question. "What are you doing here?" I ask him.

Reeve looks around the room. "In West Lake? Or here tonight?"

"Both," I answer, unsure which one I meant in the first place.

"I'm here on business," he answers. "And I guess I'm also *here* on business. What are *you* doing here?"

He's being vague. And I'm dwelling on that fact. So much so that I completely ignore his question.

"Uh . . . we live here." Zoe jumps in on my behalf. "Which means we practically live *here*." She picks up what I am pretty sure is Reeve's beer and starts to drink.

"Right . . ." Reeve nods, also watching Zoe. "Sorry. I knew that. I just figured you'd be in first year by now, so I assumed you'd be down in—"

I follow his train of thought a moment too late. I lied earlier.

I've kept two secrets from Zoe.

My night with Reeve and the application for medical school that's still sitting unsent in a somewhat forgotten file folder deep within my laptop's hard drive.

I think I mean to stop him. Clasp my hand around his mouth and halt the clarification about to make its exit.

But I forget that I'm holding a beer.

Or that thought comes a fraction too late.

Right as the amber liquid sloshes from my glass to the spot just below his belly button.

"Shit."

I regret it the moment I do it.

Reeve may be the asshole who ghosted me two years ago, but he is wearing really nice pants.

He stares down at his crotch, now soaked with Pabst Blue Ribbon.

"Wow. Okay." He shakes his left leg as wetness seeps down his pants to the floor, where it's absorbed into the carpet, becoming yet another discernible stain.

Zoe looks from his crotch back up to me and smiles wickedly. "Spicy move, Ju-Ju."

"I'm sorry," I blurt out, genuinely mortified that I've likely ruined his expensive suit.

He looks up. "It's fine." His tone is light, but the confused crinkle between his eyebrows deepens, making me wonder if he thinks I did it on purpose.

I'm not entirely sure I didn't.

"I think I'd better go," he says. "Maybe I'll see you around?"

He leaves the question as rhetorical and disappears back into the crowd, heading for the coatrack. Zoe slides back into her seat at the bar when he is out of earshot. "Spill your beans. I require immediate details."

"It's nothing," I answer automatically, knowing in my heart that it isn't. "We made out at a party a couple of years ago. It just surprised me to see him, that's all."

Zoe narrows her eyes but doesn't say a word.

"Why are you giving me that look?" I finally tear my gaze from the crowd to look at her.

She feigns innocence, holding up her hands.

"I am not giving you any look. I have a naturally curious face, but I will remind you that she did say she would send us a sign."

I'm confused.

"What are you talking about now?"

Instead of answering, Zoe looks up.

"You know me, not so much into the hippie voodoo shit, but you have to admit. A scorned ex-lover giving you bedroom eyes at her wake. It's the kind of drama she'd love."

I picture Kitty again. The Veuve spills from her glass as she leans over the edge of a cloud to wink.

What Kitty St. Clair wants, Kitty St. Clair gets.

Chapter 2

I'M DRUNKER THAN I planned to be when I leave the Legion just after nine. Especially since I have a double shift ahead of me in the morning, and a resident passing away is unfortunately not a viable excuse to come in hungover.

The street outside is dark and quiet. There are shallow puddles of water pooled in the cracks between the pavement and in spots where the sidewalk gradient is uneven. As I jump a sizable one, I hear a splash behind me, and the hairs on my arms raise with the realization that I am not alone.

I whip around, feet braced in a fight stance, even though I've never actually done so much as throw a punch. I watch as an older man steps carefully around a puddle on the sidewalk, the rubber of his galoshes squeaking as he walks.

He is my height. His frame is just as slight. My muscles relax a little with the realization that his apparent age of sixty or so means I could both outrun him or hold my own if it came down to it.

"Julia DeMarco?" He calls out my legal name, and whatever relief I had for that brief moment vanishes.

His double-breasted suit. My full name. The relentless pursuit, despite the late hour. Each gives off a succession of red flags that make me wish he were an attacker after all.

"Not the girl you're looking for," I lie.

But the man glances back toward the Legion. "The bartender told me you were her. He seemed quite sure."

Jesus, Donny.

I know he was trying to help. Donny's got a golden-retriever, help-thy-neighbor kind of heart, but this is the last thing I need tonight.

I've been dodging guys like this on the phone for two years now. I get a few months of reprieve, during which I think everything is resolved. Then there's another voicemail notification from another scripted call center agent informing me that my credit card has been sent to collections and that legal action will be taken if I don't pay it off immediately.

I don't know if my mother stared down at my newborn face at the hospital and thought, *You will be an untapped source of financial credit for me one day, so along with my emotional baggage, I will give you my name.* Either way, it has worked out much better for her than for me.

I have tried threatening to go to the police. But my mother has every excuse in the book.

You need to get in early with these types of business opportunities.
Just give it a few weeks, we'll be making six figures in no time.
Don't you want financial freedom?

Her schemes never seem to pan out. It was embarrassing enough growing up with a mother who friended all of my classmates' mothers only to "hey gurl" them a few days later about an essential oil party or an "opportunity to change their life." But since her plans started to involve me and my credit score, I've begun to reevaluate things.

I haven't gotten to the point that I'm okay with throwing the single mother who raised me in jail. But a creditor tracking me down on a dark road in the middle of the night might just be my breaking point.

"I've been trying to speak with you all day," the man says. "I'm Kitty St. Clair's attorney and executor. My name is Niles James."

He takes a step back as if he's hoping to put me at ease, and I wonder if he's suddenly following my train of thought about approaching strange women in the dark. His identification as Kitty's lawyer alleviates some worry, but Zoe has always subscribed to the superstition that you should never trust a man with two first names, and for the first time in my life, I wonder if she might have a point.

"What do you want?" It's a harsher greeting than I'd return in the light of day, but with seeing Reeve and now this, my internal compass is off, spinning in circles.

"I need to speak with you," he says. "Kitty didn't provide your phone number, and there are matters pertaining to her will that we need to discuss."

"Now?" I look around at the dampened street and wobble a little.

It's clear that Niles notices. "No, not now. This matter is better left till the morning. Can you meet me?" He fishes in his pocket and holds out a white business card. He waits until I make the move to step forward and take it from him.

"I'm staying at the Cranberry Inn in Port Logan. They have a lovely breakfast service. Perhaps we can discuss this over pancakes tomorrow at nine?"

My shift at Sunnyvale starts at nine.

"Can we make it eight and fast?"

"Eight it is," he says.

I step from the sidewalk onto the street, my heel clipping the edge of a puddle, splashing frigid water up the back of my nylons.

"I'm sorry for your loss," he calls after me. "I imagine the two of you must have been close. She talked about you often."

This revelation stops me dead in my tracks. Because although I liked Kitty—everyone did—I wouldn't consider us *close*.

I leave the conversation unfinished on the sidewalk. But when I get home and slip beneath my covers, Niles James's words from earlier worm their way through my brain. *She talked about you often.*

But why? And what did she say?

The answers don't come as I toss and turn, twisting in my sheets, then stare at the ceiling, willing sleep to take over my body.

When it finally does, it plummets me into a dream.

I'm in a long white hall. I can hear Kitty's voice calling my name over and over, but every door I open leads to an empty room. Finally, I find her. She's sitting in a chair next to the window, watching the waves roll in on the beach, with an unusually wistful look on her wrinkled face. She stretches out a hand to me—long bony fingers.

"My darling girl. Come. I want to tell you a story."

I walk toward her. My arm reaches for hers, but just before I reach her, I wake up.

Chapter 3

My car is a 1993 Mercedes E-Class in Safari Beige. I bought her last year from one of my residents at Sunnyvale, Mrs. Hail, who passed her driver's license renewal test at the age of ninety-one only to lose it two weeks later when she reversed through the front door of the Foodland out near Chippewa Beach. She sold it to me for three hundred dollars and a pinky promise to drop her over at Bogeys every Thursday after my shift so she could hit up their karaoke and half-priced wing night.

Zoe named the car Celine after Canadian legend Celine Dion because "it goes on and on" and, like her namesake, it is a classic that only gets better with every passing year.

There's frost on the windshield, which I don't scrape off because I've yet to replace my broken snow brush from last winter, so instead, I blast the heat from inside and crane my neck to see out of the top six inches of unobstructed windshield as I drive down Highway 13 at twenty kilometers over the speed limit. My hair is still wet from my morning shower, which means it will be a frizzy mess of blond waves by the time I get to work, but with Niles James LLP wanting to meet before my shift, sacrifices needed to be made, and an extra fifteen minutes of sleep seemed like the right one at seven o'clock this morning. Now, as I pull into the Cranberry Inn

Bed and Breakfast's parking lot next to a neatly trimmed hedge and stare at the Inn's large dormer windows and pitched roof covered in pristine white cedar shingles, I give myself a final glance in the rearview mirror and regret that life choice a little.

This place is fancier than I remember.

There was a time when Port Logan was just like West Lake. An affordable getaway for those from southern Ontario who couldn't afford the high prices of Muskoka. But over the years, things changed: a tennis club, then a wine bar. Almost overnight, the kitschy shops selling cheap boogie boards and beach cover-ups with cartoon bikini bodies gave way to gelaterias and cafes with NO SHOES, NO SHIRT, NO SERVICE signs in decorative gold frames. Places like the Cranberry Inn—which brought in culinary-trained chefs from Toronto to sell deconstructed hamburgers none of the locals could afford.

I step out of my car at the exact time a cold blast of easterly wind gusts across the parking lot. Instinctively, I reach to button my beige wool peacoat, but as my fingers graze the tiny nub of thread where the button once attached, I remember that it broke off last week, and I've yet to find the time to replace it. Instead, I pull the coat tightly around my body with my arms, covering the Scooby-Doo scrubs that I threw on this morning because they are always a hit with my residents but that now feel juvenile as I walk up the cobblestone pathway and pass a pair of women my age in matching Lululemon leggings and knee-length black Canada Goose coats.

There's a soft tinkle of bells as I pull open the solid oak door made even heavier by the wind. As I step through the threshold, I'm hit with the smell of cinnamon and the sound of a crackling fire and the feeling of being very deeply out of my element as I am greeted by a middle-aged hostess with an immaculate silver bob and pleated wool pants.

I don't miss how her eyes immediately shoot to the heart-shaped coffee stain over my left boob that never seems to fully come out, no matter how much bleach I use in the laundry.

"Can I help you?" Her tone also seems to ask if I'm in the wrong place.

"Yeah, I'm here to meet a guy?" My sentence comes out as more of a question when I suddenly blank on the lawyer's name. My hands skim over my butt as if searching for the business card I'm 98 percent sure is still in the pocket of the skirt I wore last night, my face pinkening until I spot him in the far corner of the dining room sipping from a dainty floral teacup, reading a copy of *The Globe and Mail*.

"Him." I point at Niles James—his name returning with the sight of his face. "We have a business meeting this morning."

The woman's brow crinkles as she follows the tip of my finger, her mouth twisting in a way that makes me think she doesn't quite buy my story. But then Mr. James looks up mid-sip, sets his cup down gently in its saucer, and smiles at her, giving me a polite *come hither* with his fingers.

"Oh, yes, Mr. James." Her voice immediately softens. "He mentioned he was expecting someone. Very well then." She steps back with no further comment, returning to her perch behind a tall walnut podium as I cross the paisley-printed carpet, pressing my shoulders back in an effort to look like breakfasting at the Cranberry Inn is something I usually do.

"Good morning, Ms. DeMarco." Niles James extends his hand as I approach—an invitation to the empty seat at his table. "Thank you for coming." He pushes a plate of what smells like blueberry scones toward me. "Have you eaten? These are quite lovely. I believe they are from the bakery down the street. I have half a mind to pick up a dozen to take home for my wife later today. She does love a homemade scone."

I bite my tongue and don't tell him that the bakery he's referring to ships in most of their stuff frozen from a commercial bakery two hours away.

I take the scone anyway. It crumbles in my mouth. The overly dry texture is only partially saved by the soured blueberries that burst between my teeth. But it fills the pit in my grumbling stomach like a comforting brick.

We both chew in silence for a few moments, forming mouthfull half smiles every time we accidentally make eye contact, until the chiming of the antique grandfather clock reminds me that these small luxuries are temporary and that I need to slip back into regular life in less than an hour. With a wash of too-hot coffee, I swallow the remainder of my scone down and clear my throat. "Thank you for this." I gesture at my now empty plate. "But I have a shift this morning and can't stay too long. Can you tell me whatever it is Kitty wants me to do?"

Niles takes a long sip of tea, nodding his head as if he's only just remembered the purpose of this breakfast. "You must have misunderstood me last night." Niles takes his napkin, wiping scone crumbs from his face. "She doesn't require you to *do* anything." He pauses, and I notice a single white crumb clinging to the whiskers of his mustache. "That's entirely my fault. It was so late. It's just I had such a hard time tracking you down." He shakes his head. "I'm getting off track." He reaches down and pulls a brown leather briefcase from under the table. He unzips the main compartment, pulls out a black leather folder, and takes a stapled stack of papers from it. "I'm not sure if you're aware, but Kitty's late husband was the heir to a large grocery chain that was sold several years ago. After his passing, the large bulk of his wealth was passed entirely to her. It's a significant estate." Flipping to the third sheet, he runs his index finger down the page, stopping halfway.

On my name.

"Along with her three children and several charitable organizations, she had named you as one of the beneficiaries. Julia DeMarco. See here . . ."

His fingers tap upon the page. The familiar letters ground me as my brain processes his words. *Beneficiary.*

As I was drifting off to sleep in the late hours of last night, I replayed my late-night meeting with this man and tried to dissect the conversation, searching for some rational reason why my name would be noted in Kitty's will.

Kitty was unpredictable. A character, you might say. Zoe and I had joked on more than one occasion that she belonged to another era. Or another place far more glamorous than West Lake. It was her flair for the dramatic.

She'd spout her life lessons to Zoe and me as we'd wheel her to her doctor's appointments—Kitty-isms, Zoe called them. "Your life isn't yours if you care what others think," or "If life hands you lemons, well, then it's time to take a break and have a cup of tea."

I remember a Meatloaf Monday a year ago when she showed up at the dining hall in a floor-length sequined gown. "Hello, my darlings," she called to Zoe and me as we spooned out mounds of mashed potatoes and gravy to her fellow residents, who seemed just as enamored with Kitty as we were.

"Nice 'fit there, Kits," Zoe said as Kitty proceeded to twirl slowly before settling into her seat.

"I felt like being fancy this evening," she said, shrugging off the compliment. "Life is far too short to wear boring clothes."

After that, Mondays became Kitty's personal fashion hour. She'd show up in head-to-toe neon pink or wearing every single bangle or bracelet she owned. There was even a week in the middle of July when she ate an entire meal in a fox-fur coat and hat.

The fashions only ended because she slipped in the shower

and broke her hip. Then, for the next month, she refused to eat anywhere but in her room. Even during that month, she'd make whoever brought up her dinner fix her a Manhattan and tell her all of the latest Sunnyvale gossip while she sipped it slowly in her silk pajamas, matching eye mask pushed up high on her forehead, her dyed-blond curls flying in all directions.

Kitty was feisty and a little demanding, so when she named me in her will, I assumed it was to task me with some wild last request. To row to some remote inlet of the lake and throw her ashes into the water or burn the naughty boudoir photos she once showed me and now didn't want her family to find. It had never once occurred to me that Kitty had left me something.

"1243 St. Mary Street." I read the words next to my name. "What does that mean?"

Niles flips the papers around and adjusts his glasses. "Kitty has bequeathed you the building residing at 1243 St. Mary Street and its accompanying property. It's a significant asset—from the look on your face, I suspect this is coming as a bit of a surprise?"

I nod, snaking my hand under the table to pinch the flesh of my thigh, not actually thinking that I'm dreaming but still wanting confirmation.

"I don't understand. . . . Why would Kitty . . . ? You said, one-two-four-*three* St. Mary?"

Niles nods, but it only adds to my confusion.

The retirement home is one-two-four-*five*. I blank again as I try to picture the property. The one next to Sunnyvale, just off the beach, with the faded asphalt parking lot, separated from the retirement home's blacktop by a long line of half-degraded cement blocks.

"That stone building?" My mind finally forms a clear picture. "Isn't it abandoned?"

I have vague memories of it being a beach shop when I was a

kid. And then maybe hosting a communal garage sale for the Presbyterian church when they were trying to raise funds for a new roof. It was definitely abandoned by the time I was in high school.

"The building may not appear to be much," Niles says, interrupting my thoughts. "I took a look at it yesterday. But it does sit on a large street-facing lot. I'd highly recommend getting a full professional appraisal once things are settled if you do plan on selling. I'm assuming that would be your plan?"

My shoulders lift, still processing the question. *Sell? What? The building.* "I have no idea. And you're sure she left it to me? I liked Kitty and everything, but this feels like . . . a lot."

Niles sets the paper down, his expression softening as he lifts one of his hands. It hovers over mine almost as if he's contemplating a comforting squeeze, but something makes him decide against it, and instead, he sets it down next to his teacup.

"Kitty was a complex woman, but I assure you she was of sound mind when she made this decision. She meant to leave the building to you. She wanted you to have it. But I should warn you . . ." Niles shifts in his seat. The brief pause in his sentence sends up a red flag. A catch.

Niles picks up the paper again and hands it to me but grips it tightly between his fingers until I meet his eyes. "Kitty's estate still needs to go through probate. It's a legal formality for any will and testament," he explains. "As I mentioned earlier, she had three children, all of whom will have the ability to contest the contents, including your claim, especially considering she was vulnerable at the end of her life and you were her caregiver—"

"*One* of her caregivers," I interrupt as I infer precisely what he is insinuating. "And I never asked for this. I would never—"

"I know, Ms. DeMarco." He finally does place his hand on top of mine. "I wasn't implying anything more than that this document has yet to be approved officially by the courts. And to be very honest with you, I don't anticipate anyone will contest it. I know the family well. Kitty's children are all financially well off and will be considerably more so when Kitty's estate is settled. I just wanted to suggest refraining from celebratory shopping sprees until things are finalized. You never want to count your chickens . . ." He leaves the analogy half-finished.

I nod along as if I'm following his train of thought.

As if I know how these things go.

As if I've lived a life where frivolous chicken counting might be something I'd even consider.

"Do you have any more questions?" Niles removes his hand as I shift my gaze from his to the safety of his mediocre scone, half-eaten on his plate.

I have a million questions. I can't formulate them into actual words, so instead, I shake my head and say, "Not right at the moment."

Niles reaches into the inner pocket of his suit jacket and pulls out a small white business card identical to the one he gave me last night. "Well, if any questions arise, please don't hesitate to reach out. I'm returning to Toronto today, but you can call or email me anytime. I'd like to file with the courts this week. However, they get backed up this time of year. Assuming things go smoothly, you'll probably hear from me before Christmas. If not, then January."

I think I stare at the scone for another minute until Niles clears his throat. I look up in time to see him glancing at his watch. My eyes follow his to the ticking second hand and then grow wide as I register the time.

"I have to go." My knee hits the underside of the table as I stand, causing the silverware to rattle and the heads of the other diners to turn in my direction.

"Sorry," I say, stepping away from the table, realizing mid-step that there is a proper exit protocol here, and I'm not following it. "Um . . . it was great to meet you. Officially. In daylight." I thrust out my hand.

Niles James stands and takes mine in between his. "Take care, Ms. DeMarco." He pats the back of my hand twice before letting go.

"Thanks. You, too."

I paste what I hope is a pleasant expression on my face.

That forced half smile stays as I retrace my way out of the restaurant, past the woman with the bob and pleated pants, into my car, and out of the parking lot. Right up until I pull out in front of a transport truck while turning onto 13 and catch my reflection while glancing in the rearview mirror.

I look discombobulated.

I feel discombobulated.

My stomach is as tight as if it's done a 360-degree flip, and my hands are so sweaty I have to wipe them on my scrubs twice to keep my grip on the wheel.

What the hell is wrong with me?

All that has happened is that Kitty St. Clair has left me a building in her will.

Possibly.

A building that could be valuable if I were to sell it.

Maybe.

My lungs swell with something that feels a little too much like hope until I remind myself of the last time I thought an inheritance would better my life, and I remember how well that turned out.

I was eleven and my great-grandmother had just passed away from cancer. Great-grandma Gillian, or Gigi as we called her, didn't have much. But what she did have was a tiny green two-story cottage a block from the lake. Gigi had raised my mother there after her own mother passed away.

The little cottage was old. It was too hot in the summer and too cold in the winter, but as a preteen girl who had lived in small one-bedroom apartments her whole life, I thought all of my dreams were about to come true.

My mother, however, had different plans.

She sold the house to the first person who offered and moved us two towns over to rent a luxury condo overlooking a tennis club, which she proceeded to join—though she had never swung a racket in her life. She bought herself new clothes, leased a new car, and introduced herself as "Julia Jane," letting strangers assume her middle name was her last.

"It will be good networking for my business," she said when I sobbed at the idea of leaving Zoe and the rest of my friends behind. Two weeks later, when the tears didn't stop, she scolded me. "You're just like Gigi," she said. "So content to live in that Podunk town. I'm showing you that there's bigger and better out there."

The bigger and better lasted until the end of August and petered out entirely by October. The dinner invitations waned, as did the sales of the German-engineered stainless steel knives that crowded half of my bedroom.

By Christmas, we were back in West Lake, in our one-bedroom apartment next to the laundromat. I was ecstatic to be back in school with Zoe, but my mom barely got out of bed for weeks.

We both avoided driving past Gigi's little green cottage for years after that. The new owners painted it white and added a large family room off the back, but it remained a visual reminder, for me at least, that hoping for something better only leads to disappointment when it doesn't work out. Life is a lot easier when you don't let yourself want something in the first place.

Chapter 4

There's an accident on 13. It appears a tricked-out Honda Civic still sporting summer tires likely hit a patch of black ice before spinning and smashing into the Ford Taurus coming from the opposite direction. Both cars seem to be in good enough shape, their drivers standing stunned on the gravel-covered shoulder, watching two tow trucks load up the wreckage. I recognize the traffic cop as Double-double Guy from a few years ago when I was a barista at Okay Cafe. I wave at him as I near the accident, then swear under my breath as he motions for me to turn my car around with a "Sorry, Miss. The road is closed." It takes me almost twenty minutes to backtrack to Old Side Road #3. By the time I get back onto 13, I realize I'm definitely going to be late for my shift. Not by much. Maybe ten minutes if I gun Celine the rest of the way.

Usually, I wouldn't be worried. I'd tack on a few extra minutes at the close of my shift and that would be the end of it, but they brought in a new administrator—Nurse Bouchard—last month from Montreal. She seems hell-bent on exercising her authority by writing up her subordinates for any perceived slips of the employee ethics code—particularly tardiness. I learned this fact a few days ago when I was late because, on my way in, I stopped Mr. Lewis trying to smuggle in a cat in his gym bag.

He was crossing the parking lot, his old red-and-white Adidas gym bag tucked under his arm, presumably on his way to visit his wife, who'd moved into Sunnyvale six months ago when her medical needs became too complicated for him to handle at home. The scene wasn't unusual. Mr. Lewis came every day to visit his wife. It was the bag that blew his cover—moving in a way that made me suspect there was more than gym socks inside.

"Morning," I called as I caught up to him in the lobby. Mr. Lewis jumped at the sound of my voice, spinning around to face me faster than I've ever seen him move.

I eyed the bag. "That's not what I think it is, right?"

"This old thing?" He shifted the bag slightly behind him. "Just my smelly old gym shoes. Nothing untoward here, I tell ya."

As if perfectly timed, his gym shoes let out an angry yelp.

His face deepened from pink to red. "It's just for an hour, I promise. Moira has been feeling a little under the weather lately, and I think a few snuggles with her sweet Pumpkin will cheer her up. It really helped last time."

I closed my eyes, picturing the last time, when sweet little Pumpkin got spooked and took out a potted ficus.

"Fine. But if you get caught, you didn't see me, and you didn't talk to me, okay?"

"Didn't talk to who?" His blue eyes grew so big and wide that I almost thought he had not grasped the plan, until he winked and patted me on the shoulder with a "Thanks, kid."

I was in a pretty good mood until four minutes later when I walked into the employee lounge to find out I'd been docked an hour's pay for being late and issued an official warning. She didn't tell me at the time how many warnings one gets before it becomes a problem, and I'm not particularly interested in finding out.

My brain is sifting through a list of half-baked but believable excuses: engine failures or failed alarm clocks. I even consider throwing Mr. Lewis under the bus and claiming my delay is due to preventing another cat smuggling, but then I clear a bend in the road and see a familiar bright red toque in the distance. Its owner walks with her back to me, gloveless hand thrust out—thumb up.

"Don't you know what happens to girls who hitchhike?" I slow as I approach, leaning over the center console to yell out the open passenger window.

Zoe spins around at the sound of my voice. "They get picked up by sexy strangers, obviously."

I stop the car fully and slide the gearshift into park. Zoe flings the passenger door open and flops into the front seat, bringing with her a gust of frigid air. "Stellar timing, Ju-Ju. The girls were getting chilly." She yanks up the zipper of her hoodie and then shivers with an audible chatter of her teeth.

"Why is your coat wide open?" I ask, cranking up the heat to its highest setting.

Zoe shrugs, tilting the heating vents on the dash so they blast her from multiple angles. "I figured I'd be more likely to get picked up. A woman with glorious tits is probably not going to hack you to bits and leave you in the woods. Right?"

"Zoe!" I look back at the road, but not before catching her shrug.

"Don't judge me. It's freezing out there. Five more minutes and I would have been a frozen Zoe popsicle."

"Where is your car?"

Zoe leans to the right, craning her neck to see her house in the side-view mirror. "Sitting in my driveway. The stupid hunk of junk wouldn't start this morning. My guess is it's probably the transmission. I'm praying it's not, though. We are beyond broke right now, and Dale is already picking up overtime at the plant. He took a night shift last night." She pulls out her phone and starts to type. "He should be home in an hour or so," she says as she continues texting. "I guess I could have waited for him to come home, but fucking Bouchard has had it out for me ever since I told her she looked like she'd be into CrossFit. She did not take that for the compliment I intended it to be." Her phone whooshes with the sound of a sent text before she tucks the phone into her hoodie pocket.

"Why didn't you call me?" I ask.

Zoe shrugs and lets out a loud huff. "It just happened now. Plus, I figured you were already on your way. I know you hate being late. The fact that the only place Dale and I can afford is in the middle of absolute nowhere is a me problem. Besides, it all worked out."

Zoe and Dale bought their cozy two-bedroom three months ago. Both had grown up in West Lake, close to the water, but during the pandemic, real estate prices skyrocketed when folks living in Toronto's downtown core had been forced to spend months with their families in six-hundred-square-foot apartments. When restrictions were lifted, they bought up lakeside properties with spacious outdoor areas in quaint little towns. Their city salaries outbid locals who couldn't afford the inflated prices. Zoe and Dale, along with a whole slew of our high school friends, have been forced to buy outside city limits—if they could afford to buy at all.

Zoe rubs her hands together and then flattens them in front of the heater as if it were a bonfire. "Not that I'm complaining, but what exactly are you doing out here this morning? I thought at first you might have hooked up last night, but you're dressed for work, so that doesn't clock."

Like my mother, Zoe is always full of glowing optimism, even on a bad day.

When Niles James warned me not to blow my unconfirmed

future inheritance on a shopping spree, he had someone like Zoe in mind. She would be thrilled to hear the news. *That's amazing, Ju!* she'd say. *Think of how this could change your life.* And maybe that's why I don't want to tell her. I don't want to spend the next few weeks dreaming with Zoe about all the possibilities that could come from a little extra money. I want to forget about it completely so that I'm not disappointed when it doesn't end up working out.

"Oh, I'm, um, feeling a little off this morning." The lie rolls clumsily off my tongue. "Thought I'd take a drive to clear my head before my shift." Zoe nods as if this is a perfectly acceptable answer. As much as last night was a party, it was also a reminder that Kitty is gone. Zoe and I have been working at the retirement home long enough to get used to losing residents, but that doesn't mean their deaths don't affect us.

By the time I flick the signal to turn into the retirement home's parking lot, it's almost 9:15.

I pull into my usual parking spot facing away from the abandoned property next door, looking in the rearview mirror to smooth my new hair frizzies with my sweaty palm before returning my attention to Zoe. "So, how do you want to play this?" I nod at the front door of the residence. "I can walk in five minutes after you if you want. Your car died. That's a pretty legit excuse, and it will give me time to think up one of my own."

Zoe flicks the handle of her door and pushes it open. "I say we go stealth. Leave our coats in the car. Sneak in through the side door. I guarantee you Mrs. Hail has left it bricked open so she can sneak out and smoke. If we run into anyone on the way in, we play it like we've been here the whole time but we're too busy to clock in yet."

Her plan is so simple it could actually work.

"You're an evil genius." I shed my jacket as she tosses hers onto the passenger seat.

She smiles as she ties back her hair with the elastic from her wrist. "Imagine what I could do if I used my powers for good."

We cross the parking lot in a full-blown sprint, dipping in between cars, seeking reprieve from the wind coming off the lake, which bites against the fabric of our thin cotton scrubs.

The side door is, in fact, propped open with a chair, and on that chair is Mrs. Hail with a lit cigarette between her lips and another, yet to be lit, between her fingers. She doesn't try to hide, either.

"Hello there, girls!" she calls when we get close. "Just out for a little fresh air." She waves at the cloud of smoke as we approach.

Zoe leans in, plucks the unlit cigarette from her fingers, lights it, and takes a long drag. "You know these things are terrible for your health."

Mrs. Hail chuckles. It's a deep smoker's laugh that morphs into a cough as she stubs out the rest of her cigarette with her shoe. "I'm ninety-four, honey. The Lord can have me anytime he wants, and I plan on enjoying the time I have left."

"Jules and me need to make a stealthy entrance here," Zoe tells Mrs. Hail. "So, if anyone asks, we've been here all morning."

Mrs. Hail takes her second cigarette from Zoe. "You can count on me, girls."

We leave her to smoke in peace, slipping past her through the door. The hallway is empty, which isn't surprising, as many residents take their breakfasts in the dining room around nine. Zoe and I slip down it silently, heading for the stairwell at the opposite end that leads up to the second-floor employee break room, where all the schedules and room assignments for the day will be posted.

Our intended pathway passes the office of Roy Taylor—Sunnyvale's general manager. He's a nice enough guy. Friendly but always looking to avoid doing actual work. If he were to catch Zoe and me sneaking in, he'd be equally as likely to ignore us as he would be to report us to Nurse Bouchard. A risk we're not looking to take.

When we near his door, I can hear a slow hiss of breath from Zoe as it becomes clear that it is firmly closed. She shoots me a thumbs-up, which I fully interpret as *See? Easy.* But just as we pass, I hear the distinct sounds of the handle turning, the door being pulled open, and two male voices caught in mid-conversation.

Run, Zoe mouths, and she takes off, sprinting the last ten feet. I follow—my legs pumping hard and fast—colliding with Zoe as she presses the latch to the stairwell door with her thumb and it flies open with a metallic bang.

We tumble through. A tornado of legs and arms, both of us out of breath and gasping.

"I think we made it!" Zoe bends at the waist before arching backward, pressing her hands to her lower back with a groan.

"Do you think he saw us?" I ask.

Zoe shakes her head. "No way. He was talking to someone. Ten bucks says he was probably too wrapped up in the sound of his own voice." And as if proving her point, a loud, Roy Taylor–like laugh sounds from out in the hallway.

Zoe raises her brows. "What did I tell you? Easy peasy, lemon squeezy." She turns and begins to climb the steps.

I move to follow but stop when a second laugh joins Mr. Taylor's, and the familiar sound makes the tiny hairs on my arms stand on end.

Zoe turns, her hand on the rail, one foot hovering above the next step. "Dude! You coming or what?"

"Just a sec." I tilt my head, resting my cheek on the cool metal of the door, and listen.

The laugh sounds a second time. Deep and throaty, it infiltrates my core as if it knows its way. As if it's been there before.

Pressing my fingers to the handle, I push ever so slightly. The door cracks just an inch. Just enough so I can see the back of Mr. Taylor's suit, and when he moves . . .

No.

I release the door, flipping around so my back is against the wall. *What is he doing here?*

"Well, that was awfully dramatic." Zoe ascends the stairs, her eyebrow raised.

"It's nothing," I breathe, attempting to look nonchalant, very aware that my half-Irish heritage has turned my cheeks a dark pink, and my heart is beating so hard I swear the *bah-boom* is echoing off the stairwell walls.

"You can't lie worth shit, Jules. Your voice gives you away, and it's doing that high-pitched squeaky thing that only happens when you're freaked out."

Before I can stop her, Zoe is down the rest of the steps and pushing the door open a crack, just as I had only moments ago.

"Hmmm," she says, peeling her eyes away to meet mine before returning them to the scene in the hallway. "Definitely didn't see that coming." She continues to divide her time between looking at me and at the crack. "I know you said last night he's in the no-fly zone, but are you sure you don't want to reconsider, Ju-Ju? I mean, those arms."

Without meaning to, I flash back to that bunk bed.

The way his muscles flexed as he braced above me.

"Let's go," I snap. My voice is unusually raw. "We're wasting time here."

Zoe takes another look before letting the door close fully and joining me on the stairs. "Are you going to explain what's really going on between you and that guy, or are you going to make me pry it out of you?"

I quicken my pace up the stairs, but Zoe anticipates this, taking them two at a time.

"There's nothing to explain." I stop when I reach the second-floor landing, knowing this conversation will happen eventually, and it's probably in my best interest to get it over with now. "He was just a hookup. A mistake, if I'm being perfectly honest. I have no idea why he's here or why he's talking to Mr. Taylor. And I really don't care enough to find out. I'm sure he'll be gone again soon. It's not worth my time to worry about it."

Zoe doesn't say anything, but she does study my face until she gives up with a disappointed click of her tongue. "I'm going to let this go—for now. But only because I have to pee."

I move to push open the door to the second floor, but before I can exit into the hallway, she grabs my arm.

"And I have a feeling when you do tell me everything, it's going to be worth the wait."

Chapter 5

Turns out, Zoe's plan had a flaw we couldn't have anticipated. Apparently, a pipe burst last night in the dining room. Minor damage.

Gunther, the head of maintenance, cut the water pretty quickly, and someone was coming in from Owen Sound to replace the corroded pipe. But since Gunther's guys were vacuuming all the water, they moved breakfast into the recreation area. A room with a full view of the parking lot, which means all twenty-three residents, along with Nurse Bouchard, watched Zoe and me tear across the parking lot like two rogue prairie dogs avoiding a hungry hawk.

We were both immediately docked an hour's wage. Our formal warnings would be issued later when Nurse Bouchard was able to return to her office (also drying out from the pipe incident). We were immediately assigned two duties at opposite ends of Sunnyvale. Zoe to Mr. McNaught, who wanted someone to alphabetize his collection of swing jazz albums. I had been assigned to hard labor—hauling Kitty's belongings down to the front lobby, as her "lawyer and trusted family friend" was picking them up later that morning on his way out of town.

"Mr. James is coming *here*?" I asked when Nurse Bouchard told me my assignment.

"Who is coming is none of your business," she said. "But yes, I do believe that was his name."

Now, as I wait for the elevator, my arms straining with the last two of Kitty's boxes, I could laugh at the irony that this morning's scheduling conflicts could have been avoided entirely if I'd asked Mr. James if we could meet in town. Still, I'm too distracted by the way the lid of the top box is cutting into my upper arms, and by the trickle of sweat sliding down between my breasts, making me shiver.

My arms give out the moment I step inside the elevator. It's empty, so I let them go with a loud crash that echoes through the chamber. The lid of the top box pops off, and as I reach down to pick it up, my eyes land on a tiny book nestled on top of Kitty's silky black robe.

The book is red and covered in satin. Tiny pink and blue flowers are stitched into the cover, forming an intricate pattern. The spine is leather-bound, or at least was at one time. What remains of the leather is worn and cracked. The book has seen better days.

I reach for it, morbid curiosity trumping my rational brain, which knows the number one rule of working in a retirement home is that you never ever touch a resident's personal belongings without permission. Still, I flip it open and find page after page of loopy blue writing.

It's a journal. Or a diary, maybe?

Suddenly, my questions from earlier this morning come flooding back. Why would Kitty name me, of all people, in her will? And why would she leave me an old, abandoned building?

What were you up to, Kitty?

If any reasonable answers are about to manifest from the pages in front of me, they are halted as the elevator dings and the metal doors slide open.

Although my eyes are on the contents of Kitty's box in front of me, I am very aware of a looming frame standing outside the doors, watching me.

"Hey."

It's a single word uttered in an indistinct male voice, and yet I can tell exactly who it belongs to, even before I look up.

The dark navy suit.

That perfectly coiffed hair.

His tie—slightly askew.

"Reeve. Hey. How are you?" My mouth goes so dry my upper lip sticks to my gums. "How . . . What are you doing here?"

If Reeve notices the squeaky pitch to my voice—my tell, as Zoe so accurately pointed out in the stairwell—he doesn't make any indication. Instead, he reaches for the box with a "Here, let me help you," just as I realize I've left Kitty's belongings haphazardly strewn about the elevator floor.

I reach.

So does he.

We're too coordinated. Too fast.

Our hands move at the same time, colliding.

The diary falls from my grip. In my haste to catch it, I kick it with the toe of my sneaker, and it skips across the lobby like a flat stone on calm water.

While I stare in a helpless haze, Reeve bends down and successfully retrieves the fallen lid, placing it back on the top box.

"After you," he says, lifting both boxes with ease. His long leg braces against the elevator door, holding it open.

I step past him, out into the lobby, ignoring how his suit strains against the flex of his biceps, trying not to think of what Zoe said earlier about Reeve's arms.

"I was hoping we would run into each other again," he says as he follows me into the lobby, letting the elevator doors close behind him. "Last night was . . . well, not how I wanted things to go. I had this whole plan to try to track you down later today. I didn't expect it would be this easy. Serendipitous, right? So are you working here? Is this like a residency thing?"

My brain catches up to all of his questions, and my cheeks flush yet again when I realize what he's asking.

Med school.

Reeve was the only person I ever told about my plans that summer. My mom had met a WestJet pilot and moved in with him more than an hour away. Zoe was preoccupied with dating half of West Lake because she had broken up with Dale, who was working up north planting trees for the summer, and she didn't want to be tied down.

Then there was Reeve. I remember how he looked at me that night. He didn't see me as Lia DeMarco's latchkey daughter. Or that quiet girl who runs around with Zoe Buchanan, always getting into trouble.

He looked at me like I was smart. Like I could be the kind of girl who could apply to medical school, move to a big city like Toronto, and become a doctor.

Like I was full of possibility, and I basked in it.

"I didn't end up going to med school." I try to sound confident—cool even. As if it were all my choice. "I got a great job here at Sunnyvale. They offer excellent benefits. I really couldn't give up the opportunity."

Reeve sets down the boxes, his face hidden by the broad span of his shoulders, leaving me to guess at his expression.

"Benefits are always good," he says as he stands, giving me that same dazzling smile from the first night on the dock.

It hits me just as it did then: hard and fast—right between the ribs.

We're caught in a moment where neither of us speaks. I mostly stare, mainly at his mouth as it parts then presses together as if he's about to say something more but the words won't come. Finally, he shakes his head. "Hey, listen. If you're free later, I was thinking maybe we could grab dinner. Or maybe a drink? I'm in town for a few days. It would be nice to catch up."

I bend down, seemingly preoccupied with securing the lid to one of Kitty's boxes but really needing a moment away from those searching brown eyes.

"I don't . . . know if that's a good idea."

There's a long stretch of silence.

"It's definitely not a *bad* one," he says softly, with an unguardedness that was absent a moment ago.

I finally look up—just in time to catch him running his hands through his dark hair. The nervous action dishevels his tresses and my resolve along with them.

I want to say yes.

Dinner. Drinks. More.

And I hate myself for it.

How I can so easily forget how he walked away and never once looked back.

"What time are you finished with your shift?" he asks. "I could pick you up here if that's easier—"

The rest of his question is cut off as the lobby's glass doors slide open, letting in a cold blast of wind—almost as if Mother Nature herself has come to my rescue.

Niles James strolls inside, his wool coat pulled tightly around his neck, but he otherwise looks the same as he did an hour ago. "Ah, Ms. DeMarco," he says, lifting a friendly hand when he spots me. "I didn't expect to see you again so soon."

He glances curiously at Reeve for a moment before eyeing the box in my hands. "Are those Kitty's things?"

I hold out my arms, creating distance between the box and my body and, in turn, between Reeve and me. "Everything is packed and ready. Can I help you carry these to your car?"

"That would be very kind." Niles takes the box with a labored grunt.

I bend down to retrieve the second just as Reeve does the same. We repeat the elevator incident—our perfectly coordinated clash—in an almost funny way.

"I can get this." I pull the box up with me as I stand.

"Are you sure?" he asks. "It's pretty heavy."

"I'm pretty strong."

Again, Reeve opens his mouth as if he is about to say something, but this time, the interruption comes from Niles. "I can show you which one is my car, Ms. DeMarco."

I nod, shifting the box to my hip to follow him to the door, but Reeve calls out after me. "DeMarco? That's your last name? You never told me."

I turn, my eyes rolling of their own volition. "Would it have made any difference?"

His eyebrows crease, a deep ridge forming between them.

I turn to leave again.

"Jules," he calls a second time. "Dinner? You never answered me. It's just one night."

I shake my head. "I don't think so."

Because that is precisely all it would be.

Reeve is gone when I get back. I'm unsure if the shrinking inside my chest is from relief or disappointment. Or maybe it's the confirmation that deep down, I knew the lobby would be empty.

Except it's not.

Not quite.

That red book is in the far corner, next to the white wall, partially obstructed by a potted ficus tree.

Kitty's book.

I half sprint over to it, then, once it's in my hand, I run toward the front doors, hoping to catch Niles James before he leaves the parking lot.

But just as I reach the sliding doors, I stop.

I think the book in my hands is a diary.

Kitty's diary.

Practically worthless.

I imagine Niles handing it over to Kitty's children, who will probably keep it stored in a dark corner of their basement until one day in the future when they've healed from their grief and feel ready to toss it in the trash. If they don't toss it immediately—many do.

But I have so many questions for Kitty and no Kitty to answer them. This book may be my only opportunity.

I stare out at the parking lot one last time—guilt puddling in my belly—before sliding the book into my pocket.

Chapter 6

My phone buzzes from inside my pants pocket as I unlock the door to my apartment, the smell of the pizzeria downstairs mingling with the leftover dining room pot roast in the Ziploc container balancing precariously on the top of my knee.

With the skills of a woman who has spent most of her life in a juggling act, I manage to slide my key out, pull my phone from my scrubs, and press it to the space between my collarbone and cheek without spilling a single drop of gravy.

"Hello?"

"Hi, baby."

My mom's voice is low and husky. I always thought it was from the pack-a-day habit she's had since she was sixteen, but Gigi used to say she came out of the womb sounding like a lounge singer.

"Mom. Hi. How are you?"

As the question leaves my lips, I inhale involuntarily and my jaw opens wide in a yawn.

"You sound tired," she says.

I nod even though she can't see me. "Yeah, long day."

I fit my key into the lock and push open the door. My apartment is dark but otherwise unchanged from how I left it this morning. "And a late night last night," I add, suddenly craving the weight of my down duvet.

"Late night, eh?" her voice teases, and it causes a knee-jerk reaction in me to shut down her thought pattern before it takes flight.

"No, I was just . . . Zoe and I went to a funeral at the Legion."

At the word *Legion*, my mom snorts.

"God. That town. Turning funerals into a reason to party. Nothing ever changes, does it?"

I don't have the mental capacity for this particular fight tonight. Especially when I know it will end the same way it always does, with her telling me how green the grass is wherever she is living and me biting my tongue to not remind her that my credit paid to water that particular patch of grass.

"What's new with you?" I attempt to change the subject.

She sighs long and hard, and I immediately realize I've made a grave mistake.

"Do you remember how Kirk and I broke up this past spring?" She doesn't pause for me to answer. "Well, he finally kicked me out of the condo. I don't know why I stayed with him as long as I did. The man was a narcissist. Anyway, I've found a new apartment. I had to move back to Keady. You would not believe the prices in Owen Sound these days. It's highway robbery."

Her voice begins to blur. This is how every one of our conversations goes. Her complaints. The woe-is-me attitude that eventually leads to the—

"It's only a grand this time, and I'll be able to pay you back as soon as I do my first survey."

Ah.

There it is.

The real reason for her call.

"I don't have a grand, Mom."

I'm still paying off the last time, when instead of asking, she just opened up a credit card using my name and social insurance number.

"Five hundred then?" my mother continues. "If you do their prep course, you get jobs faster. If I could make more money, I could get a bigger place, and maybe we could—"

"I'm sorry," I cut her off. "Mom, I can't."

The rest of our conversation lasts less than a minute. Once it's clear I'm not budging, the pleasantries fade away, and she makes an excuse to hang up.

It doesn't sting the way it used to. When I finally stopped expecting her to be something more, I made peace with what she was—a person who always put herself first.

I plug my phone into its charger, feeling almost validated. *See, Universe?* I am not the kind of girl to fall heir to a mysterious inheritance; I am the kind of girl who is in debt because her mom woke up one morning and decided she needed a waterbed.

That feeling comes over me. I start to replay all the ways in which life has handed me lemons and I have just accepted them, piled them into my proverbial fruit bowl and left them to rot.

But I don't want to go there tonight.

Instead, I pour myself a very generous glass of cheap Chardonnay and do the second worst thing—I google.

Two years ago, I found Reeve's Instagram profile.

It was Zoe's actual birthday. We celebrated by hopping all the beach bars from Fourth Street to Main. It had been two weeks since Reeve and I hooked up, and I had finally accepted that he would never call.

I had ducked out of the festivities early after one too many lemon drops. But instead of heading to bed like a responsible adult, I decided to self-inflict maximum rejection heartache by googling the one who got away.

Reeve Baldwin was easy enough to find. We didn't have any mutual friends, but I had met him at Megh Sharma's party. I found Megh, searched his followers for Reeve, and in less than ten minutes of stalking, I was staring at a pic of Reeve on the deck of a sailboat—shirtless—that golden tan looking every bit as beautiful as I remembered.

Then, I continued to click.

Deeper and deeper down the rabbit hole. He hadn't lied about the all-boys school, but he had omitted that it was private and elite. He was well traveled, and not in the drive-twenty-four-hours-in-a-station-wagon-to-Daytona-Beach kind of way. Europe, Asia, tiny remote islands with exotic-sounding names. He had the type of life I never let myself dream about.

Tonight, as I lie in bed and begin to scroll, I'm creeping for something different. A petite blonde or curvy brunette who appears in one too many pictures or stands a little too close.

I tell myself I will check only a few of his recent posts. Ha! Without thinking, I'm scrolling back a few weeks, then a few months, then to a picture I think was taken the same night we met.

It must have been earlier in the evening. The sky is still light enough that you wouldn't need a flash. It's a candid of him in that same red Muskoka chair. His eyes closed, head thrown back as if he were laughing.

Jesus, Jules.

Why are you doing this?

This form of torture is too much, even for me.

I move to swipe up with my thumb and close the whole app, but it slips, and instead, I tap a spot on the far left of my screen. A red heart flashes over the picture.

Shit.

No, no, no, no, noooooooo.

In a panic, I click again. Unliking what I liked.

But in no way reversing the clusterfuck I've just created.

You are an idiot, Jules. A first-class, grade-A asshole.

Somewhere in Cyberland, a notification is flying innocently toward Reeve's phone.

JuJuBee likes your photo.

It doesn't matter that following it is an immediate *Just kidding. Slip of the thumb. Please disregard.*

I take a single slow, cleansing breath. Then a second. And a third.

Rationalizing to myself that he might not know it's me.

My photo is of a bumblebee. And my nickname is one only Zoe uses.

For the first time in my life, I am grateful for my mom's MLM schemes.

A few years ago, when my mom started mining my social media contacts looking for followers to help her sell herbal diet pills, I privatized all my accounts, changing my usernames to JuJuBee, hoping a little bit of anonymity online would bring me a tiny sliver of peace.

Tonight, it definitely does.

By the time I polish off my wine and climb into bed, I've convinced myself Reeve Baldwin is probably the kind of guy who doesn't even turn on social media notifications.

I turn off the light, pull up my covers, and lie there, trying to will my body to fall asleep, but the feeling of falling doesn't come.

One hundred . . .

Ninety-nine . . .

Ninety-eight . . .

Ninety-seven . . .

I give up counting sheep somewhere in the upper sixties, conceding to the fact that this sleep hack is not going to work for me tonight, and move to my next idea, which is distracting my brain by reading about gruesome unsolved murders until I'm tired enough to pass out.

Rolling over, I turn my light back on, swing my body out of bed, and tiptoe over to my purse, ignoring the cold apartment floor beneath my bare feet.

I left the thriller I've been reading inside. But when I pull the hardcover from my purse, I realize it isn't my library book in my hand. It's Kitty's diary.

I pause for a moment, debating. Then my feet get too cold, and I sprint back to bed, jumping into it and pulling the blankets up to my chin. I flip the diary open and begin to read the first page.

May 21, 1949

Dear Diary,

Today is going to be the best day. I just know it! I have been waiting all year for the West Lake Dance Hall to open up for the summer season, and today is that day! Mama still doesn't want me to go, even though I'm eighteen now—a grown woman! However, I have devised the most perfect plan. I know what you are thinking, Dearest Diary. How wicked I am to disobey my mama and run off to the dance hall. But what you may not understand is that Beau St. Clair is going to be there. His family has come to the lake for the summer season, just as they always do, and I am absolutely gone on Beau. Head over heels, Dear Diary.

All last summer, I had to stay home every Saturday night while Beau would go to the dance hall without me. It drove me absolutely mad with jealousy imagining him with his arms around other girls. I told Mama I would die if I had to do it again for another summer. Mama said that I would most certainly not die and that I should forget about a city boy like Beau and find a nice boy from West Lake. However, Daddy and I were in Wiarton last week, and I found the most perfect dress in a church donation bin. It's white with the prettiest skirt that flutters every time I spin. I knew in my heart that I was meant to have that dress and the moment Beau saw me in it, he wouldn't want to dance with another girl for the rest of the summer. All I needed was a plan to sneak out and have Mama not find out.

So, yesterday, I got a new partner in my domestic education class. Her name is Dotty O'Brien. Her mama is dead, and her daddy works over at the foundry at night, and Dot sleeps at her home all alone. She told me she gets scared of being in that dark house sometimes, so I told her I would come and stay with her on Saturday, and we could go to the dance hall and then I'd sleep over so she wouldn't be alone. Isn't that simply perfect? I know tonight is going to be the start of the rest of my life. I can feel it, Diary!

xoxo
Kitty

I close the diary and set it on my nightstand with a sigh. I'm not entirely sure what answers I thought I would find, but now I'm quite certain this book does not contain them.

Flipping the light off for a second time tonight, I pull the covers to my chin and roll over onto my side. The diary may have been a bust, but by the time I count down to my eighty-second sheep, I'm already halfway to sinking into a deep and delicious sleep.

Chapter 7

"Dot."

"Dot."

"Dotty."

"Wake up, you silly goose. It's almost ten o'clock."

Warm hands grip my shoulders and shake.

My eyes fly open as panic grips my chest. I struggle under the covers, wiggling until my captor lets go, rolling until my legs are untangled from the sheets and finally free, but that sensation is immediately replaced with another—I'm falling.

My hands hit the wooden floor, protecting my face. My knees aren't quite as fortunate.

"Holy fuck!"

The intruder bounces into the bed above me. "Good grief, you sound like a sailor, Dotty. Where did you pick up that one? Have you been over to the barracks?"

The intruder flips on a lamp. And as my eyes adjust, I look up and see she's just a girl. A teenager. Maybe seventeen or eighteen? Her hair is blond, parted to one side and curled in a style that reminds me of old movies. She's wearing a white dress that falls just below her knee. It's sleeveless with a boatneck and a bright blue ribbon trimming the bottom that matches the sash tied around her waist. In her mouth is a lollipop. She pulls it out every time she speaks. I can't tell if her lips are pink from it or from lipstick.

"Who are you, and what are you doing in my bedroom?" I manage to push up onto my elbows and then get to my feet.

She rolls her eyes. "There's no need for all of the dramatics. We were only supposed to be pretending to sleep until your daddy left. He's gone, though. I heard his truck on the road. Are you ready? Maybe you should fix your hair again." She points to a full-length mirror in the corner of the room.

My mouth goes dry as panic floods my chest for a second time.

I take a frantic look around the room—the old wooden desk, the unmade bed, the mirror—and realize not only is there a stranger in my room in the middle of the night, but it's not my room at all.

"Where the hell am I?"

The girl jumps from the bed and, before I can object, pushes me toward the mirror. "Jeepers, Dotty, you can't go around speaking like that tonight. We need to sound every bit as good as any of those city girls. Do you hear me?"

I nod, even though I have no idea who this Dotty person is or why this girl seems to think I am her.

There is a long moment where I consider making a run for the door and taking my chances with whatever lies past it, but my gaze lands on the mirror and the reflection staring back. I'm me. Same blond hair. Same blue eyes. But I'm dressed almost identically to the strange girl.

She appears behind me with a brush, and as she pulls it through my hair, I realize that I was wrong. My hair isn't quite the same. It's parted to the side and curled, just like hers is.

A dream. I must be in a dream.

Except my dreams aren't vivid like this, or at least I don't think they are. They usually feel fuzzy, like bits and pieces are out of place. There's never that sense that things are real around me, yet in this one—

"Ouch!"

The brush catches on a knot, and for a moment, my head is yanked, sending a searing shot of pain to my scalp.

"Sorry." The girl sets the brush down. "You look perfect. And we should go. I don't want Beau wondering where I am."

Something in the back of my brain clicks.

Beau.

Dot.

"Kitty?"

She turns around at the sound of her name.

"Yes."

I still need further confirmation.

"Kitty St. Clair?"

Her face breaks into a wide smile.

"Oh heavens. Can you imagine? It would be a dream!" She twirls in a circle, her dress billowing out around her. "It even sounds perfect. Kitty St. Clair. Mrs. Beau St. Clair."

It must have been the wine.

And the diary.

And the day.

All three forming the perfect storm to whip me up and drop me into a wildly lucid dream.

"Are we . . . going to the dance hall?" I ask, guessing at the narrative about to play out.

"We'd better be." Kitty reaches out and places a cool palm on my forehead. "Are you sure you're feeling okay? You seem a little, I don't know . . . disoriented, maybe?"

That is an understatement.

"You know what?" I take a step back, suddenly done with this unnecessary charade. "I am not feeling so hot. Maybe you should do whatever it is you're going to do without me."

I step toward the bed with the idea that maybe if I crawl back beneath the sheets, I can will myself to wake up. However, the moment I move, Kitty moves too—with a swiftness I don't anticipate.

"No." She jumps between me and the bed, folding her arms in front of her. "I am not leaving you behind." She grabs me by the shoulders, spinning me away from the bed. "Life has opened up a door of opportunity tonight, Dotty. It's up to us to walk through it."

Now that's a Kitty-ism if I've ever heard one. And with that, she shoves me hard on the shoulder blades, throwing me off-balance so that I stumble out through the literal door into the hallway.

It takes me a moment to recover, and in that brief interlude, Kitty grabs me by the wrist and pulls me down the stairs and out the front door before I can even consider protesting again.

When we step outdoors, I immediately hear the familiar waves of Lake Huron in the distance, and it has an immediate calming effect. It even smells like West Lake. That same faint scent of earth and pine.

Kitty begins to walk down toward the water, and I find myself following along, more out of curiosity than anything else.

I was right in my earlier assessment that as far as dreams go, this one feels different. My thoughts are clear, and the world around me seems normal. My old history teacher isn't chasing me to hand in homework I never knew existed. My feet don't feel like they're walking through a pool of Jell-O. I'm not jumping from one space to another with no clear idea of how I got there. I'm just walking down a regular old street in West Lake in the middle of the night, like I've done a thousand times before.

Except the details are off.

The moment the thought forms, I begin to notice a slew of things that are close but not quite right.

The Hendersons' cottage is blue instead of white, and there's a span of wild beach grass where the new addition they put on last spring should be.

Then I see the Fry truck is missing from its spot in the far corner of the beach access lot, next to the 7-Eleven.

Speaking of the 7-Eleven. It's gone, too.

But the hardware store is there.

So is the Okay Cafe, but the sign with the giant cafe au lait on the roof is missing.

It's West Lake, but it's not West Lake.

We continue to walk, and I find myself at a loss for what to do next. I don't recall being this conscious in a dream before, but maybe I have been and just didn't remember. Kitty does not seem to share the same level of distress. She's so light on her feet that she almost skips along the road beside me.

"So, um, is Beau like your boyfriend?" I don't even know why I'm asking. It's not as if this Kitty can answer. She is a fabrication. A figment of my own imagination. She can't know things I don't.

"He will be." Kitty flips around and continues to walk backward. "He's been writing me letters since he left last August. He told me that if my mama lets me go to the dance hall this year, he'd have me as his partner for every dance. Until my feet got tired or the band packed up to go home." She twirls, letting her hands fly up over her head. "You're going to love it, Dotty. Just wait!"

The streets get busier the closer we walk to the center of town. Young women wearing dresses like Kitty's. Men, some in dress shirts and pants, others in summer suits. Everyone seems to be headed in the same direction.

I hear the dance hall before I see it. Trumpets and saxophones cutting through the night, kept in tempo by a lively, even drumbeat.

We turn the corner, and it comes into view, soft yellow light spilling from its windows. A covered wooden porch spans the entire front of the tall gray stone building.

The sight stops me in my tracks.

"Come on, Dot," Kitty calls, her walk turning into a skipping run.

I know this building.

Take away the porch out front, the music, and the soft yellow light.

"1243," I say aloud to no one but myself.

"Hey, Kitty!" I call.

This time, she stops.

"Is the dance hall's address 1243 St. Mary Street?"

She holds up her hands. "Yes? No? Maybe. Why does it even matter?"

It's a good question.

This is just a dream. It shouldn't matter. Yet I get the strange feeling that it matters a lot.

We join the line of others waiting to get inside. Kitty's hand finds mine. Her palm is hot and damp, and she squeezes my fingers, mashing them together when we finally reach the front.

"Evening, Kitty," says the young guy standing in front of the big wooden doors. His role, I gather, is to determine who is allowed in. He looks a little older than Kitty. Nineteen or twenty. A mature face with a sharp nose but a body still boyish and gangly. His hair is slicked with some kind of pomade or gel. He has a dark smattering of freckles across his nose and a faded blue-green bruise under his right eye, as if he were in a fight a few days earlier. His eyes are a bright green and very much fixated on Kitty in the kind of way that I imagine is reserved for her alone.

"Hi, Knots," Kitty replies, ignoring the way he's smiling at her, looking past him for something beyond his shoulder inside.

"I'm working the ropes inside in a little while," he tells her. "They let us dance for free once we take all the tickets. Maybe you can save one for me later?"

Kitty nods, her eyes finally meeting his. "Sure thing. I'll see you in there."

He pushes open one of the doors and lets us pass.

As we step inside, I'm hit with the smells of perfume and sweat, of stolen gin and summer.

There is a woman in a glass ticket booth. Her shoulders shake to the beat of the music as she hands out tickets to the long line of men in front of her.

In the center of the room is the dance floor. It's sectioned off with rich red velvet ropes, manned by a boy at each of the four entrances taking tickets from the dancers. Above them sits the band: ten polished men dressed in white jackets and black bow ties, with slickly coiffed hair and shiny brass instruments, led by a single conductor, all in white. His dancing is rhythmic as he moves his hands back and forth. It's almost hypnotizing.

The music picks up, drums beating out a wild tempo. This new tune draws excited gasps from the crowd and then a mad rush of bodies heading toward the dance floor.

"Over here." Kitty pulls me into the mob. We weave and duck through various groups, talking, laughing, and dancing. Closer and closer to the band.

"There!" She finally stops, spinning around to grab both my hands. "To the left. Dark hair. Completely dreamy. Do you see him?"

My eyes drift past the bassist, the trumpeter, and the trombone player to the direction Kitty was headed only a moment before. There is a group standing in a circle, talking. Three women and three men. Two of the men are of average height, blond; the third is dark-haired and very much as dreamy as Kitty described, with a strong jaw, immaculate suit, and broad chest.

And I watch him snake his arm around a very pretty brunette.

"How do I look?" Kitty fluffs her hair but doesn't wait for my answer. Before I can stop her, she whips back around, her eyes landing on Beau just as he bends to whisper something in the woman's ear. The woman laughs. Kitty freezes.

I wait to see what she will do next.

The Kitty I knew was brazen. She'd pause at the entrance to the dining room, waiting for everyone to turn in her direction before greeting them with a confident "Evening, darlings." Or when the doctor visited her to check up on a lingering cough she'd had for weeks and couldn't get a good angle with his stethoscope through the feathers on her robe, Kitty whipped it open and declared, "I'm sure this fine doctor has seen plenty of breasts in his life. I doubt mine will make the highlight reel." Then, after seeing my mortified face, she scolded me with a single pointed finger. "Don't ever let your mind bully you into believing your body isn't glorious."

She'd be the first to get up and dance to the terrible band assembled each year for the town's Watermelon Festival, in a pair of pink polka-dot capri pants. And she once lectured a two-hundred-pound tattooed biker on *courtesy toward your fellow man* when he parked his motorcycle too close to an accessible parking spot.

The Kitty in front of me seems to share her future self's confidence. She straightens her shoulders, staring Beau and his companion down until he looks up and makes eye contact. But when she finally turns away, her chin high and lifted, there's a sheen to her eyes, though not a single tear falls.

"I'm . . . not feeling well all of a sudden." She blinks twice before fully facing me again. "Would it be okay if we left a little early? I don't want to ruin your night, but I think it might be best if I go home."

I open my mouth to say something. *Yes? No? I know your boyfriend looks like a bit of a jerk right now, but I'm pretty sure it all works out in the end. Don't worry.* But a young woman interrupts, bounding into our tight little bubble, breathless and giggling and smelling like cheap gin.

"Kitty! Hello, Kitty!" Her hair is such a deep shade of brown that it's almost black. Her curls are much wilder than Kitty's, and she has a thin sheen of sweat across her brow, as if she has been dancing all evening.

Kitty wipes her cheeks with the back of her hand before smiling widely at this girl. "Lucy, gosh, I didn't see you there."

Lucy hands Kitty a square of folded paper from her pocket. "Knots asked me to give you this. He's taking tickets now but wants to know if you'll dance the next one with him."

Kitty opens the paper and reads it briefly before folding it up again and tucking it into her pocket. "I don't know. . . ." She hesitates, her eyes shifting to me.

"You should go," I tell her, not entirely sure why I'm saying it.

Kitty's eyes shoot to Beau and then back. "With Knots?"

I shrug. "It's just a dance, and you look so pretty tonight."

The band begins to play again. It's a quick and lively tune. Lucy begins to shake her shoulders to the rhythm. "The band is an absolute gas, Kit, come on! I'll see you out there." She squeezes Kitty's arm before disappearing into the crowd heading toward the dance floor.

Kitty's eyes drift to Beau again, and I can feel her reluctance returning. I'm reminded suddenly of another Kitty-ism. One she spouted after first receiving her cancer diagnosis. She had asked me to attend the appointment with her. Her daughter was supposed to be there but had a last-minute conflict, and Kitty wanted to make sure someone else was with her to get all the critical details. The doctor was direct and grim: Kitty's end was in sight. She was quiet the entire drive back to Sunnyvale, only nodding when I asked if she was okay. She returned to her suite as soon as we got back, requesting dinner to be served in her room.

I was in the dining hall a little later that night, helping to clear the remaining plates from dinner, when the lights dimmed, and the door to the kitchen swung open. A sea of orange flames danced across the dining room as a husky voice sang, "Happy birthday to you." I watched Kitty cross the carpet to set the cake in front of Mr. McNaught, then she kissed his cheek as he blew out the candles. Swing music blasted through the speakers, and she had the whole dining room up and dancing within moments. Hours later, when we were alone again, her arm looped through mine and her patent heels hanging from her other hand, I asked her, "How?"

How did she go from receiving devastating news one moment to becoming the life of the party the next? She leaned over and whispered the exact words I repeat to young Kitty now.

"Life may not be the party we signed up for, but while we're here, we might as well dance."

The young Kitty in front of me looks up, mouth open, then nods slowly as the words sink in. "You, my dear friend, are absolutely right."

Chapter 8

Beep. Beep. Beep. Beep.

The pulsating ring of my alarm clock syncs perfectly with the big band swing music still swimming in my head.

I open my eyes. Stuck between two worlds, still blended and both fuzzy.

It's dark out.

I roll my head to the side and squint. My alarm clock reads 6:30 A.M. I reach out to hit snooze, needing a few more minutes to reorient. But in my uncoordinated morning sleep haze, I miss my alarm clock completely, my hand landing on a book with a hard smack.

Kitty's diary.

All at once, my dream comes flooding back.

Usually, when I wake, any details of a dream will fade away to nothing but a vague narrative I can only half remember. But this one—the dance hall and Kitty—feels so vivid and real. It's like it actually happened.

My head rushes as I sit up too quickly. Then it clears, and I pick up the diary and flip it open to where I left off yesterday. As the pages flutter, something falls into my lap.

A note.

My heart beats hard. A steady *boom boom boom* as I recognize the square of folded paper, although this one is yellowed with age.

Nope. It can't be. It's simply not possible.

Setting the diary back down, I pick up the note and unfold it carefully before lifting it to read.

Dear Kitty,

I'd be honored to share the next dance and any more if you'll have me. Meet me at the entrance to the dance floor. I'll be the one holding the rope.

Yours,
Knots

My fingers tremble as I read the note a second time and my brain searches for a rational answer.

I must have read this part in Kitty's diary last night.

Yes. That's it. I read it and then somehow forgot.

I'm already half doubting myself as I reach for the diary again, hoping it holds an answer.

But there is no mention of Knots in the entry I read last night.

Kitty must have told me this story then. A mention, in passing, as I was tidying her things or helping her with her hair, and then reading the diary last night triggered that subconscious memory, which wormed its way into my dreams.

Except Kitty didn't talk much about her past.

"Never look in the rearview mirror"—another one of her favorite sayings—"unless, of course, you're checking your lipstick."

Still, it's the only other rational possibility.

I get out of bed, ignoring the cold floor and how my body feels jittery and off.

"It was just a dream," I tell my wide eyes and wild hair as I brush my teeth and get dressed, determined to push all thoughts about Kitty and the dance hall away and replace them with the monotony of my morning routine.

"It was just a dream," I repeat as I pull on my coat, ready for work a full forty-five minutes earlier than I need to be.

"Nothing weird is happening," I say out loud, hoping maybe if I say it enough times, I'll finally start to believe it.

But when I flick off the light to my apartment and grab for my keys from the seashell-shaped dish on the shelf, my hand knocks something beside it, which falls to the floor with an unnaturally hard clang.

"It's just a hammer." I eye the bright pink handle. I took it out a few days ago to fix a loose coat hook and never put it away.

I don't see it as a sign or as anything other than the fallout from a clumsy flick of my wrist and my never-ending to-do list, but it does give me an idea.

Niles James told me not to spend my inheritance just yet.

He didn't tell me I couldn't check it out.

Besides, I need to confirm that last night's dream came from nowhere else but my wild imagination.

My rational brain knows I really shouldn't, yet I still reach for the handle and toss the hammer into my purse.

It's not breaking and entering.

Technically.

Chapter 9

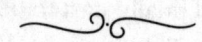

I TALK MYSELF into and out of my plan three times before the end of my shift. But by six o'clock, my morbid curiosity trumps my moral compass and I find myself standing in front of the old stone building, considering the best way to enter without actually breaking anything.

I've never noticed, but the front doors of the building are rather pretty, with intricate leafy patterns carved into solid wood. I immediately rule out my initial plan, which was to smash the combination lock with my hammer, fearing I'd miss and accidentally take a large chunk out of one of them. My eyes travel up, assessing my second and only other premeditated option: climbing up the wrought iron fire escape attached to the back wall of the building. From there, I would need to pry open one of the windows and hope there's a safe way down on the other side.

With a desire to keep from breaking both my legs, I reach for the combination lock, opting to jiggle it between my fingertips and hope the combination might suddenly come to me. As I do, a single droplet of rain falls, landing on the bridge of my nose. I look at the cloudless evening sky and think of Kitty, lounging on a cloud, laughing as she watches me and says, *You have no imagination, darling.*

I really don't. Predictability and practicality are by far my stronger suits. But with that in mind, I pick up the combination lock, spinning the numbers until they read one-two-three-four.

Nope.

Then, the building's address: one-two-four-three.

Another no.

I consider giving up, but then a memory surfaces.

A few months ago, I was listening to a voicemail that one of Kitty's doctors had left for her on her cell phone. The chemo for her cancer had damaged her hearing, and she was having trouble understanding the message.

"What's the password?" I had asked when prompted by the robotic voice.

"Zero-three-zero-five," she had said.

I computed the date while waiting to select my next option. "March fifth? I didn't have you pegged as a Pisces."

I glanced over, expecting her to roll her eyes at me the same way she did when Mrs. Hail read everyone's horoscope on Sunday mornings. But Kitty was staring at her hands.

"No. My birthday is in June."

"Ahhh. Husband? Kid? Or secret admirer?" I teased, remembering the story of how she met Paul Anka in a Berlin airport and he supposedly sent her secret love letters for years.

But Kitty didn't crack a smile, nor did she joke that she had too many secret admirers—how was she supposed to remember all of their birthdays? Instead, she got to her feet, her eyes drifting toward the window with its view of the lake.

"We can deal with this some other time," she said, her eyes still on the water. "I feel like going for a long walk on the beach. I could use a little fresh air."

With that memory still lingering, I try the same date.

Zero-three-zero-five.

The lock clicks and falls open in my hand.

I remove the chains, letting them fall to the ground with a soft clink.

Grabbing one of the handles, I brace and pull.

It takes three tugs, but then the door gives with a low grinding of its hinges.

Once again, I'm hit with a smell, but there's no trace of perfume or summer. The air inside is musty and earthy. That stale smell of old thrift shops and basement cardboard boxes left and forgotten.

I step inside, and as my eyes adjust to the dim light, I get an overwhelming sensation of déjà vu, struck by how accurate my dream was the night before.

There, in the corner, is the ticket booth. It is in the same spot as it was last night, although the glass has been smashed, and there is no longer a cash register inside. The dance floor is still there, too, sunken into the center of the room, although there is no evidence of the velvet ropes that once surrounded it. The walls are covered with spray-paint graffiti: "Tina loves Jonas" and anatomically exaggerated dicks.

I scuff the floor with my sneakers, scraping away the grime to reveal the intricately patterned travertine floor underneath.

Exactly like in the dream.

The jittery feeling I've had all day grows into more of a deep unease. I'm suddenly aware of my breath, which now requires complete concentration to draw. In and out. In and out.

Something weird is going on here. Something I can't quite grasp. It's too abstract. Too unlikely.

My jumbled thoughts are cleared by a sound.

A very distinct, very real sound of creaking wood behind me.

My unease morphs into another feeling. One far more terrifying than eerily accurate nocturnal fantasies, because this threat is very real. Someone is watching me.

I don't know how I can tell.

As the hairs on the back of my neck begin to prickle, I am very grateful for the hammer still in my purse.

I move my hand, ever so slowly, to the zipper and slide it open.

As I slip my hand inside, I listen.

There are no more creaks. No sounds at all other than the wind outside.

Still, my fingers close around the cool metal, and I take a deep breath and pull it from my bag.

I turn, arm raised, ready to take on whomever or whatever is waiting behind me.

My gaze immediately falls on the looming frame in the doorway. As recognition sets in, I let the hammer slip from my hand and drop to the floor with a loud clang. "What are you doing here?"

Reeve steps toward me, his hands held up in front of him. "I could ask you the same thing." He nods at the hammer lying on the floor. "And what exactly were you planning on doing with that?"

I ignore his question, pressing my hand to my chest. "You shouldn't just sneak up on people like that. You nearly gave me a heart attack."

"I'm sorry," he says, taking another tentative step forward. "A friend told me about this place, and then I drove by and saw the door open. I was curious. When I saw it was you, I just . . ."

"Watched me like a creep?"

He laughs. "That's one way to put it."

"What did your friend say about this place?"

He pauses as if he's considering whether to answer me. "Just that it was a cool space with great natural light. Did you know it used to be an old dance hall?"

The prickle on my neck returns, and I leave his question unanswered.

Reeve's gaze flicks to the hammer at my feet. "You still haven't told me what *you're* doing here."

And I don't plan to. "That's really none of your business. In fact, I think I'm going to go."

He watches while I pick up my hammer and give him a wide berth as I pass him on the way to the front door.

Just as I reach it, he calls out. "Hey, did I do something wrong?"

I stop. But I don't turn back, and I don't answer.

"It feels like . . . I don't know . . . that you're mad at me or something?" he continues. "And I guess I'm not really sure why."

I do turn around to face him this time. Torn between laughing and throwing my hammer, not so gently, at his head. "I don't know how you do things where you're from, but around here, guys generally call after they sleep with someone, at least once. Just to make sure there isn't a toddler running around that they don't know about."

Reeve's brow lifts. "Is there a toddler running around that I don't know about?"

"No!" I let out a frustrated growl. "And that's not the point."

"I know, Jules." He takes a step toward me. "But that's where I'm getting very confused, because I did call. I called a lot."

My heart stops—a full-blown halting of services as I turn over what he just said.

"You don't need to lie to me."

"I'm not." He takes another step forward, pulling his phone from inside his suit jacket. "Here. If you don't believe me, you can look for yourself." He swipes his screen and then types something in, scrolling for a few seconds before turning it to face me.

"I generally take the hint after one message goes unanswered—not that it happens all that often—but I think I gave up after seven with you."

I take the phone from his hands. There are texts. Exactly seven, just as he said, ranging from a simple *Hey* to *What are you up to tonight?* to *Are you okay? I'm starting to get a little worried.*

They're time-stamped from two years ago. And my name is at the top: "Jules."

But that can't be right, because I didn't receive any of them.

I click on my profile at the top, then hit info to display my details. At first glance, it looks like my number, but when I look again, I see the last two numbers are reversed.

"My number is wrong." I finally look up. "It's four-two-five-eight, not four-two-eight-five."

He lets go of a long breath as he takes the phone from my hands. "Well, I guess that explains things."

I'm not ready to accept this easy answer; it's been too many years of resenting him in my head.

"You must have put it in wrong."

He shakes his head. "You were the one who put it in. I thought you gave me a fake number." He returns his phone to his suit pocket. "I even tried to find you online. There isn't a single Jules from West Lake on X, Instagram, or even Facebook."

He's right.

My profile was well locked down before we even met. He has a logical answer for all of it.

"Did you ever try to find me?" he asks. "Online, I mean?"

My memories from last night come flooding back. I can feel my face growing hot. *Oh, you know . . . just the normal, healthy level of post-sex stalking* does not feel like the response I want to give right now.

"I didn't know your last name," I lie. "Toronto is a big city. There are more Reeves out there than you think."

He narrows his eyes. "Really?"

I begin to back up toward the door, suddenly needing to escape. It's like a spotlight has been flicked on, and I'm seeing all the events from the last two years in a completely different light.

However, Reeve is still looking at me the same way he did that night we first met. As if he can see all the way into my soul. And, *oh, god*! Now I'm that girl who poured beer down his pants.

"I need to get going," I tell him, suddenly stifled by the dance hall's stale air. "I've got an early shift tomorrow, and what we're doing here isn't exactly legal, so . . ." I take a couple backward steps. "I guess I'll see you around."

I turn and move toward the door again, and this time, I make it. Pulling it open, I welcome the cool bite of the night air as I step into the parking lot and take my first deep breath in what feels like a year. Or, if I'm being perfectly honest, two.

But just as I exhale, my phone buzzes in my purse.

It's a single buzz.

A notification.

I pull it out and look at the screen, and I get a rush of cold through my entire body as I realize how badly I've screwed up.

Reeve Baldwin requested to follow you.

Chapter 10

I DON'T ACCEPT his follow request.

But I do stand in the doorway of my apartment and stare at it for eight whole minutes while my emotions spin like that bottle on the dock.

There is a strong possibility that if I had received that very first "hey" two years ago, I would have responded with my own *hey*, which he'd follow with a *you good?*, me a *yup*, and that would have been the end of it.

But there's also the possibility—as minuscule and improbable as it may be—that something more might have happened. And although my usual tendency is to put that thought in a mental box, tape it up tight, and shove it into a dark corner of my mind, tonight I'm fighting a strange sense of nostalgia for a past that never even existed.

He had asked where I planned to live when I moved to Toronto—that night on the dock.

"I don't know," I had said. "In one of the dorms, I guess?"

I hadn't figured that part out yet.

"You should look into the Annex," he said. "I have a friend who rents a room in an old Victorian just off Bloor. He's got a dumbwaiter in his closet and a massive fireplace in his room. It's a really great area, and it's within walking distance of campus. I could get you the landlord's number if you want? There are a million great little sushi places right around there, too. I could take you sometime. Do you eat sushi?"

I had never tried sushi before, but I wanted to. I wanted every little detail Reeve described.

That weekend may have ended on a bad note, with me assuming Reeve had ghosted me. However, our talk that night had ignited something deep inside me. I wasn't going to pretend I didn't care if my future panned out. I was going to go to medical school, and I was going to live this life I'd just imagined.

I spent the next week getting my application ready to send. My transcripts, essays, and recommendation letters were all perfectly prepared and ready to give me the shot that would change my life.

Then, I made an appointment at my bank. I still had a small outstanding student loan from my undergraduate degree. But I had been making steady payments on it. I hoped they'd let me take on additional debt, leveraging my theoretical future salary as a medical professional.

I should have known something was up when the adviser looked at his computer screen and let out a long, low whistle.

"You didn't mention your line of credit," he said, his voice shifting from its previous cheery tone to something far more disapproving. "Or that you have two credit cards that have gone to collections. I'm sorry, I can't help you here."

I told him there must be some mistake. His computer must be wrong.

His computer was right, and that was just the beginning. When I called my mother out on what she'd done, she had an excuse for everything. She couldn't find work in West Lake, but there were jobs in Collingwood. She needed to put a deposit down on a place and a car to get her to her job once she found it, but her own credit was shot, so she "borrowed" from me. She'd planned on paying me back before I even noticed, but the job market took a turn and I "noticed" sooner than she anticipated.

Needless to say, I didn't end up applying to medical school that fall. There was no way to come up with the tuition money, let alone the day-to-day costs required to live downtown in one of the world's most expensive cities. It felt cruel to try, knowing I couldn't go. It was better not to know.

Tonight, I seem to be in a masochistic headspace. I sit down at my laptop and navigate to the University of Toronto's medical school website, clicking on this year's admissions information just to see.

Applications close in three days.

The requirements are the same as when I considered applying two years ago. However, as I skim the summary, I realize that my MCAT score, the one that would have set me apart from the rest of the pack, is valid for only one more year.

I wrote it in the summer of my third year of university. I took a six-month prep course, wrote three practice tests, and finally achieved a score that seemed almost impossible at the time.

But according to the web page in front of me, that score will expire in the summer. My math courses and study prep are so far in the rearview mirror that it would probably take me years of preparation before I could score even close to as high as I did back then.

A heavy, uncomfortable feeling settles on my chest at the thought of a future that was never really mine. I think a small part of me assumed I'd get my shit together one day and actually send it.

However, it looks like "one day" is today, and my shit is so far from together that I can almost hear the low whistle of the bank clerk, looking at the mountain of debt still attached to my name.

It would take a small miracle.

I climb into bed, exhausted, pulling the covers high over my chin. As I reach to turn the light off, I catch sight of Kitty's diary. Part of me wants to shove it in the drawer and never look at it again. The other part of me still wonders if it holds some clue as to why Kitty left me that dance hall. Against my better judgment, I pick it up and begin to read.

May 28, 1949

Dear Diary,

I am facing a big dilemma and I don't know who else to turn to. I had a whole plan to be Beau St. Clair's girlfriend this summer until I found out he took Ruth Eaton to her school's spring dance because their daddies are best friends. Then I overheard two of Ruth's girlfriends talking at the snack shack about how she is sweet on him but that he hasn't asked her to go steady even though he took her as his date to the dance hall last Saturday. Oh, Diary. I was so mad when I saw them together that I thought I would cry right there in the middle of the dance floor. Then this older boy from town, Knots, asked me to dance, and lo and behold, he's the best dancer I have ever danced with. We had four more dances together, and everyone kept talking about how wonderful we were at dancing. Knots is also a true gentleman. He put a chair next to his station so when he had to collect the tickets at the beginning of every dance, I could sit and rest my feet while I waited for him. He has a wonderful sense of humor, too. If it's a slower song, he tells me funny stories about all his younger brothers—he has six! And about all the bands that come to the dance hall to play. He knows all these things about the world that I don't know yet, and I want to know them all.

Now, here's my big problem, Dearest Diary. The other night, when I was dancing with Knots, I looked over and saw Beau watching me. His eyes were so dark, and his mouth was turned into a frown. I think seeing me dancing with Knots made him mad with jealousy. He approached me as soon as I left the dance floor and asked if he could have the next dance. I pretended it was already taken and told him he could have the one after that. After we danced, he stayed by my side the whole rest of the night. He isn't as funny as Knots or nearly as good of a dancer, but his friends are all so sophisticated. They go to dinner at nice restaurants and the theater or the cinema whenever they want. I am returning to the dance hall this Saturday but don't know who I should dance with. Knots? Beau? Or both of them? What do you think I should do, Diary?

xoxo
Kitty

I awake with the diary still clutched to my chest, sunlight streaming onto my face so brightly I can't fully open my eyes.

"Put that book down and talk to me, Dotty. It's bad enough I have to work on this positively gorgeous day, but there aren't even any customers to entertain me."

My eyes fly open, then squint from the bright sunlight, and I sit up so quickly I get a head rush.

It's happening again.

I'm not in my room.

Or any room at all, for that matter.

I'm at the beach. The waves of Lake Huron are crashing a mere twenty feet away.

I'm on a chair.

In a bathing suit.

Next to what looks like a wooden hut with the words SNACK SHACK painted on the side and a very bored-looking teenage Kitty

St. Clair sighing dramatically as she rests her head on the countertop.

"This part was barely even in the diary." I throw up my arms, unsure of what my brain is up to with these dreams.

Kitty lifts her head from the counter, pushing a blond curl out of her eyes. "What on earth are you talking about?"

"You." I point at her red-and-white-striped uniform with its matching hat. "There was one brief line about the Snack Shack. The rest was about the dance hall again. You were trying to decide between Beau and Knots. It didn't even mention the beach, so why am I dreaming about being in a bathing suit?"

She leans over the counter and stares down at me. "I think you've been out in the heat too long." Kitty throws her arm over her eyes and drops dramatically back down onto the counter. "But you are right. I still don't know what I should do about them. Knots is so funny and sweet, but Beau is . . . Beau. Do you know what I mean?"

She hoists her whole body onto the countertop, stretching her legs out long and leaning her head back against the wall.

I slap the side of my face with my hand in an attempt to wake myself up, but nothing happens.

"What is going on?" I groan, rubbing my now stinging cheek.

Kitty doesn't even open her eyes. "What is going on is that you're helping me, Dots. I'm in a pickle and I require my nearest and dearest friend to advise me."

"So you think I'm your nearest and dearest friend?"

Kitty's eyes open. "Aren't you? You are both dear to me"—she reaches out her arm, as if to show the minimal space between us—"and near to me."

I take her in. She looks so real. I feel so . . . real. It's as if I'm actually on a beach talking to a teenage Kitty St. Clair.

"Well?" Kitty asks, and I realize she's waiting for a response.

"I don't know," I answer her honestly. "Maybe make a pros and cons list?"

Kitty thinks for a moment, and as I wait for her answer, it occurs to me that as logical as my suggestion is, I know how this story plays out. She chooses Beau. Moves to Toronto. Raises three children. At some point moves back to West Lake and decides it will be fun to leave me an abandoned dance hall with no context provided whatsoever.

Kitty pulls her legs in to cross them, cradling her hands in her lap. "Do you ever think about a life outside of West Lake? Something bigger? Better than smelling like french fries all the time."

Her question catches me off guard. I was expecting the rest of this conversation to be about weighing Beau's blue eyes against Knots's swing dancing skills.

"I . . . I think about it." I immediately picture my abandoned med school application. "But then I also think about how great my life here is. My friends are here. It's my home."

Kitty stares at the water for a moment, and I wonder if she will say anything more. She looks so sad all of a sudden. I have this urge to reach my arm out and touch her, but before I do, she speaks.

"When I look at Knots, I can see exactly how my life will turn out. It'll be just like my parents. We'll get married and maybe live in one of those apartments on top of one of the shops on St. Mary Street. Above the drugstore, maybe? I'll work here at the Snack Shack until I have a baby. Knots will get a job at the grocery store or, if we're lucky, the foundry, and we'll save our pennies until we can afford a house, and then we'll grow old together."

"That sounds kind of nice."

Kitty closes her eyes and lets out a long sigh. "Yes, but I want . . . more. I want to see things and go places. I want to know what the Taj Mahal looks like because I've seen it with my own eyes, not just in pictures in a library book, and I want to meet people who make movies or drive race cars or run our country. I want to be fabulously interesting, but you can't be fabulously interesting if all you do is live in West Lake every day until you die."

"Hey!" Although I'm not actually Dot, whoever Dot is, I take offense on behalf of both of us.

"Sorry." Kitty winces.

"It's fine." I wave her off, but she shakes her head.

"But that's my whole point. You should be better than fine." She sits up so quickly her hat falls from her head. "We should move somewhere exciting. Like Toronto or Montreal or Paris even?"

I roll my eyes.

She shakes her head. "I'm not joking. We could pack our bags and get on a bus. We could do it tonight."

"But . . . it's not that easy, believe me." I've spent many nights lying in my bed coming to terms with this exact fact. Leaving West Lake takes money. Big cities want security deposits and last month's rent, not to mention funds to live off of until you find a new job.

Kitty throws up her arms. "Of course it's not easy. But if we just sit here and talk about it, it will never happen. I'll be a little old lady serving hot dogs with my hunched-over back, and you'll be lying on that chair all shriveled up like a raisin. Don't you want to start thinking about our futures, Dotty? Is this really the life *you* want forever?"

I close my eyes to gather my thoughts, but when I open them again, I'm back in my darkened bedroom just like I wanted to be.

The clock on my phone reads just past three.

I lie in my bed for a few moments, wondering if the memories of my dream will slip away like they usually do, but they stay vivid as Kitty's words echo in my head.

I get to my feet without fully realizing why I'm doing it. Then I'm sitting at my kitchen table and flipping open my laptop, the University of Toronto medical school site still on my screen.

I don't know if it's the conversation with Kitty or the feeling I haven't been able to shake since I realized this year would probably be my last shot.

My login still works for the university application center site. It takes a few clicks to update my information, but everything from two years ago is still relevant. All I need to do is click send.

I want to throw up.

I draw a deep breath, my eyes drifting to my ceiling as my hand hovers over my mouse.

"I hope you know what you're talking about."

I close my eyes, let the air whoosh from my lungs, and click.

Chapter 11

THE NEXT SIX weeks pass in that familiar monotony where I blink and it's the middle of November. There are no further social media requests from Reeve. No mysterious lawyers tracking me down on rainy streets in the middle of the night. No Kittys whisking me into love triangles in eerily realistic fever-like dreams.

I almost forget about all of it.

That is, until I'm at Lou's Groovy Grill, waiting on a well-deserved hot breakfast. The bell above the door chimes, and Reeve walks in.

He's in a suit again, which, unbeknownst to me until now, is apparently my Kryptonite. Covering it is a long, open wool overcoat, such a deep shade of brown that I can make out the fine dusting of snowflakes on his shoulders. His hair is perfectly coiffed, exactly like the last time I saw him, awakening this deep, primal urge to run my fingers through it.

I watch his eyes scan the busy diner, presumably looking for somewhere to sit. The moment before they land on me in my spacious, four-person cracked-leather booth, I flash back to that night in the dance hall: my lie when he asked if I'd ever looked for him online and how smugly he caught me.

In an act of self-preservation, I pull one of the menus from the plastic holder at the end of the table, whip it open, and duck—allowing Lou's fourteen different omelet offerings to hide my face completely.

My fingers stick to the vinyl. Ensnared by maple syrup or a rogue blot of jam. Reeve doesn't spot me, or if he does, he doesn't care, because his voice carries from across the diner in the direction of the stools along the counter where Donny and the other locals usually sit.

"One cup of coffee, please, Rosie. Black. And a Fit Slam when you have a moment."

I lower the menu just enough to see the back of his head.

He is, in fact, at the counter. Sandwiched between Donny's brother Bill and Zoe's cousin Clive with the perpetually sweaty hands.

I am tempted to follow my instincts, which are to discreetly mime *pack up my meal to go* motions at Rosie, slip out the front door with my white Styrofoam container, and be the unnamed culprit when Nurse Bouchard asks the orderlies who stunk up the employee break room with the smell of deep-fried potatoes.

Instead, I set my menu down, press my shoulders back, and remind myself that West Lake is my town. If anyone should be eating half-cold eggs on a saggy polyester couch, it should be him.

Twelve whole minutes pass where nothing notable happens other than Rosie pours Reeve a cup of coffee and then laughs loudly at something he says, slapping the counter between them so hard the silverware clinks.

I start to think that maybe my breakfast will play out far less dramatically than I imagined.

I'll eat. Then leave, with him never the wiser.

But then the front door opens, and the bell chimes, and I see, with almost crystal clarity, the next few moments ahead of me.

I'm about to have a problem.

A five-foot-three, two-tufts-of-white-hair-on-an-otherwise-completely-bald-head-shaped problem.

"Excuse me, young man," my resident Mr. McNaught says, tapping Reeve on the back with his cane. "You're sitting in my seat."

Reeve swivels around to face him. Their eyes are almost level even though Reeve is still fully seated.

I silently chastise myself for not predicting this snafu.

Counter seats at Lou's are sacred. The same eight bodies have filled them every morning between the hours of seven and nine for as long as I can remember. There was even a rumor once that Donny inherited his seat when his dad passed away—that it was written in his will. Reeve is understandably unaware of this delicate dynamic. Still, he slips from his seat and stands. "Not a problem, sir. I was just keeping it warm."

His gaze lifts from Mr. McNaught to the busy diner.

There is no time to reach for my fourteen-omelet shield before it lands on me.

"Would you mind doing me a favor?" Reeve says, bending closer to Mr. McNaught. "When my breakfast comes, could you ask Rosie to bring it over to that table?"

He points at the vacant bench on the other side of my booth.

No, no, no, no, no.

"Mr. McNaught." My voice comes out embarrassingly shrill. "Wouldn't you prefer to join me? The seats are far more comfortable. Excellent back support."

Mr. McNaught doesn't even entertain this alternative. He just glances at me briefly before sliding into his seat, reaching out his hand as Bill hands him the crossword section of the newspaper.

Reeve retrieves his coffee, his confident stride slowing to a more tentative step as he nears my table.

"Hey. Sorry about that, I hope you don't mind . . ." He gestures at the open seat across from me, now deciding that it's probably polite to wait for an invitation. However, my response to this awkward exchange is interrupted when Rosie appears with Reeve's Fit Slam breakfast.

"Where to, sweetheart?"

Reeve looks at me and waits.

I gesture at the empty seat across from me with my vinyl menu before returning it to its holder at the end of the table, and Reeve slides into the space across from me.

"Looks great, Rosie," Reeve says as she sets his breakfast in front of him.

"You enjoy, love." She squeezes him on the shoulder before turning her face in my direction. "Yours will be just another minute or two, hon." Then she leans in close to whisper, "No ring," wiggling both her fingers and eyebrows. "If you don't want him, send him back my way."

I can see Reeve grinning out of the corner of my eye but avoid meeting his gaze until my face returns to a less intense shade of pink. We sit in very awkward silence until the smell of his deep-fried potatoes hits my nose, and it occurs to me that he isn't eating them.

"You can go ahead and start."

He glances at the kitchen before turning back to me. "It's okay. I'll wait. It's bad enough I invited myself over. I won't make you watch me eat." He tips his head in the direction of Mr. McNaught. "Thank you, by the way."

"He's one of my residents." I tap my finger on the window in the direction of the retirement home kitty-corner to the diner. "He walks over every morning, rain or shine. Says he doesn't like the coffee in the dining room, but I think he just likes being here. Talking to everyone. He's been coming to Lou's since it opened.

His picture is over on that wall." I point to the space between the front door and the bathrooms next to the kitchen: a wall covered with photos of locals at various celebrations and the occasional celebrity customer.

Reeve twists around and looks at it until the door to the kitchen swings open and Rosie emerges with a plate in hand.

"Looks like your breakfast is here," Reeve says. But as Rosie approaches, I get a clear view of the pancakes in her hand.

"Not mine." I shake my head, and sure enough, she breezes past our booth, dropping the plate off at some other table before rushing back into the kitchen.

Reeve leans forward, resting his elbows on either side of his plate. "Yeah, I didn't figure you for chocolate chip pancakes. You feel more like . . . western omelet, white toast, buttered, and coffee with cream but no sugar." He sits back in his seat as if this is a question I'm supposed to answer.

"You're guessing my breakfast order?"

He smiles, a slow, easy spread of his lips as if he's pleased I've picked up on his game.

"One of my more underrated talents. I can be pretty accurate. Especially if I know the person well."

"I'd be a little insulted that I don't strike you as a chocolate chip pancake girl, but I guess you don't really know anything about me."

His right eyebrow lifts. It's just the slightest shift. "Is that a challenge? Jules DeMarco? Longtime resident of West Lake. Grew up here with her single mother." He holds up a hand, listing out each fact on a finger. "Next to impossible to find online until she gives herself away, decided she wanted to become a doctor at the age of ten when she slipped on some rocks down by the lake and was scooped up by a tall, dark-haired stranger and carried to his Subaru Outback, where he promptly patched up her knee, thus instilling a desire to help people and a penchant for handsome, dark-haired men."

He smiles again, this one much slower, and its effect spreads through me like a slow, creeping heat.

"I'll concede to one of those two things."

He holds up a second hand. "You drink PBRs and only rarely drink hard liquor because you don't like the feeling of losing control. You wanted a bulldog named Neil Patrick Harris as a kid, but your mom never let you have one because you always lived in apartments with no-pet policies. You have a very ticklish spot between your collarbone and earlobe."

He pauses, and my mouth goes dry.

I take a very long drink of water. "You have an excellent memory."

"I do."

"And all of this screams Western omelet to you?"

Before he can answer, Rosie appears at our table. She sets down a plate in front of me. White toast: buttered. Coffee: cream but no sugar. Omelet: goat cheese and peppers.

Reeve eyes it as I pick up my fork.

"I don't like ham."

He picks up his as well. "I'll remember that for next time."

Three bites of eggs and two of toast, and my stomach stops with the weird fluttery spasms.

"So why are you here in West Lake this time?" I ask, needing to put us on a safe subject.

Reeve reaches for the little bowl of creamers, taking two and dumping them into his mug. "I'm having breakfast with a beautiful woman."

I try to roll my eyes, but a small smile creeps across my face before I can stop it.

"I work for a developer in Toronto called Mansfield Properties," he says. "We have a few projects coming up in the area, so I'm out here scouting locations."

A large lump forms at the back of my throat. "What kind of projects?"

He takes a small sip of coffee. "Mostly residential. Low-rise condominiums. If the zoning allows, we sometimes create the spaces for small businesses underneath. Have you seen that new complex over in Port Logan?"

I have. The building is beautiful, built in the same brick style as the rest of the quaint downtown, but its construction took out an entire block of small businesses. The only shop that made the transition into the newly constructed work/live lofts was a small kitchen shop with a booming online business.

The eggs in my stomach churn. "So you're looking at locations in West Lake?"

It's a moment before Reeve can chew and swallow his mouthful of breakfast to answer. "I've been looking at locations all along the coast, as far north as Tobermory and as far south as Grand Bend. It really comes down to the area. The economy needs to be able to support the demographic we're targeting. The units will start at seven hundred and fifty K."

"Seven hundred and fifty thousand each?" I'm grateful I don't have a mouthful of coffee. "For what? A two-bedroom condo?"

Reeve looks almost sheepish. "One-bedroom. You'd be surprised what the vacation property crowd will spend."

My breakfast feels like a brick in my stomach. I drop my fork. It clatters onto my plate as I push away the rest of my food, no longer hungry.

Reeve tilts his head, lowering it to meet my eyes. "Why do I get the sense that I've just screwed up?"

I wrap my arms across my chest. "You haven't; I just don't think I could do a job like that."

He glances at me, confused. "Aren't vacation properties a good thing? More tourists means more business for the locals, right?"

He's both right and wrong. It's a complex situation. "In theory, yes. But when the people that live here can't afford to actually live here and then have to commute to jobs that still pay the same minimum wages because they have to compete with the shiny new Starbucks, or yoga studio, or cheesemonger going in down the street, it really only works out for a select few."

In a mere few moments, our pleasant-ish breakfast has turned into something else entirely. I look around for Rosie and her coffeepot and spot her coming our way with both a pot and a plate in hand.

She sets the plate down in front of me. On it is a single butter tart. "Figured I'd save you the trouble of ordering." She fills my empty coffee mug before turning to Reeve. "You want one, too?"

Reeve looks at my plate and then up at me. "I don't know. Do I?"

I move my fork to the flaky tart and cut it in half. "I'll share. I don't know if I can stomach a full one this morning."

I push the plate to the center of the table, then use my fork to pull my half of the dessert toward me.

Reeve's fork lingers over his portion. "Do you always eat dessert at eight-thirty in the morning?"

"Yup." I lift half of the butter tart to my mouth, forgoing all propriety and eating the entire thing in three bites. It's sweet, salty, and not too runny, and it drips with the correct filling-to-pastry ratio, washing away some of the awkwardness of the last few moments.

Reeve tosses his fork on the table, following my lead and downing his half in two bites.

"Wow!" he says after he has chewed and swallowed. "I think you might be on to something here."

He has a tiny dribble of filling on his chin. I reach as if I'm about to swipe it with my finger, then stop and pick up a spare napkin instead.

He takes it. "So is it just butter tarts, or do you switch it up? Cheesecake feels like it could work as a breakfast dessert."

He wipes his chin with a napkin, and I consider how much I feel like adding to his arsenal of Jules DeMarco facts. "My mom used to work at this bakery in Port Logan when I was a kid— Annie O's. I'd have to wake up super early and go with her. She'd wrap me in a blanket and set me in the corner on the big sacks of flour, and I'd sleep for a few extra hours and then wake up to the smell of fresh bread."

I look up to see him watching me with an amused half smile. "Not the worst way to wake up, I imagine?"

I nod, agreeing. "Exactly. Annie would always be in by that time, and she'd have a warm butter tart ready and waiting. *To have a good day, you should start with a good breakfast,* she'd say with a wink, which in hindsight makes me think she knew she was taking liberties with the word *good*, but it always seemed to work. Those years were good."

My mom was steadily employed, home in the evenings to tuck me into bed. They were my favorite years, until she decided she was too good to work in a lowly bakery job.

I drain the rest of my coffee to push that particular memory away. When I set my cup down, he is still watching me.

"Have dinner with me tonight?"

His question comes so out of the blue that my guard is down, and my insides flutter.

"I can't. I'm working until nine tonight."

Reeve shrugs like he doesn't see the same problem. "Nine still works for me."

"You want to hang out at *nine*?"

Reeve pales slightly as he follows my thought process. "I wasn't implying . . . I assumed you'd be hungry after work. I promise I made that statement with the most gentlemanly of intentions."

I dwell on the word *gentlemanly* and wonder if he remembers our night together and how he couldn't make that promise back then. And that memory reminds me of the bigger problem here. "What did you think of this butter tart?" I nudge the remaining crumbs with my fork.

Reeve tilts his head, unsure of where I'm going with this. "It was delicious."

"It was good, but not great," I correct him. "Lou's used to get their butter tarts from Annie O's. There would be lines out the door on weekend mornings when Annie would send over a fresh batch. A good butter tart is practically worshiped up here. But two years ago, a developer bought the block where Annie O's was located, and she had to shut the bakery down and move it three hours north where she could afford to live."

Reeve swallows, his face slightly paler than a moment ago.

"It wasn't your complex in Port Logan," I tell him. "But it could have been. Now Lou's brings in butter tarts frozen from some big bakery in Toronto. He makes practically no margin, but people come to little towns like this expecting butter tarts."

Reeve stares at his plate and then up at me. He doesn't say anything, and I open my mouth to shift our conversation somewhere less awkward, but then he scoops up the last forkful of eggs and holds it up. "Let me tell you about my breakfast."

I shut my mouth again, wondering where he's taking this.

"I love chocolate chip pancakes," he continues. "They are hands down my favorite food—of all time, not just breakfast—yet I ordered scrambled eggs with a side of tomatoes. So that tells you . . ."

He holds out his fork and waits.

"You don't want to die of a heart attack?"

He laughs. "Well, yes, but also that I'm prone to doing what is expected of me instead of what I want." He holds up his butterless whole wheat toast. "Dry and boring, like my job. The job my father got me after I failed to find what he deemed 'suitable employment.' Also, I am lactose intolerant."

He takes a bite out of the bread, and when he swallows I expect him to continue, but he doesn't immediately.

After a pause, he continues. "I am also the middle child of three boys. A people pleaser both by birth order and by nature. That unimpressed look you're giving me with your eyebrow right now is both killing me and turning me on."

My mouth falls open, which I quickly try to cover by taking a long sip of my coffee.

"What about the hash browns?" I ask as I finally set my mug down.

He shrugs. "I just like hash browns." Then he spears the last forkful and bites, fighting back another smile as he chews.

I'm smiling, too, despite myself, and despite still grappling with the idea that I hate everything about his job and yet I like more and more about him.

As if he can sense the thoughts in my head, he reaches his hand out like he's going to cover mine but stops, and instead sets his hand next to mine so only the backs of our fingers brush.

"It's my job, Jules. But it's not *me*."

His eyes lock with mine. Two pools of a deep mahogany brown.

But instead of him looking into my soul, this time it's me looking into his, and although I can't explain why, I know exactly what he means.

"Reeve, I—"

Someone clears their throat.

I turn to see Rosie placing a black plastic tray on the table with two bills, leaning away as if she's trying her best not to interrupt.

"I know you gotta run, honey, so I'll just leave this here." She gives me a not-so-discreet thumbs-up before rushing off.

Reeve tries to reach for my bill, but I stop him, setting cash down on the table.

"I'm sorry, but Rosie's right, and I really need to get going. My shift starts in ten minutes."

I slide out of the booth, as does Reeve. There is an awkward moment where I don't know if I should hug him goodbye, shake his hand, or awkwardly wave and walk away.

What I do know is that I wish I didn't need to go yet. Despite our rocky start, I remember why I fell so hard the first time.

"Do you still have my number?" I nod at his cell phone sitting on the table. "The wrong one. From before."

Reeve nods. "Yeah."

"If you reverse the last two numbers, it should be right. Four-two-eight-five."

He picks up his phone and begins to type, then turns the screen so I can confirm the number is correct.

I double-check it and nod. "For the next time you're in town. Maybe we can have dinner then?"

"I like that plan." He takes the phone back, types something into it, and then returns it to his pocket. "I guess we'll talk soon."

Chapter 12

November 23, 2024

Reeve: (Link: Grey Bruce This Week) Brawl over butter tart! Two local West Lake men arrested.

Reeve: You weren't kidding about people taking butter tarts seriously up there

Jules: I actually went to high school with one of those guys. An ex-girlfriend and an ATV were also involved, but I like that they went with the butter tart angle.

November 28, 2024

Reeve: I know you knocked Toronto butter tarts, but I found an amazing place in the Junction. I had one with walnuts that I swear I had dreams about.

Jules: I will entertain the idea of raisins in my tarts, as I am more liberal than most, but nuts are a hard no. You're only reinforcing my point here.

December 6, 2024

Reeve: Jean L. from Markham claims they're better than sex

Jules: I think Jean L. from Markham needs to have better sex

December 8, 2024

Reeve: I have in my possession Nana Baldwin's prized butter tart recipe. I told her I needed to woo a beautiful woman, so she said she'd let me have it on the blood oath that I only use it once and then destroy it by fire.

Jules: You bake?

Reeve: I'm trying

Jules: I'm impressed

Reeve: You might not want to get too impressed quite yet.

Jules: You'll have to give me the recipe if it works out

> **Reeve:** Can't. I will be burning it once these tarts are made. A blood oath is a blood oath.

December 25, 2024

> **Jules:** How's the baking going?

"Who ya sexting?"

I look up from my phone, my face the same color as Zoe's velvet stocking hanging next to me in front of the fireplace.

"No one." I set down my phone as Zoe hands me a boozy white drink that I think is supposed to be eggnog.

"Your face is a full-on smitten kitten. You never look like that, Jules."

I attempt to school my face into a more neutral expression. "Just read something funny, that's all."

Zoe eyes my phone but lets it go. "If you say so. And in that case, I still think you should hook up with cousin Clive. He's still single. We could be family. Even though we basically already are." She climbs into my lap, wrapping her arms around my neck and pressing our foreheads together.

"I love you, Ju-Ju."

I can smell the faint hint of eggnog on her breath.

"I love you too—"

My phone lights up on the coffee table next to us.

I grab for it before Zoe can see.

It's another text from Reeve. A picture of a very sad-looking butter tart, the pastry cracked and the insides crumbly, less "gooey filling" and more "dried brown crust."

> **Reeve:** This is not going well

I quickly type back.

> **Jules:** Looks to me like you need to add more love.

I go to set my phone down again, but Zoe is staring at me, arms crossed.

"Either share the meme or spill the beans. Who are you talking to?"

She is still in my lap, her bony butt bones digging into my leg.

"It's Reeve," I concede, flipping my phone around to face her.

Zoe scrunches her forehead. "Hot funeral guy? I thought we hated him."

"Not anymore. We've been texting. A little."

"For how long?" Her voice is a teasing singsong.

"A few weeks."

"Weeks, huh?" Her gaze shoots to the opposite side of the room. "Poor Clive."

Poor Clive is chugging a tall boy of PBR to the rhythmic chants of his two brothers.

Zoe turns back to me. "So. Reeve. Tell me more."

I shrug, not wanting to get into details. "It's nothing."

Zoe glances at my phone. "It doesn't look like nothing."

I pick up my phone and try to shove it into my pocket but can't with Zoe still sitting on me. "Yeah, well, it can never be anything."

Zoe wiggles out of my lap and plops down on the couch beside me. "And why not?"

I avoid her eyes. "Because he lives in Toronto. This is just..." I wave my phone around.

Zoe gives me a single, unimpressed eyebrow. "He has been texting you for weeks, Jules. That feels like a little more than..." She mimics my phone movement from a moment ago.

"Zoe." I roll my eyes, but she catches my head between her hands.

"What I want to know is why I'm finding out about this now. After I practically forced it out of you."

"You didn't force—"

"Jules."

"Because of this." I point at her. The way she's staring me down. Looking at me like I should expect more.

Now it's she who rolls her eyes. "Ohhhhhh. Me pointing out how a guy sees all your wonderful qualities and wants to have more than hot, sweaty sex with you? Yes, then I am a terrible friend. I don't know how you put up with me."

I wrap my arm around her shoulders. "It was a vocation. I was called."

"Speaking of calls." Zoe nods at the lit-up phone in my hand. "You'd better answer that."

I glance down at the screen. Reeve's name is there next to *Incoming call*.

I stand.

Actually, jump.

My legs move toward the tiny screened-in porch outside the front door. There is a rush of cold air as I push it open, biting against my thin wool sweater. I can see my breath when I take a long exhale before swiping and pressing the phone to my ear.

"Hey."

"Jules?"

There's a tiny pause while neither of us speaks.

"Is this okay?" he finally says. "I figured since we were texting, you might be home."

My heart is beating double time. A fitting drumbeat to the new mantra I made up as I stepped outside. *He's just a guy. This is just a casual conversation. Don't get ahead of yourself.*

"I'm actually at my friend Zoe's. You met her that night at Kitty St. Clair's wake. The tiny brunette. I think she stole your beer."

He laughs. "Yeah. She's not one I'd easily forget."

"Well, she has this party every year. Takes in all of us Christmas orphans who have nowhere else to go. It's a weird collection of misfits. My mailman, Marv, is here. We have lasagna."

I am very aware that I am babbling like a prepubescent middle schooler.

My voice is a full octave higher than normal. I have underarm sweat.

"Are you at home?"

There's a sound on Reeve's side like crunching leather. I imagine him settling on a sofa, stretching his long legs out onto a coffee table in front of him.

"I am. My brothers all do dinners with their in-laws or friends tonight, so my parents go out. I'll see them all tomorrow for Boxing Day."

There's a loud cheer from inside Zoe's living room, followed by another round of "Clive, Clive, Clive."

I can hear Reeve's low laugh on the other end of the line.

"Sounds like a good party. I don't want to keep you from it, and I should probably get back to my baking, but I wanted to say hey and merry Christmas."

My insides melt despite the cold.

"Merry Christmas, Reeve."

There's a pause on his end of the line. "Maybe I'll see you in the new year?"

He's just a guy. This is just a casual conversation. Don't get ahead of yourself.

"Maybe you will."

Chapter 13

We get our first big winter storm on December 30.

It blows off the lake, blanketing the town in two full feet of wintry white. By the next morning, New Year's Eve, the plows have made enough headway that I can make my way to Lou's for breakfast. The diner is packed with townies who all had the same idea.

I have a hot coffee warming my hands when Rosie stops at my usual booth to take my order. I open my mouth to tell her, "Just my usual," but stop myself.

I have never been one for resolutions: optimistic declarations given for no other reason than a calendar date and prone to be forgotten before spring. But as my eyes skim the menu, they stop on a section they usually skip right over.

"I'll have the chocolate chip pancakes, please."

Rosie doesn't blink twice at my new revelation. "Coming right up."

Perhaps this year will be different.

The pancakes are delicious. I don't feel any different by the time I'm two-thirds of the way through, but I definitely am stuffed.

Rosie comes to refill my coffee and eyes my unfinished plate. "Room for dessert?"

I groan involuntarily. "I don't think I can do it this morning. I'm so full."

"Are you sure?" says a different voice.

One that is not Rosie's.

One that is very deep.

I look up as Rosie turns around.

Reeve stands behind her with a white paper box in his hands. There is no suit today. Just jeans, a gray zip-up hoodie, and a mid-length wool coat, one shade of gray darker.

Maybe it isn't the suits that are my problem.

"I'm hoping you have at least a little room." He holds out the box. "Although we can freeze them, Annie was pretty insistent that they be eaten the same day."

He slides onto the bench across from me, placing the white box in the center of the table.

"Did you say Annie?" My fingers tremble as I reach for the lid. I have to stop and squeeze them into fists.

Reeve reaches for the white butcher's twine, slipping it off the box to lift the lid. "Yeah. I tried to do it myself, but it turns out I'm a terrible baker. I think that's why she gave these to me. I showed her my best attempt, and she took pity on me."

I look up, my head all of a sudden so dizzy that I'm not entirely sure if I'm hearing him correctly. "You met Annie?"

Reeve nods. "Yeah, and she still remembers you. I think that's the other reason she agreed to give these to me."

I stare at the two tarts nestled in the center of the box. So perfect. Exactly like I remember.

"I don't want to guilt you into eating them if you don't have—"

"No," I interrupt, finally finding enough steadiness in my fingers to reach into the box and lift one out. "I can't wait."

Even before the tart reaches my lips, I know it tastes exactly like how Annie used to make them. I can smell the sweetness. It's the same sugary scent I used to wake up to. That warm comfort. The feeling of being safe.

I close my eyes and bite.

The pastry flakes in my mouth, and as the filling hits my tongue, a single tear falls down my cheek.

Reeve reaches out and wipes it with the pad of his thumb. "It's really that good, huh?"

My eyes fly open. "You have no idea. You need to try one." I push the box with the second tart toward him, but he shakes his head.

"No, that's yours. I was hoping for more, but she had sold out of almost everything over the holidays. I'm pretty sure these two came from her own personal stash."

His words register. "You went to Orillia?"

He shrugs as if it's not a big deal. "I have an artist friend up there. He had some new pieces he wanted me to look at. When I realized I couldn't make the thing on my own, I had to go to plan B."

The gravity of what he's done hits me. "Thank you, Reeve. I don't think you know how much this means."

My hand covers his, my cold fingers curled around to his warm palm.

"Have dinner with me?" The words come out of my mouth the same way they did his a few weeks ago.

He smiles like he's been waiting for this. "Tonight?"

I nod until I remember.

"Wait. No, I can't. There's this big New Year's Eve thing at the Legion. Zoe is going to jump out of a cake. She's been working on it for weeks, and I need to help her get into it and potentially out of it."

He nods, understanding, and a thought settles over me.

I don't want to wait to see him again.

"Come with me?"

Chapter 14

The Legion is decked out for a party.

Streamers are strung up across the top of the bar in black and silver waves, and air-blown balloons with HAPPY NEW YEAR printed on them are gathered into bunches and taped up into every corner. There is even a disco ball on the ceiling, secured with a patch of color scheme–approved silver duct tape, sending hundreds of tiny shreds of light onto the walls and floor. Donny's even dimmed the lights—so if you squint your eyes and let the whole scene blur a little bit, it almost feels magical.

Donny's brother Bill, who runs a wedding DJ business on the side, has set up his equipment on a folding card table in the corner of the room. His Justin Bieber mash-up pumps through the speaker system as we make our third attempt to fit Zoe's giant cake through the front door.

Dale, Zoe's husband, sets his side of the cake down to step back and assess our progress. "We should have spent more time on logistics instead of all those hair tutorials, eh, Zo?"

Zoe fluffs her Marilyn Monroe–style curls, which suit her jet-black hair. "I regret nothing."

"What if I lift from the bottom, and we tip it?" Reeve offers, already bending at the knees.

Dale and I join him. The angle works, and with a few grunts and groans, we're able to slide the cake inside.

Zoe cups Reeve's chin with the palm of her hand. "You are more than just a chiseled jaw there, Reeve Baldwin." She taps the side of his face lightly. "Keep doing what you're doing with my girl Jules and I may even start to like you. But remember, if you screw with her again . . ."

She pulls his face toward her, which, because of their height difference, has Reeve bending almost fully at the waist. She whispers something in his ear that, knowing Zoe the way I know Zoe, is almost definitely a graphic death threat.

When he straightens, he meets my eyes with a funny look I have no time to decipher because Zoe is grabbing me by the wrist and tugging me toward the kitchen with a "Be back in a bit, boys. Prepare to be dazzled."

I help her into the cake without smudging her lipstick. When Bill's voice booms through the speaker system, "It's time to light up this party," I light up Zoe's sparklers and wheel her into the center of the room, praying that the Legion is nowhere near up to fire code.

Zoe emerges and dazzles.

Singing in her husky Marilyn Monroe voice a "Happy New Year to you."

Her routine, for the most part, goes off without a hitch. About halfway through, Dale has to dump a few sparklers into a half-empty beer glass when they sparkle too close to a paper tablecloth. Still, by the time Zoe takes her final bow, the entire bar has full glasses and is ready to party.

Bob cranks the Biebs. One of the women from the Ladies League hides the darts behind the bar while the rest of her crew moves a bunch of tables to create a dance floor.

By 11:50, there is a pile of high heels in the corner, including mine. There are some sleeping children on makeshift beds made of coats under tables, and Bill has abandoned his DJ booth to Donny's Celine Dion CD, which is playing on repeat.

I have barely seen Reeve since we got here. Every time we seem to find each other, one of us is whisked away into another conversation.

My eyes skim the room, looking for his now familiar frame as I attempt to pay attention to the two Ladies League members discussing the proposed changes to the Summer Beach parking regulations.

"Excuse me?" Reeve's deep voice plucks that sensitive spot inside my chest as he slides up next to me, his fingers pressing ever so slightly to the small of my back. "Would you mind if I stole Jules away?" he asks them. "They're playing our song."

The women nod, that open-mouthed, stunned expression I've seen happen more than once around Reeve.

His hand skims along my back, then down my arm, before cupping my hand in his. I let him lead me to the dance floor, where I reach my arms up around his neck as his hands come around my waist, only realizing once there that it's been two years since we've been this close and yet it feels so natural.

"'All Coming Back to Me' is our song?" I ask, registering the lyrics.

Reeve laughs, a single soundless *ha*. "I needed an excuse to steal you away, but now that I've said it, it feels fitting."

His thumbs stroke the back of my rib cage. "When I touch you like this."

His hands tighten, pulling me closer. "And when I hold you like that."

Our swaying slows to more of an off-beat rock. I lift my head until my eyes meet his, very aware of the mere inches between our mouths.

"You really know all the words."

He laughs, flattening his palms to the small of my back. "That's all I got."

I tuck my head under his chin and close my eyes. As Celine sings about it all coming back, I can't help but think how easily it does.

I'm in that dizzy haze again. It's exactly like two years ago, where all I want is him. I don't care what happens tomorrow or the day after that. Consequences be damned.

The song finally ends, but instead of a new one starting, the countdown begins. A chorus of voices shouting together. Ten ... nine ... eight ...

Reeve bends down, his lips brushing the side of my ear.

"I was thinking about kissing you at midnight." He asks it like a question, pausing to wait until I answer.

"I think I would like that."

His hands travel up my arms to my neck, then gently brush away a sweaty strand of hair.

Seven ... six ... five ...

Oh, how badly I want to fall right now, hard and fast. Give myself over to that rush that comes when there's no fear of hitting bottom.

"I need you to promise me something." I claw my way out of the haze. Just enough to see that there is a bottom, and as badly as I want to ignore it, to forget it, I can't.

"Okay," he says as the chanting grows louder.

"This is just a kiss," I tell him. "For now, I think ... that's just what I ... need it to be."

He pauses for a moment, and I worry I've ruined everything.

Four . . . three . . . two . . .

He leans close, his breath hot in my ear as singing erupts around us.

"Then I'd better make it a good one."

Chapter 15

I'm in the dance hall again.

Wearing that same white dress. Standing. Watching.

The crowd around me dances and laughs with that carefree air of a summer Saturday night party.

My own New Year's party hasn't entirely faded into a memory yet.

Reeve's kiss.

The quiet walk home in the snow, where, in the shelter of my doorway, he asked if he could kiss me again to say good night.

How he tilted my chin with the tips of his fingers, brushing his lips with mine.

The soft growl as he pulled away.

How it was everything, and yet I wanted it to be so much more.

I close my eyes and sigh, remembering my determination when I finally said good night instead of inviting him in.

My resolve when I didn't text him *I changed my mind come back*, and instead climbed into bed and read Kitty's diary until I was tired enough to fall asleep.

Now I'm here.

My eyes scan the crowd for Kitty. I find her on the dance floor, in the arms of Knots, her rope boy, head tipped up toward him with a dreamy and content smile on her lips.

The song ends. The dancers clap. Kitty presses up on her tiptoes to kiss Knots on his cheek. The next song starts, and I lose sight of her as more bodies flood the dance floor until the crowd shifts again and, like an apparition, she reappears in front of me.

"Are you a ghost?" The thought pops into my head and out of my mouth at the same moment.

"Not the last time I checked?" Kitty fluffs her curls, only half paying attention to me, her eyes back on the dance floor where Knots is taking tickets from the next group of dancers.

"I think you might be a figment of my subconscious," I tell her, working a theory out in my head. "That, or you're haunting me. You always seem to appear when I . . ."

When I read your diary before bed.

Kitty doesn't notice my unfinished thought. The band has started up again, and Knots is free to do what he wants, which is to stare at Kitty in a way where I half expect cartoon hearts to pop out of his head.

"You two seem awfully smitten," I tell her.

It seems to be what she wants to hear, because she clasps me on the shoulders and squeezes.

"Really? Do you think he likes me?"

I have to consciously stop myself from rolling my eyes, because I'm pretty sure it's a serious question. "Yes, I think that's a pretty safe call. He can't stop looking at you, and you can't stop smiling at him. It's rather adorable, actually."

Kitty's eyes fall to her hands. "He kissed me, you know."

With the events of the last few minutes, this revelation doesn't exactly shock me. "As I said, you two seem pretty into each other."

"No." Kitty looks up, shaking her head. "Not Knots. I meant Beau."

Kitty's gaze drifts away again, but this time, it's not to the dance floor but to a table to the left of the bandstand, where a set of dark eyes are also watching her back.

"Oh." My brain fills in the missing plot. "And how do you feel about that?"

Kitty doesn't answer my question. She seems to be lost in thought. The band has struck up a new song. It's a slow foxtrot, played by just the two horns and bass.

"The St. Clairs own seven grocery stores," she says, her eyes still on Beau. "They have a summer house here and a big house right in the middle of Toronto, with a housekeeper and everything. Mrs. St. Clair doesn't even have to work. She throws dinner parties and travels the world. She's even been as far as China."

We both watch as Beau stands, bending to say something to the gentlemen next to him before he excuses himself from the table.

"My mother has never even been farther than Toronto, Dot." Kitty's expression becomes suddenly flat. "She spoke to Mrs. Minard. She needs another girl to clean rooms over at the lodge. I'm supposed to start next month. I don't want to be a maid for the rest of my life."

There's a desperation in her voice that I know too well.

"You could do something else," I offer with no real idea of how or what. "Maybe you could move to the city like you said? Get on a bus. There's got to be loads of jobs there."

Kitty throws her head back and laughs. It sounds almost bitter. "You and I both know that was nothing but a silly dream. I have no money, only a little education, no skills. But I am pretty, and I like to think of myself as charming when I need to be." Her eyes shift to the dance floor, where they catch her rope boy's. He waves. She smiles, but when her eyes return to me, I swear she looks almost sad.

"Have you ever been kissed?" she asks.

I immediately think about my doorstep and how it felt to be in Reeve's arms tonight.

"Yes."

"And was it like they always say it is in the movies?" Kitty asks. "Did your head get dizzy and your insides fluttery and light?"

"I don't know if I'd use those exact words, but yes, it felt . . . right."

"Oh." Kitty's mouth turns down. "With Beau, it wasn't like that. It was nice and all, but . . ." She offers a small smile. "You must really like this boy you kissed."

I think about her words and Reeve and the undeniable fact that feelings are forming that are deep and real and terrifying.

"I think I do. A lot. It's just that . . ." I can't finish the thought. I'm too afraid to say the next part out loud—as if saying the words will somehow manifest them into existence.

Kitty's small fingers slide in between mine and squeeze. "You can tell me."

Kitty is a figment of my imagination. A person that I barely even know, and yet I find myself wanting to tell her.

"He kind of broke my heart once before," I admit. "It was an accident." *A communication error that you probably won't fully understand for another sixty years.* "But I'm . . . I don't know—scared, I guess."

Her thumb strokes the back of my hand. "You're worried he will do it again?"

I nod and, in doing so, catch a glimpse of Beau moving across the dance floor toward us.

Kitty follows my gaze, then shifts hers to Knots before leaning in to whisper, "Our hearts were meant to love, Dots. Even if love is fleeting. I would rather endure a lifetime of heartache for the briefest moment of knowing what it means to be truly loved."

I shake my head, hating that I know what I know about her future.

"Even if you know it will one day fall apart?"

There's no time for her to respond because Beau has reached us. He offers his arm to Kitty, who smiles taking it. "You look beautiful tonight," Beau says. "I was hoping to have the next dance and maybe the one after that."

Kitty's smile slips. It's the slightest twitch of her cheek, only noticeable because I am watching so closely.

"That sounds lovely, Beau."

She lets go of his hand to place both of hers on my shoulders.

I inhale the sweet scent of her perfume as she leans in close to place a kiss on my cheek.

"Yes, my friend. Even then."

She pulls away, then turns again, placing her hand in Beau's so he can lead her to the dance floor.

Chapter 16

January 1, 2025

> **Jules:** So I made the mistake last night of telling Zoe that I had a verified Annie's butter tart in my possession. This is basically the equivalent of announcing something on that giant billboard you see driving in on 13. Half of West Lake has texted this morning. Top bids include $50 cash, the taxidermied buck from the Legion, and the right to name Zoe's theoretical firstborn, which might be a kindness, seeing as the current front-runner is Dale Jr.

> **Reeve:** I'm very worried for all of you

> **Jules:** Wait. Just got another one. Bill's counter seat at Lou's is now up for grabs.

> **Reeve:** Are you going to go for it?

> **Jules:** I am going to sit here in my kitchen and devour every last crumb

> **Reeve:** Are you still up for dinner? And in a very related question, any chance you're free this Saturday?

> **Jules:** I very much am up for it. However, I've picked up double Saturday shifts for the next two weeks. But I am only working a half shift next Wednesday. Could I meet you halfway?

> **Reeve:** No, let's wait. I want to do this right.

> **Jules:** Are you sure? It will be two weeks, almost three.

> **Reeve:** I've waited two years, Jules. A few weeks won't be a problem.

On the day of my big date with Reeve, my phone rings as I walk through the retirement home's front doors. I pull it from my purse and see that it flashes the 416 area code of a Toronto number. My heart picks up speed wondering if it's Reeve calling me from his work number until I press it to my ear with a breathy "Hello" and hear a voice that isn't his on the other end of the line.

"Ms. DeMarco. It's Niles James. Am I catching you at a bad time?"

I check my watch. It's 8:45. I have fifteen minutes to clock in for my shift, and this is a conversation I don't want anyone who may be lingering around the break room to hear.

"I have a few minutes." I pull the collar of my coat tighter, step back out into the cold, and huddle into the small alcove in the retirement home's brick exterior where the smokers stand to shield themselves from the wind.

There's a soft shuffling of papers on the other end of the line. "Good. Good. Well, apologies for taking so long to reconnect. As I suspected, the courts were all backed up with the Christmas season and whatnot, but I have some good news for you."

My chest fills with an icy cold. It grips my lungs and forces me to take slow, shallow breaths.

"As I anticipated," Niles James continues, "there were no objections from any beneficiaries on the division of Kitty's assets. You are now entitled to inherit the property located at 1243 St. Mary Street."

I hear his words. I understand their meaning individually, yet strung together they sound so foreign I have to ask him to repeat.

"The property," he says, slower this time. "Kitty St. Clair's will has been finalized. You will officially own the property as soon as you fill out the needed tax and banking information. I will have my assistant send them over, which reminds me, there is one small issue I would like to bring to your attention."

The brief euphoric moment as I process this good news quickly fades to an impending sense of dread.

"Kitty left provisions to cover all estate and other administration taxes, including the property taxes for the initial year after her death. As her executor, it was my responsibility to take care of this." He pauses, and I know, even before he begins to speak, that the thing he is about to say next will not be good.

"However, moving forward, you will be responsible for the annual property taxes. I wanted to make sure you were aware of this fact well in advance."

He may be using lawyer speak, but I am all too familiar with the core of his message.

"How much will I owe?"

There's another pause before Niles answers. "This is a matter you should discuss with your municipality directly, but using this year's figures as an accurate comparison, I would estimate somewhere in the neighborhood of five thousand dollars."

He waits. And when a moment goes by with nothing but heavy breathing on my end of the line, he clears his throat. "Did you hear me, Ms. DeMarco?"

"I got it."

I own a plot of land with an abandoned building that requires me to come up with $5,000—cash that I don't have.

"You are more than welcome to contact me with any further questions," he continues. "As I said, there will be some paperwork to sign, but I hope to have all of it straightened out by the end of the month."

He hangs up.

Almost immediately after, my phone pings with an email from a generic Niles James LLP address with a formal lawyer-esque greeting and line-by-line details of what to do next.

The instructions are clear and precise, with underlined links to forms and notes on their desired completion dates. It details exactly what to do about the legal matters that need attending to. What it doesn't tell me is what to do with my hands, which are shaking, and my teeth, which are chattering—and not, I suspect, from the cold.

Chapter 17

Despite my early morning news, I have big plans to show up for my first official date with Reeve as the hottest, most pulled-together version of myself.

I even endure a stern look from Nurse Bouchard when I remind her of my approved request to leave at 4:00 so I'll have time to blow out my hair and apply the jelly eye patches Zoe ordered in bulk on Amazon.

The day passes in a way that cannot be described as anything but an absolute gong show. There's another pipe burst on three and a faulty fire alarm on five. The chair yoga teacher calls in sick, as does the "Art with Your Heart" instructor, leaving me downward dogging and decoupaging during the moments I'd typically reserve for deep breaths or, lately, thinking about Kitty's will or, more important, my date.

By 3:45, I'm a walking zombie, but I snap out of it quickly when I walk into Mr. Minard's room and find him still in bed, looking the wrong shade of gray and breathing a little too heavy for my liking.

"I think we'd better call the doctor," I tell him when I check his forehead with my palm and find it both hot and clammy.

"Oh, there's no need." He waves me off.

He begins to cough, and it becomes clear that there is, in fact, a big need.

"Well, I think we need a second opinion." I pick up the phone and call the doctor in Southampton. He happens to be on his way home and promises to stop by.

The clock on the wall ticks past 4:00 and then 4:30. At 4:45, the doctor finally arrives. He checks Mr. Minard's temperature and listens to his lungs.

"I think we need to take a little trip to the hospital tonight," the doctor says to Mr. Minard, then, later to me in the hallway, "You made a very good call. He's okay for now but may not be in an hour or two."

When Zoe gets off after her shift, she finds me in the lobby watching the paramedics rolling Mr. Minard out to the waiting ambulance.

She kisses him on the forehead as he rolls by. "What's happening with Bernard?"

I catch her up on the doctor's prognosis.

"I'm going to ride with him," I tell her. "I don't want him going all alone."

Zoe glances at the time on her phone. "Don't you have a date with Reeve tonight?"

"Yes." I calculate his estimated distance away. "I'm going to have to cancel. I feel terrible, but—"

"Nope!" Zoe turns my shoulders toward the elevator. "I've got this one. You go . . ." She sniffs me. "Have a shower. Then have a swooningly romantic evening that I will live vicariously through when you tell me all about it tomorrow."

She taps me on the butt.

"Are you sure?"

She waves me off. "You can repay me with eternal devotion."

By the time I get home to my apartment, I have a mere thirty-two minutes remaining before Reeve is set to pick me up.

My keys are in one hand. My purse and lunch bag are in the other. I'm moving so quickly up the stairs that I almost step on the bundle lying in front of my door as I shove my key into the lock.

It's a small wicker basket filled with three wax-covered cheeses, a box of crackers, and two miniature pots of jam, all wrapped in clear cellophane. Stapled to the top is a hot-pink Post-it with a note scrawled across it in blue pen.

> You didn't tell me West Lake already had a cheesemonger.
> What it really needs is a florist.
> I can't wait to see you tonight.
>
> Reeve

I don't think I breathe the entire time it takes me to read the note twice. When I finally do, it's deep and gasping, accompanied by a dizziness that I am not entirely sure is from the temporary lack of oxygen.

I recognize the handwriting—and the cheese, for that matter. Baskets just like it sit in the window of A Shore Thing: the gift shop on the corner, which sells everything from seashell-covered tea towels and handmade tea cozies to beef jerky and, as Reeve pointed out, an assortment of locally sourced cheese.

The gift shop doesn't deliver. Its owner, Lizzy Gowdie, barely leaves her chair behind the counter, especially during the winter months when she opens only between the hours of ten and two—if she opens at all. I can almost picture Reeve charming her over the phone. His honey tone convincing her to deliver this to my doorstep, and the names she would have called him before begrudgingly agreeing.

My Reeve-inspired daydreaming costs me another ten minutes. By the time I get into the shower, it's twenty to six. I have no time to debate my outfit and opt for my black jeans and a slinky black blouse, which I inherited from Zoe, who bought it online and passed it to me when it came three sizes bigger than the XXS she ordered.

My intercom buzzes as I'm drying my hair. I abandon it, still damp, and use the precious few seconds as I buzz Reeve up to apply a single coat of mascara and lip gloss. The result is not how I imagined looking for our first date, but it's a lot better than how I looked twenty minutes ago.

"Hey." I open the door to find him standing in a suit and that same brown wool coat from a few weeks ago, his hair back to its perfectly polished coif save for a single dark lock curling over the center of his forehead.

"You look so nice. Are we going somewhere fancy?" I look down at the outfit I deemed cute and a little sexy only moments ago and suddenly find it less so.

He steps inside, ignoring my question and producing a bouquet of twenty-four perfect red roses from behind his back.

"I know I sent the cheese, but I wasn't one hundred percent confident it would show up. And as I said, I want to do this right."

I take the roses from his hand, a matching blush crawling up my cheeks.

He produces a bottle of wine from a bag I missed with the distraction of the roses. "I figured we could have a drink before we go."

He holds up the bottle. It's a fancy French champagne with a name I wouldn't dare to try to pronounce. I nod, flushing again, this time from the realization that I have never owned a champagne flute and am about to make us drink from two red wine glasses I bought on sale from the home section of the Superstore.

Reeve pops the bottle but doesn't comment as he fills the glasses and hands one to me.

"Cheers." He clinks his glass with mine.

I drain mine quickly, avoiding his eyes. "Are you sure I'm dressed okay?"

He steps toward me, taking the glass from my hand. Our bodies are so close now that I can smell the scent of his expensive aftershave. I linger, simultaneously wanting to bury my nose in his neck and also regretting that the only thing I smell like is the ambiguous mound of fruit on the bottle of my drugstore body wash.

"You look beautiful." His hand drops, dangling next to mine until he hooks my pinky finger with his ever so lightly. "I had to go into work this morning. My boss asked me to prep a last-minute presentation, and I didn't have time to change. But unfortunately, that also means I need to go back tonight. He's called a Sunday morning meeting for the whole team to prep for the client presentation on Monday."

It's a moment before what he has said fully hits me.

"You drove three hours just for dinner? You could have canceled."

He shakes his head, abandoning my pinky to lace his whole hand with mine. "I had it in my head that I would see you tonight. I lied the other week. I couldn't wait. But we should get going. Our reservation is for six-thirty."

I nod, weighing the sweetness of his gesture tonight with the practicalities. We live three hours apart. That's six hours of commuting just for dinner. He seems willing to do that now, but this relationship is still shiny and new. Pheromones and hormones are still weighing heavily in our decision-making—*but how long will that last?*

Reeve's car is parked on the street in front of the pizzeria. It's still warm inside as we climb in and take Main Street out onto the country highway. The drive to Port Logan takes almost twenty minutes. It's a dark stretch of country road where only a handful of cars pass in the opposite direction.

"I think you're really going to like this place," Reeve says as he pulls to a stop at the traffic light just before the downtown stretch. "I might be biased, but I swear it's the best food in Bruce County."

"Pro tip from a local. You don't wanna let Rosie hear you say that—unless you want to eat a cold Lou's breakfast for the rest of your life."

He smiles and flicks his right blinker, taking us toward the Cranberry Inn. My heart sinks a little, but Reeve doesn't slow as the parking lot nears. Instead, he drives past, taking a quick left down a side street and pulling in behind a blue-sided building.

"Have you ever been here?" He cuts the engine and unclips his belt, shifting in his seat to face me.

"You're taking me to the Moose?"

His face lights up. "I should have known better. Of course you know it."

"Best food in all of the Bruce Peninsula. And yes, my warning about Rosie is from learning the hard way."

He opens his door, slips out, and is around the back of the car and opening mine before I have my seatbelt fully off. He reaches out his hand and helps me to my feet, and I have this urge to kiss him again.

I am not usually one to make the first move. Especially since whatever we are doing is still so undefined.

But my body takes over.

It's just a quick, soft brush of my lips over his.

A taste. A fix.

But when I pull away, his arm comes around my back, and he presses me hard against the side of the car. His hand is in my hair, tongue parting my lips. It's a kiss I can feel all the way down to my toes.

One kiss turns into two, then three. Until I lose count, and he pulls away, out of breath.

"We should really go inside." His thumb runs the length of my lower lip. But then he kisses me again, this one too brief, before pulling back with a groan. "Quick, before I change my mind."

I lead him from the back parking lot down a narrow alley to the front of the building.

The outside of Nona Sardo's Italian Eatery looks like a simple residential cottage.

There's no sign indicating it's an Italian restaurant, or any restaurant at all, but there is a large, life-sized statue of a moose. Its head is brown and lifelike, with large light brown antlers. Painted on its body is a Toronto Maple Leafs jersey, rainbow-colored knee-high socks, and a black-and-yellow pirate hat. It was once part of some public art display in Toronto in the early 2000s, then somehow made its way up to Port Logan and the front sidewalk of Nona Sardo's, giving the restaurant its nickname. Tourists might be able to find the place if they stumble across the right Tripadvisor recommendation. But only locals call it "the Moose."

We open the front door to a blast of warm air that smells like tomato sauce and garlic bread. The Moose has only six tables, plus a room at the back reserved for family celebrations, and only if you know Nona Sardo well enough to ask. The tables are covered with red-and-white tablecloths, with old bottles of Chianti in the middle. Each has a long white candle inside, dripping layers of white wax over the side. It's homey, romantic, and perfect.

"Hey, Jules." Danielle, Nona's youngest daughter, greets me as she emerges from the kitchen, a plate of creamy fettuccine in each hand. "You can have that table back in the corner. The other one is a reservation."

The corner table is one Nona always keeps open for locals wandering in. I'm surprised to find it vacant.

"Actually, I think we are your reservation," I tell her. "But that table looks great."

Danielle tips her head sideways, looking past me. "Oh, hey, Reeve. I didn't see you there. Mom wanted to say hello tonight, but her hip is bad, so she's at home. She sends her love, though. I'll be over in just a minute." She sets the plates in front of two guests I don't recognize.

I move to the table, slip off my coat, and place it on the back of my chair, trying to fit this new piece of Reeve into the unfinished puzzle of him in my head. "Okay, how do you know Nona?" I ask as I pull my chair back and we sit.

Reeve settles into the spot across from me. "We had a place near here in Southampton when I was a kid. There was a solid summer where the only thing I wanted to eat was gnocchi, so I always came here with my nana."

I try to picture Reeve as a little kid but can't.

"I came here as a kid, too, every Friday night. My mom would get paid and then pick me up from my after-school babysitter, and we'd drive down here and split a giant plate of spaghetti. You never know. You could have been sitting at one of the tables next to me and I never even noticed."

Reeve leans forward, his forearms resting on the top of the table. "Maybe. But I think I would have noticed."

My stomach fills with that fluttery feeling that has become synonymous with being around Reeve.

"Do you try to be charming?" I ask. "Or does it just ooze out of you naturally?"

He smiles. "With you, Jules, I'm always trying."

We're interrupted as Danielle comes to take our order. We select a bottle of red to split and both choose the gnocchi as our main. Danielle immediately brings the wine over and pours it into two stemless glass tumblers.

Reeve tips his glass toward mine. "I know we did things a little out of order, but I'm glad we ended up here." He lifts his glass for a cheers. "To our first date."

I clink my glass with his, trying to find the right words to respond. Instead, I pick up our conversation from where we left it a moment ago. "So, does your family still come up here?"

Reeve shakes his head. "No, they've rented the place the last few years and sold it last summer. My oldest brother is an orthopedic surgeon and works all the time, and my younger brother just finished law school and joined my dad's firm, so the place was sitting empty most of the year."

My eyebrows lift involuntarily. "Wow! Impressive family."

Reeve offers what feels like a forced smile. "They like to think so." He sets his glass down next to mine, and whether intentional or not, when he pulls his hand away, his fingers brush the back of my hand.

"What about you?" I ask. "Where does all that love for art come from? Your mom?"

Reeve leans back in his seat and shakes his head. "My mom is a CFO for a big telco. She's probably the least interested in art. I thought I might be adopted for a while, but we all look alike, which puts a big hole in that theory."

"Did you ever end up working in a gallery?" I think back to our conversation on the dock. "I remember you said you were trying to get an internship."

Reeve nods. "I did. Best three months of my life. They wanted me to stay on longer, but their budgets were limited and they couldn't guarantee when the position would become paid. My dad golfs with Howard Mansfield. They go way back. So when he had an opening at his company, I was strongly encouraged to take it."

The way Reeve smiles makes me think it was a little more than strong encouragement.

"Do you like your job?"

Reeve thinks about my question. "I wouldn't say *like*. Real estate isn't really my thing, but I do get kind of a rush when I close a deal. It's kind of the same feeling as when I find a really great piece of art, so I figure that counts for something. What about you? Do you like working at the retirement home?"

"I do." I nod, taking a sip of water. "I applied to work there thinking it would be a good way to pad my résumé for med school and then I fell in love with the place. The residents are great, and I feel like the work I do is actually helping people."

Reeve takes a sip of his wine. "Do you think you'll ever go?" he asks. "To med school, I mean."

He is looking at me like I'm still that same girl I was on that dock. The one who saw the future she wanted and wasn't afraid to admit it out loud—as improbable as it might be.

"I actually applied for next fall." It feels surprisingly good to say it out loud. "So I guess that's up to U of T."

His eyebrows lift. "That's amazing. When will you find out if you get in?"

I lift my wineglass to my lips and drain the last of it. "Final decisions are made by May, but I need to get invited to the interview round first."

Reeve nods, picking up the bottle of wine and topping off my glass. "And when do you find out about that?"

My stomach squeezes. "They said we will hear, either way, by the end of January. So any day now, I guess."

Reeve's eyes go wide. "So are you checking your email every hour?"

My hand instinctively reaches for my coat pocket, closing around the hard edges of my Samsung phone to confirm it's still there. "I glanced at it this morning for about thirty seconds for something unrelated, but other than that, I have avoided checking it completely."

Reeve eyes me as if he's waiting for some sort of punch line. "Seriously? Not even once?"

I shake my head, pulling my phone from my pocket and setting it on the table as if presenting evidence.

Reeve stares at it. "You mean, your answer could be sitting in there right now waiting for you."

I shrug. "Theoretically, yes."

Reeve shakes his head, smiling. "What are you waiting for?"

"I don't know. . . . The right time? The nerve." The honest answer is probably some deeper Schrödinger-based explanation. Right now, that email could be in there, or it could not.

"Why not do it now?"

The way he says it makes it seem so easy. "Open your email. Take a look. Rip the Band-Aid off," he teases.

"That sounds like a terrible idea."

He nudges my phone closer to my hand with his fingers.

Now that I've considered the idea, I can't unthink it. I could do it right now, and then I'd at least know either way.

"Fine." I slide the phone over to his side of the table. "But you have to do it."

Reeve stares at the phone and then at me. "You want *me* to check your email?"

I fold my arms across my chest. "I was ready to come here tonight and enjoy my wine in pure, ignorant bliss until you suggested ripping Band-Aids off." I pick up the phone, swipe it open, click on my Gmail, and hand it to him. "Here you go. Rip away."

He takes the phone tentatively as if trying to figure out how serious I am. "I think you should be the one doing this."

I close my eyes, unable to watch. Afraid to see an expression cross his face that I'll never be able to unsee. "I can't. Right now I need to focus on not throwing up."

I wait for a moment. With my eyes closed, I can't tell if he's looking or still staring at me.

"It's here," he finally says, and my heart jumps straight up my esophagus and into my throat.

"Do not joke, Reeve, please." My voice cracks.

I hear Reeve's chair scraping across the floor, then I feel his warm hand on my back.

"I really think you need to read it."

I open one eye and then the other.

He's holding my phone in front of me. My eyes scan the screen and stop.

The University of Toronto Admissions Office; Update to Medical School Application

The preview cuts off after *application*. No hint of the contents or which way they will go.

It's like time halts around me.

After what feels like an eternity, I find my ability to speak. "They really should be more detailed in their email notifications. It's like they're already trying to weed out those of us with weak hearts."

Reeve strokes my back in small, soothing circles.

My thumb hovers over the screen, shaking.

I click.

The words in front of me blur.

"Jules." Reeve rubs my back a little firmer. "Jules, look at it."

I open my eyes. I hadn't realized I'd even closed them in the first place. The letters in front of me come into focus enough for me to read in small chunks: *congratulations . . . interview . . . Toronto.*

My heart hammers hard as I look a second time.

"Holy shit. This is real, right?"

Reeve's lips lightly press my temple. "Congratulations."

My heart, which is still relocated north of my esophagus, begins to beat even harder and faster. I'm not sure if I want to let out a loud, celebratory scream or retract my knees into the fetal position until I calm down.

However, before I can decide, Danielle arrives with our pasta. Reeve scoots his chair back to his side of the table, and the only thing I manage is to sit and watch as she places our plates down with a "Buon appetito."

I pick up my fork, but I'm shaking too hard to actually eat. Instead, I set it down, pick up my phone, and reread the email.

It's still there. It's still real.

"Does it tell you when your interview is?" Reeve asks.

I scan to the end of the page. "The end of March."

"In Toronto, I assume?"

I nod, clicking through the various links. "Yes, at the St. George Campus."

Reeve holds up his wineglass, his pasta still untouched. "Congratulations, Jules. I remember how badly you wanted this, and I'm glad it's happening."

I set the phone on the table to pick up my wineglass and clink it with his. The shock has worn off just enough for some reality to seep in. "It's not happening yet. I still need to make it through the interview and figure out if I can actually pay for four years of atrociously expensive school, not to mention food and housing."

Reeve takes a drink. "My brother went through it a few years ago. There are lots of loan programs, and most banks are eager to get the business of a future doctor."

I sip the wine still suspended in midair from our cheers. "Yes, I looked into them before—back when I was about to apply two years ago—but . . ." I consider how much I want to tell him. How the next part may change things between us. But if this part is going to make him run, it's better he runs now. "My mom had some trouble with her credit score, which became my trouble when she started using my SIN to try and get herself out of it." I pause to gauge his reaction, but his face is blank and unreadable. "I am now what banks call a *subprime borrower*, so I'm going to have to figure something else out. Maybe buy lotto tickets, hope for a miracle, or figure out how to sell pictures of my feet."

My lame attempt to lighten the mood doesn't seem to work. If anything, a concerned ridge forms between Reeve's eyebrows.

"Is that why you didn't apply?" he asks. "Two years ago, I mean."

I nod. "It's how I discovered my mom's spending in the first place. But I have it under control now." I feel the need to explain that, unlike my mother, I do have my life together. "I've been on a payment plan. I need another year or two of steady payments to repair the rest of the damage. . . ." I leave my thoughts unfinished and instead study Reeve in an attempt to dissect what he's thinking.

His wineglass is paused halfway to his lips. I swear he's about to say something, but instead, he sets the glass down and reaches for his phone. He scrolls for a moment and then places it back in his suit pocket.

When he looks at me again, I know something is off. There's a feeling in my chest that is sending off glaring red alarm bells in the back of my mind. So when he reaches for his wine and stops a second time, I burst.

"Okay, what are you thinking?"

Reeve picks up my phone and sets it on the table between us. "I saw something in your email when I was looking for your application update."

My stomach drops so hard, I swear I hear it thunk.

"I wasn't trying to snoop," Reeve continues, "and I wasn't going to bring it up tonight because we're celebrating, but now I wonder if it might be relevant."

I'm mentally combing through my emails, wondering what could be in there. Another creditor notice? Or maybe some X-rated porno foot spam. *Oh, god! What if he thought I was serious about the foot pics?*

"Can I ask why you have an email from Niles James about 1243 St. Mary Street?"

"Oh, that." Relief rushes through me. "Niles James is a lawyer. He works for one of my former residents—she died a few months ago and left me that property in her will. There were some legal things that needed to be worked out before everything was final. But I found out this morning it all went through."

"*You* inherited that property?" Reeve's fork clanks against his plate. "Jules, that's amazing."

I shake my head. "No, actually, it's not. The place is a mess. It's completely abandoned, and I just found out that I will have to start paying property taxes on it next year, which is a lot of money—money, as you now know, I can't really afford."

Reeve shakes his head as if clearing it. "Jules, I have been looking for you."

His words don't quite register.

"What?"

He draws back in his seat, then immediately leans forward again. "That property has been on my radar for months. It was why I was up in West Lake the night of Kitty's funeral. I had been talking to her about selling it, but then she passed away before we could reach an agreement, and then the executor—Niles James—wouldn't tell me who inherited it until it went through probate. I can't believe it's been you all along."

Suddenly, the events of the last few months look very different in my head. "Wait, *that's* why you were up here?"

Reeve takes a long sip of his wine. "Yes. West Lake was on our short list for possible locations for the new build, and when the St. Mary property stalled, we started looking elsewhere, but now that it's potentially back on the market—" He pauses. "Wait, are you planning to sell it?"

I don't know.

I don't know anything right now.

"No? Maybe? You want to buy it? To what, build condos?"

"Yes." Reeve nods, and I'm grateful for the short, uncomplicated answer.

Sell the property to a developer. To Reeve.

My heart starts beating hard. I can't help but think it's saying *bad, bad, bad*. I have feelings about developers. They are not good ones.

"I don't know if I can do that," I tell him honestly. "Condos in West Lake . . ."

Reeve does nothing but take my hand.

Developments are evil leeches on the local economy. I know this. But I also know I have no way to pay these property taxes if I don't sell it to someone.

"Hey." Reeve gently squeezes my hand. "I know I've put you in a weird position, and I really should talk to my boss before we talk about this too much more, but I think you should know that your property is worth a lot of money."

My heart double beats. "It is?"

Reeve nods. "You should get a good lawyer, Jules, and a real estate agent. They'll be able to advise you without any conflict of interest."

The price tags of both send a wave of acid up my throat. "I can't afford a lawyer."

Reeve pushes a glass of water toward me. I drink three big gulps, but it doesn't help.

"If you sell, you will. You'll be able to afford a lot more."

A thought occurs. "Like a four-year medical degree?"

Reeve smiles; it's the first one that doesn't feel forced since the turn in conversation. "You could definitely afford that."

"Oh, god." I reach for the water again, change my mind, and take a big swig of wine.

Reeve waits for me to swallow. "Take some time and think. You don't need to decide anything right now. It will take a few weeks to get my team together anyway. I can even show you a model of the development if you think it will help. It's going to be a really beautiful space."

I must nod because Reeve lets go of my hand.

My brain recites that long list of reasons on why condos in West Lake are a terrible idea. But my heart travels back to that night on the dock and the girl who pictured herself at medical school, her entire future bright in front of her. She's been lost to me these last two years as I've lived on autopilot, showing herself for only a few brief, disorienting moments to press send on my application. I knew that night that going to medical school would require a Hail Mary—a miracle. I just never imagined the dance hall would be it.

Reeve reaches for his wineglass. "I think we should get back to celebrating. Getting a med school interview is a big deal." He raises it up. "Here's to you, getting your dream."

My dream.

I manage to lift up my own glass and clink. And drink. And

eventually, pick up my fork and eat an entire plate of Nona's famous gnocchi.

I stay in a half-catatonic, half-euphoric state throughout dinner and the boozy tiramisu Danielle brings out for dessert. By the time we climb back into Reeve's car, the unsettled feeling in my stomach has shifted to being just plain stuffed.

It starts to snow as we drive back to West Lake. Teeny-tiny white flakes that blow across the windshield without sticking to it. I check my weather app, ensuring it's just a little blip and not a storm, realizing how dark the roads get at night. As if I haven't lived here all my life.

"You really need to go back tonight?"

Reeve lets out a long sigh. "Yeah. I've spent the last twenty minutes trying to come up with some believable excuse to tell my boss, but it's a big meeting, and I really can't." He reaches to turn the heat down slightly, quieting the car. "But I've also been thinking, when you come down for your interview, you could stay with me for a few days? I can take a day or two off if it's midweek, or you can spend the weekend. What do you think?"

My head reels with everything else that would bring. Reeve's place. A glimpse into Reeve's life. Reeve's bed.

"Yeah. Great. That sounds like fun." I pause, and I can feel him staring at me. "Sorry, I just . . . need to process everything a little more. Maybe sleep on it for a night or two or five, but then I'll text you, and we can plan."

He pulls the car up in front of my place, again opening my door before I have a chance to. We linger on the steps of my front stoop, the lights of the pizzeria reflecting in his eyes.

"Do you want to come up?" The question comes out of my mouth before I fully think through the consequences.

He throws his head back with a groan. "You don't know how badly I want to say yes." He steps in closer. "But if I come up now, I don't know if I'll be able to leave, so I think it's better if I say good night here."

He leans forward, resting his forehead against mine.

"I'm sorry you came all this way," I tell him. "I know it's a lot."

His hand reaches up to cup my chin as he plants a soft goodbye kiss on my lips.

"That's the thing, Jules. It's not nearly enough."

Chapter 18

When I get into my apartment, I close the door behind me and, with the lights still off, bury my face into my coatrack, thinking about the night with the tiny bit of perspective I gathered as I walked up the stairs.

I just had, arguably, the best official first date of my life, with a man so hot he gives me repeated heart palpitations.

Not only that, but I also got a medical school interview, and the weird old building I inherited is potentially worth enough that if I did get into medical school, I might actually be able to go and move within reasonable dating distance of the aforementioned heart-palpitating man. If I'm willing to sign a deal that would almost definitely screw over my entire town in some way.

It all feels too complicated. Too intricate. It's a precarious tower of blocks where if one slips, it could send the entire structure to the ground. I hate how most of this feels so out of my control. Reeve. My interview. Even the dance hall still feels like a wild card. I still have no more answers on why Kitty left it to me. She obviously knew it was valuable and that Reeve's company was interested in buying it.

I wish I could talk to her. Ask her what she was thinking and what the hell she wants me to do.

But I can't.

At least, not the Kitty I once knew.

I walk to my bed, open the nightstand drawer, and stare at Kitty's diary. All three times I read it previously, I ended up in one of my weird dreams. Perhaps tonight, I can *make* it happen? Catapult myself into a past I'm not sure actually existed. But this time, I can demand answers.

I open it to the entry where I left off. It is a very lengthy pros and cons list with Beau's name on top of one side and Knots's name on the other. I laugh a little at how well I predicted the criteria. *Beau: handsome face, Knots: wonderful dancer.* I skim through more of the same: *Beau: sophisticated and worldly, Knots: funny and kind,* until I reach the last entry under Beau, and it makes my breath catch: *I could leave and never look back. I could be the person I'm meant to be.*

That phrase *never look back* reminds me of something I once read. A phrase written in a diary in a similar teenage scribble—but the diary in my memory belonged not to Kitty but to my mother.

I was twelve or thirteen when I found it, at home by myself one night, snooping around my mother's closet more out of boredom than anything else. The diary was in a box with a few of her other childhood things that she took from Gigi's house before she sold it. I spent the next week reading it with a flashlight under the covers of my bed on the nights when my mom was out late and I was scared of the dark and the weird muffled yelling that always came from the condo above us.

It wasn't the usual entries you'd expect from a preteen. No angsty love letters about her crushes or angry venting about a fight she had with a friend. Her entries were all about wanting to leave West Lake. *I hate it here. I will never be like Grandma Gigi, doing the same stupid things day after day. As soon as I can, I'm going to leave and never come back.*

I memorized that passage, wanting to understand her but never quite fully comprehending why she hated our home so much.

So it's my mother who occupies my thoughts as my eyelids begin to droop and I slip toward sleep.

But when I awaken a little while later, in that hazy state that isn't quite a dream but also isn't fully awake, it's not my mother but Kitty St. Clair beside me.

We're on a bus.

It's dusk outside. And quiet inside. Kitty's head is pressed against the window, but I can see, from the reflection in the glass, that her eyes are open.

"What's happening this time?" I whisper.

Kitty lifts her head at the sound of my voice. "Oh good, you're awake. I think we must be almost there."

She points to something outside the window. I follow the direction of her finger to an outcropping of buildings in the distance.

"Can you remind me where 'there' is again?"

Kitty lets out a long, dramatic sigh. "Honestly, Dot. Sometimes, I can't tell if you're telling a joke or being serious. It's Toronto."

I can count the number of times I have been to Toronto on one hand.

Once with my mom and one of her boyfriends when I was little. Then, a grade twelve field trip to a Blue Jays game. Then, twice more with Zoe, who was dating a guy she met who lived in Etobicoke until she decided that long-distance relationships were a form of self-inflicted torture because absence only made her heart think about the orgasms she wasn't having. She dumped the guy at the Greyhound bus station at the end of one of our weekend visits, declaring from then on that she was going after only "local dick." Neither of us has been back to Toronto since—until now.

I know the area south of the Eaton Centre well enough to identify it, and yet the closer we get to the core, the more I realize it's not the same city of my youth. The streets are still covered with large bricked apartment buildings and office towers. But they aren't quite as tall, and there are fewer than I remember. The skyline is missing notable landmarks, too. There's no CN Tower or SkyDome, but as our bus pulls up in front of Union Station with its imposing stone columns, I do recognize the iconic green roof of the Royal York Hotel across the street.

"So, are we running away?" I ask Kitty, who is checking and rechecking the contents of her purse.

"Can you imagine?" Kitty pulls out a piece of paper and hands it to me. "Beau said that we are to go into the hotel and ask the concierge to call this number, and then he will come down to fetch us and take us to his cousin's house."

"Ah, so we are back on Team Beau again?"

Kitty rolls her eyes. "What on earth are you talking about now?"

I shake my head. "Sorry, what I meant to ask is what happened to you and Knots? I thought you were super into him, and now . . . well, now we're on a bus."

"I don't know why you keep asking me this." Kitty flushes pink. "I told you, Knots and I aren't officially going steady yet. Beau invited me to visit, and I thought it would be the perfect opportunity to get a taste of city life. Get out of West Lake for once. See if Toronto is right for us. If we could picture ourselves here."

This, at least, is something I can relate to.

If I get into med school, I will have to move here to Toronto for at least two years to attend my foundational classes and labs. Then, when I move to the clinical part of the program, I could theoretically be assigned to a placement anywhere in Ontario for another two years. Not to mention residency after that.

"It's busy," I say as we step off the bus and onto Front Street.

"What is?" Kitty looks around.

"The city. It's busy. Too many cars. Lots of noise. And people."

As if to illustrate my point, one of those people comes flying by on a bicycle so close that Kitty shrieks.

Once the bike has passed and Kitty has taken a safe step back from the road, she removes her hand from over her heart and uses it to brush back her curls. "Well, I happen to like people."

She smiles past me at the bus driver unloading luggage from a storage compartment below the bus. When he pulls out two small canvas suitcases, she calls to him, "Yoo-hoo! Those belong to us," to which he responds by stopping his unloading job to bring them over, setting them down at our feet with a "You be safe now, girls."

Kitty eyes me as she reaches for one of the handles, as if she's just presented irrefutable proof to her point: that she likes people, and people, in turn, like her back.

I pick up the other suitcase and follow her as she crosses the street toward the hotel.

"It's also expensive," I call out after her, not quite ready to drop my side of the argument. "Way more expensive than West Lake."

Kitty stops on the sidewalk. "Well, Beau has lots of money."

I shake my head. "Fine, but what if, in the future, Beau decides he's not interested anymore? What then?"

Kitty glares at me like it's a preposterous thought to consider. "Why are you being so negative? The glass doesn't have to be half-empty all of the time, you know. Sometimes it's half-full with room for opportunity."

"I'm not being negative," I argue back, wondering how this figment of my imagination has pegged me so accurately. "I just . . . recognize how much I've been served in this aforementioned glass. Maybe I've learned there's no point in asking for more."

Kitty stops on the steps and turns to face me. The way she carries herself with her shoulders pressed back and that determined set of her jaw makes her look so much older than eighteen.

"Then that's the difference between us, Dot. You can be happy in the life you were handed. But when I am an old woman, ready to die in my bed, I want to know that I chose my life—I didn't settle for it."

With that, she turns and marches toward the hotel entrance, leaving me speechless on the steps.

That felt harsh, even for Kitty.

Despite the fact that I am already in a weirdly vivid dream, I close my eyes and, in a very *Inception*-y way, picture Kitty as an old woman in her last days and wonder what she thought about her life. I remember her playing gin rummy with Mrs. Hail against Mr. McNaught and Mr. Minard. After being dealt her hand, she picked up her cards and sighed. "These simply won't do," she said, shuffling the cards. Mrs. Hail made a comment. Something about cards being like your lot in life and how you play what you get.

I remember Kitty setting her cards on the table and staring at Mrs. Hail. "I don't know about you, but I chose my life, darling. I did exactly what I wanted when I wanted to do it. If opportunities weren't there, I simply created them." Mrs. Hail waved her off. I did, too, at the time, but now it makes me think about how Old Lady Me would see her life. She'd probably stare out her window for a moment at the same view of the lake she'd looked at since she was a girl and say something perfectly practical like, "It's not *settling* to be content with the hand life has dealt you."

Except, as I dwell on the thought for another heartbeat, I realize that's exactly what settling is.

While I have been having an existential crisis on the steps, Kitty has continued to the hotel door without me. I run after her, reaching her just as the doorman pulls it open. He's so immersed in watching her that he fails to see me coming. Once she's inside, he lets it go, and the door starts to close with a slow, even swing, forcing me to sprint the last few steps and maneuver my body sideways to slip in behind her. I'm so preoccupied with not getting hit by the door that I nearly knock Kitty over as she stands just inside, mouth agape, looking up.

"What's wrong?" I ask, curious as to the reason for the sudden stop.

Her only response is a small, soundless gasp.

I follow her gaze, tracing the high mahogany ceilings with their intricate moldings to the large crystal chandeliers glittering above, then down to the plush velvet sofas on the intricately patterned marble floors.

"That there. Dotty," she finally says, "that's your answer. Look at this place. Everything about this hotel feels like it earns the word *opulent*." She reaches for my hand, tearing her gaze from the ceiling to meet my eyes.

"I want so badly for this to be my world," she says, squeezing my fingers so hard I almost yelp.

"I want to wake up every morning and put on a pair of heels and a smart outfit. And I want to know all about interesting things and dress in the best fashions, and when people see me coming, I want them to say, 'Here comes Kitty, gosh, isn't she just the most fabulously fascinating girl you've ever met?'"

"But, Kitty, don't you think—" I begin to argue, but Kitty cuts me off, her eyes shifting to something over my shoulder.

"Them!" She points at two women walking through the middle of the hotel lobby. "Would you look at them, Dotty? They are so beautifully glamorous I'm absolutely positive they must live fascinating lives."

I turn to watch the women in question cross the lobby floor. It's true. They have that air of pulled-togetherness that I have often aspired to but never come close to achieving. The taller of the two wears a light knee-length pencil skirt and fitted blouse accessorized with pearls, white gloves, and a matching handbag. Her shorter friend is in a lavender day dress with a cinched waist and a full A-line skirt. They laugh as they walk, their tall pump heels clacking on the marble floors, unaware of Kitty, who watches them wistfully. "If only I could be exactly like them," she whispers, more to herself than to me.

"But you are," I tell her, unable to separate this Kitty in front of me from the one I knew not that long ago. The Kitty who once, during arts and crafts hour, pointed at the television and a young Mikhail Baryshnikov as he wooed Carrie Bradshaw in an old *Sex and the City* rerun.

"I danced with that man once," she had said with the same easy tone she used to describe the weather. "I was at Studio 54, celebrating my dear friend Estelle's birthday, and this man came up and began doing the Hustle with me. He was a marvelous dancer and quite charming as well. He invited me back to his hotel. I had to decline, of course, because I was a married woman. I had given birth to three children by then! But imagine my shock when I returned to Toronto and he was on the front page of the paper's entertainment section—dancing in *Giselle*." She went back to painting her birdhouse or whatever craft we were working on that day while the rest of us stared and gaped.

Kitty St. Clair was fabulous.

Or at least she becomes fabulous.

Right now, I am at a loss on how to explain this to the Kitty beside me, who is still a girl. The one who stares wide-eyed at the beautiful women and shakes her head. "No, Dotty, I am not like them. Not yet, anyway. But mark my words, one day, I will be."

Once the women leave, we find the concierge, who takes the paper with Beau's number and calls it to let him know we've arrived. About twenty minutes later, Beau picks us up in a shiny black Cadillac, driving us north, away from all the looming downtown buildings and into a more suburban area.

"My cousin Eleanor is looking forward to hosting you," Beau says as he turns onto a street with large bricked estates and sprawling lawns.

"Well, we are looking forward to meeting her as well. She seems like a . . ." Kitty leaves the thought unfinished, her mouth gaping in another soundless gasp as Beau pulls the car onto a long paved driveway and stops in front of a large Tudor-style home.

"Well, this is it," he says, ignoring or not noticing Kitty's half-open mouth.

She manages to close it before Beau comes around to open her door. Still, when he leans to open mine, I catch her wide eyes over his turned shoulder as she silently mouths to me what looks like *Oh my heck!*

We stare at the large two-story stone house with its big glass windows and steeply pitched roofs, then at the manicured gardens and three-car garage. At the same time, Beau jumps the front steps two at a time to ring the front bell.

"Good grief! It looks like a castle," Kitty whispers to me when Beau is out of earshot.

I glance around and find that this time, I can't argue with her.

Beau takes us inside, where he introduces us to his cousin Eleanor, then leaves with a promise to return in two hours to take us to dinner. Eleanor escorts us up the wide swirling staircase to the east wing on the second floor.

Six bedrooms, Kitty mouths when Eleanor gives us a quick tour.

"And this one is yours," Eleanor says, turning around just as Kitty schools her face back into a cordial smile.

Eleanor pushes open the heavy oak door. "I assumed you two would want to share, but let Henrietta know if you prefer your own rooms."

She waits outside while Kitty and I step in and stare at a large four-poster bed that looks big enough for the two of us to do synchronized snow angels and never touch fingertips.

"I think we will be just fine," Kitty answers.

"I've left a few of my old dresses in there"—from the hallway, Eleanor points to a large wooden wardrobe in the corner of the room—"in case you don't have anything suitable. We are going to the club tonight."

Kitty nods as if she knew this was the plan all along. "Thank you, Eleanor, and thank you for inviting us to stay."

"It's nothing," Eleanor says with a polite half smile before leaving and closing the door behind her.

"*Did* she invite us?" I ask Kitty, who rolls her eyes in response.

"Beau invited us. When I told him I'd never been to Toronto, he insisted on hosting us, but you know how my mother gets. She didn't feel it was appropriate, and I would rather die than have her act as my chaperone, so staying with Eleanor was a happy compromise."

Kitty hoists her canvas suitcase onto the chest at the end of the bed, unclicks the fasteners, and lifts the lid.

"I brought my dancing dress to wear tonight, but I wonder . . ."

She shuts the lid of her suitcase and moves toward the wardrobe Eleanor pointed to a moment ago. "We should probably take a look."

She opens one of the doors, which hides her from my view. A moment later, I hear an "Oh my heavens" before Kitty's arm—and only her arm—juts out from behind the door, holding a pale pink chiffon dress.

"Dotty, you have to come and see these with your own eyes. I've never seen such beautiful gowns in my entire life."

The rest of her body emerges from behind the door, holding a second dress up to her body, this one a pale blue made of some sort of silk or satin.

"Here." She hands me the pink dress. "Try it on. You look so lovely in pink."

Turns out I actually do.

Kitty fixes my hair. It's the very same curled style from the first dream. When she finally deems us ready, we stand in front of a full-length mirror where I'm forced to admit that if being pulled together and sophisticated was our aim, we've come pretty darn close.

She wraps her arm around my waist, laying her head on my shoulder, her eyes still fixed on her reflection. "I'll bet you anything Eleanor looks like this every single day. Not just on special occasions. Can you imagine?"

The question remains rhetorical because we're interrupted by a knock on the door.

Eleanor's housekeeper, Henrietta, informs us that Beau is here and waiting for us downstairs.

We're ushered outside toward another fancy black car. This one is a little bigger than the one Beau picked us up in earlier.

He steps out, as does the driver, an older gentleman wearing a long black coat and matching black patent driving cap.

Beau reaches us first, extending his hand to Kitty with a "You look beautiful tonight."

Kitty takes it and then dips underneath, twirling in a slow circle. Beau watches her with a look Zoe would describe as *smitten kitten* as he presses the back of her palm to his lips, dissolving Kitty into a fit of giggles.

Eleanor emerges from the house a moment later in a silvery gown even more beautiful than the ones Kitty and I are wearing. Kitty doesn't say anything but watches Eleanor for longer than a beat before turning her attention to the car with a "Shall we?"

The four of us climb into the car, where another of Beau's friends is waiting.

We reverse our earlier drive, heading south into the heart of the city. The lights from the buildings filtering through the windows illuminate the car in tiny, fleeting pockets.

Beau points out notable landmarks to Kitty, who oohs and aahs, as his friend and Eleanor engage in a whispered conversation that appears intimate.

The car continues to wind through the city until we pull to a stop in front of an old stone building, even larger and more intimidating than Eleanor's home.

"This is Beau's social club," Kitty whispers as we step out of the car. We're ushered along a stone path covered by a long awning into a small lobby area where our coats are gathered and given to a coat check girl.

"He comes here three times a week," Kitty continues. "Two days to curl and one to play tennis. It's incredibly exclusive; you need to be invited to join."

I nod, my face an expression of awe, although not at the exclusivity of the place but at how unbelievably different Beau's life is from mine.

It's a thought that lingers as we are escorted into a small but beautiful ballroom with glittering crystal chandeliers and dark mahogany floors, where we're seated at a table next to the currently empty dance floor. We're brought a round of elegant-looking drinks in fancy cocktail glasses, and intricate canapés served on silver trays by men with white dinner jackets and black bow ties. The dream, the night, whatever this is, continues to roll on as we are joined by more and more of Beau's friends dressed in elegant evening wear, bearing bottles of champagne or shiny crystal glasses of dark liquor.

I sit back and watch it all as if it were a movie playing out right in front of me. The crowd gathered around our table, with Kitty holding court in its center. The careful way she drops her voice, low and conspiratorial, as she tells a story. The way the crowd around her leans in close, hanging on her every word. Her brief pause, just before the punch line, that causes everyone, including myself, to hold their breath.

She's magnetic.

Even I am drawn into her orbit, wondering what she will say next, until she throws her head back and laughs, declaring, "You have all been such wonderful company, but I do think it's time for someone to ask me to dance."

There is a ten-person band set up in the opposite corner. They've been here since before we arrived. Yet, I only now notice that their subdued jazzy notes of earlier have been replaced by lively swings and jitterbugs. One of Beau's friends, a tall ginger-haired man, quickly takes up Kitty's ask and offers her the first dance. Then Beau himself takes the second and third. Song after song ripples through the ballroom. Kitty dances them all, barely leaving the dance floor before she's swept back with a new partner.

At one point, I lose track of her completely, but then, I walk into the ladies' room and see her sitting on a plush sofa in the corner, reading a piece of paper, her eyes red and puffy.

"Kitty! What happened? Are you okay?"

Kitty looks up at the sound of my voice. Her fingers fumble with the paper before shoving it into her evening bag. She pulls out a small white handkerchief, which she uses to dab at the corners of her eyes.

"I'm fine," she says, smoothing out the wrinkles in her dress. "Just needed a little break from all of the dancing, that's all. This place is fabulous. Don't you think? I'm having the best time."

Best times don't usually lead to crying in a bathroom.

"What's that?" I drop my gaze to her evening bag.

Kitty hesitates, looking from me to her bag twice before slowly prying it back open. She reaches inside, pulls out the piece of paper from earlier, and hands it to me.

"He gave it to me just before your daddy drove us to the bus station. I didn't tell him why we were coming here, but I think he knew."

I unfold the paper carefully. The loopy blue handwriting is vaguely familiar.

Dearest Kitty,

I had a dream last night. You were in it. We had a quiet little cottage down on the beach. It wasn't big, but it was nice, with a stone fireplace in the kitchen and a big veranda where we could sit out and watch the water. You were sitting in my lap, and my arms were around your waist, and I swear I could even smell the flowers of your perfume. It's like you were really there. I've been working hard at the dance hall. Mr. Scott says he's considering retiring soon, and I hope he will make me manager. Whatever happens, I'm saving all of my extra money so I can buy a nice place one day. I don't know what I meant to say with this letter. I think I may have gotten a little off track. But I did want to tell you that I think you're swell and I hope you think the same of me. I'll be working at the dance hall this weekend and will save every dance for you if you'll have them.

Sincerely yours,
Knots

My stomach does a funny flip as I read the sign-off. When I look up, Kitty watches me as if waiting for my reaction.

"I think he might be in love with me." She reaches for the note.

I fold it back up and hand it to her. "And are you in love with him?"

She tucks the folded paper into her purse, avoiding my eyes.

If an answer was coming, it's interrupted when the door to the bathroom swings open, hitting the wall with a bang. I watch as Eleanor strolls in, heading straight for the mirrors above the sinks. She leans in close to apply a tube of deep red lipstick, not noticing Kitty until she appraises her own reflection and spots her in the mirror.

She spins around to face the couch. "Kitty, there you are." Her voice reflects the gin fizzes she's been drinking all evening. "I have been looking for you everywhere. I want you to come meet my friend Darlene. She is a riot." Eleanor returns to the mirror to give herself a final look, too preoccupied with her own reflection to notice Kitty dabbing her eyes a final time.

"There." Eleanor steps back, making a quarter turn left and then right. "Come." She holds out her hand to Kitty, who takes it.

I don't get Kitty alone again till well after midnight.

Not until Beau has dropped all of us off at Eleanor's house, and Kitty and I are tucked in next to each other in the giant four-poster bed.

The room is dark, but the moonlight filtering through the window gives me just enough light to make out Kitty's face.

"Hey, Kitty..."

I slipped into this dream intentionally tonight so I could ask her a question. But now that I have her here alone, in the quiet, I don't know where to start.

She doesn't yet know she marries Beau.

She doesn't even know who I really am.

"What's the matter, Dotty?" Kitty runs her finger along the crinkle between my eyebrows. "You look so worried right now."

Worried isn't quite it.

"If you had to decide whether to do something that was good for you and could one day enable you to help people, but it might make life a little harder for many people you care about, what would you do?"

Kitty yawns and snuggles deeper into her pillow, making me wonder if she will answer. But she opens her eyes and looks into mine. "Thinking about what's best for you doesn't mean you don't care about other people, Dot. It means you're smart enough to realize that you can't help anyone if you don't first help yourself."

Chapter 19

My dreams stay Kitty-free for the rest of January and February and into the first two weeks of March, replaced with almost-as-vivid med-school stress dreams where my teeth crumble into dust, or I'm back in high school and unable to find any of my classes.

I see Reeve three more times. I meet him halfway at the Tipsy Fox in Mount Forest for hot wings and an even hotter make-out in the parking lot. Then, a week later, when he has meetings in the area, we both sneak away for a quick lunch at Lou's, but my strictly monitored lunch break allows for only a single slow kiss in the retirement home's parking lot and a murmured "You're gonna need to kiss me longer next time" from Reeve. We plan another dinner at the Moose, but five minutes into the dessert course, I get a call from work telling me the stomach flu has hit the retirement home and taken out the staff. I cut our date short, then cancel our next one when that same flu inevitably takes me down the following weekend.

When I'm finally back at work, it's the week of my interview. I'm feeling as prepared as I can be, having spent most of Sunday lying in bed, reciting aloud to my empty bedroom the answers to my prep guide questions, hoping I sounded more intelligent and less like I was moments away from heaving up the toast I had for lunch.

The retirement home, however, has spent the last two weeks understaffed. Although we've thankfully been able to cover all the necessities, none of the little things have been done. I spend every minute of my Monday shift, including those normally reserved for breaks or lunch, watering plants, painting fingernails, and making gin and tonics.

I don't even see the break room until an hour after my shift officially ends. So when I finally check my phone for the first time all day, I am not entirely shocked to see three missed calls and three text messages from Reeve.

> **Reeve:** Hey! Any chance you're free tonight? I had a meeting cancel, so my afternoon is free.

> **Reeve:** I'm guessing you're working. I'm going to take the chance and hope you're working a regular shift today. I'm on my way. Call me when you get a second.

> **Reeve:** I'm in West Lake and I have a friend I'd love you to meet. I'm going to head over to his place at six. Hopefully, I can see you at some point.

I dial as soon as I finish reading.

He picks up on the second ring. "Hey. Are you at work?"

As I slip on my coat, I press my phone into my shoulder with my cheek. "Just finished my shift. Are you still in town?"

There's the sound of muffled voices on Reeve's end of the line. "I'm actually across the street at Lou's. I'm just about to place an order for takeout. Can I get you something?"

My stomach growls as if answering for me. "Oh my god, I love you. I haven't eaten all day. A burger and fries, please."

There's a pause on Reeve's end of the line.

It's just long enough for me to replay what I just said.

"I didn't mean—"

"You got it—"

We both speak at the same time.

There's another beat of silence. My mortification flushes my cheeks an even deeper shade of red.

"So I guess—"

"Are you on—"

This time, we laugh.

"So, I'll meet you over there?"

"Sounds good," he says. "But we're going to need to eat in my car. I promised my friend I'd be there by six, and there's something I want to show you first."

I push open the stairwell door and step into the hallway, curious as to why he's being so vague. "Who's this friend?"

Reeve hesitates. "He's a lot easier to explain once you see him."

My burger is delicious. I make multiple moaning sounds while I eat and draw amused looks from Reeve as we drive out of West Lake and head toward Port Logan. I'm in that gleeful kind of mood that comes when something good happens unexpectedly, like the guy you've been seeing showing up on a random Monday.

I have a smile on my face when I finally shut my now empty takeout container and let out a satisfied *ahhh*. It stretches even further when Reeve places his hand on my knee and squeezes.

"So you're not going to give me any hints on where we're headed?"

Reeve flicks his blinker. "I don't really need to, seeing as we're already here."

He pulls off the country highway onto a recently paved road, then turns into an empty parking lot and cuts the engine. There is a small building in front of us. It's simple, with white siding and big windows, the land around it a large lot of mud, half dug up, with large construction trucks abandoned for the evening. There's a big sign out front: MANSFIELD PROPERTIES.

The burger in my stomach roils. "Is this your . . . office?"

Reeve undoes his seatbelt and opens his door. "It's the sales office. I wanted to show it to you, remember? I spoke to my boss about your property. He's really interested in discussing it further, but I thought you might want to see the plans before I introduce you to him."

I follow him out of the car, my rational brain reminding me that selling the dance hall is the only way that I'll be able to pay for school. However, something settles in my stomach. It gives context to why they always say *pit*. It feels like a stone. An uncomfortable presence, reminding me that Reeve works for Mansfield and this—I—am part of his job.

"We just broke ground on this one a few weeks ago." Reeve nods at the trucks in the distance, then locks his doors with a high-pitched chirp. "It's going to be beautiful."

"Looks like it," I lie as the pit doubles in size.

Reeve pulls a key from his chain, unlocks the door, then holds it open as he punches in a code to a beeping alarm box. Once the alarm stops, he flicks on the lights and holds out his hand. "Come on in."

The inside of the office is white, with artists' renderings of various projects framed along the walls. I recognize the six-plex from Port Logan and a strip of townhouses down on Cayuga Beach where an old bowling alley once stood. Then I see, in the middle of the room, encased in Plexiglas, a full 3D rendering of a low-rise condo complex. The structure is also all-white, with tiny trees in pots out front and even tinier people walking little model dogs and lounging on red-and-white doughnut-shaped floats in the pool at the building's center.

It is beautiful.

Reeve joins me at the Plexiglas-covered model, getting more animated as he points out where the gym will go, the roof for sunbathing, and the sustainable features he's working to introduce: solar panels, automatic sunshades that gauge the sun's angle and reduce the need for air-conditioning, and a water system to recycle rainwater for the plants.

It all blurs in my head because all I can think about is how that giant gleaming building looks like it belongs somewhere glamorous like Miami or Malibu, not West Lake.

"So what do you think?"

I blink, snapping out of my haze to find Reeve leaning in, watching my face for a reaction.

"It looks like a big project."

He takes this as a compliment, nodding as his hand caresses the Plexiglas. "It was supposed to be managed by one of the senior partners, so when they gave it to me, I took it as a good sign. It might give me grounds for a promotion."

"Oh. Wow." I force the kind of smile you'd expect from a girl who was just told the guy she's dating is up for a big promotion. But my insides are not that same level of okay. They hear the word *promotion* and begin to think about that night at Nona's. Reeve was so excited when he found out I was inheriting the dance hall. But now I wonder, was that enthusiasm for me or for him?

It's an ugly thought. And before it can fully take shape, Reeve reaches for my hand.

"We should get going. Marcus is easygoing when it comes to almost anything, but he's an absolute stickler when it comes to time."

I'm too worried to ask who Marcus is as we get back into the car and pull onto the highway. *What if he's a real estate agent or a lawyer?* I'm not prepared to have a conversation with either of those people yet. I'm considering telling Reeve that I'm feeling sick—that my stomach flu is relapsing—when we turn down a dirt driveway and head into the woods.

The driveway is bumpy and uneven. I have to grip the handle above me as the road twists and turns for a good half kilometer until the trees open up to reveal a small cedar-sided cottage up ahead. The cottage almost blends into the surrounding pine trees. Next to it is what looks like a large garage. The wooden siding looks a little older than the house, aged gray with mossy bits in a few places. Its carriage-style doors are open, and a small orange light illuminates the inside. It's filled with what looks like tables and tables of random stuff.

"Where are we?"

Reeve pulls the car into a clearing next to the trees.

"This place belongs to my friend Marcus Landers." Reeve pauses, and I wonder if I'm supposed to recognize the name.

"He's an artist," Reeve explains. "I met him when I was interning at the gallery. We carried several of his pieces. He's a potter and a sculptor and is incredibly talented."

We get out of the car and start to walk toward the garage. When we are about halfway there, a man comes out to greet us. He looks to be in his mid-sixties—a mixture of Bob Ross and Fred Penner, complete with a bushy gray beard and wild curly hair. He has paint on his pants and clay under his nails, and smells like sandalwood. I like him the moment he shakes my hand.

"Jules, eh? I once had a dog named Jules. She was the best girl."

He shows us around his garage, which is actually his artist's studio. It's filled with wooden tables stacked high with plates and vases and bowls. There are carvings made from wood and rock and molded from clay. Tiny fish and birds with details so intricate you expect them to swim or fly away. Abstract pieces with beauty drawn from delicate curves or stunning blends of color. Every few steps, Marcus picks up a different piece to show us.

"The inspiration for this one came from a seashell I found on the beach."

"I saw a squirrel just like this the other week. The little guy jumped right out in front of my truck."

"My cousin Bert told me I couldn't make a vase that felt like a summer night, and man, I proved him wrong."

We wander for almost an hour before Marcus invites us back to his cottage for hot chocolate. "It's an old family recipe," he says, winking at me while tearing open a pack of Swiss Miss.

We sip our drinks around his kitchen table while a fire crackles in the old stone fireplace beside us.

"This is beautiful." I lift my mug; it's a stunning blend of ombre green, the handle shaped like one of the pine trees outside.

Marcus smiles at my compliment. "I did a whole series of those. They sell fairly well with the tourists. I kept all the ones where things went a little wonky." He points at the imperfect shape of the tree trunk. "The shops don't like them, but to be honest, they're my favorites. The most beautiful parts of nature are found in the flaws. I'll send you home with one." He leans back in his chair, dropping his feet on the stone hearth of the fireplace. "So, do you live down there among the chaos with this one?" he asks me while clapping Reeve on the back.

It takes me a moment before I register that he's asking if I live in Toronto.

"No." I shake my head.

"Not yet." Reeve taps my arm with his. "Jules lives in West Lake, but she will hopefully be in the city for school in September."

"Hmmm." Marcus raises a brow at me. "OCAD? Are you another artist?"

I try to imagine myself at the world-renowned art school. "No, U of T medical school."

Marcus takes a sip of his hot chocolate, masking his expression.

"I moved down there once, back when OCAD opened. I was accepted into their inaugural class, ya know?"

I nod, impressed.

"Wasn't the place for me," he says, placing his mug down and pushing it away. "I didn't even make it till Christmas. Too many people."

I picture him in his wool socks and sweater and can't imagine him in the city. I look down at my own North Face hoodie, bought secondhand and weathered with years of use, and wonder if I'll fit in any better.

"Speaking of the city"—Reeve checks his watch—"I have got to head back there tonight, and it's a bit of a drive, so we should probably get going."

Marcus hugs us both goodbye. He and Reeve disappear while I put on my shoes, and when they return, Reeve has what looks like a wrapped vase in his arms. Marcus waves at us from the frame of his doorway as we make our way to the car through the light layer of snow that has fallen since we went inside.

Reeve starts the engine. He blasts the heat and insists I wait inside while he brushes off the windshield. When he finally joins me, the air has warmed enough that I can no longer see my breath.

"Thanks for coming with me," he says, leaning across the center console.

"I like him," I say. "I can see why you're friends."

Reeve smiles slowly, and I can tell he likes what I've just said. "He understands what I'm about, and when you find people in your life like that, you keep them close."

We're talking about Marcus. I know this. I'm the one who made the comment in the first place, but the way his eyes linger on my neck, my lips, and then my eyes, it makes me think we're also talking about me.

And as if confirming that theory, he cups my cheek in his hand, pulling my head to his. I can smell the chocolate on his breath. "I hate that I have to go back tonight, but at least I don't have to wait too long until . . ."

Until I'm in Toronto and we're alone for an entire weekend.

He reaches for the zipper of my hoodie, his chilled fingers dragging along my skin, sending a shiver up my spine.

"Sorry," he says. "They're cold." His nose skims along the curve of my neck. "And you're so warm."

He bends so his lips hover over the spot—his spot—just along my collarbone, the heat from his breath teasing the surface of my skin.

"Thursday," I say as he finally places a kiss just there. Exactly where I want it.

"Thursday." He kisses a tiny trail all the way to the corner of my mouth, where he kisses me again a little longer. A little harder.

I pull him closer. His hands slide under my shirt and up my back. Our tongues intertwine as my hands slide into his hair. I'm contemplating climbing up and over the console into his lap and am working out the logistics of my move when there's a loud *tap tap tap* on his window.

Reeve lets go of me with a frustrated growl.

The sudden absence of his touch makes me acutely aware of the chill still lingering in the car.

He reaches over and tugs up the zipper of my hoodie with a grin that sends another wave of pulsating heat through me, before he turns and presses the button to roll the window down.

Marcus stands on the other side.

"I'm glad I caught you." He holds up the green tree mug. "Didn't want you to leave without this." He hands it to Reeve, who sets it down in the cup holder.

"I just heard on the radio there's some weather coming in later tonight," Marcus says. "I'd get on the road sooner rather than later." He taps the side of the car. "You kids be safe!"

Marcus lingers as Reeve rolls the window back up.

It becomes clear he intends to see us off.

I clip my seatbelt into the latch, and Reeve shifts the car into drive. He looks over at me, his foot still on the brake. "Thursday?"

I nod. "Thursday."

Chapter 20

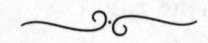

I PLAN TO wake early on Thursday, take a soothing walk on the beach, then drive to Toronto to spend the night at Reeve's, mentally preparing to dazzle at my interview Friday morning.

However, on Wednesday night, Mr. Minard, who was supposed to return from spending the night at the Orillia hospital, has his medical transportation cancel at the last minute. He calls the retirement home, upset that the only alternative is for him to spend yet another night in the hospital, which he hates because the beeping machines and loudspeaker announcements keep him up. I decide to pick him up in Celine instead. That part goes smoothly enough, but then we have to visit two different pharmacies to fill his new prescriptions. Which means I get home late, which means I sleep in late. And since sheer exhaustion prevented me from packing my bags the night before like a sensible human, I have to scramble to find suitable undergarments, which means yet another trip to the drugstore. Needless to say, I am far from the absolute best version of myself when I finally close the door to my apartment and a *call me it's an emergency* text comes through from my mother.

I have to call twice before she picks up.

"Julia?"

"Mom, hey, what's wrong?"

I can hear music in the background. It sounds like the piña colada song.

"Nothing's wrong, sweetheart." The music seems to lower. "Why would you say that?"

I take a deep breath in an effort to take my emotions down a notch. "You texted and said it was an emergency."

My mother laughs. "Oh, that! Yes, I wanted to tell you about my new friend."

I take two more breaths. Neither of them helps.

"I met her at the nail salon the other day," my mother continues. "And it turns out she is a very successful real estate agent, and her office is throwing a new client party this afternoon, so I am going to swing by."

I can see the red flag coming. "You're buying a house?"

My mother laughs. "Of course not, but they don't know that."

The band around my chest loosens at the thought that some mortgage isn't being taken out in my name.

"Anyway," my mother chatters on. "This woman has a son your age. He's a lawyer and looking to buy a place over in Collingwood, and I think it would be fun if you two went out. From the sound of it, he's very single. I could plant the seed today—"

"Mom, no." I cut her off.

"I'm not asking you to marry him, Julia. Although a son-in-law with a chalet would be a nice little bonus. I've always wanted to learn to—"

"I can't, Mom," I try again.

Her response is an audible sigh. "Why not? Because Zoe Buchanan hasn't given her official stamp of approval or because god forbid he has a life outside of West Lake?"

"Because I am seeing someone." I had no intention of telling my mother about Reeve—at least not for the foreseeable future—yet here I am.

"Seeing who?"

I lower my phone to check the time.

"His name is Reeve, and I'm actually on my way to visit him for the weekend and am running very late. I really need to go, so if there isn't an emergency—"

"Visit him where?" It's she who cuts me off this time.

"He lives in Toronto."

"Oh! And what does he do there?"

I move down the stairs and out onto the street. If I don't leave now, I will completely miss the campus tour I signed up for.

"He's in real estate development."

She doesn't so much as take a breath and yet I can hear her excitement. "Commercial or residential?"

"He builds condos." I rush the words out. "I'm sorry, but I really need to go. I'll call you when I'm back, and we can talk then. Okay. I love you, bye!"

I hang up before she has a chance to protest.

I shove my phone into my purse but miss the open slot completely. It clatters to the sidewalk. I'm so concerned with making sure I haven't cracked the screen as I pick it up that I don't even notice Zoe on the sidewalk next to my car watching me until she asks, "What's with the suitcase?"

Her voice startles me so badly that the strap from my gym bag slides off my shoulder and the bag falls onto the sidewalk.

"Jesus Murphy, what are you doing here?"

She bends down, picks up my dropped bag, and hands it to me. "I think you meant to say: Good afternoon, my dearest Zoe, you look absolutely radiant today. What a pleasure it is to see you so unexpectedly."

I take the bag, open my car's back door, and toss it onto the seat. "You're right. I'm sorry. You just scared me. What are you doing here, though? Aren't you supposed to be at work?"

It's just past noon. Zoe and anyone else on shift at Sunnyvale is usually in the dining room at this time, seeing as Thursdays are always butterscotch pudding day and, therefore, kind of a big deal.

Zoe holds up her phone. "Mrs. Hail wandered off without signing out. Bouchard got worried and sent me out to find her. Turns out she's just getting her hair done, so I'm on my way back to catch the end of lunch. What are you doing?"

I haven't told Zoe about applying for med school yet. Or even that I'm spending the next two nights with Reeve. Up until now, I have justified my lies as acts of omission even though she's known every detail of my life since we were seven. I told myself that Zoe has a big mouth and that telling her is like telling all of West Lake my plans. It will be hard enough to let myself down if this doesn't work out. I don't need pitying glances at Lou's or the post office when I'm still here come fall.

However, Zoe is now on the sidewalk waiting for some explanation, and as much as I don't want her to know, I also can't lie to her face.

"Promise me you're not going to get mad."

Zoe crosses her arms. "Does anyone ever say yes in response to that question?"

I sigh. "No, but I thought I'd give it a shot. I'm actually headed to Toronto for the weekend."

Zoe rolls her eyes. "Why would I be mad about that? A forty-eight-hour booty call is something I'd fully support. Do you not know me?"

I fake a laugh, which Zoe immediately sees through.

"That's not why you're going, is it?" She narrows her eyes.

"It is," I counter. "I am spending the weekend at Reeve's. It's just not the only reason." I consider the best way to tell her and decide straight up and fast is my best bet. "I also sort of applied to medical school back in October. It was kind of a whim at the time, and I didn't think anything would come of it. But it has, and now I have an interview tomorrow. It's at U of T, so I'm driving down there now."

I wait, attempting to look nonchalant. As if it's no big deal, even though I know it's a huge one.

Zoe closes her eyes and draws in a breath so deep and so loud that I can hear the hiss of her inhale through her nostrils.

"Okay, just so I have this right: you applied to med school on a whim, are planning to move to a completely new city to live this whole new life with your boyfriend, and just casually tossed it into conversation, as if this isn't something you've been thinking for months and somehow forgot to inform your best friend about?"

"Reeve isn't officially my boyfriend."

Zoe growls. "That's not the point, Jules."

I have rarely seen Zoe angry. Pissed off—sure. Annoyed—all the time. But a pure, unabashed rage is not in her usual arsenal of emotions.

But the way she spits out the word *point*. And the way she glares at me, nostrils flared, feet planted wide, as if it isn't above her to swing a wild punch at my head, makes me think I've probably not broken the news in the best way.

"What has happened to you these last few months?" She doesn't wait for me to answer. "It's like you have this whole other secret life, and I don't get to be a part of it."

"I don't have secrets. I've always wanted to be a doctor."

"Yeah, but in the same abstract way I've always wanted to be Shania Twain. And that's not what I'm talking about. I'm talking about all the *No, nothing's new with me* and *My life is same old, same old* you've been feeding me when you're secretly planning your escape."

"It's not like that at all."

"So how is it then?" She crosses her arms over her chest and waits.

I am very aware that I was late before and every second I spend arguing is making me later.

"Nothing is certain. It's all just ideas at this point. I didn't want to tell you until I knew it was a sure thing."

She throws up her arms. "So, what? You were going to wait until your car was packed and wave at me on your way out of town? 'See ya, Zoe, thanks for having my back for every major milestone in my life, I'll send you a freaking postcard.'"

"Zoe."

"No." She turns and crosses the street, heading for the retirement home.

"I'm sorry," I call after her. "I didn't mean to . . ." I don't finish the thought. Mostly because I don't know how to end the sentence. Lie? Hurt her feelings? Get into a blowout fight in the middle of the sidewalk?

I get into my car and start it. Pulling a quick U-turn, I catch Zoe just as she's crossing the street in front of Sunnyvale.

Rolling down my window, I call out, "Hey, I'm really sorry and I love you."

Zoe doesn't turn around. But she does lift her hand.

To give me the finger.

Chapter 21

I AM A miserable wreck of a human being the entire drive to Toronto. The sour feeling in my stomach is eased only when I exit the Gardiner Expressway and loop around to turn onto York Street, where it's replaced with yet another feeling of déjà vu.

Whether subconsciously or just from following the Google Maps directions, I'm taking the same route as the bus in my last Kitty dream. However, instead of pulling into Union Station, I pass the Royal York Hotel. And by pass, I mean drive by, only to come to a complete stop half a block farther when the traffic in front of me grinds to a complete halt.

Fuck.

I don't actually swear out loud. But the woman in the business suit cutting between my car and the one in front of me has no trouble reading my lips and gives me an unimpressed single eyebrow raise.

I glance at the clock on my dash: 3:45. I planned to be at the U of T campus just after three, giving me plenty of time to park and freshen up before the 4:00 campus tour.

I naively assumed the traffic on the highway would be minimal, seeing as it was the middle of the day, but I failed to check the sports schedule. Both the Leafs and the Raptors have home games tonight. Apparently, every single person attending those games decided to head downtown early to avoid the congestion.

I pick up my phone to email the campus coordinator and let them know I'm not going to make it, rationalizing to myself that the student center and the medical admissions committee likely do not cross-reference who failed to make their completely voluntary tours. No sooner do I hear the whoosh of the email flying through cyberspace than there's a *tap tap tap* on my driver's window and a police officer on a humongous brown horse signaling me to roll my window down.

"It's illegal to text and drive, ma'am," he says, pointing at the phone now sitting in my cup holder.

I want to tell him I'm not driving as much as sitting, going absolutely nowhere, but think better of it as he writes and hands me a two-hundred-and-eighty-dollar ticket.

As I roll up my window, the car behind me blasts its horn, then the driver flips me the finger as they pull around, racing down the next fifty feet, only to get stopped by another bout of traffic.

Even though that move feels far more dangerous and illegal than texting while stopped, horse cop does not pursue.

It's almost five o'clock by the time I make it to the St. George campus. I have to circle three times to find a parking spot on the street, and when I finally do get out, the sky opens up and begins to sleet. I wander the campus for thirty minutes on my own, in the rain, growing less and less enamored with it all and more and more intimidated by my interview scheduled for the next morning.

As weird as it sounds, I wish Kitty were here. To point out with her glass-half-full optimism the architectural beauty of the Gothic buildings and remind me of all the opportunities a med school degree could bring, then wrap it up with another of her Kitty-isms: "The beauty of uncertainty is that anything is possible, darling."

Because it all feels impossible right now.

My phone rings just as I'm getting back into my car.

Reeve's voice comes through so even and solid. "Hey. Are you here? How'd it go?"

I resist the urge to recap the day's woes that seemed to fall like dominoes, rationalizing that whatever is happening between us is still so new.

"It was a bit of a journey to get down here, but I made it." I force a false, sunny tone. "Where are you? Still at work?"

There's a sound like an elevator ding in his background.

"Yeah, just leaving now. It's about a ten-minute walk. If you're still at St. George, I will beat you home. Why don't I wait by the entrance to the parking garage? I can jump in and buzz you into the visitor parking. I have the pass in my bag. You've still got the address, right?"

I glance around the street for more horse cops before putting the phone on speaker to pull up the map.

"Google says I'll be there in fifteen."

There's another ding of an elevator, and then the quiet background of Reeve's phone shifts to the sounds of traffic noises.

"Sounds good. I'll see you soon. And, Jules . . ."

He hesitates just enough for me to become aware of my heavy heartbeat.

"I'm really glad you're here."

Chapter 22

THE RIDE TO Reeve's condo is far less dramatic than my earlier drive. When I turn off Bloor Street onto a narrow side street, he's waiting just as promised, hand outstretched, looking like he walked off the front of a J.Crew catalog and making me very aware that I still haven't replaced the buttons on my coat.

He jumps inside and leans across the console as if he's about to kiss me, but the hard beep of the annoyed driver behind us stops him.

"Easy there, buddy." He flashes an acknowledging wave. "Here." He pulls a set of keys out of his pocket. "Use this." He hands me the keys, holding them by a black key fob, which I tap against the black box at the garage entrance, causing the door to lift.

Reeve directs me to a parking spot with a serious sign that details the repercussions of not having the correct permits for parking. He places an official-looking parking pass on my dash, swiftly grabs my overnight bag from the backseat, and holds out his hand as he waits for me to lock my car.

When my fingers find his, I feel the best I have all day. That feeling is only topped when we step into the empty elevator and he drops my bag to the floor, tugging me closer and slipping his arms under my coat and around my waist.

"Today was torture." He places a light kiss on my lips. "I watched the clock all afternoon, resisting the urge to call you."

"You could have." I hook my fingers through his belt loops and press onto my toes to kiss him back.

"I didn't know if your car was hands-free. I didn't want you to get in trouble."

I'm about to tell him that despite his good intentions, that premonition still came true, but he leans in and plants another kiss on my neck, just below my earlobe, and all bad thoughts fly away.

"Can you do that again?" I ask.

"I plan on doing that quite a lot, actually," he says, but before he can make good on his promise, the elevator dings, and the door slides open.

I have thought about what Reeve's apartment might look like on multiple occasions. Yet, I have no idea what to expect as he leads me to the end of a long hallway, where he uses a different key fob to open his door. It beeps and clicks, and he pushes it open with a "Home sweet home."

I have no idea why I'm holding my breath. Still, my head swoons with a dizzy, offset feeling as I step into a brightly lit foyer, my emotions churning with apprehension and straight-up curiosity.

At first glance, everything seems to be in the realm of what I anticipated. The foyer area is simple and clean: white walls and white tiled floor. But then I follow Reeve down the hall to his open-concept kitchen and living area, ignoring the marble counters, the wide-planked wood floors, the art, and the modern sectional sofa that looks like it came straight out of a Crate & Barrel catalog, because my eyes are fixated on the windows in front of me. They span upward two stories to the loft above and run the entire length of the south-facing wall.

"Wow, you can see the whole city from up here."

Reeve sets my bag down next to the kitchen island. "Yeah, it's the main reason I bought the place. You can see all the way to the lake on a nice day. That, and the building has an infinity pool on the roof."

He smiles, and I nod as if I, too, would have considered this.

"Are you cold?" Reeve reaches out, and the backs of his fingers skim down my tightly hugged arms.

I nod, not wanting to tell him that temperature-wise, I'm fine. It's just the rest of me that feels so completely out of my element.

He walks over to the wall and clicks something on a keypad. It beeps, then there is a whooshing sound as a giant glass fireplace set into the wall fills with dancing flames.

I stare momentarily, mesmerized by the orange glow, and return to reality only when Reeve clears his throat. "Want the rest of the tour?"

He picks up my bag again and I follow him up a staircase. It's one of those modern artsy ones with only the step and no backstop that makes me grip the railing tight in fear of losing my balance and falling through.

When we reach the top, Reeve hesitates.

"That's my room." He points to his left, to a door open enough to see a perfectly made bed and the same view as below. "And this is the guest room." He walks over and opens the door to a second room. This one has a spacious queen bed and a beautiful oak dresser with a mirror.

"I got it ready for you," he says, tilting his head, his eyes searching my face. "We didn't really talk about . . ." His voice trails off, and my cheeks flush with a mortified heat.

Reeve's right. We didn't discuss sleeping arrangements. I definitely thought about them when I imagined where he lived. Assumed he, like me, had a tiny one-bedroom and that this weekend would mean only one bed, inevitably leading to sex, but now I'm second-guessing things. Second-guessing him.

"It's great." My voice comes out in a rush as I realize I've taken too long to answer. "It's beautiful. So clean."

My cheeks are absolutely on fire now, and I attempt to hide them by looking out the window at yet another breathtaking city view.

"Are you hungry?" he asks. I can see him in the window's reflection, setting my bag on a small chair. "I made a reservation at a place nearby, unless you want to hang in. I wasn't sure if you'd need more time to prep."

Right. Tomorrow.

Just a day that has the potential to change my life forever.

"I would like to keep myself as distracted as possible." I turn from the window. "I'm as prepared as I can be. All I need is to relax and get a good night's sleep."

Reeve's eyes linger on my face for a moment before he nods and says, "I can definitely help with that."

We walk to the restaurant, taking Bloor Street most of the way, passing Hermès, Dior, and a slew of other high-end shops that I've never heard of but that look expensive, then cut down a pedestrian path between two tall buildings and come out on a quieter street with small independent shops and a few bars. The street has that "trying not to be pretentious" vibe while very much still being so. A little like Port Logan in the summer when the wealthier tourists come to stay at their summer cottages.

We stop at a crosswalk next to a group of women in long wool coats carrying designer bags. Their effortless sophistication makes me feel less pulled together and more thrown together, which quickly morphs into another eerie feeling of déjà vu as I am reminded of Kitty in the Royal York Hotel. She stared at an equally intimidating pair of women and said in much more eloquent words, *I want to be like that.* As I pull my peacoat tighter, eyeing their four-inch heels from the comfort of my flat, comfortable boots, I realize that, at my core, I don't share Kitty's aspirations.

We continue to walk. Reeve stops in front of a pale yellow stucco building with a cobblestoned side patio shut down for the winter save for a single tall heater with two men in suits smoking underneath. "This is it." Reeve holds out his arm to let me take the stairs first. "The food is amazing, especially the dessert. I think you're going to love it."

I pull open the front door and step into dim lighting and low-key house music. A hostess in a strapless black dress is standing behind a Plexiglas pedestal. Her lips are a bright shade of red, the bottom one caught between her teeth as she studies an iPad in front of her.

"Reservations for two under Baldwin," Reeve says, helping me out of my coat. I am caught between loving the sound of those words and noticing the way the hostess's eyes drop to my jeans and then my knockoff Costco UGGs. It makes me reconsider that what I thought was comfortable but cute might, in reality, be screaming, *Not from around here.*

Reeve, whose suit fits in beautifully with this business casual crowd, holds out his arm, seemingly oblivious to my slow slide down this self-esteem spiral. When I step closer, he places his palm on the small of my back. We follow a different hostess through the crowded restaurant to a small table near the window.

Reeve pulls out my chair, but this sweet, chivalrous act is lost to the panicked band of sweat breaking out across my forehead as I fully take in my surroundings. The restaurant is even fancier than I thought. There are cloth coverings on the tables set with two types of wineglasses and three different forks.

I sit down, hold the menu open in front of me, and try to smother the *Jesus Christ* that wants to word-vomit its way out of my mouth at the sight of the prices in front of me.

"Forty-five dollars for a hamburger?" I accidentally say out loud. "Is the bun plated in gold?"

"I know." Reeve folds his menu and sets it down beside him. "I try not to think too hard about it, but they're famous for it. And it's really good."

I can't fathom what one could put on a hamburger that would make it taste twenty-eight dollars better than a quarter-pounder special at Lou's, and I have no intention of finding out tonight.

"What are you in the mood for?" Reeve asks, picking back up his menu.

My mood and what I can afford after my unbudgeted parking ticket are very different things.

Our server arrives. He's wearing a dress shirt rolled up at the sleeves to show off just a hint of the tattoos on each of his forearms. Its pristine whiteness makes me wonder how long I'd last working here before having a run-in with a chicken cacciatore.

"Hi, I'm Micah, I'll be your server today. Can I start you off with a cocktail?"

Reeve lowers his menu to look at me. "Do you want to split a bottle of wine? Or something else?"

I can't bring myself to look at the wine prices.

"Maybe just a beer?" I say to Reeve, then realize it's probably our server I should be talking to. "PBR?"

Our waiter smirks, then schools his face. "I don't think we carry that, but we have a great craft lager on tap that you might like."

My seat feels even more uncomfortable than it did when I sat down. "You know what, I'm good with water."

A cool trickle of sweat runs down my back, and my stomach

does a complete 360-degree flip, sending a wave of nausea up into the back of my throat. It's just a stupid beer. It doesn't mean anything. Order something else. It's not a big deal.

"Where's your bathroom?" I have this sudden, overwhelming sense that I cannot sit at this table a moment longer.

He points to the back left corner of the restaurant. I stand with an "Excuse me," ignoring the questioning lift of Reeve's eyebrows as I make a panicked dash for the back.

I can't breathe.

And my body is way too hot.

And it's taking too much of my concentration to force air into my lungs. In and out. In and out.

I slam into a stall. The fancy wood door hits the wall with a loud bang. There's no lid on the toilet, so I press my back against the tiles, feeling the coolness seep through my cotton shirt.

What am I even doing here?

What was I thinking?

That I'd just move to the city. Start med school and become a person who eats gourmet hamburgers and drinks microbrews.

That's exactly what I was thinking.

My knees start to wobble and give way. My back continues its slide until my butt hits the floor. I remove my phone from my back pocket, fearing crushing it, and, in doing so, I notice a text.

It's from Zoe—a GIF of a slug on a leaf that looks very much like a dick, followed by the words *I'm sorry.*

In less than a second, I'm dialing her. Two rings later, her voice is on the other end of the line.

"I'm the dick in this relationship, not you," I tell her before she has a chance to say anything first.

She lets out a long and breathy sigh. "It wasn't a shining moment for either of us."

"I'm sorry I didn't tell you about applying to med school."

She pauses a beat. "I still don't get why you kept it such a secret."

I've asked myself the same thing every time we've hung out—whenever she's asked her usual *What's up, Buttercup?* and the only thing I said back was *Not much, you?*

I don't have a straightforward answer other than Zoe would act like my entire plan was going to happen. Say things like *When you're down in Toronto*, or *Easy there, Dr. DeMarco*, inching my hopes up a little higher with every well-meaning comment and making the fall all that much farther when it inevitably didn't work out.

"Do you remember my fourteenth birthday when my mom promised to take us to the Drake concert?" I ask.

Again, Zoe pauses, likely wondering where I'm going with this. "Uh. Sure."

"I obsessed about it for weeks. Picked out my outfit. Told everyone at school. Made that stupid sign on the poster board, only to have my birthday come and my mom pretend she had no idea what I was talking about. Not only did I have to live with the crushing disappointment for weeks, but I also had to hear all our friends' questions on how good the concert was."

There's a quiet shuffle on Zoe's end of the line, as if she's changing positions. "Your mom has always been the worst. There's no denying that. But I'm not making the connection."

I change my tactic. "To actually go to med school next year, I need to beat out more than four thousand applicants for one of two hundred spots. Then, if by some miracle I actually do, I need to come up with a hundred thousand for tuition and at least a hundred more to cover four years of living expenses. The odds are slim of being able to do one of those things, let alone both. I didn't want to tell you about it because I know you'd get excited for me and I thought it might be easier to handle the crushing disappointment solo."

There's background noise on Zoe's end of the line, quieted by a closing door. "Well, you are right that I will always get excited when something good happens to my best friend. That is simply a fact that we both need to deal with. Where you're wrong though is with all this negative talk. You are going to get in."

"Zoe—"

"Do not 'Zoe' me. You know I'm right. You are Jules fucking DeMarco. You're smart, and incredibly capable, and every time life has handed you shit, you've figured it out. You'll get in, and then we'll figure out the money thing. There has got to be a way."

I know I need to tell her about the dance hall, but Zoe more than anyone has reason to hate this next part of my plan.

"Don't get mad at me, okay?"

"Jules. We've talked about that question."

I tentatively choose my words. "You know that building next to Sunnyvale?"

Zoe pauses as if thinking. "The abandoned one?"

I nod even though she can't see me. "It belonged to Kitty St. Clair, and I found out a little while ago that she left it to me in her will."

Zoe lets out a breathy *No shit*. "Okay, so what does that mean?"

I consider how to phrase the next part and decide to rip the Band-Aid right off. "Reeve works for a developer, and he says it's worth a lot of money. They want to buy the property from me and turn it into condos."

Again, Zoe's end goes quiet.

"I'm not going to sell it." I jump in before she can. "At least, I haven't decided if I will sell it. I know what it means. If I do sell it, I know it could affect the town, and I'm not the kind of person who can throw away her morals like that, I just—"

"Jules." Zoe cuts me off. "You don't need to tell me what kind of person you are. I'm your best friend."

The tightness around my lungs loosens enough that I take a deep breath.

"And so take this as coming from a very best friend place," she says. "You should do it. Sell that building. But squeeze those assholes for every single penny they will give you and then go to med school and become the fabulous doctor you were meant to be."

Her answer is so far from what I was expecting that I'm sure I've heard her wrong. "Seriously?"

"Serious as a heart attack. Which I would be terrified to have right now, given the state of our healthcare. This town is changing. It is what it is. I hate it, but I love you more. And with all of these tourists clogging up the urgent care centers, we need as many doctors up here as we can get."

I mean to laugh, but it comes out more as a sob.

"It's true," Zoe says. "Dale cut himself the other day and had to wait eight hours for stitches at the urgent care. He's a bleeder. We need you."

There's a loud flushing sound from the stall next to me. It's so loud I have to wait to continue the conversation, but when it's finally silent again, it's Zoe who speaks first.

"Where are you?"

I wait until I hear the bathroom door open and close before answering. "Sitting on the bathroom floor in a trendy restaurant I have no business being in."

I expect some comment about how nasty bathroom floors are, but Zoe's voice is unusually soft. "Are you okay?"

"I think so. Definitely getting there."

"Where is Reeve?"

I glance at the clock on my iPhone, realizing I've been in this stall for almost ten minutes. "He's back at the table. Probably regretting inviting me down here right now."

"Hey." She draws out the word. "Putting aside the whole evil developer thing, that guy adores you. I watched him make lovey googly eyes at you all New Year's. I almost called him out, but you were doing the same thing."

"I was?"

"It was gross."

"I should probably get back out there." I get to my feet, resisting the urge to wipe my hands on my pants.

"You deserve good things, Jules. Remember that tonight and, more important, tomorrow."

I draw my first easy breath since entering the bathroom. "Thanks."

"Kick some doctor ass at that interview thing. Show no mercy."

"I'll try."

"I love you."

"I love you, too. You are a good friend."

"I am the best. You won't find a better one, so don't bother looking in Toronto."

Although I've always known it, there are no circumstances where I would ever want anyone but Zoe as my best friend.

"I'd never even try."

Chapter 23

Fourteen minutes later, I emerge from the bathroom, still working out what I will say to Reeve. But when I reach our table, it's empty.

Not only that, it's been reset.

I look around, wondering if maybe I got turned around exiting the bathroom, and spot him standing at the front door with his coat on.

All of the feelings I managed to quell during my talk with Zoe come back in a rush.

He's leaving. He realized what a mess I am and got out while he still could. I almost turn to go back to the bathroom, but then he reaches out his arms and takes something from the hostess, and before I can tell what it is, he turns in my direction.

In his hands is my coat.

We lock eyes as I walk toward him. He holds the coat up, waiting for me to slip my arms into it. I move toward him, my legs on autopilot and my head still processing what is happening.

"I'm sorry," I say as I turn, letting him help me into my coat.

Reeve's hands linger on my hips as he brings his mouth to my ear. "You have nothing to be sorry about. I think I picked the wrong place. It's pretty loud in here, and you have a big day tomorrow. What do you say we head back to my place and order in? I've got some beer in my fridge."

I think I manage a nod. Either way, he grabs my hand. Then we're out the door and on the street, and the entire time I'm wondering how he knew, how I never even had to say anything.

It starts to snow as we walk back. We're taking a slightly different path, down a quieter street instead of the busy one. We stop on a corner to wait for a break in traffic, and I find myself drawn to the sound of a tinkling acoustic guitar. I look up and see what looks like a rooftop patio.

"It's like minus two out. Are people actually sitting outside?" I ask Reeve, who looks up as well.

"Yeah. They keep that thing open all year round. It's nothing fancy, but they have some pretty serious heaters."

I don't know why, but I have this sudden urge to see it for myself. "Can we go up?"

A small smile breaks across Reeve's face. "This is your night. We can do whatever you want."

We open the door to a typical-looking small pub, then climb a steep flight of stairs to another door that does, in fact, lead out to a rooftop patio. As we step out, I am blasted with a wave of heat.

It is, as Reeve described it, just a simple rooftop patio. The floor is made from wooden boards, the same kind that Dale used a few months ago when he built a backyard deck for his and Zoe's yard. Clear Plexiglas walls and what looks like a yellow vinyl roof give enough shelter from the winter and the wind that, with the help of my jacket, the temperature is bearable—even pleasant. Whether it's the crisp night air or the familiar laughter of the crowd in toques and parkas, I feel as if I can breathe easy here. It looks nothing like the Legion back home but somehow feels like it.

A waitress walks by with a tray full of beers. Addressing me more than Reeve, she says, "We're pretty full tonight, but there is a bit of space at the bar if you don't mind."

Reeve looks at me as if asking me that same question.

I nod. I don't mind. I don't mind at all.

I can see PBRs in the fridge behind the bartender as I slide into my seat. And as stupid as it seems, it sends me a signal. Maybe I'm not so out of place. As Reeve said, the earlier restaurant was a bad call.

The bartender doesn't even blink when I order my beer. He reaches into the fridge, cracks the bottle open, and hands it to me, not even asking if I need a glass. Exactly as I like it.

"I like this place," I tell Reeve after a long sip. "It reminds me a little of the Legion." He clinks his bottle with mine. "And I'm sorry about earlier. . . ." I feel the need to explain, but Reeve waves me off.

"You don't need to apologize," he says. "It was busy and loud—definitely not the right place for the night before your interview." He shakes his head. "I just got so wrapped up trying to impress you, I didn't really think."

His comment catches me so off guard that I snort, causing beer bubbles to shoot up my nose and forcing me to clamp my hand over my mouth to prevent a cartoonlike spitting on the bar top. When I finally swallow, I begin to laugh. "Why on earth would *you* ever need to impress *me*?"

I expect him to smile back, perhaps saying something Reeve-like and charming. Instead, his eyes meet mine without so much as a hint of a smile. "Because I like you, Jules—a lot."

I hold my breath, waiting for the *but* or the *however*, or even the *except*.

It doesn't come.

Because that's it, that's the sentence. *I like you, Jules.* Hard stop.

There are probably a hundred suitably appropriate things I could say back, but the only thing I manage is an ambiguous "Oh."

He stares at the bottle in his hands, rolling it between his palms before peeling the corner of the bottle label with his thumb. "I didn't tell you that on the dock two years ago, and that was a mistake." His gaze returns to mine. "So I'm saying it now. On the off chance it isn't already painfully obvious."

The only painful thing is how badly I wanted to hear it.

I take a swig of beer to distract myself from this overwhelming swelling in my chest. "I like you, too, a lot," I tell him. "And the restaurant was great. I was just coming off a rough day, I guess. I had a big fight with Zoe and then a run-in with a horse cop who gave me a very expensive ticket, and then that forty-five-dollar hamburger became this symbolic reminder of how expensive this city is."

Reeve pauses his beer halfway between the table and his mouth. "I didn't even think—I was planning on paying for—"

"No," I interrupt again. "It's not about the money—well, it's a little bit about the money. It's more . . ." I consider how to phrase my thoughts.

"I really, really want to go to med school." I start with the most straightforward part. "And I don't think I realized how much so until a few weeks ago. But up until now, my money issues have always been the thing that stopped me."

I pause, as the next part is more complicated to explain. "Now I have this dance hall, and all of a sudden, a pretty hopeless situation is now a lot more hope . . . full? And I know I should be thrilled, but all I can think about is that if I sell the dance hall, it will make life harder for all the people I love. It might just be condos today, but then the people in those condos will want fancy coffee that isn't Folgers from Lou's and microbrews that you can't get at the Legion."

"And forty-dollar hamburgers?" Reeve offers, leaning his shoulder into mine.

I look over at him, relieved that he gets it. "Yes. So I am in this weird place where I'm stuck between making a decision I don't feel good about or going back to pretending I'm okay with my life when I've finally admitted to myself I'm not. And all that uncertainty seemed to surface tonight on the restaurant bathroom floor."

I smile in an attempt to lighten our conversation.

Reeve also smiles, his eyes dropping to his beer before meeting mine again. "When it happened to me, it was on the Yonge subway line."

I stare at him for a moment, confused, then realize what he's telling me.

"I had just left the art gallery," he continues. "It was the last day of my internship, and I had just told them I wouldn't be extending my contract. They were really great about it. Wished me well and even got me a cake. Told me I was welcome back anytime. I took the subway home that night, and when it was time to get off, I couldn't do it. It felt like it made my decision final, so I rode all the way to North York and then back again before I was finally able to get off."

He looks up, forcing a smile, as if trying to bring us back to easier conversation.

"Is this the part where you tell me it all works out in the end and then offer sage advice?" I ask.

Reeve shakes his head. "I don't think I'm the best guy for advice. Maybe just the guy who understands."

I scoot my chair closer. He helps, pulling it the rest of the way so it's flush with his, and our knees touch.

We're interrupted by the bartender, who stops to eye our half-drunk bottles.

"Can I get you guys anything else?" He nods at the menus in front of us we've yet to open.

Reeve leans forward, his arm resting on the back of my chair. "What do you recommend for two people trying to figure out what the hell they're doing with their lives?"

The bartender thinks for a moment. "Loaded nachos."

I look at Reeve. An entire decision is made with a simple lift of our brows.

"Loaded nachos it is."

Chapter 24

"I THINK THAT may be my new favorite bar," I say to Reeve as we cross the street toward his condo. There is a paper bag dangling from my right hand, inside of which is a white takeout container with the remaining scraps of the best nachos I have ever eaten.

"I would have thought that honor would have gone to the Legion," Reeve says as he opens the front door to his building with his key fob.

"The Legion is less of a bar and more of a lifestyle choice." I smile at the concierge, who gives me a bored look before returning to something far more interesting on his phone.

We head toward the elevator, the soles of my boots making squeaking sounds on the marble floors.

"This is a very fancy building," I tell Reeve as he presses the elevator button and the doors slide open.

We step inside. When the doors close, they shut out all the sounds of the outside world, making it even more apparent that it's just me and Reeve in a very small space. "So," he says, stepping toward me, and I notice a hint of cologne that I hadn't noticed earlier. "Your interview tomorrow is at ten, right?"

I am quickly reminded of the reason I'm here visiting him. Still, just as quickly, that thought seems to disappear as his hand slides inside my coat and comes to rest on my hip, his fingers magically finding that tiny strip of exposed skin between my sweater and my jeans.

"I'm guessing you'll want to get there early?" He leans in, pressing the softest kiss to the side of my neck, and although I know he just asked me a question, I am far more concerned with how I can make that happen again.

"Hmmm." My fingers trace the hem of his coat until they find the lapels and tug him closer.

"So?" He kisses me again. In that exact spot, giving me exactly what I want.

"I can't think when you kiss me like that," I tell him. "It does something to my brain. Makes it very hard to concentrate."

The elevator bell dings. Reeve and his lips pull away. I recover just enough brain cells to tell him, "Nine. I want to be there early, just in case."

We step into the hallway and walk toward his door, but he stops and presses me against the wall just before we reach it. His hand cups my chin, and his hips slide against mine, and my brain is stripped of all thought except the sweep of his tongue and the way his thigh presses between my legs. My hands roam down his back until my thumbs hook the waistband of his pants, but as they move toward the buckle of his belt, he pulls back.

"Why are we stopping?" I ask, slowly opening my eyes.

"That was our kiss good night," he says. "Because if I kiss you again after I open that door, I'm not going to stop, and you need to be up early."

He plants another kiss. This one is softer and sweeter than the last, but when my hands reach for his waist, needing his body closer, he stops me, trapping my hands between our bodies.

"This is killing me. I want you to know that. But you need to get to bed."

He kisses me on the forehead before pushing away from the wall, unlocking his front door, and holding it open.

I watch him for a moment, not sure if he is serious. When he doesn't budge, I concede, walking into his foyer, where I shed my boots and coat.

He waits for me at the bottom of the stairs.

As I pass him on my way up, I search his face for any hint that this is all one big joke. But there's nothing. His hands stay in the safety of his pants pockets until I'm halfway up the stairs, and only then does he climb up after me.

I stop when I reach the top step, arms crossed, blocking his way like a petulant toddler.

"You're really sending me to bed?"

He pauses three steps down. "It's a big day. You're going to want a clear head."

He's not wrong. But I want something very different right now.

I try a different tactic. "I'm not tired yet. Are you at least going to tuck me in?"

"I am going nowhere near your room," he says. "In fact, I'm not moving until you're safely behind that door."

I eye the three closed doors in front of me, almost certain that the center one is mine.

"Is that another bedroom?" I point at the third door. The only one Reeve didn't show me on my tour earlier.

"In theory, yes," he answers. "But . . ." His voice trails momentarily, and I hear him climb the two steps between us. His warm hand finds the small of my back. "If you're not tired, I guess I can show you. But please don't judge until I can explain."

I plant my feet, suddenly wondering what I'm walking into. "Do I want to know what's in there?"

Reeve passes me and crosses the hallway, pausing with his hand on the doorknob. "It's not weird. Actually, it is a little weird... but I'm guessing less so than what is going on in your head right now. Come on."

He pushes the door open. I follow him inside, unsure of what I'm about to see.

I definitely don't expect shelves filled with bowls, plates, and mugs. Rows and rows of figurines and vases.

In the center of the room is a black leather stool. Beside it is a small square table with what looks like a massive bowl on top covered in a claylike substance.

"Is that a pottery wheel?" I ask, putting it all together.

Reeve sits on the stool and presses a pedal on the floor with his foot. The bowl comes to life, whirring in a circle.

"You asked me once how I got into art, and I guess this is the answer. I started throwing pottery when I was in my second year at Queens. I had some anxiety issues, and my therapist suggested it as a way to relax, and I've been hooked ever since."

I examine the shelves again in a new light. "Did you make all of these?"

Reeve nods to the shelf behind him. "Almost everything on that one is mine. I kind of rotate pieces in and out, depending on how I feel about them. The rest of the pieces in here are ones I've collected over the years. Just stuff I've seen and liked that makes me happy."

I step over to one of the shelves, my eyes attracted to a tall vase with a forest scene painted on the outside.

"This reminds me a little of West Lake." I pick it up to show him.

He takes it from my hand. "It should. That's one of Marcus's."

My fingers run along the edge of the shelf. The pieces he's collected are truly beautiful. "Do you ever think about going back to work in a gallery?"

"All the time." He stares for a moment at the vase in his hands before meeting my eyes. "But what I'd love to do is open my own gallery at some point."

"Really?" I can suddenly picture it. "You should do it."

"Maybe someday." He sets the vase down carefully back in its place and then pulls a white Tupperware from one of the shelves, opens it, and takes out a plastic bag. "Want to try?" He rolls down the plastic to reveal a large mound of rust-colored clay. Taking a piece of what looks like wire, he cuts a grapefruit-sized clump off and sets it on the table.

"Come here." He slides off the stool, refits the plastic over the remaining clay, and returns the box to the shelf.

"It's easy." He pulls out the stool and waits. When I don't move, he holds out his hand. "Come on. I promise. I'll show you."

I slide into the stool, slightly more curious than nervous. Reeve kneads the clay a few times before setting it into the center of the bowl.

He steps behind me, placing his hands on top of mine and guiding them to the clay, which feels cool to the touch.

"I need to add a little water." He dips his fingers into a small white bowl on the corner of the table. Cupping the water in his palm, he drips it over mine, making the clay soft and slimy.

"I'm going to turn the wheel on. Are you ready?"

"No," I answer, my stomach suddenly nervous and fluttery.

Reeve's hands slowly slide down my forearms, then cover mine as his breath brushes my ear. "Don't worry, I got you."

As his foot presses the pedal, I hold my breath, and the wheel again rolls to life.

The whir, the heat, and the way my skin buzzes beneath his fingers make any natural talent I may have secretly possessed disappear. I squeeze my hands too tight. The clay beneath them spins into a tall cylinder and then flops to the side.

"Oh no, I ruined it already."

I can feel the shake of Reeve's quiet laugh at my back. "Nothing is ever ruined with clay. It's all about the process. You figure things out as you go and sometimes the figuring out *is* the point." He squishes the toppled cylinder back into a ball.

"I get why this is therapy." I take the clay back into my hands. "Do you do this a lot? The pottery, I mean."

There is a slight hesitation before he answers. "With my job . . . yeah. I'm in here all the time. Here—" He grabs a second stool from along the wall and pulls it up behind me. He sits down, his legs straddling mine, knees pressing ever so gently into the sides of my thighs.

"We may need a little more water." He reaches for the white bowl again, his chest pressing into my back, his other hand grazing my hip bone as he leans.

"Place your hands on top again, but this time with just the lightest touch."

I do as he asks as his fingertips graze the back of my wrists. "I'm going to hit the pedal again. Don't move. Just get a feel for it."

The bowl begins to whirl again, but I keep my hands lightly on the clay, barely touching it, just as Reeve instructed.

"Okay." His lips brush the side of my ear as he leans closer. "Now, just the smallest bit of pressure. Take your time. You're in control here."

I'm not.

I am desperately trying not to think about sex or the strength of his hands—the confident way his body guides mine exactly how he wants me.

I close my eyes, but it only heightens the sensations: the hairs on my neck standing on end, the tingles that have traveled from my earlobe all the way down to my belly.

The clay beneath my hands starts to shift, molding into a cylindrical shape.

"Good girl," Reeve coaxes, his hands slipping farther up my forearms, giving me more control. "Just keep that perfect pressure. You want it to stay nice and thick. Just like that."

My head suddenly floods with thoughts that are not pottery-related.

"For a guy who seemed very adamant about not having any sexy activity within these walls tonight, you are making very interesting word choices."

Reeve laughs, his chest pressing against my back. "I'm sorry, I got a little carried away. Do you think you're ready for the next step?"

The deepness of his voice reverberates all the way to my core. I'd agree to almost anything at this point.

"Place your thumbs in the center." His hands glide over mine, easing my thumbs into the middle of the clay. "And give it just a little more pressure. Right there. You've got it."

His nose brushes against my neck, and his thighs press against mine. My head falls back. He turns, his lip brushing that sensitive spot just below my ear. He kisses it—and any remaining concentration slips along with my hands, which flatten my creation into a rust-colored pancake.

"Ahhhhh!" I stare down at the messy brown lump still spinning on the wheel.

"That was my fault," Reeve says, kissing me one last time before pushing back his stool.

The wheel begins to slow. My head clears just enough to notice the curve of Reeve's pants as he clears away the scraps of mangled clay. The sight gives me some consolation that at least I was not the only one affected.

He opens the door to a small powder room painted a soft buttery yellow, with just a toilet and sink. Turning on the faucet with his elbows, he scrubs his hands quickly and then waits for me to do the same. As I rub my arms with the soapy water, I half expect him to slip behind me like he did at the wheel, sliding his hands down mine, pinning me between the hardness of his body and the sink; however, my soapy sex fantasy is interrupted when he clears his throat and hands me a towel.

"I didn't realize it's past eleven already. You should head to bed. Is there anything else you need?"

There is one thing I very much need right now, but Reeve does not seem to want to give it.

"I think I'm good."

He nods, looking at me in a way that makes me wonder if I may have telepathically communicated that last thought.

"Get some rest," he finally says, his voice suddenly hoarse. "You have an important day tomorrow, and then it's going to be a very late night."

Chapter 25

It takes a while for me to fall asleep. The night-before jitters mix with that undeniable want of something I can't have, leaving sleep more of a theoretical concept than something I'll be drifting off to anytime soon.

More than once, I consider knocking on Reeve's door, wondering if he'd be so quick to turn me away if I kissed him in the oversized tee I use as a nightgown. Instead, I open Kitty's diary, needing the distraction of problems that aren't mine. I flip to where I last left off.

Dear Diary,
 What does sex feel like?

I slam the diary shut, immediately regretting my decision to read it in the first place. The last thing I need tonight is to wake up in a dream where Kitty wants to have "the talk." I revert to my tried-and-true sheep counting, eventually succumbing to Reeve's sheets, which feel like silk, and drifting off into a deep sleep.

Or so I think.

My eyes open, and I'm in a strange room again. There's no panic this time. I'm used to the discombobulated feeling.

I should have known better.

"Okay, Kitty. What are we up to this time?"

There's no answer at all, and I sit up and gaze around what appears to be Dot's darkened bedroom.

It's empty, but the bedsheets are crinkled beside me, and as I smooth my hand over the empty space, I find it warm.

"Kitty?" I call again, but the only sounds in the otherwise quiet night are a loon calling somewhere out on the lake and the soft flutter of leaves blowing in the breeze coming in through the open window.

I slip out of bed. The floor is cold on my bare feet, but the full moon gives me enough light to find my way to the window. However, as I reach up to shut it, I catch a flash of movement crossing the yard.

Kitty.

Unlike me, who is in a nightgown, she is dressed. I wonder momentarily if she's sneaking out to the dance hall again. But her dress is plain and dark, and for no reason other than a sixth sense in my gut, I don't think that's where she is headed.

She opens the front gate slowly, but the hinges emit a low, rusty groan despite her efforts. She freezes. Then, her head turns toward the still-open window. I swear she's looking right at me for a moment, but before I can call out to her, she turns and darts across the street.

My role in these dreams has never been clearly defined, but I get the strong sense that I was not brought here tonight to hang out alone in Dot's bedroom. With a groan, I follow her out of the house, across the yard, and to the street. I catch another glimpse of her blond head running toward the water just before she disappears behind a grass-covered dune.

I doubt when Reeve sent me to bed for a full night's rest tonight he had any idea that I'd be playing hide-and-seek with a teenage Kitty St. Clair. But here I am, feet sinking into the cool sand, hair blown by the gentle summer breeze, allowing my eyes to adjust to the dark.

I scan the beach, grateful for the moonlight reflecting off the softly rolling waves. Everything to my left is dark, but when I turn to my right, I can make out the dancing orange flames of a bonfire up ahead and the outline of Kitty standing in front of it.

"Got you!" I whisper as I walk toward her, but I stop just before I reach the circle of light cast by the fire.

Maybe it's instinct.

Or my brain slowly putting together why Kitty might be headed to a half-hidden late-night bonfire.

"Oh, god." My brain connects the diary entry with the scene before me just as a second body comes into view.

He's taller than Kitty, but the shadows obscure his identity.

He opens his arms, and she steps toward him. Their two bodies become a single, indistinguishable form backlit by firelight.

I watch them for a moment, trying to make sense of it.

Beau or Knots?

Her rich city boy or her sweet country love?

There's no denying that I'm rooting for someone in this story. My loyalties lie with my West Lake brethren—team Knots—despite knowing it's a losing one.

So when they finally pull away, and he turns his face just so, his profile catching in the light, I let out a deep exhale.

"Good choice, Kitty," I whisper.

Knots sinks to his knees, and only then do I notice the blanket spread around his feet. When he holds out his hand to Kitty, and she takes it, sinking down next to him, I get an even clearer picture of the scene in front of me.

"I don't think I need to be here for this," I say to no one but the night as a shirt comes flying toward me. "I can figure this part of the story out alone."

I begin to walk backward toward the road.

Although I'm feeling a small solace that at least one of us is having sex tonight.

When my feet are safely on the pavement again, I hear Kitty cry out.

I can't help the smile that curves my lips.

She always did have the best stories.

Chapter 26

When I wake in the morning, back in reality, it's to the smell of coffee and bacon and the sight of a sweaty Reeve in gym shorts in the kitchen with a spatula in hand.

"Are you one of those morning exercise people?" I descend the steps dressed for my interview but not quite the same level of bright-eyed and bushy-tailed.

He pours me a cup of coffee. "Not usually, but I didn't sleep that well last night." He hands me the cup and an understanding passes between us, and I wonder if he had his own sexy sand-dune dream.

"Are you ready?" he asks.

Having not yet had a sip of coffee, I figure he's asking about breakfast, but then I realize he's referring to my interview.

Am I ready to stand up in front of arguably the most intimidating audience I've ever been in front of and convince them that I, more than any other candidate, belong in their fine institution?

No, I'm terrified.

But I paste on a reassuring smile, open my mouth, and say, "As ready as I'll ever be."

Reeve places a red pepper omelet in front of me that I am too nervous to eat.

I'm also too nervous to have anything more than polite, surface-level conversations with him as he walks me to the U of T campus a whole hour before I need to be there.

He waits while I get checked in. Although he seems to want to stick around to be there when I get out, he nods when I ask if we can meet at a coffee shop on the corner at eleven when I'm done.

"I think I need some time alone to get in the zone."

And maybe some buffer afterward if I bomb and need to cry in a bathroom stall.

He kisses me on the forehead, saying all the right things before leaving me alone in an empty waiting room with nothing but my thoughts.

The first negative one creeps in as I watch him walk down the path and pass a group of students. It brings the reminder that if I get into med school, I will find myself amidst a sea of new faces. I have lived in West Lake my whole life. Even my undergraduate degree was online, keeping me in the comfort zone of the friends I'd known since middle school. That coming-of-age experience where you move away from home for the first time and grow into that better, more improved version of yourself as you shed all your high school insecurities—I skipped over that part.

I start to regret telling Reeve and Zoe about my dreams and even admitting to myself how much I wanted them, but then my phone begins to ring in my pocket.

I pull it out, more so to avoid the death glare of the stern-looking woman behind the desk, but then I see the name on the display.

Kitty St. Clair.

My stomach bottoms out completely. My heart begins to hammer so fast that I have to turn and sit on the windowsill for fear I'm about to pass out.

What has she done now?

I press the phone to my ear. "Kitty?"

"Jules!" says a voice. "I'm glad I caught you."

"Who is this?"

There's a notable pause on the other end.

"It's me. Zoe. I would have thought my voice would have been burned into your brain by now. Oh shit! I didn't call during your interview, did I?"

"No," I tell her, my heart slowing down enough that I can stand again. "Why does it say *Kitty St. Clair* on my phone?"

"Oh . . ." There's a pause on Zoe's end. "Ohhhhhhhhh. Yeah, I'm calling you from her old room. I guess they never changed the call display. Shit, that would have been creepy. But that's not why I'm calling you. Hold on."

There's the sound of static on Zoe's end, and at one point, I think she may have even dropped the phone, but then a voice comes on.

"Hello, Jules? Norman Samuel Sr. here. Zoe told us all about your big day, and I wanted to tell you that I think you'd make the most wonderful doctor. We all do, honey."

"Tell her about my granddaughter," says a gruff female voice in the background.

"I shall do no such thing," Mr. Samuel says.

There's some indecipherable arguing. Then the female voice says, "Give me the phone."

This is followed by more static. More scuffling. Someone definitely drops the phone before the female voice picks it up and clears her throat.

"Hello, Jules. How ya doing, sweetheart?"

"Mrs. Hail?" I ask, still very confused.

"Heard you're in need of a land shark. I wanted to tell you my granddaughter is the best in the business. Out for blood. I'll give you her number when you get back."

"Um . . . thank you?"

A third round of static before I hear Zoe again. "Sorry about that," she says, lowering her voice. "Just in case it wasn't clear: I'm pretty sure Jean's granddaughter is a real estate agent, so she might be able to help you out with the . . . other big thing in your life. I will clarify that before you get back. Anyway, I hope you know that everyone here is thinking about you and rooting for you today."

"Thank you, Zo," I say, and I really, really mean it.

"How are you holding up?" Zoe asks, as if her best friend radar still works from two hundred kilometers away.

"I'm hanging by my last thread," I tell her honestly.

"Yeah, but you're a West Lake babe. We're made of fishing line. A hell of a lot stronger than we look."

The woman at the desk looks up and catches my eye. "They're ready for you now, Julia."

"I have to go," I tell Zoe.

"I heard," she says. "Hey, Jules . . ." There's a hesitation to her voice, and I find myself holding my breath.

"Knock 'em dead."

Chapter 27

"So, Jules, what draws you to medicine?" The head of immunology research stares at me from behind a pair of thick black glasses. The two other doctors beside him form a formidable wall of navy-blue blazers and intellect.

I clench my hands into fists to keep from wiping them on my skirt and remind myself that there is a reason I am here—or, if I'm being exact, twenty-three of them.

I think of Mr. Minard spending nights away from his own bed because he can't get the care he needs in West Lake for a simple case of pneumonia, or of Mr. McNaught and his morning trips to Lou's and how for him, coffee and hash browns are the best forms of medicine. I even think of Mrs. Hail and her cigarettes.

"I have worked in a retirement home for the last two years." My voice cracks, and I catch the immunologist wincing, but I pause, take a deep breath, and clear my throat. "I have seen the difference access to good quality healthcare can make in a community, not only in diagnosing illness quickly but also in building trusting relationships with patients so that they are not afraid to seek out treatment because of long wait times or being transferred out of town for overnight stays."

I think about Sunnyvale and how, even though there are big holes in the healthcare system, our residents are mostly thriving.

"I read a brilliant paper once that said loneliness is as harmful to our health and longevity as smoking fifteen cigarettes a day. And the population that is at most risk is older adults. But I have also seen what happens when seniors feel like they have a special place within their community and people of varying ages they can talk to—it can make such a tremendous difference when it comes to quality of life. My hope is to advance my education in medicine so that I can work hand in hand with those in geriatric care positions to further these types of programs with the idea that the best type of medicine is often preventative care."

I finally look at the panel. I see the head of immunology exchange glances with a leading neurologist at one of Toronto's most prestigious hospitals. If I were to describe their expressions, I'd say they look surprised. Dare I say it—even a little impressed.

"So, is that where you envision using your medical education?" The head of immunology checks her papers. "In West Lake?"

"Yes." I have zero doubts as the answer leaves my mouth. "We need more qualified doctors in Bruce County, although we are in a better position than some remote communities farther north, where there are still thirty thousand people without a family doctor. My ideal scenario would be to work hard, become the best doctor I can be, and then return home—hopefully, to put a dent in that statistic, or at least the urgent care wait times."

This answer earns me a laugh. The tension breaks enough that I unclench my hands and draw my first full, deep breath of the day.

My interview continues for the better part of an hour. I'm asked about what I think are the best qualities in a physician, my experiences working with sick people, and my own qualities that would enable me to succeed in the field.

I talk about compassion and communication and recognizing that especially when it comes to planning for end-of-life, "a doctor needs to clearly lay out the risks and outcomes but also respect that quality of life plays into a patient's decision."

I even manage to turn my glass-not-always-full realism into a strength. "I am not an optimist. But I am straightforward and able to clearly outline the most likely outcomes and their probabilities, which often helps families create a realistic plan when faced with a serious medical concern."

My answers draw more impressed eyebrows and encouraging nods, almost as if they can tell that I'm not spouting the bullshit they want to hear—as if they can sense it comes straight from my heart.

When I finally shake their hands and leave, I'm feeling like all the best parts of me showed up—if U of T rejects me, that's on them, but if I lose out, it isn't because I held back.

I make my way through the winding paths of the downtown campus in a sort of residual euphoric fog, imagining myself grabbing a coffee as I take a break from an all-day study session or zipping from building to building because I've scheduled myself in back-to-back classes.

I somehow make it to the coffee shop, my cheeks stretched so wide that they ache as I push open the door.

Reeve stands when the bell above the door dings, as if he has been watching and waiting. When our eyes meet, he raises his hands in a victorious V, whooping so loud half the coffee shop turns their heads as he opens his arms, waiting for me to crash into them.

And I do. Oh, how I do—my body trembling with all of the adrenaline it's been holding all morning.

"So it was good?" he breathes into my hair, still holding me tight.

"So good."

"Everything you hoped for then?" He pulls away, his palm gently tracing the length of my jaw before he presses a kiss to my forehead. And I feel it—that little flicker of hope igniting. Normally I'd expel it. Extinguish it. Banish it to some dark corner where it could never burn me. But today, I hold on to it and bask in its glow.

Chapter 28

My nap that afternoon is long, luxurious, and completely dream-free. I awaken refreshed and starving. Reeve orders in Thai. I spend significantly longer than usual getting dressed for a celebration that Kitty would undoubtedly approve of: dancing, cocktails, and acknowledging that I am proud of what I did today, no matter what happens.

I descend Reeve's terrifying staircase, feeling pretty, smart, and hopeful about my life, especially as I take the last few steps into the living room and catch him watching me.

"You look great." His eyes start at my silk cami, drop to the same knee-length black skirt I wore to my interview, and move past my nylons to my fancy black heels, usually reserved only for weddings, before they reverse their way back up to my face again.

"You are far less fancy than you normally are." I eye his simple fitted T-shirt and jeans. "I think I like this look on you."

When we put on our coats, he holds mine, then brushes my hair out from under the collar, his fingertips leaving soft tingles on my neck. In the elevator, we're forced to press close as it fills with other twenty-somethings out for the evening. He grabs my hips possessively, pressing my back into his front. A position that would be far more obscene if not for the thickness of our coats. On the

Uber ride to the club, Reeve points out various landmarks from the windows as they blur by: his office in the distance, his favorite shawarma spot, the corner where he once stood next to Dustin Hoffman, not fully realizing who he was until he crossed the street. His thumb strokes the back of my hand the entire time, a rhythmic back-and-forth that distracts me from the conversation.

By the time we pull up in front of the club, I am ready to dance. No, I am ready to press up against Reeve, run my hands all over his chest, and feel how his body moves under my fingertips.

The line is short enough that it takes only a few moments until we are at the front of the line, showing the bouncer our IDs. The club is deceivingly bigger than I anticipated from the narrow front entryway. The lights are low, and the music is so loud that the bass reverberates under my rib cage as we weave through the sea of bodies toward the dance floor at the back.

"Do you want to grab a drink?" I ask Reeve, only to realize his attention has shifted to someone standing at the end of the bar: a tall, good-looking Asian guy with broad shoulders and a nearly shaved head who raises his hand and smiles.

"Baldwin. Buddy, what's up? It's been a while."

Two women turn at the sound of Reeve's name. The short one, also Asian, has long brown hair, red lipstick, and a short leather miniskirt. The other woman is white with chin-length blond hair, wearing tight black pants and a black strapless crop top. Both are so effortlessly cool they look as if they've been plucked from some Netflix TV drama.

"I hope you're in the mood to meet some of my friends," Reeve says, dipping his head to my ear as we approach.

My heart flutters in a brief panic as the guy sticks out his hand for a fist bump.

"How's it going?" he says. "I'm Anders."

"Jules," I reply, almost missing his fist, our knuckles hitting at an awkward angle.

He shakes his hand, laughing it off before reaching for Reeve and pulling him into a half hug, giving his back a loud but friendly slap.

"Jules, this is Keshe"—Reeve introduces me to the brunette, who smiles—"and that's Kendra." He waves at the blonde, who acknowledges me with a slight raise of her drink.

"We all went to Queens together."

"So, Jules." Anders leans against the bar. "How do you know my man Reeve?"

I automatically look to Reeve as I attempt to summarize our history into a single digestible sentence.

"We met at a party two years ago," Reeve answers. "It just took until now for Jules to finally agree to go out with me."

Anders laughs, throwing his head back. "Smart woman."

Our conversation is paused as Anders gets the bartender's attention. Reeve abandons me momentarily, following Anders to the bar and whispering something in his ear. They return a moment later. Anders with two vodka sodas, which he gives the girls. Reeve with two more and a PBR, which he hands to me.

Kendra holds out her glass toward Reeve for a cheers. "I thought you were working this weekend?"

Reeve clinks his glass with hers and shakes his head. "No, I said I was busy. Jules is in town visiting for the weekend. I didn't plan on inflicting you guys on her so quickly. I'm trying to make a good impression."

Kendra drops an arm around my shoulders, pulling my head to hers. "Then you made a big mistake bringing her here, Baldwin. Three more drinks, and I'll be spilling every one of your secrets." She winks at me and laughs. Then she drops her arm and links it with mine. "Come on." She inclines her head toward the dance floor, holding her other arm out to Keshe. "That dance floor is calling our names."

She pulls us into the crowd, weaving through the dancing bodies until she finds a small clearing in the center. Turning, she spreads her arms wide and backs up, pushing the other dancers away to make room for Anders and Reeve, who have followed us out onto the floor. She raises her arms above her head and begins to sway her hips. Keshe and Anders join in with an ease that makes me painfully aware of my lack of natural rhythm until Reeve's hand snakes around my waist, pressing his body against mine. He lowers his head so his mouth is at my ear. "Sorry about all of this. I know it's not what we planned. If you're not into it, let me know. We can go somewhere else."

I begin to dance as well, moving as best I can with the beat of the bass. "This place is perfect. Cold beer, excellent music, and . . ." I dance across our little circle away from Reeve and closer to Kendra and Keshe. "I need to hear more about these secrets."

Kendra lets out a laughing "Yessss." I can smell the vodka on her breath. It mingles with the vanilla of her perfume when she leans in close. "Remind me later to tell you the streaking snowman story."

"And why his nickname is Bobby Gorgeous," Keshe chimes in.

They both look at Anders, who holds up his hands. "I can't be a part of this. It violates the bro code." But then he reaches over and pulls Reeve into a headlock, covering his ears with his arm, and says, "Come find me later, Jules, and I'll tell you why Reeve is permanently banned from Red Lobster." He releases him with a loud laugh and a quiet "You're in trouble, buddy."

We dance for almost an hour, singing off-key to the songs we know, taking turns going to the bar for the next round of drinks. I'm sweaty and happy and slightly dehydrated, so I'm not upset when the DJ makes an unexpected foray into an ambient house set and we head for a small bar table tucked around a corner, far enough away from the speakers that there is a little relief from the thumping music.

"Hey, man." Anders slaps Reeve on the back. "I think it's our turn to grab the next round." He nods toward the bar, not waiting for Reeve to answer before taking off.

"I just need water," Keshe says to Reeve, wiping her sweaty forehead with the back of her hand.

"Me, too," I agree.

"Wimps," Kendra yells, smacking her palm on the table. "I will take a double tequila soda, *s'il vous plaît*. Somebody has to keep this party going."

"I'm on it." Reeve squeezes the side of my hip before following Anders to the bar.

Kendra sighs, her eyes following Reeve as he goes. "I really missed him," she says, then turns to me as if explaining. "I don't think I've seen Reeve in months. I'm so glad you guys came out tonight."

"Really?" Reeve has mentioned his friends only in passing. Still, I'm surprised by this.

Kendra gives me a knowing look. "His job is the worst. He missed my birthday in September because of some work trip and Anders's birthday in December because of a company party. He made it out for Keshe's in January but only because he felt terrible because he bailed on her engagement party back in October."

"To be fair, he was at a wedding that day," Keshe says as if defending him. "I can't get mad at him for that."

Kendra rolls her eyes. "Yeah, some random wedding with some *client's* daughter he barely knew. That still counts as working."

It's a beat before I fully register what she just said.

"Reeve went to a wedding with a client's daughter?"

Keshe shrugs as if confused by it, too. "She needed a date. It was a favor to his boss or something. They were looking to close some big deal, and his boss wanted to keep the client happy. Reeve called me and explained everything." She directs her last comment at Kendra.

"They basically pimped him out," Kendra argues back. "And Reeve went right along with it." She turns to Keshe. "You know that if the situation were reversed, Reeve would be the first one calling it out. Telling us we shouldn't put up with that shit."

"Okay, okay." Keshe links her arm through Kendra's. "As you can see, Jules, Reeve's work is a bit of a hot topic with Kendra, especially when she's fueled by vodka. But we love Reeve, and we're just glad he's out tonight and happy."

I get the impression Keshe wants to change the subject, but I want to know more.

"Does that kind of thing . . . happen a lot?" I ask Kendra, trying to sound nonchalant.

Kendra throws an arm around me. "Girl, yes! It's mostly Reeve's boss being a dick and Reeve not doing anything about it." There's a noticeable slur to her words. "I swear to god the guy used to be able to say *no*, but the last year it's been like anything his boss wants, Reeve does it—no questions asked. I just hope he never gets asked to, like, bury a body."

"Okay, that's enough of that for tonight." Keshe pries Kendra's arm off me and steers her toward the dance floor. Keshe holds out her other hand to me. "Why don't we all go dance for a little bit?"

I shake my head. "I'm going to sit this one out. I'll wait for the guys."

"We'll be out there if you change your mind." Keshe pulls Kendra into the crowd. I watch them go until the sea of dancing bodies swallows them.

I close my eyes and try to get lost in the music, but Kendra's words keep playing over and over in my head: *Anything his boss wants, Reeve does it—no questions asked.*

It makes me wonder what his boss has asked of him with the dance hall.

Then it makes me wonder if his boss has asked anything of him with *me*.

I shake my head as if the motion will erase that thought.

You know Reeve, I tell myself. *He is a good guy. He isn't like that.*

But if Kendra's right and Reeve took someone to a wedding to close a deal, that would mean Reeve *is* very much like that.

Before that terrible thought entirely takes hold, a warm hand slides along my hip bone.

"I am ready to get out of here." Reeve's breath is hot in my ear. "What about you?"

I nod, all of a sudden very much done with this place. "Should we go say goodbye?" I think of Kendra and Keshe on the dance floor, but Reeve shakes his head.

"I'm known for my Irish exits." He smiles. "It hasn't been a good night if I don't slip out without a trace. Come on."

He takes my hand, leading me toward the coat check, then, once we have our coats, out the front door and onto the sidewalk.

A fresh layer of snow has turned into a wet gray slush from the steady stream of passing cars.

"It's a busy night," says Reeve, looking down the street. "We may need to walk to the corner to get a cab." He reaches for my hand.

"That's fine." I pretend not to see him do it, folding my arms across my chest, feigning cold.

They stay there as we run across the street and onto the opposite curb, where I am so caught up in thinking about what Kendra told me that I fail to see the thin sheet of ice when I step onto the sidewalk.

My feet come out from under me. My arms, still crossed, splay a fraction of a second too late. I plummet hard toward the pavement, but just before I hit, Reeve's arms grab hold of me. "Whoa. Are you okay?" he asks as the world rights itself again, and I catch my breath.

I nod, leaning into him until my feet find their footing again and I can stand.

When I do, he pulls me to his chest, his arms coming around me tightly.

"I think that scared me almost as much as it did you. Are you sure you're all right?"

I'm not.

Although my body has recovered, I'm still reeling from the emotional whiplash of the last few minutes.

I want to ask him about all those terrible thoughts that began to take shape inside the bar.

I want to know if I'm just another way to impress his boss. The key to his next promotion.

"Are you dating me so I'll sell you the dance hall?" I say, not able to keep it in any longer.

His smile disappears. "What? Of course not. Why would you think that?"

My voice takes on a cool tone I didn't know it was capable of. "Because you've done it before. Your friends told me you took some guy's daughter to a wedding as part of a business deal."

He pulls back, his expression confused until it clears, and he closes his eyes and groans. "Jesus, Kendra."

It's not what I wanted to hear.

"Okay . . ." I draw out the word, and his eyes fly open.

"No," he says. "It wasn't like that."

I wait to hear what it was like then.

"She was the daughter of a client whose property we were trying to buy," he explains. "We met at a business dinner at my boss's house. She asked if I would go with her."

The adrenaline draining from my body is leaving me surprisingly bold. "And you thought, what? I'll lead this poor girl on and hopefully land the deal in the process?"

He steps toward me, his hands reaching for mine then backing off at the last second. "I don't want to lie to you, Jules. Yeah, I agreed to go because I knew it would make my boss happy. But before I even said yes, I made it very clear to her that I wasn't interested in her romantically. She said she felt the same. She lived on the West Coast and didn't know anyone attending the wedding besides her parents. All she wanted was someone her age to hang out with."

"Okay." I suddenly regret this whole conversation. "I shouldn't have brought it up. Let's just go."

I move to walk past him, but he steps in front of me, blocking my path. "No, wait. Ask me what we talked about."

I don't want to know anymore. I'm tired, and I'm cold, and I want to be doing anything but this.

"It's fine," I tell him. "It's really none of my business. I don't need to know."

"You do, Jules." His voice is suddenly raw. "Ask me what."

I have to blink a few times before I can meet his eyes. "What did you talk about?"

He swallows, the intensity of his gaze never breaking with mine. "Well, she talked about her girlfriend. They'd only been together for three months, but she was sure she was the one. And I talked about how I'd just been up in West Lake and run into this woman I never thought I'd see again and how I couldn't stop thinking about her."

I stop breathing completely.

"I told her about the dock," he continues. "And how it was one of the best nights of my life. How some bad luck prevented it from being more than just a night, and how I fell even harder when I finally found her again, and she called me a creep and poured beer down my pants."

I breathe now. It's a staggering breath followed by a quick, short laugh.

"I'm serious." He steps closer, taking both my hands in his. "How I feel has nothing to do with my job. I haven't stopped thinking about you since that night, even when you still hated me."

I shake my head. "I never hated you. I just didn't trust you."

"Do you trust me now?"

I hesitate.

He reaches into his coat pocket and pulls out his phone. "I will call Howard right now and tell him I can't work on the West Lake project anymore." He taps on the screen and then scrolls, and when he holds out his phone to me again, Howard Mansfield's name is on the screen. "I want this deal to happen for you. But if I have to choose between the deal and you knowing where my intentions lie, I choose you, Jules. I want you to know you can trust me."

There's a way out here. I leave. I go home. I go back to being the girl I was before Reeve came along. Chalk all of this up to another lesson on how hope in the wrong hands always ends in hurt. I can do it. I've done it once before.

But just like before, I'd be lying to myself. I'd be pretending I don't want him when, in truth, I haven't stopped thinking about him since that night on the dock, either.

"I trust you," I finally say. The relief is a shared emotion, vibrating back and forth along the invisible string between us.

His arms come around me. I tuck my head under his chin. The comforting warmth of his body and the feeling that things are really good right now give me a full-blown body shudder.

"Are you cold?" He leans back to study my face.

"Not really. I think that was more like an emotional exorcism. It's been a really big day. A good one," I clarify.

"We should get back then." He looks around for a cab. "You're probably exhausted."

He reaches for my hand, and when he takes it, another emotion surfaces from earlier. "Actually, Reeve, I'm not tired at all."

Chapter 29

It turns out the only available Uber is a rideshare. Reeve and I squish into the backseat of a Toyota Corolla with a very large man named Caruso, who proceeds to lovingly unwrap and eat his haddock burrito while his girlfriend, Tina, hits on the driver from the front seat.

I'm forced to half sit on Reeve's lap, both my legs strewn across his right leg. His arm is slung around my shoulders, protectively keeping my body close to his and away from the chili lime burrito sauce dripping off the side of Caruso's foil wrapper.

"It shouldn't be too much longer." Reeve leans his head in close, his arm slipping behind my back then under the hem of my coat to my hip. I lean my head against his shoulder, but with my weight shifting, my legs start to slip. He grabs them before they hit the ground, slipping his hand over my thigh, his fingers dipping just slightly under the hem of my skirt.

They brush the lace at the top of my thigh-high stockings as if they're not quite sure what is causing the sudden change in texture. His fingers trace the seam between the silky nylon and the lace before creeping upward slowly until they meet the skin of my inner thigh.

"Dear god," he growls into my ear. "Have you been wearing these all night?"

"All day, actually," I clarify. "I had meant to buy the full, pantyhose-style ones, but the West Lake pharmacy doesn't exactly have a big selection. I had to make do."

The Uber slows to a complete stop and the driver lays on the horn at the sea of red taillights up ahead.

"Fuuuuuckkkk," Reeve moans at the traffic, then tilts his head, his mouth once again at my ear. "I just want to get you home."

His nose trails down the side of my neck before he plants a kiss at the base, just above the collarbone. His fingers continue to trace a line along my skin, following the edge of my nylons. The competing sensations lull me into a haze where I forget for a moment that we are in an Uber. His fingers feel so good. I mentally urge them up farther and farther, my want intensifying with every quarter inch. When he kisses my neck again, I have to grit my teeth not to moan.

"Ahhhhhhhh."

My eyes fly open, wondering how that sound could have escaped.

But it isn't me.

"That was fucking great." Caruso crumples the empty foil of his burrito into his fist. "Where the fuck are we?" He looks around. "Teens," he calls to his girlfriend in the front. "Let's get out. This is taking forever."

They abandon the Uber mid-block. Reeve and I decide to follow. He tips the driver, who doesn't seem too fussed about this change in plans, pulling a U-turn and driving off down the less busy side of the street.

We walk hand in hand for half a block until Reeve tugs me around the corner of a building—pressing my back against the brick, his hand once again sliding up my leg to that spot just beyond the lace.

"Sorry," he says, leaning down to kiss me. "I couldn't wait."

My fingers run through his hair, pulling him closer. His tongue parts my lips as his hand moves up another blessed quarter inch, the heat of his fingers a stark contrast to the cold night air.

I arch, pressing my back against the brick, inviting his fingers higher, but before he can give me what I want, a car passes, and a drunk male voice yells out a "Yeah, baby" before zooming off.

The distraction is just enough to break our kiss and pull us back.

"My place is three minutes away," Reeve says, glancing down the street.

"Let's see if we can make it in two," I challenge, taking off at a questionable pace for heels.

It takes us four. Only because we stop to kiss again at a stoplight.

By the time we reach Reeve's building, I have made multiple plans for what I want to do in his bed. I have a dozen more by the time we step into the elevator.

It makes the ride up excruciating.

Six different passengers get off at six different floors. Every ding of the doors only increases my want, so when it's finally Reeve's floor and we tumble out into the hallway, I have no patience left.

I throw my arms around his neck and kiss him. He slides my skirt up and over my butt so he can pick me up and carry me the rest of the way to his door.

Just before we reach it, he glances down at my exposed thigh. "Fuck. It's even hotter than I imagined." He lets me down slowly but holds on to that thigh, hitching my knee high as he presses me hard against the door.

The angle of our bodies is filthy. If anyone were to step off the elevator now, there would be no mistaking what we're up to. No denying exactly what we're about to get up to next.

"We should go inside," I tell him, not because I'm ashamed of anyone finding us in the hallway but because I can't wait any longer.

He kisses me. And with the distraction of his lips and his hand reaching under my skirt to cup my ass, I don't notice him remove his keys or press the fob against his lock. I register only the door swinging open, my balance temporarily lost until a second hand snakes under my knees, lifting me into his arms.

"You are a magician," I tell him as he closes the door with a kick of his foot and carries me down the hall toward the kitchen. We bump against the wall, knocking one of his art pieces on an angle. I try to fix it, but he growls at me, "Leave it. I need to get you in my bed."

I weave my fingers into his hair; the ends have curled because of the snow, and I can smell his spicy shampoo as I nip his earlobe.

"Fuck, Jules." He sets me down on the kitchen countertop. His body lingers between my legs.

The counter height brings us even. I enjoy this new angle, pulling his face to mine, kissing my way along his jawbone, making my way toward his lips as his hands slide under my camisole, thumbs tracing along the edge of my bra.

I shiver. "You're distracting me."

He uses my break in focus to kiss that spot in the dip in my neck. I'm helpless, my head falling back as my body arches toward him. His thumbs graze my breasts, brushing ever so lightly over my nipples. I inhale—shallow and quick. "You're finding all my weaknesses tonight."

He runs his tongue all the way up my neck to my ear, where he whispers, "Not finding. Remembering."

My heart surges at his words, and at his hands, which have left my breasts in favor of slipping my camisole up over my head. I lift my arms, enjoying the feeling of silk sliding over my skin and the soft, long "fuuuuuccckk" that escapes his lips as he tosses it somewhere near the couch.

His hands return to my body, firm and purposeful. They reach for the zipper of my skirt, undoing it as far as it will go until I have to lift my hips so he can slide it off the rest of the way.

When it joins my shirt, he steps back, his eyes traveling the length of my body. I reach for one of my nylons, but he stops me, his hand gripping my wrist as he shakes his head.

"Let's leave those on."

He lifts my arm, kissing it lightly below my wrist, following the pulsing beat of my blood to that tiny dip inside my elbow, leaving a soft bite on my shoulder, then trailing his lips along my skin to the base of my neck.

"You know if you kiss me there, I'll do anything you want."

He stops only to trace his fingers along the waistband of my underwear, hooking a finger underneath, tugging me ever so slightly toward him.

"I think that's where you have it backward, Jules. You've had me since the moment we met. I've been completely at your mercy this entire time."

And with that declaration, my tiny black thong joins the ambiguous pile of clothes no longer on my body.

If I didn't believe his words before, I believe them now in the greedy way his hands glide along the skin from my thighs to my knees, and in the urgency as he parts my legs, forgoing any teasing, to taste me with his tongue.

Each lick, each stroke, each tiny nip of my thigh tells me over and over what he said earlier on the street: what's happening between us is real and good and on its way to being so much more.

My head falls back, and I barely register the green 1:43 on his microwave clock before it blurs as two fingers enter and then curl.

"Holy shit." My head snaps back up, but my coherence lasts for only half a second before the sensation overtakes me and my head drops again, the microwave clock this time a distant blurry green.

He twirls his tongue over my sensitive spot, and the sensation, combined with the pressure of his fingers, brings me right to the edge.

"Reeve." His name comes out in a moan. "If you don't stop, I'm going to come."

He pauses only long enough to kiss me quick and hard on the lips. "That was my plan."

"I thought you wanted me in your bed?"

Reeve laughs, his fingers and tongue resuming their positions. "We will do that, too. I have all sorts of plans."

I succumb to the plan of the moment. The delicious friction building between my thighs. My hips drive off the counter. Allowing his hands to slide under me. To grip. To pull me closer. To give him all the access he needs for one final flick of his tongue, one last curl of his fingers to drive me around that final bend, tip me over the edge, where I free-fall.

I linger in that blissful state where everything in my body feels light. I'm only half aware of Reeve, who is kissing his way along my thighs to my stomach. Carving a slow, soft path from my navel to my lips.

"How you doing there, Jules?" His voice is so deep it acts as a tether for my soul as it slowly returns to my body.

"I'm good. No, I'm great. You said something about going

upstairs?" My eyes open just as his lips meet mine, and I can taste myself on him.

His arm snakes under my knees as he lifts me off the counter, pulling my body to his, setting me down slowly, every inch of him pressing against every inch of me.

"We can do that," he says. "But I want to kiss you first."

His hand cups my jaw as he tips my face to meet his. His first kiss is soft. His second is a little deeper. The third makes me forget every kiss that came before him.

It is like every cell in my body resets. Forgets the bliss of the last few minutes. I ache for him as if I've never touched him.

"One of us is practically naked"—my hands reach for his dress shirt—"and one of us is not."

I undo his buttons, one by one, until the final button gives way, allowing me to remove his shirt and toss it in some dark corner of the room. My hands, now free, roam the hard planes of his chest, the curve of his biceps, his abs—all of the places I have only allowed myself to fantasize about occasionally for the last two years.

"If we don't go now"—his hands cup my ass and pull me to him—"I may have to break my promise about making it upstairs. And I'm a man of my word." With that, he bends down and picks me up, scooping me into his arms. When we reach the stairs, I close my eyes and try not to think about the death trap we're climbing. But my fears are unfounded. He keeps me close and tight and safe until he lays me down in his bed with all the care of handling something precious.

"You distracted me downstairs," I say as I reach for his belt. "I was trying to get you naked." He lets me take off his pants, and I let him remove my bra. My thigh-highs stay, and his fingers return to ensure I'm still wet before he reaches for the nightstand for a condom.

He plays between my legs as he rips the condom open, pausing only to roll it on, then bends to kiss me behind the ear. "You still want this?" he whispers.

"I need this."

"Thank god."

He pushes inside me. His thickness fills me in a way that makes me cry out and cling to him.

"You okay?"

"So good."

It's so, so good as he picks up speed, the bed beneath us rocking along in rhythm.

"I've waited—" He groans.

"Me, too."

"It's even better than—"

"I know—"

The rest of the words are lost to the pounding of our bodies, his fingers intertwined with mine, and the way he kisses me, as if he needs every part of me closer. He waits for me to come, and when I cry out, giving in to the euphoric rush, he gives one last hard thrust, his body collapsing onto mine, his heart beating so hard I can feel it all the way to my core. He kisses me softly on the temple before he rolls out of bed to dispose of the condom. Then he returns a moment later, slipping under the covers and pulling my body into his.

"I like you in my bed," he whispers as his breaths slow and become even.

I snuggle in closer, thinking only how much I like it, too.

Chapter 30

I don't dream of Kitty.

My sleep is dreamless and deep.

When I awake in the morning, sun streaming through the windows, my only memories of the night before are of waking to Reeve—sometime in the early hours—kissing me softly while I slept.

Now I'm curled up beside him. A little spoon to his big one.

His arms tighten as I open my eyes, and I'm not sure if I've woken him or the other way around.

Then I hear it. A soft buzzing from Reeve's nightstand, followed by silence.

"I think that's your phone." I try to turn over, but he holds me to his chest, nuzzling his nose into the nape of my neck.

"The only person I feel like talking to this morning is in my bed," he grumbles into my skin.

The buzzing, however, continues. A rhythmic *zzzz zzzz zzzz* of metal vibrating on wood.

"It could be important," I tell him, to which he groans, letting go of me just enough to roll onto his back so he can reach over and tip the screen toward us.

"It's just my mom." He clicks decline, sets the phone back down, then remains on his back but pulls me on top of his chest.

"How did you slee—" His question is cut off by another round of phone buzzing.

Reeve growls, pulling one of the pillows from behind his head and plopping it on top of his nightstand.

"What if it's an emergency?" I ask, suddenly concerned about the need for two consecutive phone calls.

Reeve kisses the top of my head. "It's not. Trust me."

The buzzing happens a third time, its annoying persistence cutting through the pillow. I prop myself up onto my elbow and stare, my head filling with gruesome scenarios, car crashes and kitchen fires. "Maybe you should answer it. Just to be sure."

Reeve snakes his arm under the pillow, clicks the phone, and brings it to his ear.

"Hey, Ma."

I hear a female voice on the other end of the line. I can't make out her words, but her tone is very nonemergency.

Reeve looks over at me. "You called me three times to invite me over to brunch?" he repeats, as if giving me a recap of their conversation.

"I can't make it," he says, rolling onto his back, bringing his other hand behind his head, and flexing his biceps, to my delight and pleasure.

"Why?" He stares up at the ceiling above. "Because my girlfriend is here for the weekend, and I haven't yet mentally prepared her for you and Dad."

My stomach bottoms out at the word and how he so casually tossed it out there, like it wasn't the first time he'd thought it. To his mother, nonetheless.

I'm a girlfriend.

Reeve's girlfriend.

With that idea still sinking in, I lose the plot of Reeve's conversation until he rolls onto his side, saying, "Fine. I'll ask her." Then he presses the phone to his chest. "Do you want to go to my parents' for brunch today?"

My previous elation is replaced with curiosity at the prospect of filling in yet another piece of the Reeve puzzle. "Yeah, kind of."

He lowers one of his eyebrows. "Are you sure? I was planning on us staying in bed all day, ideally naked."

As much as I love the sound of that plan, I'm even more curious to learn more about Reeve. "We would have to eat at some point, though. You know how I feel about breakfast."

Reeve leans forward, kissing me softly on the lips before returning to his back and pressing the phone to his ear again. "Okay. We'll see you in an hour." He lifts the phone away as if he's about to hang up but quickly brings it back to his ear. "Wait, is Brodie going to be there?" He pauses as his mom presumably answers his question. "Liam and Lorraine or just Liam?"

There's another few seconds of indiscernible mom talk before he clicks off the phone and sets it on the nightstand.

"Does this mean I get to meet the brothers as well?" I ask, piecing together his half of the conversation.

"The whole fam, except my brother's wife, Lorraine. She's on call." He rolls out of bed. "We should get dressed then. You'll need a cup of coffee before you go, possibly a shot of tequila."

"Are they really that bad?" I ask, following him out.

Reeve turns, and I notice the smile has slipped from his lips. "They're something."

We take Reeve's car to his parents' house. About halfway there, I get that now too familiar *been here before* feeling as I start to recognize a few of the homes before I realize it's in the same neighborhood as Beau's cousin Eleanor from my Kitty dream.

However, the house we pull up in front of is newer and more modern than Eleanor's old Tudor-style mansion. Its exterior is covered with big gray stone slabs, huge arched windows, and an impressively tall entryway. I can feel Reeve watching me as we park in the driveway.

"Ready?" He holds out his hand, which I take, even though we're still sitting in the front seat. He brings our entwined fingers to his lips and kisses the back of my hand before reaching for his door handle and stepping out.

It occurs to me as we walk up the front steps that I've never before met parents in such an official capacity. Most of the guys I've dated over the years are from West Lake, with parents I've known most of my life who had no clue when the line shifted from us just hanging out in their basement to making out in their basement.

The front foyer of the house is empty. It reminds me a little of Reeve's condo with its white-and-gray marble floors and sleek, sharp lines.

We toss our shoes and coats in a large closet and walk the long hall to the back of the house toward the sounds of sizzling pans, cupboards being opened and closed, and the trickles of multiple conversations.

Reeve takes my hand again as we walk in. A woman sits at a large kitchen island the same shade of marble as the floor. Her chin-length blond bob is cut at a sharp angle that reminds me of her house. She's thin and fine-boned and bears little resemblance to Reeve until she looks up, and her eyes light up in surprise.

"They're here!"

Standing at the stove, a man turns at the sound of her voice, flipping a tea towel over his shoulder. He raises a spatula in greeting, and I instantly see where Reeve gets all of his features. Both men sport the same broad shoulders and dark hair, although Reeve's dad is a little rounder in the waist and has a little more salt and pepper at his temples.

"Mom. Dad. This is Jules."

I wipe my hands as discreetly as I can on my jeans as Reeve's mom comes around the island, but she ignores my outstretched palm and instead pulls me into a tight hug.

"So happy you could make it, Jules. I'm Cheryl, and that's Reeve's father, Bill. Reeve has told us all about you."

My cheeks flush at the idea that his mother knows my name.

"Thank you for inviting me. It smells wonderful in here," I say to Bill as Cheryl moves on to Reeve for a hug.

"We're still a few minutes away from being ready," Bill says, holding up a metal flipper. "Why don't you grab some coffee and see what your brothers are up to?"

He goes back to tending a frying pan of bacon. Cheryl inclines her head toward a small living area off the kitchen where two men are sitting reading their phones.

The one lying on the couch looks up as we walk in. "Reevey Boy, nice of you to show up for once." His tone is joking, and his smile is wide, yet I feel Reeve stiffen beside me.

"I don't know why you're giving me shit," Reeve says, his eyes drifting to the guy still on his phone. "Liam's the one who hasn't been here since Christmas."

The guy on the phone, presumably Liam, continues to type as he talks. "He pretended not to recognize me when he answered the door. It was all very hilarious," he says dryly before looking up and realizing Reeve is not alone.

"Oh, hi. I'm Liam." He extends his hand.

As we shake, the other brother waves at me, still lying on the couch. "Brodie."

"Jules," I reply, the formalities now complete.

We sit down on the love seat across from Brodie. His splayed form is a notable contrast to Liam, who's straight-backed in the chair.

All three Baldwin brothers look like their father. Although Reeve got more of the height and broad shoulders, they all inherited the strong jaw and honey-hued skin.

I know Reeve is the middle child, but I can't remember if he told me which of his brothers is the oldest. However, I can wager a decent guess. "So Liam, then Reeve, then you?" I say to Brodie.

He flashes back an all-too-familiar smile. "Only if you're going in birth order. If you're going by who's the best-looking, it's me, then probably Reeve and Liam way at the end."

Liam doesn't even look up from his phone as he says, "Let's go by who makes the most bank. That would be me, then I guess Brodie. Reevey, are you even on the list?"

Brodie laughs. Reeve stares straight ahead, unimpressed.

Brodie sits up, swinging his feet to the ground. "Or we go by who has the biggest di—"

"Boys!" Cheryl yells in that universal mom-tone. "We have a guest. Now, go get your drinks. Breakfast will be ready in a moment."

We fill our coffee mugs and settle around a kitchen table that is yet another shade of light marble. On top of it is a breakfast that looks like it came out of a '90s-era sitcom: big plates of pancakes, scrambled eggs, and an entire platter piled high with crisp bacon.

Once plates are filled, Cheryl turns to me, her eyes kind as she says, "So, Jules, Reeve tells me you're here this week for your medical school interview."

I take a sip of coffee, swallowing down the half-chewed bite of pancake in my mouth. "Yes, it was yesterday."

"And how are you feeling about it?" she asks.

"Good." My answer isn't even a canned response. I do feel good about it, even with twenty-four hours of perspective. "I guess I'll find out what they think in the spring."

Cheryl shakes her head, astonished. "I forgot they make you wait that long."

Liam nods, taking a sip of his coffee. "Do you know what you want to specialize in yet?" he asks.

"If I go with the answer I gave yesterday, yes. General medicine with a focus on geriatrics."

Liam seems to think about my answer for a moment. "If your interest lies in geriatrics, you might want to consider specializing in orthopedics. There's a lot of money to be made in replacing knees and hips."

"She said she's interested in general medicine," Reeve cuts in on my behalf. His voice is unusually combative, although this doesn't seem to faze his brother, who shrugs off his outburst.

"All I'm saying is the money is good. Med school is expensive; not everyone can do what they want and live off a trust fund."

An awkward silence follows that only I seem to be aware of. The rest of the Baldwin family continue to serve and eat their breakfasts with an ease that makes me wonder if I'm imagining the tension.

But there's an unusual clench to Reeve's jaw that I've never seen before. The same goes for the tiny pulsing vein in his right temple. I wonder if I should change the subject, but Cheryl beats me to it.

"So, Jules," she says, and her voice seems an octave higher

than before, "Reeve tells us you're from West Lake. We absolutely love the area."

I nod, thankful for the safer conversation topic. "I've lived there all my life."

Bill reaches for a stack of toast. "Don't they have that great little tapas place right down by the water?"

"No, honey." Cheryl shakes her head. "You're thinking of that place in Southampton."

Bill holds his toast as if he's about to take a bite but is still thinking. "What's in West Lake then?"

"My new project," Reeve pipes in. "The condo development I've been working on."

Bill finally takes a bite of his toast, chewing and swallowing it. "You're working on the marketing team, right?"

Reeve seems to pull in a deep breath before answering. "No, I'm leading the whole project, remember?"

Bill raises an eyebrow. "They let you do that with a fine arts degree?"

Both of Reeve's brothers laugh, tucking their chins and exchanging glances. It feels like a bad inside joke. One I don't want to be a part of.

Reeve remains stone-faced. The only indication that anything is off is the tiny vein going *pump pump pump* on his temple.

Silence descends over the table again. I become acutely aware of Liam's knife scraping as he butters his toast and Brodie's silver spoon stirring his coffee. I look to Cheryl to see if she will come to the rescue again, but Bill breaks the silence.

"Did Brodie tell you he's already building his book?" It's unclear if his comment is directed at Reeve or Liam, as they both look up. "Six months in, he's already bringing in a new client. Billed two hundred and fifty hours last month."

Bill looks to me like I should know what that means.

"That's a lot of hours," I reply, which seems to be the answer Bill was looking for, as he nudges me with his elbow, smiling. "Chip off the old block."

My eyes flick to Reeve, whose gaze is on the butterless toast in his hand. I wonder if he wishes he, too, were a chip.

I watch him slowly bite his bread and then swallow it with a sip of coffee—this passionate guy who sends cheese baskets and has a secret pottery room—and can't help but think I'm really glad he isn't.

The rest of the breakfast passes with less contentious conversation: the odds of early spring, the likelihood the Leafs will make the playoffs, and the email about the food and beverage minimum hike at Reeve's parents' golf club. Although Reeve doesn't say anything, somehow I feel his tension—like a sixth sense—wound deep and tight.

His silence continues as we help clean up the dishes and walk to the front hall to retrieve our coats. In fact, the only words that come out of his mouth are a gruff "Thanks for breakfast" when his mom hugs him goodbye, followed by a stiff wave at his brothers as we exit the front door and climb into the car.

I don't know how to navigate this side of Reeve. What I want to do is pull him tight to me. Kiss him. Remind him that he's intelligent and funny—the kind of person who leaves people better than when he found them. But I place my hand on his thigh instead.

Reeve's eyes focus on the road as we pull out of the driveway and onto the street. When we hit Yonge Street and he still hasn't said anything, I assume I've done the wrong thing. But when I try to retract my hand, he stops me, gripping my fingers in his, returning it to his leg, and pressing my hand to his thigh.

"Sorry," he finally says as we turn onto Bloor Street. "It usually takes me until Davisville to calm down. I guess it took a little longer today."

"Are you okay?" I ask, somewhat understanding where his head is at but realizing there are still a lot of blanks left to fill.

He lets out a long breath. "I'm fine. That's actually a pretty normal Sunday at the Baldwin household. I was mentally prepared for it, though I had hoped since you were there, they might have laid off a little. Talked me up a bit." He smiles, but it doesn't quite reach his eyes.

"My dad just has this very specific idea of what my life should look like," Reeve continues. "We didn't talk for three months when I decided to pursue an arts management diploma instead of an MBA. I had inherited some money from my grandma, which allowed me to do it. When he finally started talking to me, it was to tell me that I was squandering my future."

"I'm sorry," I say, squeezing his leg.

He shakes his head. "I really thought things would get better when I took the job at Mansfield. Howard loves me, and he and my dad are tight, but you saw how he was. I'm not Liam, and I'm not Brodie."

I turn my palm so our fingers can lace together. "I know it's not the same, but I happen to be a big fan of Reeve."

This time, his smile is genuine. When we stop at a light, he turns his head to meet my lips for a quick kiss. "It makes for an exponentially better experience to have you sitting there beside me. And I know I've done a pretty shitty job of selling you on the idea of spending time with my family, but my parents are having an anniversary party at the Granite Club in a couple weeks. It's a Saturday night. Do you think you'd want to come with me?"

"Of course," I answer before fully thinking things through. "I will need to check my schedule. We're down a staff member, so I'm picking up a few more shifts than normal, but I will let you know. I'd like to try and get down here more."

He reaches his arm behind my shoulders, the pad of his thumb kneading gently at the tight muscles at the base of my neck. "I have a meeting in Port Logan on the Friday after next. I was thinking I could come after and stay the night?"

"Yeah," I tell him. "That would be great." But my heart sinks a little at the timing. "Two whole weeks, huh?"

His thumb stops kneading and, instead, rubs gently back and forth. "Yeah, I know. But I have meetings in the city until then. You don't have any time off?"

I mentally calculate my schedule. "Wednesday this week and then Monday and Tuesday next week, but I'll be coming off a weekend of night shifts. So not ideal."

Reeve blows out a long breath. "No, it's not." He slows the car to a stop as the light in front of us turns red. His hand curls around my neck, bringing my face to his, and he kisses me longer and deeper than I expect.

"That was nice," I say as he pulls away. He reaches up and wipes a drop of moisture from my lip with the pad of his thumb. "Two weeks," he repeats. "I needed another good one to hold me over."

I glance at the clock, calculating how much time we have left and what I need to hold me over. Reeve seems to follow the same train of thought.

"What time do you need to head out?"

I take my phone from my pocket and navigate to my weather app. "It looks like there is snow coming in tonight. It's probably best if I'm on the road by four. Four-thirty at the latest."

Reeve glances at the clock again. "I don't love the idea of you driving home in the dark."

"I'll be fine," I argue. "Celine is a beast in the snow. She's used to it."

"I know. I just worry about you, Jules. I . . ." Reeve reaches out, his fingers cupping my chin, and the way his eyes find mine, I swear he is about to say something. But instead, he releases a breath and presses another quick kiss to my lips.

"You like me a lot?" I attempt to finish his thought.

The slow spread of his smile tells me I've completed it perfectly.

"Yeah."

My hand covers his, and I lean across the console, my heart beating wildly at the implication that maybe I didn't complete it so perfectly after all. "I like you too—a lot," I whisper, kissing him on the temple. "In case it isn't painfully obvious."

His hand reaches up, brushing a stray strand of hair from my forehead and lingering. "It's only a few more months until September. St. George Campus is a lot closer than West Lake."

It is. If I were to get into med school, we could be in the same city. We could be within walking distance.

The admissions part of med school is now out of my hands. It is at the mercy of the committee. It will be, or it won't.

But there's a part two that needs to happen, and *that* decision is very much up to me.

I'm suddenly remembering yet another Kitty-ism, that same advice they give you when you board a plane. *Help yourself first so you can then be in a position to help others.*

I can't be a doctor unless I go to school, and I can't pay for school unless I sell the dance hall.

"Hey." My eyes find Reeve's, the decision already made in my head. "Do you think you'd have more meetings in West Lake . . .

let's say, if a prospective seller was ready to put their property on the market?"

Reeve eyes me as if he's not sure he's interpreting correctly. "Are you saying you want to sell?"

This is me putting on my oxygen mask.

"I'm ready. Let's set it up."

Chapter 31

I RETURN TO West Lake a new woman. It feels clichéd to think about it, but something inside me has changed. Maybe it's hope. I've given up my knockoff Ray-Bans in favor of rose-colored glasses. Where before I refused to let myself even think about the possibility of getting into medical school, now I'm making plans.

The Thursday of the week I get back, I hire Mrs. Hail's granddaughter, Miranda, as my real estate agent. She has her grandmother's blue eyes and easy laugh and, as Mrs. Hail promised, a lust for blood when working with developers.

She convinces me to list the property publicly, instead of entering into a private deal with Mansfield Properties. "If they want it badly enough, they'll make it worth your while," she tells me. "I can think of only one scenario where you want your back up against the wall, and this ain't it."

The following week, Miranda refers me to a real estate lawyer she's previously worked with who agrees to take a commission once the property is sold. They put up the official listing on Wednesday morning. By Thursday afternoon, we have a meeting set up with Reeve and his boss for the following day.

The night before my meeting, I'm a nervous wreck. I know that selling the property to Mansfield is my right. It's legal. The property itself will be beautiful, and I could—if I really wanted to—focus on the "pros" side of the list: It will drive up property value ... for those who already own property. It will encourage retail businesses to move to the area ... where they will cut prices and drive out local businesses. It will allow me to afford school finally.

I concentrate on that last shining pro as I put on my pajamas and climb into bed.

Kitty's diary sits in its usual spot on my nightstand. I reach for it instinctively as I slide under the covers. I tell myself that I'm giving it one last try—a final chance to find a reason behind her mysterious gift, but I'd be lying if I also didn't admit it's an unfinished story and I want to know the ending.

Dear Diary,

The most wonderful thing in the world has happened. Mr. Scott, who owns the dance hall, has decided to retire. He is almost seventy now and finds the late nights too long. But guess who he thinks is perfect to run the dance hall in his place? Knots! It's such fabulous news. I have never seen Knots happier. His new job comes with a big raise, too! He loves the dance hall more than anyone in West Lake and has all of these wonderful ideas for bringing more and more tourists to the town. I think this is the beginning of something extraordinary for Knots, me, and everyone here in West Lake.

Yours forever,
Kitty

I awaken in Dot's bed, in that same dark room, wearing that same white dancing dress, yet there is no Kitty sleeping beside me.

I don't call out for her this time.

The bed is cold, and I can sense she isn't there.

But I know exactly where to find her.

I run all the way to the dance hall, toward the music and the yellow light, until I'm inside and weaving through the dancing bodies. I spot her next to the stage, her lips curved into a dreamy smile, watching the dancers as they spin and sway.

I don't recognize Knots beside her until I'm almost upon them. He is in a new black suit with his hair slicked back and smart. However, it's not the suit that's thrown me off. It's the notable difference in how he carries himself from just a few dreams ago. His head is a little higher, his stance a little wider, and his smile seems to say, *Welcome to my party*.

Knots spots me first, calling me over with a friendly wave of his hand. "Evening, Dotty. You're looking lovely." He reaches for my hand and kisses it, causing me to fight an unexpected blush.

"Hey," I say back. "Good to see you, too."

Knots inclines his head toward the stage. "Have you had a chance to listen to the band yet? What do you think? Swell, aren't they?"

The band in question are all dressed in white jackets with thick black lapels and matching tiny bow ties. A tall Black man stands as he plays the piano, periodically pausing to point at the trombonist and trumpeter, who seem to be squaring off in a back-and-forth battle of the horns. But it's the drums that capture my attention. It's not the usual steady rhythm I've gotten used to here at the dance hall. The wild, syncopated thumping seems to capture the essence of a summer night.

"Are those bongos?" I ask.

"It's called the mambo." Kitty shakes her shoulders to the music. "It's all the rage in New York City, and now we have it here in West Lake, thanks to Knots." She smiles, nudging Knots with her elbow.

"Just wait until you hear the band I am bringing in next weekend," Knots says. "They are a sensation down in Chicago. We'll be the first to have them up here in Ontario. I heard their new record on the radio, and I thought—"

Knots is interrupted by a young rope boy who has intruded into our tiny circle, pulling something from his pocket.

"Hey, Knots . . . I mean, sir . . ." he stammers, handing a note to Knots. "I'm supposed to give this to you. It's from the boss. I mean, the old boss." He shakes his head. "It's from Mr. Scott."

Knots unfolds the paper. His smile slowly fades, and then his mouth presses into an expressionless line. "You'll have to excuse me for a moment." He tucks the note into his jacket pocket. "Mr. Scott needs to see me in the office. I may be a little while."

He cups Kitty's elbow, holding it and her gaze for an extra beat before turning and following the young rope boy back into the crowd. We watch as they bob in and out of view then eventually disappear entirely behind a door next to the ticket booth.

The band starts up with another lively tune. Kitty turns to me, inclining her head toward the quickly filling dance floor. "Shall we?"

She reaches into her evening bag and pulls out a long strip of tickets. "There are benefits to going steady with the manager, you know."

She laughs and rips two from the strip, handing one to me, then pauses as if waiting for me to put two and two together.

"You're going steady with Knots?"

Kitty rolls her eyes. "Don't look at me that way, Dotty. I know I might have said a few silly things about how I imagined our life. But I've come to realize it's not going to be like that. Knots is going to run the dance hall and I will help him. We are going to bring all sorts of fabulous people here to West Lake. I can practically see our future in my head. It's going to be grand."

She twirls around, her smile so hopeful and bright that it makes me suddenly sick. I can see her future, too. The dance hall abandoned. Kitty living her fabulous life but far away from West Lake and far away from Knots.

"What happened to Beau?"

Kitty's smile falters. "What do you mean?"

She hasn't mentioned him in her diary since that trip to Toronto.

"Does he know about this new life plan?" *And how he's no longer a part of it,* I want to say.

Kitty's cheeks turn a bright shade of pink. She brings her fingers to her face as if she, too, is aware that she is flushed.

"I haven't told him yet," she says quietly. "I haven't had a chance to. He has been back in Toronto the last little while, and it's not something I want to explain in a letter. But you're right." Kitty's hand reaches for mine and squeezes. "I will tell him the next time I see him."

She keeps hold of my hand, pulling me behind her. We weave and dip between dancing bodies on our way to the dance floor entrance, but just as we reach the velvet rope, Kitty stops.

I step quickly to the right to avoid running into her back.

"What's going on?" I try to see past her to the problem, but the crowd is too thick. "Are we not dancing?"

My question remains rhetorical because the crowd thins enough for me to see the office door is open again. Knots is reentering the dance hall. Following him is an older man with two tufts of white hair and wearing a summer suit. The older man pats Knots on the back and whispers something in his ear. Knots responds with a slow nod of acknowledgment, his eyes fixed on the floor in front of him.

The scene is brief and unextraordinary.

Under any other circumstance, I wouldn't look twice.

But as I watch them, I feel the significance of the moment.

This is when it happens.

This is when Kitty learns what I have known all along. That you can dream all you want of something bigger and better, and just as you feel that future within your grasp, life comes along and knocks you hard on the ass.

Kitty stiffens beside me, as if she, too, can sense something has changed. We both watch as Knots shakes the man's hand and then watches him leave out the front door. The moment it closes, Knots's eyes find Kitty's. His shoulders deflate. His complexion turns an eerie shade of gray. There is no trace of the man who stood so proud only minutes ago.

"What's wrong?" Kitty asks when Knots gets close enough to hear her.

"The dance hall." His voice is thick. He coughs to clear his throat. "Mr. Scott is selling the building. He says he can't afford to keep it running any longer."

Kitty stifles a gasp with her hand. "Oh, Knots." She steps toward him, ready to wrap him in her arms, but he holds out his hand.

"I can't right now, Kit. I need to tell the guys. This is going to be an awful blow for all of them. Zeb's pop is out of work, and Stu has a new baby on the way. I gotta let them know before word gets around and they hear it from someone else."

Kitty's hand reaches for mine. Her palm is hot and clammy. She nods. "Of course," she says, and swipes the corner of her eye with her hand, dislodging a single tear that rolls down her cheek. She stands stiff and stoic as we watch Knots make his way to the dance floor, where the rope boys have begun taking tickets for the next dance, tapping their feet to the mambo music, blissfully unaware of everything that has happened.

"This is going to be awful for the whole town." Kitty tips her head to rest it on my shoulder. "The Minards just built three more summer cabins to accommodate all the weekend tourists, and Lou just opened his diner. He was counting on a busy summer to bring in enough extra money. I don't know if it will be the same without a dance hall, do you?"

I open my mouth to tell her I'm not exactly sure but stop as a familiar face appears in the doorway.

He steps inside, and there is a moment where he is completely swallowed by the crowd, but I know exactly where he is headed, and we have only moments.

"Kitty." I poke her hard with my elbow. "Beau—"

"I know. I said I'll talk to him," she hisses back. "But there are far more important things I need to worry about right now."

"No. He's—"

I don't finish the sentence.

Because he has made his way to us. A dazzling smile breaks across his face as he closes the last few steps.

"Kitty. Darling." He leans down to kiss her on the cheek.

I don't see her reaction.

Because a terrible sound yanks me back.

I open my eyes and wake up.

Chapter 32

It takes three tries before I successfully turn off my alarm. My eyes feel bleary and swollen, and my stomach feels as if it's shriveled up like a raisin. I don't know if I should blame my dream and how it ended in a cliff-hanger worthy of a television season finale, or my nerves, which have only now clued in to the fact that it's morning, and I'm meeting with Mansfield in a few short hours, and the outcome will likely shape—oh, I don't know—my entire future.

The two cups of coffee I drink while waiting for Miranda to pick me up do nothing for my stomach other than make me more jittery.

It doesn't help that when Miranda picks me up, she hands me a to-go cup from Okay Cafe. I drink it, despite better judgment, and it cranks my heart rate up another notch so that I'm very aware of its rapid beating as we drive from West Lake to Port Logan. Miranda, however, seems calm, cool, and collected as she reviews some last-minute thoughts on how she expects the meeting to go. "We'll get you sorted, honey," she says as she pulls the car into the parking lot of the sales office. "There's no need to look so worried." She pats my knee. "You'll have a few more pennies to calm those worries pretty soon."

Despite her reassurance, my mouth is dry, and I'm distinctly aware of my heartbeat as we climb the steps of the same white-sided building Reeve took me to a few weeks ago.

He opens the door just when we reach it, flashing a warm smile and a "Welcome" as he shakes Miranda's hand and then repeats it with me.

I'm caught a little off guard by this sudden formality in our relationship, comforted only slightly when he takes my coat and rests his hand on the small of my back, letting it linger for a breath before removing it as his boss enters the room.

Howard Mansfield is shorter than I imagined, with a salmon-colored polo shirt and a deep tan that give me the impression he plays a lot of golf in Florida.

He introduces himself with a voice that feels a little too smooth and a handshake that feels a little too firm before he escorts us to a large boardroom-style table where he and Reeve take turns walking us through a very polished sales pitch. They use catchy phrases like *hot market, redevelopment,* and *up-and-coming* as they hand us glossy photos of the rendering Reeve showed me during my last visit. There's even one transposed onto a real-life picture of the dance hall's lot, although they've erased any trace of the old stone building. It makes the latte Miranda bought me curdle in my stomach.

"I won't beat around the bush here, Ms. DeMarco," Howard says. "We are very interested in purchasing your property."

He smiles. It's the kind of smile where I know he expects me to do the same. However, my impulse is to glance at Reeve, who nods encouragingly. I mirror him, a slow, even nod, even though the rest of me is not quite as convinced.

"We would love to get the papers signed quickly," Howard says to Miranda, sharing a knowing look that she does not return.

"We are putting forth a very generous offer to demonstrate our interest." He pushes a pile of papers toward us.

"My client and I will need time to go through this." Miranda merely glances at them. "We'll be in touch."

Howard nods, but the stiffness in his movements makes it clear this isn't the answer he wants. "We'll chat later today then?" he offers with a false cheeriness to his tone.

Miranda picks up the papers and puts them in her briefcase. "We're making it a long weekend. Let's say early next week."

She inclines her head toward the door. I walk that way as well but once again look toward Reeve, hoping he will follow and we will get a moment alone.

He walks us to the door like I hoped, holding it open and stepping out after us.

Miranda turns to me. "I need to make a quick phone call, honey. Would you mind if I did it now?" She glances at Reeve. "Or would you prefer I wait?"

I shake my head. "No, you go ahead. I'm great."

She shoots Reeve one more look before pulling her phone from her purse. "Okay then. I'll meet you at the car." She presses her phone to her ear and wanders to the corner of the parking lot, leaving Reeve and me alone.

"How are you feeling about all of this?" Reeve steps toward me but doesn't take me in his arms like I want him to.

"Your boss is a little intense," I joke. "But otherwise, everything is what I expected. I want to go through the details with Miranda, but I guess I'm feeling okay. I think I just want it all to be done."

Reeve smiles sympathetically. "I should probably get back in there." He nods back toward the office. "Howard is going to want to debrief. We drove up together, which means I need to take him home, so I won't be able to stop by tonight." He reaches for my hand and holds it, his thumb brushing the back of my palm. "I'll call you later, though."

I nod. "I have an overnight shift, but it's been a pretty quiet week so far, so I will hopefully get a break tonight."

He glances at the office before leaning in and pressing a soft kiss on my lips. "I'm glad you're taking the weekend to think. We can talk more tomorrow night, too."

I nod, still unsure if any amount of talking will ever make this feel right.

"It's all going to work out, I promise." Reeve squeezes my hand, as if he can sense my uncertainty. He kisses me one more time before disappearing back inside.

I start to walk back toward Miranda's car. I can hear her on the phone. She's talking fast and her arms are moving animatedly. It doesn't seem like she will be done anytime soon.

I reach into my pocket and pull out my phone, scanning my email. There's one from Nurse Bouchard. The all-caps *REJECTED* in the subject line makes my heart sink even before I open it.

Ms. DeMarco,

Unfortunately, I will not be able to accommodate your request for a shift change on Saturday. As you know, we have a staff shortage and I am unable to fill your position. I should also remind you that company policy requires written requests for vacation a minimum of four weeks before the event. In the future, please be proactive when making requests.

Yours,
Marie-Soleil Bouchard,
RN, BScN, NP, CNO, OIIQ

I shove the phone back into my pocket, sadness swelling in my chest. Reeve is going to be so disappointed.

I glance quickly at Miranda, who seems to still be on her phone.

Maybe it's better to tell Reeve the news now, instead of waiting until tonight when he calls.

Turning, I head back to the sales office. The main area is empty, so I head toward the conference room, but the sound of Howard Mansfield's now familiar voice makes me pause.

"Things are shaping up well, Baldwin," he says. "Nicely done."

His words are followed by the sound of a hearty pat on the back.

"Thank you, sir," Reeve answers.

"I had my doubts about whether you could pull all this off," Howard says. "But I'm impressed. It's important we stay on track, though. This West Lake project will be the launching point of some future deals I'm working on. If all goes well, there will be more Mansfield projects with you at the helm."

I don't know why, but I'm holding my breath, and it allows me to hear the next words out of Reeve's mouth with absolute clarity.

"Thank you, sir," he says. "I'm on it. Don't worry. It'll get done."

There's something in his tone that sets off a warning, like a storm gathering in the distance. I can't see the clouds yet, but I can smell it.

Turning, I abandon my plans and instead walk slowly back to the door, taking my time to close it behind me so it doesn't make a sound. When I'm safely outside again, I close my eyes and remind myself that Reeve cares about me—I know he does. But it's clear he also cares about his job more than I thought. I'm having a hard time separating my feelings for him from how I feel about this deal, and I worry he's having the same problem.

When I get back to the car, Miranda is ending her call. "All set?" she asks, unlocking the door with a click of her key fob. She glances back toward the sales office. "We should probably talk, but I don't want to do it here."

If she says anything more, it's drowned out by the sound of a giant backhoe digging into a mound of nearby dirt.

I glance one more time at the sales office. Howard and Reeve stand shoulder to shoulder in the window. In unison, they raise their hands and wave, watching me as I get into the car.

"I agree," I say to Miranda.

I want to do it as far away from here as possible.

Chapter 33

My overnight shift at Sunnyvale starts off rather peacefully, just as I had hoped.

I set up the recreation room for bingo night, a resident favorite activity. We have only one minor incident, when Mr. McNaught calls bingo having heard B8 instead of G48. This causes a small uproar when half the residents clear their bingo cards prematurely and lose out on the coveted prize—a king-sized Coffee Crisp and a coupon for two-for-one hotcakes at Lou's.

We quiet the riot with a complimentary round of hot toddies. The warm whiskey and honey combo makes for a smooth final bed check. I even take my fifteen-minute break on schedule, checking my phone just in time to see a *Got your message about the party. I'll miss you. Heading to bed in half an hour. Call me if you can* text from Reeve. However, when my thumb moves to call him back, I get a 911 text on the Sunnyvale phone.

I sprint to Mrs. Lewis's room, fearing she's in mid–heart attack or possibly having another stroke, but when I reach her door, she's standing on her bed in her flannel nightgown, a bright orange Dorito in her outstretched hand, looking otherwise perfectly fine.

"Mrs. Lewis?"

She drops her hands with an exasperated sigh. "He prefers cheese," she says, "but this is all I've got." Once again, she stretches her hand out toward the ceiling, this time making clicking sounds with her tongue. Only then do I notice the ceiling panel slightly askew and the yellow eyes peering down through the dark gap.

"What is that?" I reach for her, fearing it's a raccoon or rat. However, a tiny *meow* escapes the hole, bringing my panic down a notch.

"Pumpkin?"

Mrs. Lewis presses up on her tiptoes, waving the Dorito at the gap. "We were watching a little *CSI Miami* before bed. A gator jumped out, and the poor thing got spooked."

"Okay," I coax Mrs. Lewis rather than the cat, worrying one misstep will have her toppling off her single bed. "How about you let me give it a go?"

It takes me ten minutes to convince Mrs. Lewis to get off her bed, then another thirty to lure the cat out with a can of tuna fish from the kitchen.

Despite Mrs. Lewis's insistence that Pumpkin is usually a *well-behaved little man*, I have to call Mr. Lewis to pick up the cat.

I wait for him out front, the cat tucked into the space between my scrubs and my coat, until he rolls up in his station wagon, window down and arms outstretched.

"I told Moira that was a bad idea." His grin is sheepish as I hand him the cat through the window.

By the time I get back upstairs, it's time for another round of bed checks, and it's long past my window to call Reeve back.

Thankfully, the rest of the night passes without any more cat-related or other dramas.

When I clock out, it's just past 6:30 in the morning. I call Reeve back, hoping to catch him before work, but my call goes straight to voicemail.

By the time I get home and ready for bed, he still hasn't returned my call, and part of me is a little relieved. Reeve will ask me about yesterday's meeting. I know we need to talk about it, and I want to, but not until I've followed Miranda's advice and slept on it—ideally for eight solid hours.

I plug my phone into the charger and settle under the covers, but as I reach for the light-blocking sleep mask I usually keep in my nightstand drawer, my eyes land on the diary instead.

I have been so worried about Mansfield and my own problems that I haven't even thought about my last Kitty dream. Obviously I knew Beau would have to make another appearance and the dance hall would eventually close given its current abandoned state, but is that really how it all ends? What happened to poor Knots?

Despite my tired eyes and aching body, I open the diary to where I left off the other night, knowing I won't be able to fall asleep unless I know how it all turns out. I thumb the remaining pages. There are only a few left unread. An apprehensive feeling settles over me. It's that same one you get when you're at the end of a book and there aren't enough pages left for the plot to take much of a turn.

Dear Diary,

I watched the waves today.

They rolled against the sand one by one. Over and over, never changing.

I found myself wishing one would rush forward, crash onto the beach, and continue to roll down Main Street, taking everything in its path along with it.

But every time it felt like one was about to escape, it was sucked right back into the lake.

I want so many things, and all of them feel so out of reach. When-

ever I feel like I might just be able to break free, I get pulled back—powerless.

I hate being powerless.

Kitty

It's a big departure from Kitty's usual sunny entries. For anyone else, I'd consider it a healthy, if not excessively poetic, expression of teenage angst. However, as I read her words again, something in my chest gives a painful lurch.

They were so happy, she and Knots. They were going to be together. They had a plan, and I wanted so badly for it to work out.

I know it's irrational. The dance hall now lies abandoned and shuttered, and Kitty lived her last days as Kitty St. Clair, not Kitty . . . whatever Knots's last name is.

I know their future doesn't end in a happily ever after, no matter how much I want it to.

I close my eyes and sink into my pillow, knowing exactly where I will go.

Kitty's fate was sealed long ago.

And all I can do is watch.

There's a line by the time I get from Dot's empty bedroom to the dance hall.

The dreamy yellow light spills from the windows, and the catchy and upbeat music echoes through half of the town. However, as I stand in line, waiting to get inside, I notice that the mood doesn't translate to the crowd around me.

I'm still surrounded by freshly pressed suits and skirts that flutter with every light breeze from the lake. The summer air still smells like perfume and gin. But there's something else that hangs heavy in the night. An intangible feeling that something is off.

It isn't until I get closer to the entrance that I fully understand why.

> ***West Lake Dance Hall—one last hurrah!***
> ***Join us for one final twirl around***
> ***the dance floor.***

The banner is painted in swirling black letters.

All of the air stutters out of me as I read it, and my own mood joins the collective air of melancholy around me.

It's over. The dance hall is closing.

"Oh, I just can't believe it," says a weeping redhead in front of me. She rests her head on her partner's shoulder. "What are we going to do now?"

Her partner shakes his head. "It's such a shame."

The line moves forward. An unfamiliar rope boy opens the front door, and I step inside, knowing deep down that this will be the last time.

My eyes scan the dance floor, looking for Kitty. She isn't among the foxtrotting bodies or sitting at the tables or standing in a ticket line. I even open the door of the tiny back office, hoping that she and Knots might be stealing a quiet moment inside, but there is only a man hunched over a desk, his head resting in the palms of his hands.

"Knots?"

He looks up at the sound of my voice.

"Hey. Um . . . have you seen Kitty anywhere?"

His head returns to his hands at the question. "She's gone," he finally says.

Gone?

"Where? What happened?"

His shoulders begin to shake. The music is too loud for me to hear if he's crying or simply breathing, but when he looks up again, his eyes are glassy, and his cheeks are wet.

"She left with him. I don't know where she went, but I don't think she's coming back."

He looks so lost—so forlorn—that my arms ache to hold this man I barely know. When his chin begins to tremble, I step toward him, encircling his heaving shoulders with one arm and making slow, soothing circles on his back with the other.

"It's okay," I coax. "Everything's going to be all right."

Although I'm not sure it will be.

We stay like that until his breaths begin to deepen, and he finally pats my arm with his hand. "Thank you, Dotty."

I stand and watch as he wipes his cheeks with the sleeve of his jacket, then pushes back his chair and stands. "I should really get out there." He clears his throat. "I am still the boss—for one more night."

He attempts a smile, but it fools neither of us. As he steps past me toward the office door, I'm struck with an awful thought. This could be the last time I ever see Knots.

These dreams haven't exactly come with an instruction manual, but I have to think they will end when I finish the diary.

"What is going to happen to you?" I ask, not caring that I'm breaking the third wall between this dream and my own reality.

Knots forces another strained smile. "I've got some maintenance jobs lined up in a couple of weeks. My brother needs help closing up some summer cottages, and then, who knows?" He shrugs. "I may head up north. I have a cousin up in the Bay who can get me a job on the rails."

He pauses to see if I have another question. When I don't say anything, he pushes open the office door and waits for me to walk through.

I step back into the dance hall, sad, lost, and unsure of what I'm supposed to do next.

I don't want to be in this dance hall any longer.

If I'm being honest, I don't really want to be in this dream any longer, either.

I leave and head back toward Dot's house, but when I get to her gate, something compels me to keep walking.

Maybe it's the sound of the waves that calls me. Or the imagery from Kitty's diary entry still swimming in my head. But I continue down toward the beach, my feet sinking into the sand until my toes touch the edge of the water.

Above me the moon is beautifully full, and it sheds just enough light to see the outline of two figures just around the bend of the next dune.

My body shivers with a sense of déjà vu, and a line of goosebumps prickles up my arms.

It feels like I've been here before.

Watched a scene just like this one unfold.

And just like Knots, Beau drops to his knee. He reaches into his back pocket and pulls something from it.

I find myself holding my breath.

A few moments pass before he removes the lid.

I hear Kitty's gasp as the stone inside catches the moonlight.

I want her to run. To laugh. To be that brazen, unapologetic woman I know. To throw up her hands and tell him, "No!" She's taken. Her heart belongs to someone else.

But she nods and holds out her hand. I can't make out her yes through the wind; all I can hear is annoying repetitive ringing.

I open my eyes and wake up.

Chapter 34

"Hello?"

My voice is still thick with sleep when I pick up my phone, my heart still beating wildly from the panic of being ripped from my dream so quickly.

"Julia?" says a female voice. "It's Nurse Bouchard. I realize I have likely woken you. My sincerest apologies for that, but I seem to have found myself in a bit of a situation and require your help."

I think I grunt an *okay* or maybe a *fine* as I push myself onto my elbows.

"I have had a small family emergency," Nurse Bouchard says. "I have to go to Montreal immediately. I have a replacement from corporate on her way, but she will still be a few hours. I need someone to cover for me until she arrives. Are you able to come back in?"

I pull the phone from my ear to glance at the time. It's not even noon. "I just came off a night shift, and I have another tonight—"

"I am aware," she interrupts. "I've managed to do some shuffling with the schedule. You only need to come in until my replacement arrives, but I'll make sure you're paid for a full twelve hours. Please. I would consider this a great personal favor."

I consider pointing out how quick she is to flex the rules now that it's her situation that requires bending them. Instead, I stretch my arms, awakening my body.

"Yeah, okay. Give me twenty minutes."

There is a rush of breath on her end of the line. "Thank you, Julia. I knew I could trust you."

My heart begins to warm for the briefest moment until she adds, "I will see you in eighteen minutes. Please don't be tardy."

I throw on a pair of clean scrubs, scrape my hair back into a ponytail, and arrive back at Sunnyvale sixteen minutes later.

Nurse Bouchard runs me through a checklist of the items that need covering before reassuring me her replacement is only three hours away.

I spend the first two hours methodically running through the items she asked me to do, completing them just as Nurse Bouchard's replacement arrives—an hour earlier than expected. I catch her up on all the basics, and when I'm formally excused, with a full twelve-hour shift clocked on my pay card, I head downstairs to catch the tail end of happy hour in the recreation room.

The lights are dimmed to give maximum effect to the tiny laser machine plugged into the corner. It flashes blue, purple, and green specks onto the ceiling and walls and the temporary bar set up on one of the wooden tables in the corner.

I wave at Zoe, who is acting as head bartender this afternoon, flipping liquor bottles up in the air to the delight of Mr. Minard and Mr. Samuel. They *ooh* as she catches them and *aah* as she misses, sending a thankfully closed bottle of vodka rolling across the carpet.

"There you are, Julia." Mrs. Hail dances over to me, her shoulders shaking in time with the music from Mr. McNaught's record player. "Come and dance. Everyone else here is acting like party poopers, and you know how I love a good mambo."

I take her hand and spin her, then attempt to follow the rhythmic shuffles of her feet. I last all of half a minute before she stops and pats me softly on the cheek.

"Actually, maybe you should help out Zoe instead. I think I'm better off as a one-woman show."

She dances away, and I find Zoe at the bar pouring two martinis with the recovered vodka.

"Hey there, big shot," she says as she pours. "Heard you made it to the Oval Office."

I laugh and pull an empty folding chair over so I can sit. "It was great while it lasted, but alas, I return to being lowly support staff tomorrow at nine A.M. sharp."

"So, are you off for the night then?" Zoe holds up the vodka bottle as if asking if I want one, but I shake my head.

"I'll wait until I get home. I'm going to make myself stay up so I can get back on a normal sleep schedule. I may have a glass of wine when I call Reeve."

As soon as I say it, I remember that I can't call Reeve. He has his parents' anniversary party tonight.

A party I can all of a sudden make.

I check my phone. It's not even three. If I move fast enough, I could go home, change, and make it to the party just in time for seven.

"Actually"—I jump to my feet—"Reeve's parents are having a thing tonight. I was invited, but I didn't think I could make it. Do you think it's weird if I show up?"

Zoe's lips curl into a small, knowing smile.

"You are asking this question of a person who has zero issues crashing a party she wasn't invited to—but with that context, no. I think you absolutely should go. Go home and shower. Put on a hot dress—the black one, not the pink one you think is hot—and dance the night away, my little Cinderella. Tell me every detail in the morning."

I call Reeve when I'm outside of the city limits, on a quiet country road where there is little chance of running into a traffic cop looking to bust me for not being hands-free. He picks up on the fourth ring right as I'm starting to panic a little at the last-minute nature of my plan.

"Jules?"

The sounds of the city are in the background, an indistinguishable hum of car engines and honking horns.

"Yes, hey. It's me."

"I was thinking about you but didn't call because I assumed you'd still be sleeping. Are you on your way to work?"

I instinctively glance at the dress I threw on and then at the gym bag on my passenger seat, packed haphazardly with clothes and toiletries.

"Actually, I'm on my way to Toronto. My shifts got switched, and now I'm off for the night. I have to be back by nine A.M. tomorrow, which means a very early morning, but I really wanted to see you." I'm babbling now, the words pouring out in a rush. "I was going to show up at your parents' party and surprise you like they do in the movies," I continue. "But I don't have the address, so . . ."

There's a pause as he catches up to everything I've spewed out.

"You're coming?"

There's a loud honk in the background, and I'm not sure if his question is a clarification or sheer surprise.

"Yeah." I mentally calculate the remaining distance. "I should be there right at seven. I missed you."

"Shit." His curse is soft, but it hits me hard.

"Oh." I instinctively look for a place to pull off, a driveway or dirt road to turn my car back around. Clearly, I haven't thought through this romantic gesture.

"No, no, no. That wasn't about you." I hear static, as if his phone is brushing up against his clothing. "I just have a few things going on at work."

I see a dirt driveway off to my right and pull into it. My blinker ticks as I make the turn.

"It's okay, I can turn around."

"Do *not* turn around." The force behind those words covers any soreness from before like a balm. "I just need a second to figure this out."

I hear him draw a deep breath.

"Okay." The word comes out in an exhale. "I need to run into this meeting now, but I will meet you outside the Granite Club at seven. I'm texting you the address now."

"Are you sure? I can turn around. It's fine. I—"

"No." He cuts me off. "It's been a really, really shitty day, and seeing you is going to be the only good thing about it."

My heart feels like it's grown a size.

He fills the pause before I can. "I'll see you in a couple hours then?"

I nod even though he can't see me. "I'll be there."

Chapter 35

Round two of battling Toronto traffic goes significantly better than my attempt a few weeks ago. I make it to the Granite Club with zero distracted driving tickets and only one irritated honk, which was deserved, as I tweezed a few rogue eyebrow hairs while waiting at a red light.

I arrive exactly two minutes ahead of schedule; I skip the valet service and instead park Celine under a shady tree, where I apply a coat of mascara to my lashes, swipe deodorant under my arms, and give my hair one last fluff. My walk from the car to the club gives me a moment to fully appreciate the modern-looking building. Its architecture is imposing yet beautiful, with sharp angular lines, black bricks, and big glass windows, but it holds my attention for only a brief moment before I'm drawn to the man standing out front, hands shoved into his pockets, watching the stream of cars drive in.

"Has anyone ever told you how good you look in a suit?"

Reeve spins around at the sound of my voice. Two strides and I'm in his arms.

"Fuck, I missed you," he whispers into my hair.

We kiss in a way that is not appropriate for a public sidewalk.

"Let's skip the party," Reeve murmurs as his lips trace a trail from my lips to my neck. "We can go back to my place, and I can take you straight to bed."

"Won't your parents be upset?"

"I really don't care what they think."

He leans in but then stops, a slamming door turning his attention to a black town car parked beside the sidewalk. We both watch as the back door opens and Reeve's mom, Cheryl, climbs out. Reeve's dad, Bill, follows behind.

Cheryl opens her arms when she spots Reeve. "Hello, my sweet boy."

She stops just short of a hug. "Sorry, lovey." She holds out her hands, blowing him two air kisses instead. "This face took forty-five minutes to put on. No smudging the lipstick until after I've made my entrance."

Her eyes flick past Reeve to me, and I can tell the moment she registers my face: she makes a dramatic lean to the side, her eyes growing wide. "Jules! You made it! Reeve told us you had to work."

Despite her earlier declaration, I get an actual hug. It's a firm squeeze with a lipstick-pressed kiss on my cheek.

"There were some last-minute shift changes," I explain as she takes her thumb and rubs at the spot where she made contact. "I hope it's okay just showing up like this."

"Of course, honey." She loops her arm through mine, leading me toward the front door—leaving Reeve to walk in behind us with his dad. "The more the merrier." She tips her head toward mine, lowering her voice. "With everyone coming tonight, Bill's a little wound up. And with Reeve being so sensitive, I'm—" She pauses. "I'm glad you're here, Jules."

I get one more squeeze of my hand before there's a loud "Cheryl!" from the other side of the room, and she is whisked off into a group of women.

I'm alone for only a moment before I feel a soft kiss pressed to my neck. "Can I get you a drink?" Reeve asks, nodding at the beautiful modern bar in the corner.

I loop my hand through his arm. "One glass of champagne. Then I need to be cut off for the night. I have to drive home in"—I turn his wrist so I can check his watch—"less than nine hours."

Reeve cups my face between his hands and pulls me in for another questionably public kiss. "Here's my plan. We hang out here for a bit. Then, right after dinner, we sneak out and make the most of our nine hours. Deal?" He kisses me again lightly on the lips.

"Deal."

I turn toward the bar. "Shall we?"

Reeve starts to walk and then stops suddenly. "Actually, maybe we should wait. If you're only having one, we should save it for dinner."

I shrug, fine with this new arrangement. "Okay, but we can still get you one—"

"No." His eyes shoot from the bar to me. "I'm fine. Let's go over there." He points at a group of people on the other side of the room. "I'll introduce you to a few of my cousins."

The next hour is a blur of introductions and polite conversations.

Reeve's hand stays on the small of my back, leaving only to rub my neck or shake someone's hand or pull my body closer to his.

I stay tucked under his arm, and as stupid as it sounds, it feels like we're no longer a "Reeve and Jules" but an "us."

And I love it.

So when he leans in and whispers, "Are you sure I can't persuade you to take off? They've seen us here. I'm sure they won't even notice we're gone," I almost say yes. The only thing that stops me is the deep male voice announcing through the speaker system that we are to take our places at our tables for dinner.

"Let's stay." I take Reeve's hand. "A girl's gotta eat, and I still need my glass of champagne."

Reeve nods, but I sense a little reluctance as we follow the crowd heading into the ballroom and find our table.

The room is stunning in that way achieved only by wedding magazines and carefully curated Pinterest boards. Each table is set with crisp white linens, fine china, and silverware. The only thing informal about our table is Reeve's two brothers, their suit jackets already off and strewn over the backs of their chairs.

Reeve's older brother, Liam, greets me with a "Nice to see you again, Jules" and an introduction to his wife, Lorraine.

Brodie reaches out his hand for a fist bump and introduces a blond-haired Amanda, who he later tells Reeve is his hookup from the weekend before.

We're served a dinner of beef and delicate vegetables, followed by a sweet and light dessert that practically melts on my tongue. All of the friction from brunch a few weeks ago is absent, replaced by wine and laughter and expensive Scotch. Even the tense lines around Reeve's eyes relax.

But just after our plates are cleared, the room fills with the sound of clinking glass.

The *ting ting ting* of knives being tapped on champagne flutes.

It's followed by a brief microphone shriek, then a few surprised gasps and a "Well, that was not the introduction I was going for, but I think we're sorted now" from Reeve's dad, Bill.

The room quiets. Their attention is rapt on our host this evening, who smiles with the quiet confidence of a man who knows he can control a room.

"I'd like to thank you all for being here this evening," he says, bringing the last few voices to silence. "It's hard to think that it's been forty years since we gathered in this very ballroom and this—" He gazes down at his wife. "This beautiful woman agreed to have and hold me for the rest of her life." He pauses. "I'd like to think she has only regretted that decision a handful of times."

There's a murmur of laughter from the crowd. Bill holds up his hands as if conceding to the joke, then waits for the room to quiet again before continuing.

"We have been blessed with so many gifts. My late father, William Senior, left an extraordinary legacy in both the value of hard work he instilled and the financial stability he passed on that allowed me to invest in and grow my firm of Baldwin Barrington and Crouch.

"I am incredibly grateful to be able to pass that same legacy and hopefully a few of Pop's life lessons down to my youngest son, Brodie, who is following in my footsteps and proving to be a hardworking and promising lawyer." Bill raises his glass in the direction of our table.

Brodie, in return, lifts his glass with a shout of "Love you guys!" They mime a cheers, although Bill doesn't drink, instead returning to his speech.

"My oldest son, Liam, is breaking medical ground every week," Bill continues, "as he tirelessly serves his community and the patients at Mount Sinai Hospital." Bill pauses, his glass held out in front of him. "Liam, you may refuse to be called Bill like your old man, but you got a lot more from me than just my eight-handicap golf swing, and I'm proud of you." The crowd laughs again.

Liam raises his glass and shouts, "Not all of us work summer hours," drawing an even bigger round of laughter from the room.

"And finally, Reeve." Bill's eyes lock on his middle son. Reeve stiffens beside me, the tiny vein pulsing in his temple. "Reeve is our dreamer. Our nonconformer. Growing up, he was the one who gave his mother and me the most heartburn at night." More laughs, but not from me this time. "We used to joke that the stork must have had an address mix-up with our middle child, but I'm proud to stand here and tell you that he's about to break ground on a massive project up in West Lake, Ontario—a small community on Lake Huron. Howard Mansfield"—he points at a table on the opposite side of the room—"my oldest and dearest friend, says Reeve is one of the brightest, most ambitious project managers he's ever had at his firm."

My mouth goes completely dry. I take a sip of water, but it does nothing but make me cough as I struggle to swallow it down.

"Reeve's new project will be a crowning achievement for the firm over the next year," Bill continues. "Maybe even a legacy he passes on to his own children one day." He raises his glass. "Reeve, I'm proud of all the incredible work you've done. Maybe next year we'll celebrate this anniversary at the new condo complex in West Lake."

I turn to Reeve, my face searching his for answers. Did his dad make a mistake? Maybe he misunderstood? Or is Reeve so confident the deal is done that he has no problem hearing it announced to a room full of people?

Reeve's face, however, is impossible to read. His lips remain pressed in a thin, firm line, even as Brodie leans over and throws an arm around his neck. "Look at you, Reevey Boy, climbing the ranks. You'd better be careful, Liam," Brodie calls across the table to his older brother. "Reeve may take your spot as Dad's second favorite." Brodie ruffles Reeve's hair.

Reeve doesn't so much as flinch, moving only as we are called to raise our glasses for a cheers.

"To Mom and Dad," Liam says.

"To Mom and Dad," we all echo, clinking our glasses together in the center of the table.

The champagne is dry and tickles the back of my throat on its way down. As I set my glass on the table, the band begins to play a slow foxtrot, and the rest of our table gets up to head to the bar.

"We need to talk." I hold my hand out to Reeve. He takes it and nods.

"Yeah, we should—but not here." He's turned an unnatural shade of white, and although I could chalk that up to the overhead lights, I don't think that's it.

Reeve grows even paler. "Have you signed the papers yet?"

"No." I shake my head. "I still need to talk with Miranda. We told you we were taking the weekend—"

Reeve stands so abruptly the silverware clinks. I push my chair back and stand as well.

"What is going on, Reeve?"

He glances at the exit, then the dance floor. "I really want to be alone with you. Let's get out of here."

He turns toward the ballroom doors but runs straight into Brodie, who catches him by the shoulders. "Whoa! Easy there, big guy. Can't take off yet. Mom wants a family photo."

"We're on our way out." Reeve grabs my hand, but Brodie throws his arm over Reeve's shoulders.

"It will take two minutes. We all want to get out of here. You know what Mom will be like if we don't do this. We'll be hearing about this until Christmas."

Reeve sighs. "Fine." He begins to follow Brodie, his hand still holding mine, but I let go.

"Why don't I get our coats? You can meet me out front when you're done?"

Reeve glances at the door and then at his impatient brother. "Okay. I'll see you out front. We should only be a couple minutes."

Reeve reaches out, cupping my chin in his hand, his thumb

slowly stroking my cheek until Brodie slaps him hard on the back with a "Come on, dude," and Reeve reluctantly lets go.

Once they're gone, I stick to the plan and join the coat check line in the foyer. There is only one couple ahead of me, so the coat check attendant takes just a moment to collect my tickets and retrieve our coats.

Just as he places them on the counter in front of me, I feel a cold hand on my back.

"You were fast," I say, spinning around, expecting to see Reeve, but it's Howard Mansfield.

"Ms. DeMarco. Good to see you. I didn't expect you to be here tonight." He holds out his hand toward a middle-aged blonde in a sparkly dress. "This is my wife, Celeste." He addresses his wife. "Celeste, Ms. DeMarco owns one of the properties we are buying up in West Lake."

She smiles but does not extend her hand.

I grab our coats, but as I do, something about what he just said registers. "I'm sorry. Did you say *properties*? Is there more than one project?"

Mr. Mansfield laughs. "Oh no, no. Just the one you saw earlier this week. We finally managed to secure the lot adjacent to your dance hall, so we are expanding the build. We'll now have room for the tennis courts. I don't know how you invest, Ms. Demarco, but you may want to consider purchasing one of our premium units for rental purposes. The property is going to be a hot commodity."

He starts to say something else, but my brain is no longer listening. It's mentally computing which lot he's talking about. The beach is beside the dance hall. The only other lot he could be referring to is—

My heart seizes like a cold engine in my chest. "You don't mean the retirement home? That big redbrick building?"

Howard Mansfield thinks for a moment. "I thought it was apartments. But yes, that's the one. Reeve was working on them for months. They were hesitant at first to sell, like you, but eventually couldn't deny our offer was too good to pass up." He continues talking, but I block him out, my eyes too busy scanning the foyer.

I catch Reeve's eye right as he exits the ballroom. I watch him look from me to Howard, and I can tell when he realizes what has just happened.

Reeve knows.

He knows they're going to demolish the retirement home—and he purposely kept it from me.

All of a sudden the odd moments from the night make perfect sense. The vagueness. The weirdness. He didn't keep me close because he wanted to be near me. He kept me close to keep me away from Howard.

I look at him one last time. He's too far away to hear, but I can read his lips perfectly as he says, *Jules, I'm sorry.*

If he says anything else, I don't see it because I turn around and run.

Chapter 36

I LEAVE REEVE and the rest of the party as a blur in my rearview mirror, turning my car out of the parking lot and taking city streets until I reach the highway. As I take the on-ramp, tiny raindrops begin to fall from the sky, smattering across my windshield.

My phone buzzes in my purse. I let it go to voicemail. When it happens again, I press the power button until the phone goes completely silent. The only sounds in the car are the soft pattering of rain on the roof and the rhythmic *thwack thwack thwack* of my wipers.

I wait for the tears to flow and the pain to wash over me. Or the denial, or the anger—whichever of those stages of grief is supposed to hit first. But all I feel is a hollowed-out numbness.

I don't want to think about how long Reeve has lied to me or how much of the last few months was real.

I can't yet.

His betrayal tonight has put me into shock, but that is only a surface wound. A scratch.

If I were to dwell too long on the idea that Reeve could have been lying to me from the very beginning, that he was always nudging me along, subtly, in his desired direction—that thought would split me open completely.

The tiny sprinkle that coated my car turns into a full downpour as I finally leave the city limits and hit the country highway. Then, and only then, when I'm back among the cornfields with the empty dark road ahead of me, do I let myself truly cry and allow my darkest thoughts to surface.

My foot presses against the pedal. Celine roars her engine, and I roll my windows down, letting the rain spatter my face and wash away the stream of tears rolling down my cheeks.

I hate you, Reeve Baldwin.

I hate that when I told you my worst fears, you looked me in the eyes and told me it was all going to be fine—that I could trust you.

I hate that you convinced me it was okay to be selfish, that I deserved this big life I imagined in my head, when all along I was just a way for you to close another fucking deal.

I roll my window back up and succumb to the sobs that rack through my body. My chest heaves so hard I worry my ribs will break, and a part of me wants them to. Then at least there would be a good reason for the aching pain that fills my chest, instead of the stupid one before me: that I believed him and fell hard even when I knew better.

Eventually, I return to numb.

The dark road and the quiet night lull me into a trance where I convince myself if I stay just like this, then maybe I'll be fine.

Deep down I know I won't.

And, as if the universe agrees, my car hits a pothole with an audible *bang*.

Celine swerves left, and my veins rush with adrenaline as instincts kick in and I counteract with a hard right turn of the steering wheel. There's a loud drumming in my ears, perfectly timed with the heavy thumping in my chest, as I slow the car to a more reasonable speed, suddenly aware of a bumpiness to the road that wasn't there before.

"No, no. Please, no," I plead as I pull the car off to the graveled shoulder, still clinging to a faint hope that the damage may be all in my head.

When I get out and confirm my tire is no longer a perky O but now a sad C, I almost laugh at how well aligned my life is in falling both literally and figuratively to shambles.

"Okay." I breathe deeply, forming a plan. "I just need to figure out how to change a tire. It can't be that hard."

I turn my phone back on and a few moments with Google confirms that it is that hard, and not only that, I don't have the tools to do it. I consider calling Zoe's cousin Clive, who owns a garage in West Lake, but it's almost midnight and the garage is long closed.

"Fuck" slips from my lips, followed by a few more profanities. I kick the flattened tire with my toe, which provides no relief other than a temporary reprieve from thinking about my problem as I shake my stinging foot.

"What the hell am I going to do now?" I say to the dark night sky. It doesn't answer back, but my phone does.

My home screen lights up with an incoming call. I almost throw it into the dark cornfield, but it's not Reeve's name on the screen.

"Mom?"

My greeting is met with static and a series of thumping sounds, as if the phone is tumbling around the inside of a washing machine.

"Mom," I yell a little louder. Whether she hears the desperation in my voice or what little parental instinct she has kicks in, I hear more scratching and then her voice.

"Julia. Is that you? Why are you calling me so late?"

I consider telling her it was the other way around but abandon it.

"My car broke down. I'm stranded on the side of Highway Six." I consider my location. "I'm actually not too far from you, I think." I can't believe I'm even considering the next part. "Is there any way . . ."

I don't have to finish my sentence.

"Send me your exact location. I'll be there as soon as I can."

It's twenty minutes until she arrives. Reeve calls twice while I'm waiting for her, but I'm too afraid to turn my phone off in case my mom gets lost. When her old Toyota pulls up behind me, I feel an unusual sense of comfort.

I get out, lock my doors, and make my way to her passenger door, which pops open just as I reach it.

"Thanks for coming," I say as I settle into the front seat and tip the heating vents toward me. "I know it's really late."

"What are you going to do with the car?" my mom asks, glancing at it before signaling and pulling a U-turn on the empty highway.

"I called and left a message for Clive. He'll come out and get it tomorrow. I'll take a cab to work in the morning."

My mom nods. "Or I can drive you?"

We drive for a few moments in silence. The adrenaline from the last few hours is finally exiting my body, and I'm exhausted. I tip my head against the window and consider closing my eyes, but my mom clears her throat.

"What are you doing out in the middle of the night?"

I desperately do not want to answer her question, but I know my mother, and if I say nothing, she will continue to pry until I give in.

"I was in Toronto at a party. I had to come home for work tomorrow." I leave it there, hoping it's enough.

"Was it with this new boyfriend?" Her voice teases with the word *boyfriend*, and it sends a physical pain through my chest.

"He's not . . . We're not . . ."

I am saved by the sound of crunching gravel under the wheels. We pull up in front of a small detached house with weathered white siding and an overgrown yard.

My mother catches me eyeing the sloping front porch. "I know it's not much, but it's temporary."

"No, it's great." I try my best to sound enthused—sunny—then grab my overnight bag and get out of her car.

As soon as we're inside, my mom immediately starts tidying: loading the sink with dirty dishes, gathering strewn-about clothes and yesterday's socks and tossing them in the closet. It gives me time to take in the generic Berber carpeting and white walls without her watching me. Although I've never been to this particular place, the worn IKEA sofa and the wall of cityscapes in mismatched frames give me a strange nostalgia for the various rentals we lived in when I was growing up.

"There's a guest bedroom." My mom points at one of the three closed doors. "It's just a twin bed, but it's comfortable."

"That's perfect," I reassure her, grateful to have a place to sleep. "And thank you again."

I stand there for a moment letting the awkwardness hang between us before picking up my bag with a "I guess I'll head to bed then."

The room is exactly what I expect. A single bed in an old

wrought iron frame spray-painted white. An old wooden desk with nothing on it. A single framed poster of Audrey Hepburn on the wall.

I yawn at the sight of the white bedspread with its polyester frills, hoping the universe will grant me a solid and sleep will come quickly tonight, but no sooner do I toss my bag on the floor than my mom appears in the doorway.

"So are things serious . . . with your boyfriend?" she says, stepping into my room.

I close my eyes to prevent any tears from forming. "It's done."

I hear her sigh and then sigh again.

"Not tonight, Mom, please," I beg, noticing how raw my voice sounds.

I feel the bed indent as she sits down next to me. "Relationships aren't all sunshine and roses. He sounded like he had so much promise. Did you at least give it a chance?"

"I don't want to talk about it."

"It's just that you have this tendency to do this, Julia. You could have so many opportunities if you branched out a little, hung out with someone other than Zoe Buchanan, and let yourself think about a life bigger than West Lake."

I hate this argument. I hate that we are still having it after twenty-four years.

"I always tried to encourage you to expand your horizons, but you are so set in your ways."

Like a switch has been flipped, the sorrow simmering in my stomach boils into a full-blown rage.

"You want to hear a funny story, Mom?" I pause for effect but not long enough for her to answer. "I tried to leave West Lake. Branch out like you said, and *you* screwed that up for me."

I allow her to rebut now, but she only rolls her eyes dramatically, removing her hand from my leg with a "Come on, Julia."

"It's true." I shake my head, needing to tell her what I should have told her two years ago. "I had a plan to go to medical school in Toronto. I was finally ready to start this exciting life you always wanted, but when I tried to inquire about financing from the bank, I was informed that *my mother* ruined my credit and there was no way in hell they were ever going to give me any more money."

My mother goes still.

"Yeah, ironic, isn't it?"

"Julia . . ." She reaches her arms out, but I stand.

"I need to go to bed. It's been a really shitty night, and I am exhausted."

"Julia, I—"

I don't let her finish the sentence. I grab my bag, head for the bathroom, and slam the door behind me.

When I come back in, she is gone.

I open my bag and stare at the cute pajamas meant for a night in Reeve's bed, and I can't bear to put them on. Instead, I pull out my scrubs for tomorrow's shift to get them ready for the morning. When I throw them over the back of the chair, something falls from between the folds and lands on the floor with a hard smack.

Kitty's diary lies open. Her loopy blue writing looks so innocent and adolescent.

While I once may have thought of the diary as a welcome distraction—maybe even a friend—tonight, it brings no comfort at all. Quite the opposite.

I lift my face to the popcorn ceiling above me, as if Kitty herself can hear me from the heavens.

"This is all your fault," I tell her. "I was fine. My life was fine, and then you came along and . . ."

Changed things?

Changed me?

I grab the diary and slam it shut, shoving it back into my bag and zipping it up tight. "I'm done with this, and I'm done with you," I say to Kitty, wherever she is.

I keep to my word, and it's not Kitty I'm thinking of as I climb into bed, close my eyes, and try to slip into sleep.

It's Reeve. My sweet summer boy.

My tears return, soaking my pillow, and I try to stifle my crying, fearing the thinness of the walls.

I knew it was all too good to be true.

I hate that I'm right.

Chapter 37

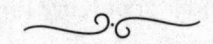

I AWAKEN IN a bedroom. The ceiling and the darkness and the crispness of the sheets are so familiar it's a moment before I realize I'm not in my own bed.

"No," I say out loud. "I didn't read it tonight. I'm not supposed to be here."

I squeeze my eyes shut and try to will my body back to sleep. Nothing happens. I count sheep. I recite the alphabet twice from Z to A. Finally, I resign myself to counting the knots in the wood on Dot's pine-planked ceiling, which soothes me somewhat until I am startled by the sound of a car engine outside.

"I'm not going out there," I say to no one in particular, and as if the universe is answering back, I hear the soft *plink* of a rock hitting my window and then Kitty's whispered voice.

"Dotty? Dotty, are you there?"

I pull the covers up and over my head, but the rocks continue to come.

Plink.
Plink.
Plink.
Plink.

I get up with the idea that I will shut the curtains and thus shut

Kitty out of my life for good. But as I reach up to close them, I catch a glimpse of her.

The moon illuminates her finely made wool coat, her fancy hat, and the gleaming town car with its engine still running. Suddenly, I no longer want to hide here in Dot's bed. I want to give Kitty a piece of my mind.

I don't bother trying to keep quiet as I stomp down the stairs, pulling open the front door and slamming it behind me.

Kitty smiles when she sees me. She extends her arms as if she expects me to fall into her embrace, but I stop short, folding my arms across my chest.

"What do you want, Kitty?"

Her face falls as she registers my tone.

"I'm leaving now. I've come to say goodbye."

If there was any uncertainty about which part of the story I stumbled into, it is cleared.

"So that's it? This is how it all ends? You move to Toronto, marry Beau, and leave all of us behind to pick up the pieces of our lives?"

She closes her eyes and draws in a deep breath. "I don't know what you want me to say. This was always my plan. You knew that."

"In the beginning, yes." I throw up my arms. "But you have to admit there was a while where you . . ."

Fell for him. Chose love. Made me think this was all going to work out.

I give in with an exasperated growl. There is no use fighting a past that has already happened. "I just thought that this was somehow going to be a love story."

A single tear runs down Kitty's cheek. She makes no attempt to wipe it away. "I hoped for a while it might be, too. I really wanted it to be."

She glances toward the waiting car. "And you never know.

Maybe one day it will be. But for now, I like to think of this as not an ending, just maybe a new chapter."

She reaches toward me, trying to take me in her arms again, but I take a step backward.

"Dotty. Don't be mad at me, please."

She sounds so young and so sad. And part of me knows she's just eighteen. A kid, really. But the rest of me is thinking only of how Kitty St. Clair has inserted herself into my life without permission, leaving me a dance hall and sucking me into these dreams that have brought nothing but more heartache.

"I believed you, Kitty. All that crap you said about carving out your own destiny—never settling. Despite my better judgment, despite knowing the ending, I . . ."

I hoped.

With my whole heart for everything to end differently. For Kitty. For me.

"Did you even love him?"

It's a full minute before she answers, and her voice is so quiet that I almost don't hear her. "Of course I did. I do. But it's complicated."

"How is it complicated?"

She stares down at her feet, but her chin is high when she lifts her head again.

"I love him, but I love *me* even more."

I laugh. It's a single, bitter "Ha" that I cling to in hopes it will hold back the tears threatening to fall.

"At least you're honest about it." I throw out my arm in the direction of the waiting car. "Go. Be the fabulous Kitty St. Clair. Live your exciting life."

I continue to back up toward the house. Done with Kitty. Done with the dream. Done with everything.

She turns and walks back toward the waiting car, pausing with her hand on the door.

"Take care of yourself, Dotty," she says. "And if you have a moment, take care of him, too."

With that, she gets back inside, and the car pulls a slow U-turn, its tires crunching against the gravel road as its taillights disappear into the dark.

I awake to the smell of coffee.

Then to the panic of thinking I must have slept through my seven A.M. alarm, and the brief relief that comes when I check my phone and see 6:50 on the screen.

That reprieve lasts only until I spot two voicemail notifications from Reeve—which I don't listen to—along with two text messages, which I refuse to read.

Instead, I roll out of bed, throw on the scrubs I laid out the night before, grab my bag, and follow my nose to the kitchen, where my mom sits, fully dressed, mug clasped between her hands.

"Oh good, you're up." She stands and begins to pour me a cup, adding just the right amount of cream. "You didn't tell me last night what time you needed to leave. I assumed it was early, but I wasn't . . ." She leaves the thought unfinished as she hands me the coffee. "I can drive you home. You won't be able to get a cab this early."

Assuming Keady is like West Lake—one random Uber driver who has a habit of playing *Call of Duty* until dawn—I trust that she is probably right. I take a sip and nod. "Okay, thanks."

She grabs her mug and heads to the front door. I grab my things and follow her, realizing she means we're leaving right now. We get back into her little Toyota and begin to drive. The only sounds are of the wheels on the road and the sipping of coffee as each of us nurses our drink.

When we get into West Lake and she pulls onto Main Street, I begin to compose something to say. My emotions range from lingering anger from our fight to gratitude for her midnight pickup to emotional exhaustion. I think I'm going to go with a simple "Thanks, I appreciate it," but then she zips right past my apartment and keeps driving.

"I still live back there." I point at the pizza parlor, wondering if she forgot.

"I know," she says and makes another quick turn, and it dawns on me exactly where she's going.

She pulls up in front of Gigi's cottage and puts the car into park.

We both stare at it silently for a moment before she finally speaks.

"My mother died in that little green house." Her voice is quiet. "And her mother died in that little green house. I was hell-bent on getting as far away from it as I could."

I snort at the bluntness of her statement. "Really? I hadn't noticed."

"Did you know I lived in Toronto once?" she asks.

I don't answer her question, but she takes my silence for a no.

"I was there for a year, right after high school," she continues. "My apartment was the cutest little bachelor above a laundromat on Queen Street. During the day, I worked at a twenty-four-hour diner—which I told myself was cooler and far more sophisticated than Lou's, but now, with a little perspective, I see it was exactly like Lou's—and on the weekend, I bartended at this gloriously dingy dive bar with live music. It was the best year of my life."

My eyes remain on Gigi's front porch. "So then, why did you come back?"

"Well." She hesitates. "I met your father. And as you know, he didn't stick around for very long, so when I found out you were coming, I knew I wanted to care for you but I wouldn't be able to do it by myself. So I moved back in with Gigi, and I guess you know the rest."

I am very aware. "You spent the next twenty years resenting being here and trying to get out again."

She finally turns to me, waiting until I, too, make the move to meet her eyes.

"No. I didn't resent it," she says. "I made my choice. No one forced me to come back. What I resented was that when I was growing up, neither Mom nor Gigi supported me in wanting to have a life outside this town. They didn't push me to meet new people or get an education past high school. I wanted you to grow up seeing that there was a big, beautiful world out there. I wanted you to know you could have a life that was more than just West Lake."

The silence stretches between us, and I think this conversation is over. I adjust the strap of my seatbelt, hoping she gets the hint that we should get going, but she places her hand over mine and squeezes, waiting again for me to look at her.

"I thought about what you said last night about how you couldn't pay for your school." Her eyes drop momentarily before returning to mine. "It made me realize that I went too far. I wanted more for myself, and I made some very bad choices. I know I don't have the right to ask you to forgive me, but I am sorry. I really thought I was doing the right thing for both of us."

I hear her apology, and I get it sort of. While I can appreciate what she is saying, I'm not ready to open my arms and tell her everything is forgiven. Maybe I'll get there someday, but right now my insides are too raw and too hurt from everything that has happened.

"Well, at least I've learned to be happy here," I tell her. "And I guess that's a good thing, seeing as I am not going anywhere."

My mother is quiet for a moment, then two moments, then three. The clock on her dash starts ticking too close to nine.

"I need to go to work."

My mom shakes her head, shifts the car from park to drive, and circles the block until we pull up in front of my apartment, where she cuts the engine.

I grab my bag, but her hand finds my arm as I push open the passenger door.

"If you're truly content here, then be content." Her voice wavers slightly. "But if you're not, I hope my mistakes won't be the things that stop you, because trust me, Julia, you will regret it."

Chapter 38

I LEAVE MY phone off and in the break room with the idea that if it's out of sight and out of mind, I won't spend the day moping about Reeve.

This strategy works until lunchtime, when the dining room serves gnocchi, and the smell of oregano and garlic bread sends a wave of fresh grief through my body.

From there, it all goes downhill.

When I check in on Mrs. Hail, she's blasting "It's All Coming Back to Me Now." She holds out her hands and says, "Come and dance with me, darling. It's just a slow one. I think you can handle it."

I can't handle it. I think of Reeve and New Year's and that single perfect kiss, and I have to excuse myself to cry in the bathroom and then tell everyone my red puffy eyes are from allergies.

As the hours creep on, I keep picturing what he's doing and what he's thinking.

My thoughts become so intense—so vivid—that when I spot Reeve in the lobby standing by the elevator, I think he's a hallucination. His dark suit is rumpled. His hair is a mess of wild locks. He's unshaven. The last time I saw him like that was the night we first met, and that memory makes me want to run the backs of my fingers along the scratchy texture of his jaw. But before I move, the door to the main office opens, and Sunnyvale's manager, Roy Taylor, steps out. He greets Reeve with a booming "Mr. Baldwin," and I realize this is no delusion. Reeve is actually in my lobby.

I duck into the stairwell before he can see me.

I slump down on the stairs as the tears return. It's no grand gesture.

My hollow sobs bounce off the empty walls. They echo through the stairwell, so I don't hear Zoe until she sits beside me, holding out an open foil bag. "Cheeto?"

I shake my head. Zoe reaches inside and pops an orange puff into her mouth, then wipes her hand on her scrubs, leaving a streak of orange powder behind. "I heard you had a rough night."

I lean against her shoulder as her arm comes around me.

"I guess no one's buying the allergy excuse?"

Her hand makes small circles on my back. "No. I think the early April pollen might be working in your favor. But I talked to Reeve this morning. When he couldn't get a hold of you, he called me. He wanted to make sure you were okay. Are you?"

The question makes the tears come even faster.

Zoe lets me cry with no further explanation needed until I compose myself enough to take a full, deep breath.

"I just feel so stupid, Zoe. I really thought he—" I can't even finish the sentence. The sob that rips through me seems to get stuck in my throat, and for a moment, I worry I'm going to vomit.

"You know I have your back always," Zoe says. "No questions asked. Would bury a body, take a bullet, drive off a cliff holding hands in a cute little Miata, all in the name of friendship, right?"

I nod, still not quite able to speak.

"Reeve told me about Mansfield and Sunnyvale. After I told

him in perfect anatomic detail where Mansfield could shove their offer, he told me Howard went behind his back. Reeve only found out it was happening a few hours before you did. He was going to tell you everything, but you caught him by surprise when you decided to go to the party, and he ran out of time."

I shake my head, the scene from outside still fresh. "If that's true, then why is he in the lobby right now, talking to Roy Taylor?"

Zoe's eyebrows scrunch. "I don't know. What I *do* know is that he drove up here last night because he was worried about you, Jules. He must be talking to Taylor about something else. You know me. I do not give people the benefit of the doubt."

The sound of a vibrating phone interrupts us. Zoe pulls it from her pocket. I see Reeve's name on the screen before she hits decline. A moment later, a text notification flashes.

> **Reeve:** Did you find her? Did she get home okay? Make sure she doesn't sign until she's talked to me or her lawyer. Mansfield won't buy Sunnyvale if they can't also get her property.

Zoe tips the phone so I can see it. "I really think you should talk to him."

I shake my head, the panic climbing my throat again. "I just don't think it's going to work out, Zo."

"Why not?"

"Because." I recite the laundry list of reasons I've ignored all these weeks. "I'm never going to sell to Mansfield. Reeve isn't going to get his deal. Which means he's in Toronto and I am here in West Lake for the foreseeable future. Stories like ours, they don't work out."

Zoe crumples the empty foil bag in her hand. "Okay . . ." She draws out the word. "I think you need to talk to Reeve about those first two reasons. As for the distance . . . we are living in a beautiful age, Jules. We have the internet, and, more important, we have sexting."

"It's not that simple."

Zoe narrows her eyes as if she is trying to figure me out. "Can I run a different theory by you? It's just a hunch." She shifts her body around to face me. "I think you're afraid that if you get any more invested, he could really hurt you."

Her words hit the tender spot between my ribs. "It's not like it's an unfounded theory." I can't keep the sarcasm from my voice as I think about Reeve and my mom—and even Kitty.

Zoe tips her head, her temple touching mine. "I'd like to think there is someone who has shown you that if you put your hope in the right person, you will end up with a soulmate who will always love you no matter what bonehead choices you make or how much you try to push them away."

A single tear slides down my cheek, catching on my chin before it falls and absorbs into my shirt.

"That person is me." Zoe pokes me with the butt of her elbow. "If that wasn't super clear. I will always and forever have your back, Jules. You deserve to be loved."

I wrap my arms around her, pulling her head to my chest. Despite the awkward angle, she stays, letting me cry it out into her hair. When I finally let her go, she wipes a tear-soaked strand from my cheek. "You also deserve a lifetime of orgasms, another reason why I strongly suggest you call him or, better yet, go find him."

I shake my head. "I don't know. I—"

My thought is halted by the banging of the stairwell door above us.

I freeze, expecting Reeve to somehow come down the stairs, but it's just a voice that calls out.

"Ms. DeMarco, are you down there?"

Nurse Bouchard.

Zoe slowly gets to her feet, motioning as if she wants us to make a bolt for the door, but I answer. "Yup, I'm here. What's up?"

"It's Mr. McNaught. He isn't in his room, and he's scheduled to go to Port Logan for his doctor's appointment at four. Would you locate him and ensure he's prepared to leave on time?"

I nod and say, "Yup, no problem," shaking the stiffness from my legs and getting to my feet. I hug Zoe one last time before heading back into the now empty hallway.

Mr. McNaught may not be here, but I have a strong suspicion I know exactly where to find him.

Chapter 39

I BARELY HAVE the chance to inhale the smell of bacon before I spot Mr. McNaught in his regular seat at the counter, just as I suspected. He has the *Toronto Star* in front of him, open to the crossword puzzle, where he looks to be lingering on the last few clues.

"I had a feeling you'd be hiding out here." I settle into the empty stool beside him. "You know the coffee in the dining room really isn't that bad."

He sets his pencil down, turning to me, his lips curved upward in a small smile. "I'll let you in on a secret. I don't come here for the coffee. I come here for Rosie." He lifts his mug in her direction and gets a swat with the rag as Rosie rolls her eyes.

"This one is far too smooth, Jules," she says as she takes the pot and refills his cup. "You have to be careful around him."

Mr. McNaught takes a sip with an approving nod of his head. "The coffee *is* better here." He motions at the pot, as if asking if I want a cup, but I shake my head.

"The older you get, the less willing you are to put up with bullshit in your life," he says. "And that includes people. I like it here. I like my friends." He points to the shelf above the coffeemaker. "I've already told Lou when I die, I want my ashes left right up there."

Rosie turns her head, following the direction of his finger, then whips back around with a shake of her head. "That's a little too close to the Folgers, hon."

Mr. McNaught chuffs. "Fine. Over there then." He points to a shelf a little farther from the coffee, filled with photographs of various patrons of Lou's. It was put up last year when they ran out of room on the far wall.

Mr. McNaught leans close, tipping his head so only I can hear. "When I go, do you want my seat?" He taps his leg on his stool. "No one has asked for that yet. I'll leave it to you if you like?"

I shake my head, my new philosophy firmly being that I don't want to be named in any wills and testaments for the foreseeable future.

"Thanks, but I'm good. And I wouldn't be giving it away too soon. I don't think you're going anywhere for a while."

Mr. McNaught shrugs, his smile highlighting the wrinkles around his eyes. "You never know; life throws you curveballs when you least expect it."

A lesson I've learned this year.

"Well, why don't we do our best to get ahead of one of those curveballs? You've got a doctor's appointment in . . ." I check my phone. "Twenty minutes. What do you say? Should we try to get there on time?"

He waves me off, taking another sip of his coffee. "Oh, don't worry. I'm an old man. I'll act a little confused in the waiting room. The doctor will cut me a break."

I get to my feet, hoping it will prompt him along. "That might work for you, but I need to answer to Nurse Bouchard."

He sighs and nods. "Then I guess I'd better finish my coffee and come with ya."

I wait while he does just that, then takes a trip to the bathroom because "Port Logan is a ways away, and my prostate isn't what it used to be."

I wait for him by the front door, busying myself by skimming all the pictures on the far wall. Lou's whole history with this town. There are so many with Sunnyvale residents. Most of them were taken long before they came to live at the home.

I close my eyes, the full weight of the day taking hold. When I open them again, my gaze catches on a black-and-white photo. It's taken in front of what I now recognize as the dance hall. Two women and two men, arms around one another, laughing. I must have passed this photo easily a hundred times on my way to and from the bathroom over the years. However, as I brace my hand against the wall to lean closer, I wonder if I've ever really looked at it.

"Good-looking fella, wasn't he?"

I jump at the unexpected voice.

"Yes. Very good-looking." I glance at the next photo over. It's of Mr. McNaught, sitting at his spot at Lou's counter, Mardi Gras beads around his neck, posed in front of a giant plate of chocolate chip pancakes. "And still is." I reach up to wipe a smudge from the glass, but Mr. McNaught shakes his head.

"Not that one. He's an old fart. But he used to have a little more hair back in his day." I follow his gaze to the dance hall picture, to the tall, gangly teen with the big nose and slicked hair, and only then do I see the resemblance.

"That's you."

He's smiling in the photo, although he isn't looking at the camera. His eyes are on the beautiful blond girl standing next to him in her white dress.

"And that's Kitty," I whisper.

Mr. McNaught nods. "Now, *she* was a looker."

The word triggers something. A memory. Or a dream. In less than a breath, my kaleidoscope of memories spins and then clicks—forming a completely different picture.

Knots.

McNaught.

"You're . . . Knots." I don't fully believe it, even as the words leave my mouth.

Mr. McNaught laughs softly to himself. "I haven't been called that in years."

I guess I assumed all along the nickname was a rope thing. Ropes and knots. I feel so stupid.

He smiles. "They used to call my father by that nickname, too."

He reaches up and taps his finger on the other woman in the picture, the one I don't recognize. "I've always thought you look a little like your great-grandmother."

"I'm sorry . . . what? Who?"

He taps the glass. "Dotty. It's the eyes. Your mother had them, too. Must run in the family."

I shake my head, not following. "Dot wasn't my great-grandmother. My great-grandmother's name was Gillian."

Mr. McNaught brushes his thumb over her face.

"She had the cutest freckles. Like a smattering of polka dots across her nose. She was never a fan of the nickname. Made us call her Gillian again when she married your great-grandpa."

Dotty.

Not some figment of my imagination pieced together with snippets of Kitty's diary.

A real person.

Not only that, but my flesh and blood.

Mr. McNaught steps toward me, taking me by the elbow. "You're looking a little pale there, honey. Maybe you should come with me to the doctor."

"I'm . . . okay."

Mr. McNaught ignores my words and leads me to an empty booth, where I sink into the leather as my knees give out.

"You and Kitty," I whisper, still not fully understanding. "I didn't know."

He settles into the seat across from me. "Most people didn't. It was so long ago."

I am filling in the remaining blanks. All those years after the diary and before today.

Kitty comes back to West Lake.

Knots is still here.

They've been living the last two years under the same roof.

So *was* it a love story after all?

"Is that why she came back?" I ask. "Because of you?"

Mr. McNaught looks up at my question, a surprised lift to his eyebrows. I half expect him to ask why I seem to know their history so intimately, but instead, his eyes shift to the window, first to the old abandoned dance hall, then to the retirement home next door.

"She wanted her last days to be spent in her hometown." His eyes drift back to meet mine. "And I think she wanted to remember the girl she used to be."

I have so many questions. Even with the diary and the dreams, there are so many gaps.

"Can I ask a personal question?" My curiosity overwhelms my conscience. "Did you ever ask her why . . . why she said yes to Beau? I mean, you had to know she loved you."

His eyes return to the window, and a moment passes, then two.

I open my mouth to apologize, but he clears his throat, his gaze dropping to his hands.

"Oh, I asked myself that question more than a few times over the years." He looks up, giving me a half smile. "For the first few, I assumed it was simply that Kitty wanted a life I couldn't give her. . . ."

Mr. McNaught pauses, his voice suddenly choking up. I go to the counter and fill a glass of water, Rosie giving me her nod of approval from the other side of the restaurant before I return to the booth and hand Mr. McNaught the water glass.

"Thank you." He takes it from me with shaking hands, drawing a long sip before setting it down in front of him. "But when we finally closed the place down in sixty-four, I came across the paperwork that named her as the owner. I saw the dates and put two and two together."

I've lost the plot.

Mr. McNaught tips his head to the side, studying me. "When I realized who Mr. Scott sold the dance hall to all those years ago, I understood why she left."

"Kitty bought the dance hall?" I ask, still unsure if I've got it right, but Mr. McNaught nods.

"It was her wedding present from Beau. She knew the town needed it, and . . ." His voice cracks. "I think it was Kitty's way of telling me she loved me."

It's like the world has all of a sudden shifted, and I'm seeing everything from a different angle.

"I didn't know." My voice is a whisper.

"That was Kitty's way."

He reaches for the water again, his eyes glassy and an even lighter shade of green.

"Do you think she ever regretted it?"

It's a question I've wondered since I first began reading the diary.

Mr. McNaught stares at the half-empty glass for a moment before answering. "I think she always wondered what life would have been like had she . . . chosen me. I think it's perhaps why she came back in the end. We had our last few years together. She died knowing . . ."

His voice cracks, and there is no water left. I move to stand, but his hands reach for mine, pulling me back into my seat. "I loved that woman." His eyes meet mine in time for me to see his glassy gaze turn into teardrops that he doesn't try to hide as they spill down his cheeks. "I'll take my last breath—not too long from now—and I will still love that woman. But to answer your question, I think the thing she regretted most of all was that she had to choose in the first place. She couldn't do it all on her own."

"She left it to me when she died," I whisper, my gaze automatically shifting to the lot across the street.

Mr. McNaught's does the same. "Did she? I wondered about that."

Suddenly, a new thought surfaces.

"Do you think she did it because of Dot? Gillian, I mean. She and Kitty were close. That would make a lot more sense."

Mr. McNaught shakes his head. "I don't think so. They lost touch after Kitty left. Kitty lost touch with most of us."

"Then why . . ." I try to finish the thought but can't find the right words, and before I do, Mr. McNaught's hands cover mine. They're aged with brown spots and skin so thin that I can see his blue veins underneath.

"I think she saw herself in you." He squeezes my hands. "The both of you were born and raised in West Lake and maybe a little stuck. I think she wanted to make sure that if it came down to love and your future, *you* could choose both."

Kitty never had a choice. It was live in West Lake with Knots but give up all of her dreams or marry Beau and live them out. *I love me even more.*

He removes his hands from mine to check his watch, an old digital Timex with big orange buttons. "Shall we get going? It's getting a little late. I'm charming, but I don't think I should push my luck with the doctor too much."

He pulls a napkin from the metal holder and holds it out to me. That's when I feel a single tear roll down my cheek, landing on the table with a quiet *plop*.

Mr. McNaught stands and waits. Holding out his hand to me, he says, "I can walk back on my own if you want to sit for a little longer."

Another tear falls, landing almost on top of the first, forming the shape of a heart for a brief moment before I smear it into the tabletop with the pad of my thumb.

"Honey?" Mr. McNaught picks the napkin up again. This time I take it, pressing it to my cheeks.

It took Kitty almost a lifetime to choose love.

Luckily, it hasn't taken me quite as long.

Chapter 40

I RETURN MR. McNaught to Sunnyvale in time to board the minibus to Port Logan, then immediately begin my search for Reeve.

With West Lake being not much more than a crossroads of two main streets, and knowing Reeve isn't at Lou's counter chatting with Rosie, I'm left with only a handful of options for where he might be.

I check Ron's office in case they're still meeting, but it appears to be locked up for the night, so I walk to Clive's garage, pick up my car, and drive to my apartment. Although the street in front of the pizzeria is empty, I still check to ensure he isn't waiting for me in the hallway. I troll Main Street and then St. Mary Street twice, checking the Legion, the 7-Eleven, and even the gift shop. With each pass, my heart gets a little heavier. On the third, I finally consider the most obvious answer: I'm too late, and he's on his way home.

Out of options, I turn into the parking lot of Sunnyvale, where I silently curse the light blue Honda Civic parked in my usual spot. But as I make a quick U-turn and park near the dance hall, I catch a glimpse of silver just visible around the far corner of the building, and my heart stops.

I'm not entirely sure if I turn off my engine.

I definitely leave my doors unlocked as I unclick my seatbelt and sprint to the tall wooden doors, pulling them open and taking just a moment to let my eyes adjust to the dim interior light.

He's sitting on the edge of the stage, feet dangling over the dance floor below, looking at his phone cradled in his hand.

"Hey," I call out.

He looks up. "Jules! Are you okay?"

I consider the events of the last twenty-four hours. "I don't know if I'd use the word *okay* yet, but I'm here."

He slides off the edge of the stage to his feet. "I was going to tell you, Jules, I swear. I just ran out of time."

"How long have you known?"

He shifts his weight as if he's considering stepping closer but then stops and shoves his hands into his pockets. "I found out yesterday—a couple of hours before the party."

I nod, and he takes a step closer. "Roy and I met back in the fall when Kitty passed away, but Sunnyvale wasn't interested in selling, so I moved on. Then, on the way home after meeting with you, Howard and I drove past the dance hall. He asked about Sunnyvale. I explained they weren't interested, but Howard . . . well, he doesn't like to hear the word *no*. I guess he called Roy after we got back and offered him double what I had. I found out with the rest of the team when he called a Saturday morning update meeting."

His words make sense. It wasn't months of betrayal, only hours. "I was with you all night, Reeve. You could have pulled me aside. I should have heard it from you."

He lets out a long breath. "I know. You are right. I just . . . I wanted to fix things before I told you. I wanted to at least have a plan or an idea of what you could do. I have this friend. He's a lawyer. He's trying to see if you could write some sort of clause into the sale to ensure they couldn't touch Sunnyvale. It's unconventional, but Mansfield doesn't want the retirement home if they can't also get the dance hall with its water access. He thinks it's possible for the deal to still happen. You just need to—"

"It's not going to happen," I interrupt him. "I can't. Even with that clause or whatever. I've decided I can't go through with it."

There's a notable stillness in the room as he processes what I've said and I figure out what I want to say next. "I know this screws up your project," I continue. "And now you're going to have to tell Mansfield and your dad after he made that whole big speech, and I'm so, so sorry, but I can't—"

"Jules," Reeve interrupts. "I quit. Didn't Zoe tell you?"

I freeze. "What?"

Reeve nods. "I handed in my resignation to Howard this morning."

"Wait, why?"

He takes a tentative step toward me. "I didn't want to be a part of it anymore, either. I've been thinking about it for a while now. The only parts of the job I enjoyed were when I had excuses to come up here and see you. So when I found out about Sunnyvale, that was it."

I hear his words and process them. They're just so very different from the narrative in my head that I have trouble fully grasping what he means.

"But you met with Roy like an hour ago. I saw you."

Confusion crosses his brow. "You saw me? Why didn't you . . ." He shakes his head, and his expression clears. "I came looking for you at work. I didn't really have a plan, and I ran into Roy in the lobby. When I saw him, it clicked that me just showing up might get you in trouble, so I chatted with him for a few minutes and then left."

It's the simple, logical explanation Zoe promised, yet I still can't get my head around it. "But you wanted that deal so badly. You really just walked away?"

"I wanted the deal to happen for you, Jules."

He closes the final few steps so that his toes nearly touch mine. "I have been thinking a lot about that night we first met," he says. "Not just meeting you, but the things we told each other, and I realized that that guy on the dock would look at my job at Mansfield and be horrified. He'd wonder what the hell happened— why I was telling myself I was happy when in truth, I gave up on my dreams."

He reaches out, his hands framing my face. "But you hadn't given up, and I wanted to do everything I could to help. A little redemption for those kids back on the dock."

I swallow. "It's not going to happen for me this year." I tell him the hard fact I've already come to accept. "I'm not going to sell, so I won't be able to get the money together in time." But as I say it, Reeve's words from a moment ago blend with my mom's, and I realize something I think I've known for a while. "But I'm not ready to give up yet. I just need a new plan. One that likely involves writing my GMAT a few more times and Saturday night shifts for the foreseeable future."

Reeve leans forward, pressing his forehead to mine. "What can I do?"

I shake my head. "I'm not sure yet. But for now you can kiss me. You're the only thing I have figured out."

He's already bending down, his lips searching for mine like he had the same idea.

His arms wrap around my back, squeezing me tightly as I lay my head on his chest. My eyes roam the empty dance hall, thinking of Kitty and Knots. That very first night, they swayed together not too far from where we stand now, completely unaware of how their story was about to unfold.

"I wonder what those two kids on the dock would say if they could see us now." I kick an empty beer bottle with the toe of my shoe and watch it roll away. "I'll bet they never would have predicted this."

Reeve leans away so he can look at me thoroughly. "Maybe not the abandoned dance hall part, but I think Dock Reeve would have hoped to be standing next to you."

My heart flutters. "Really?"

Reeve cups the side of my face in his hand. "He fell pretty hard. Not as madly in love as he is right now, but he knew."

My heart stops for a moment as I hold my breath, replaying the words in my head, sure that I must not have heard him correctly. "I'm sorry, but you need to back up a little and maybe drop the third person."

"He fell hard?" Reeve offers, smiling like he wants me to say it.

"The part right after that."

He reaches so that both hands now cradle my face, leaving no place for me to look other than into the deep brown of his eyes. "That I'm madly in love with you?"

I attempt to nod.

"It's true," he continues, the pads of his thumbs stroking my cheeks. "I love you, Jules. I wanted a future with you that night on the dock, but it's only a fraction of what I feel now."

My brain gets stuck on those three words—those beautiful words—repeating them over and over, but as much as I love to hear them, I want to say them even more.

"I think I spent the first half of our relationship waiting for you to realize it wasn't what you wanted, and then the next half terrified you would," I begin. "I didn't want to admit to myself that I loved you because if I did, there would be no going back.

But I want to tell you that now because even though I think we have a long love story ahead of us, I don't want to wait until the last chapter for the happy ending. It should come now."

I pull him to me, not bothering to linger this time. We kiss with that perfect, practiced tilt to our heads that says this isn't our first kiss and the slow, savoring exploration that says we know there will be an entire lifetime before our last.

When we finally pull away, he keeps me close, pressing my cheek to his chest, nestled perfectly into that nook under his chin.

I stare at the dilapidated walls of the dance hall; its future is still so undefined.

"I wonder what will happen to this place."

Reeve lifts his head, presumably to look around. "Do you have any idea what you will do with it now?"

I shake my head, stepping back to survey the whole room. "Keep it on the market, I guess. Keep my fingers crossed that dance halls come suddenly back into fashion. Kitty's estate paid the taxes for the next year, so at least I have some time." I take Reeve's hand. "What do you say we get out of here?"

He adjusts his grip so his fingers lace with mine. "Yeah. It will be dark soon." We walk hand in hand to the big wooden doors, but just as we are about to step through, Reeve pauses and turns around. "And I know it's weird to say, but I've always gotten a feeling about this place. I think it might be a little haunted."

Chapter 41

When I awaken, it's to the feeling of Reeve's lips brushing softly against mine.

"Sorry," he says when my eyes flutter open, sunlight pouring into my bedroom and the sheets tangled at our feet. "I just couldn't wait. . . ." His words fall away as he looks down at me in that way I've waited all my life to be looked at.

"Me neither." I reach up and pull his head to mine. We kiss until he collapses down beside me and I pull the covers up and over our heads, creating a down-filled layer between us and the rest of the world.

We make love. A quickie before we indulge in a breakfast of homemade blueberry pancakes and French press coffee, and then again after, where we take our time. I want him close. Maybe to make up for the emotional distance of the last few days. And Reeve—with his hands always reaching for my hips, and his lips always seeming to find that spot on my neck, just above my collarbone—seems very content with this plan.

Sometime just before noon, we crawl out of bed and get dressed. Our romantic fantasy morning will meet a grim reality sometime later this afternoon when Reeve has to head back to the city to fulfill his two weeks' notice, and I have an overnight shift at Sunnyvale, but until then, we enjoy our last few moments of domestic bliss, lazing around on my secondhand couch: Reeve on his phone sifting through the last of his work emails; me on my laptop, paying bills.

"That's a very deep sigh." Reeve leans over and kisses that spot before returning to his end of the couch.

"Sorry." I'm staring at the only damper of the morning: my online banking site. All of my mother's damage from the last two years is consolidated into one easy payment.

"Anything I can do?" Reeve asks. I shake my head, minimizing the screen, no longer wanting to look at my sizable hill of debt, although it's considerably smaller than the mountain it was a year ago.

Reeve flips his phone around so his screen is facing me. "Check this out." He hands me his phone. On it is a photo of the two of us from his parents' party this weekend. We're talking. Not looking at the camera, instead gazing into each other's eyes and very clearly looking like we are in love.

"Can you send that to me?" I hand his phone back.

Reeve clicks on something on his screen. "Looks like my mom already did. It should be in your inbox."

I pull up my email to see the photo on a bigger screen and find it, just as Reeve said, sitting with my other unread messages. But before I can click it open, another email catches my attention, making me gasp.

"What's wrong?" Reeve rubs the side of my arm with the back of his hand, and when my only answer is a strangled gurgling at the back of my throat, he scoots closer to see what's on my screen.

"Are you going to open it?"

My eyes comb over the subject yet again. *University Admissions: Update to Your Recent Application.*

I consider my plan. Delete the email or banish it to some dark corner of the internet. I could go on with my life as if it never existed. Never having the hope that maybe some miracle could happen that would allow me to go. It's what I've always done. But it's also the reason I wouldn't let myself fall in love with Reeve. Hope may be a dangerous thing, but living without it is . . .

I click on the email before I talk myself out of it. It takes me to a generic message that provides no further hints on my application status other than a direct link to the application portal, where my username and password auto-populate in their respective boxes.

"Here we go." My mouse hovers over the submit button. Reeve's lips find my temple. He presses a kiss right as I click, and the screen becomes a blur in front of me until I hear his sharp intake of breath. I read the word *congratulations*. Then the phrase *welcome you to the class*. My eyeballs make it all the way to the end before the implications fully set in.

"I got in." The words come out alongside a sob.

Reeve's arms come around me as he whispers, "Congrats, Jules. You did it."

I expect to be devastated. To be overwhelmed with the feeling of everything being within my grasp for a brief moment before it slipped through my fingers. But all I feel is proud.

"I did it." The tears that cloud my eyes are happy ones.

Chapter 42

"What if I gave you the money?"

We are getting into Reeve's car on our way to Lou's for breakfast and having the same argument we've had all week.

"Tuition is thirty thousand a year; add in meager living expenses and I'm looking at two hundred thousand at least. Don't tell me you have two hundred thousand sitting around." I've gone from politely declining to being just plain blunt.

"Well, it's not sitting around," he counters. "But I could sell—"

"No."

"Jules—"

"This isn't up for negotiation." I close the passenger door and fasten my seatbelt, watching Reeve as he pulls a U-turn and heads toward Lou's.

"It would be a loan." Reeve tries a new approach, the same one he tried yesterday.

"No."

"It's for your future," he argues. "It's for *our* future."

Now, that is a new tactic. It makes my breath catch in a way that makes me unable to respond immediately, which Reeve uses to his advantage.

"I love you, Jules. I know how important this is to you. I want to do anything in my power to help."

"I know you do." My voice softens. "But I can't take your money." I consider the best way to phrase the metaphorical elephant that has always existed between us, knowing that what I am about to say is going to make things awkward but also that it needs to happen if we are going to be together.

"You know I didn't have a whole lot growing up." I start with the basics. "When I was a kid trying to figure out where to go to university, I didn't argue with my mom about which program I should take. I argued with the bank about a student loan and justified it by doing an online degree to stay home and save on living expenses. Even now, my financial situation is far from where I'd like it to be. I check the prices of items at the grocery store and thrift my clothes, and I think long and hard about every single major purchase because I don't have anyone who can bail me out if I make a bad financial decision."

Reeve's brow creases, and I know he's taking this little speech in a way I don't want him to.

"This isn't a dig at you," I tell him. "Or your trust fund, or the way you grew up. Please don't take it that way. I know that having money comes with its own set of challenges. I just want you to understand that I will always be the person who checks the prices on menus at a restaurant, and I will wear the same old winter coat because a new one isn't in the budget—and that is not a bad thing."

As the words come out of my mouth, I realize how true they really are. "All that stuff with my credit and my mom was awful, but it had a silver lining. I know I can take care of myself. My financial planning skills are pretty stellar now, but that comes with making financial decisions I know I can handle independently. I am *really* good at this now, Reeve, and I don't want you to . . . save me."

Reeve opens his mouth. I know a firm denial is about to exit his lips, so I cut it off before he can get it out. "I know that's not what you're trying to do, but if you just gave me the money, I would always know that I couldn't figure this out on my own—and I have, Reeve. I talked to the admissions office, and they will let me defer a year. That gives me twelve more months where I can reduce my debts and hopefully get myself in a situation where the bank might be willing to lend me money again, and as a backup, I will try to figure out another plan for the dance hall. It's far from foolproof, but it's what I've got."

Reeve nods and doesn't say anything further. It makes me think our conversation is over, but as we approach Lou's parking lot, he slows the car and puts on his hazards just shy of the turn-off. "I get it. You want to do this on your own. But would you be open to hearing about a different idea?"

I stare at him skeptically. "As long as it doesn't involve you or your money."

He turns off his hazards, flips his blinker, and pulls us back onto the road. "It does involve me, but not in the way that you're thinking."

We drive for forty-five minutes. Despite my pleading and moaning that I'm starving and cannot survive a moment longer without pancakes, Reeve gives me no clues as to where we are going or what we are doing until he turns down an unfamiliar wooded road.

"This is the second time I've allowed you to take me into strange, dark woods. Don't ever say I don't trust you completely."

He takes a right at the fork. "You might want to hold on to that thought."

I see the blue lake glimmering through the trees before the road opens into a large clearing with a small parking lot. Like a tiny farmers market, seven or eight small wooden kiosks are gathered in a large circle.

"What is this place?" I ask Reeve when we get out of the car, and Reeve waves across the circle to a man I immediately recognize.

"It doesn't have a name," Reeve explains as he takes my hand and leads me to the stall where Marcus Landers is showing off a large blue platter to a woman in a humongous white straw hat. "There's a big sign that says 'Local Art' back on the road, but I've never heard it called anything officially."

Reeve waves at a woman with long red hair in paint-spattered overalls. Her kiosk is filled with local landscapes and tiny watercolors of local flora and fauna.

The rest of the kiosks are also filled with art, ranging from homemade wind chimes to intricate pottery like Marcus's and—

I pick up a very familiar cylindrical vase. "Wait. Is this one of yours?" I turn to Reeve, his wide smile confirming my suspicions without him saying a word.

"Marcus convinced me to share a few pieces. He actually sold something the other day."

I hug the vase to my chest. "Well, you're about to make a second sale. I'm taking this one home with me."

He takes the vase from my hands and puts it back on the table. "I have an entire closet full of these things. Next time you come over, I'll send you home with five."

I consider ignoring him and buying it anyway but relent, justifying it with the thought that someone else is going to see it and fall in love.

The woman with the hat decides to buy the platter. As Marcus rings up her purchase, I peruse the rest of his table, spotting a few pieces I noticed when we visited his studio and a new piece that knocks the breath from my lungs.

It's of a couple in a dancer's hold. He's in a summer suit. She's in a white dress. Her skirt is billowed out as if frozen in mid-twirl. They are looking at each other in a way that cannot be described as anything but true love.

Marcus, who has been watching me take in the sculpture, picks it up. "I call it *The Lovers*." He hands it to me. "I made it after I learned about these dance halls they had all along the coast of Lake Huron. Pretty much every town had one. There were hundreds in their heyday all across southern Ontario."

I run my fingers over their faces to try to hide my surprised smile. His slicked-back hair. The sparkle in her blue eyes. So familiar. "Did you model these two after anyone?"

Marcus looks at me, surprised. "It's the funniest thing. I had a dream about these two and couldn't get them out of my head. Then, the next day, the sculpture felt like it had molded itself. It happens like that sometimes. I call it divine intervention. If you're interested, I can throw it in as part of our deal."

I look from him to Reeve, not fully following. "What deal?"

Marcus points to the kiosks. "This place is only open April through August. Reeve has been trying to get a few of us to put together a more permanent show. We've been dragging our feet, not having a good place in mind, but we heard your dance hall is available for rent."

"You want to *rent* the dance hall?" I'm still not sure I'm following him correctly.

Marcus looks at Reeve before returning his gaze to me. "You look confused," he says to me. "I may have jumped the gun a little. I assumed our new gallery manager would have already filled you in. But yes, I hope you're open to it. I know you are looking for a buyer, and we may be able to get there eventually, but we're hoping for a four-year lease to ensure we can get things up and running. I'll have Reeve fax over our formal offer to your real estate agent, but I hope we can do business together, Jules. I have a good feeling about this."

Before I can say anything back, Marcus excuses himself to help a middle-aged couple who have stopped by his kiosk to find an anniversary present for their friends.

With Marcus gone, Reeve nods toward the woods. "Can we sit and talk?"

I nod back, follow him to a knocked-over log near a pretty spot at the edge of the woods, and sit.

"So what do you think?" he asks.

Although I'm watching a little green bug climb along a maple leaf in front of me, I can feel Reeve studying my face.

"About Marcus's offer? Or your new job?"

I can hear Reeve take a deep breath, and when the answer doesn't immediately come, I turn to look at him and do some face studying of my own.

"I wanted you to consider the offer before I told you about the job." His words come out in a rush, as if he's held his breath this entire time. "I really want you to make this decision for yourself. I know a lease isn't what you were hoping for, but by continuing to own it, you'll have the certainty that no one will develop the land."

What he says makes sense. I like the idea of knowing for certain what the building will be used for, and I can picture the space as a gallery.

"And you're going to manage it?"

Reeve smiles. "Marcus has been trying to convince me to do it for a while. The pay is abysmal. The hours are long, and my dad probably won't speak to me for months, but I need to do it. I owe it to Reeve from the dock."

I take his hand and squeeze it, loving how happy he looks as he tells me his plan. "I'm really glad you're doing this."

He nods, but then his smile slips. "But if you don't want to lease, or if the gallery doesn't feel right, I don't want you to do it. We will find another space if we need to. I don't want you to feel obligated—"

"I don't," I say, cutting him off. "I really like this idea. I mean, I will need to talk it through with Miranda, of course. But it feels right."

I think Kitty would approve.

A smile returns to Reeve's face as he pulls me to my feet and plants a soft kiss on my forehead.

"Are you going to be okay with having a starving artist for a boyfriend?"

I pretend to think about it before sliding my arms around his waist. "You are all I need, Reeve Baldwin."

He leans closer to kiss me again but stops. "There's just one other problem. If this all works out the way I hope it works out, I'm going to be living up here most of the year, but you'll be in Toronto for school. We're going to be long-distance for a while."

I lean over and press my lips to his with nothing but hope in my heart for our future.

"I think we can make it work. We are living in a beautiful age. We have the internet, and, more important, we have sexting."

Epilogue

Two years later

"I ALWAYS THOUGHT I'd be one of those cute pregnant ladies who looked like I had a beach ball shoved up my dress. I should have known better when I married a McCullough."

Zoe rubs her enormous belly, shooting Dale a death glare, to which he responds with a stupidly happy grin. Dale Jr. is about to make an appearance any day now, and I'm grateful my spring break at the U of T first-year medical program has allowed me to be back in West Lake to mark the occasion.

These past two years have been busy. I worked another full year at Sunnyvale, saving my pennies anywhere I could, deferring my acceptance into the U of T medical school until this past September—when I was able to pay my tuition with the additional income from leasing the dance hall to Reeve and Marcus, along with an unanticipated scholarship courtesy of the West Lake Royal Canadian Legion executive committee, headed up by committee chair and favorite barman Donny Buchanan.

Reeve has been living in West Lake since he left his job at Mansfield almost two years ago. He and Marcus have been working slowly but surely to transform the dance hall from its abandoned state into one that pays homage to its beautiful and eclectic past.

Since he had to sell his Bloor Street condo to invest in the gallery, he has been renting my former apartment above the pizza parlor. He now spends his weeknights at the Legion and, after enough teasing from Donny and Zoe, has even taken to wearing flannel button-ups. He looks very good in them—almost as good as he looks in a suit (which he still puts on every weekend he comes to visit me in the city).

I love medical school. I don't know any other first-year who has come out the other side using the L-word, but it's true. My courses are grueling. Some of my peers are so competitive I feel like I'm running a marathon but always three steps behind, with no finish line in sight.

But when I pull myself out of the fog of labs and practicums and all-night study sessions, I can see where I will be in three years, and I know it was the right choice.

"You are going to need to strap these babies to my sausage feet," Zoe says, handing me a pair of silver ballet flats. "I am doing this for you." She stares momentarily at the hot-pink Crocs she's worn exclusively for the last month. "Your man won't forgive me if I show up in those."

"Reeve doesn't care."

Zoe shoots me a glance that says she disagrees. And as much as I think that's the case, Zoe does have a point. Reeve has poured his heart and soul into preparing the gallery for tonight's opening. He's been obsessing over lighting and spacing, and if I hear the word *ambience* one more time, I might have myocardial ischemia.

But I have never seen him happier, either.

I think if you asked him, he'd say the same thing. We don't get to spend nearly enough time together. The three-hour drive is tedious and long. The parking lot of the Tipsy Fox has seen things this last year, and we've made an art out of seven A.M. sexting. But every single day only reinforces what I know in my heart. He is my best friend. He is the person I am meant to be with.

The parking lot of the dance hall—or Meraki, as it's now called—is so full of cars I have to park in my old spot at Sunnyvale. I glimpse Nurse Bouchard giving me a disapproving frown for my trespassing. Still, she doesn't say a word as Zoe, Dale, and I cross the pavement and join a group of Sunnyvale residents waiting in line to get in.

One resident is missing from the pack, and the thought of him still makes my heart ping with grief. Mr. McNaught passed away in March, just shy of his ninety-fifth birthday. March 5 . . . zero-three-zero-five. He fell asleep one night and never woke up, and though neither he nor Kitty has infiltrated my dreams since the spring before last, I still think about them both often.

I wait patiently to be let in, not feeling right about using my girlfriend card to cut in front of a bunch of senior citizens, despite Zoe's loud complaints about her sausage feet.

When I finally do step inside, my breath catches. I have been inside the gallery many times these last few months, the most recent being last night, but there's something about the lighting—or, dare I say it, the ambience—that has transformed the place into something magical.

My eyes slowly dance around the room, gliding over the local art, which I know will be a huge attraction. Until they land on Reeve, who is watching me from across the room.

He opens his arms just before I reach them, and when I crash against his chest, he pulls me into an embrace, as if it hasn't been only hours since we last made love.

"It's incredible," I tell him, my words slightly muffled by the fabric of his navy suit.

"It's everything I hoped it would be." He kisses the top of my head before turning my face upward to press a long, slow kiss to my lips.

"Did your parents decide when they are coming?" I ask.

"My mom should be here tonight with some of her friends, and my dad is hoping to make it out next week," Reeve replies.

His dad was not thrilled with Reeve when he told him about quitting his job. It didn't help that a few weeks later he broke the news that instead of returning to the corporate world he would be running a small-town art gallery. There were a few weeks where Reeve's dad called daily to convince him that he was throwing his future away, then a few more where it was complete silence. But he has slowly come around to the idea, especially with Reeve's mom being so supportive.

As for my mom, since our talk, things have slowly started to get better. She's put herself on a payment plan to pay back the money she owes me. I still roll my eyes when I catch her referring to us as her "doctor daughter and her partner who owns a renowned art gallery." But I also understand her a little better.

A small quartet begins to play up on the stage. It's a tune I can't quite place. As the crowd all turn to the stage, I get the weirdest sense of déjà vu, and for a moment, I swear I see Kitty and Knots in each other's arms, gliding across the dance floor.

"Hey there, lovebirds." Zoe appears beside me, interrupting my thoughts, with a bottle dangling from one of her hands, half-obstructed by her giant belly.

"Are you drinking?"

Zoe holds it up. "We're playing spin the bottle, you in?"

"Zoe."

Her face cracks into a wide smile. "Relax. I'm joking. Besides, the moment this kid is out of me, I'm having a beer, not this crap."

She flips the bottle so I can read the label.

"It arrived a few minutes ago. All the note said is: *There in spirit. Have a drink for me.* I figure it would be rude for you all not to. What do you say?"

Dale steps out from behind her, a sleeve of red Solo cups tucked under his arm.

We pour the Veuve and raise our glasses in a cheers, and I can't help but let my eyes drift skyward, where something tells me there's another party happening.

Touché, Kitty St. Clair. Touché.

Acknowledgments

IF ANYONE IS following along on my author acknowledgments that double as post-book therapy sessions, you'll know that I struggled with my second book (thus fulfilling the ancient prophecy that sophomore books are the absolute worst to write). I wondered if this was just my writing process from now on: write, curse at the universe, question if *This Spells Love* was just some margarita-fueled fluke. I was so happy to be wrong. Writing *Kitty St. Clair's Last Dance* was a joy from start to finish. I loved Jules and Reeve with my entire heart, and I adored seeing Kitty become this character who was nowhere near what I initially imagined but everything she needed to be. Kitty was personal to me, and my wonderful editor, Emma Caruso, understood that from the moment she heard the idea. Her enthusiasm in championing Kitty from the start and persistence (no one loves editing more than Emma) made Kitty come alive in ways I could have never done alone. I am incredibly grateful to be one of her many talented "Kates." *Kitty St. Clair's Last Dance* was also a special book in that I got a two-for-one deal on working with amazing editors and had the pleasure of working with Talia Cieslinski. Talia, I think you are an incredible talent now, so early in your publishing career. I look forward to watching all of the incredible work you will bring into this world.

In a world that seems to want to squash anything different or diverse, I am so proud to be part of an imprint that celebrates underrepresented voices, poetry, empowering women, happily ever afters for all, and cheese plates! I know all that would be impossible without an amazing team that wants nothing more than to put great books into this world. Whitney Frick, they say the greatest leaders build strong teams, and you continue to have the hands-down best team in publishing. From my stunning covers (thank you, Diane Hobbing, Donna Cheng, and Petra Braun) to the thoughtful marketing and publicity plans (Jordan Hill Forney, Vanessa DeJesus, Avideh Bashirrad, and Debbie Aroff—you are marketing and publicity goddesses) to the copy editors of my heart (Laura Dragonette and Cindy Berman, thank you for putting the perfect finishing touches on this baby, and for not judging my deep love of em dashes). I am honored to continue being counted among the incredible authors that Dial represents.

To my agent, Bibi Lewis. You are a true champion in every sense of the word. With each book, I feel like I figure it out a little more (and also realize how much more I have to learn), but what I have learned is how valuable it is to have a trusted partner in your corner. You are publishing gold, Bibi Lewis, and I count myself so lucky to have you.

I am on my second glass of prosecco now, so things are going to get weepy. I started writing because I wanted to find myself again. Becoming a mom was a bit of an identity crisis, and I forgot how to do things for me. I went into this as a solo mission, but I found this incredible community of readers, writers, librarians, and booksellers who have changed my life in a million different beautiful ways. To all of the readers who have blogged, Bookstagrammed, Booktoked, or shared their copy with their bestie.

Thank you! It gives me life to hear your thoughts, sign your books, and sometimes, when I'm lucky, talk books with you in person. To all the incredible authors who have imparted little pearls of publishing wisdom, volunteered to blurb my books, or shared a bottle of wine: this community is amazing because of you. To my people (you know who you are), whether we came together through Toronto Romance Authors, Toronto Area Women's Authors, The Boners, SF2.0, The Mouse Jigglers, or just hanging out in The Bird Booth, I love you with my whole "hjeart." I could not have done this without your highly inappropriate DMs, coordinated outfits, cardboard dance parties, and quickly consumed cocktail talks.

To my wonderful friends and family who are continually relocating my books to the front bookstore tables, you are the best kinds of people and I love you dearly. Mama, I hope you saw a little piece of her in this. Dad, your keenness to understand publishing when I still don't fully understand publishing is the best kind of love. Howie, you are the butter tart queen. Glencoe Fair can blow it out their shorts! Andrew, hearing you repeatedly hype my books on your Zoom calls is true love. My boys, you make me proud every single day.

One last shout-out to Peter Young, author of *Let's Dance! A Celebration of Ontario's Dance Halls and Summer Dance Pavilions*: your research is a true treasure, and I hope I did it justice.

Kitty St. Clair's Last Dance

Kate Robb

Dial Delights

LOVE STORIES FOR THE OPEN-HEARTED

I could write an essay on the culture of the butter tart in small-town Ontario or debate the additions of raisins (acceptable) and walnuts (should never be added under any circumstances). I could tell you a long story about how my sister (baker extraordinaire) and her perfect tarts were disqualified from the Glencoe Fair, causing a small riot and the permanent addition of rule 17: "Tart shells to be circular, not folded." But because I have just written an entire book, I am going to keep it short and sweet and instead encourage you to find your perfect butter tart. If you happen to be in Ontario cottage country, stop by the Luscious Bakery in Sauble Beach or Doo Doo's Bakery in Peterborough, or if it's June, the butter tart festival in Midland or find someone with a nana who has a secret family recipe (always the best). If you have skills in the kitchen, I will leave you with this recipe. It may not have a blue ribbon, but I think it's "chef's kiss."

Bon appétit!

ALY'S WORLD-FAMOUS AWARD-LOSING BUTTER TARTS

Recipe yields 24 servings

PASTRY
- 3 cups sifted all-purpose flour
- ½ teaspoon salt
- 1 ¼ cups shortening
- 1 egg
- 2 teaspoons distilled white vinegar
- 6 tablespoons ice water

Step 1: Combine Dry Ingredients. In a large bowl, whisk together the flour and salt.

Step 2: Cut in Shortening. Using a pastry blender, cut the shortening into the flour mixture until it resembles coarse crumbs, about the size of peas.

Step 3: Add Wet Ingredients. In a separate bowl, whisk together the egg, vinegar, and water. Gradually add the wet ingredients to the dry ingredients, one tablespoon at a time, mixing with a fork until a dough ball forms. You may not need to use all of the liquid.

Step 4: Refrigerate. Create two disks of dough, flatten and wrap in cellophane. Put in fridge overnight.

FILLING

½ cup unsalted butter, softened
1 cup packed brown sugar
½ teaspoon salt
1 ½ teaspoons vinegar
1 ½ teaspoons vanilla
2 eggs
1 ¼ cups corn syrup
⅔ cup raisins

Step 1: Prepare the Filling. Cream together butter, sugar, and salt in a bowl. Add vinegar, vanilla, eggs, and corn syrup. Mix gently. Chill the filling for 30 minutes.

Step 2: Roll Out and Shape. Roll out the dough and cut out four-inch circles of dough. (If your soul tells you to flute those edges, then flute them, baby! Screw rule 17.) Place the dough circles in greased muffin tins. Chill the filled tins for 30 minutes.

Step 3: Assemble and Bake. Preheat your oven to 350°F

(177°C). Stir the chilled filling. Place 1 teaspoon of raisins in each pastry shell. Fill each shell with ¼ cup of filling. Bake for 25–30 minutes.

Step 4: Cool and Serve.

P.S. If I have inspired any sort of pastry-inspired cross-Canada road trip, you should also check out Nanaimo, BC, and their infamous Nanaimo Bar, and St. Donat, Quebec, for their Sugar Pie.

Who Are You, Kitty St. Clair?

THE QUESTION I most commonly get asked is if I base my characters on the real people in my life (particularly by my neighbors who fear I secretly write them into my books). The answer is no. I steal little pieces from people for sure: interesting mannerisms, catchphrases, and a secret fear of owls. However, everyone in my books is fictional, and Kitty St. Clair is no exception.

However, Kitty's origin story is much more based on my real life than any character before her. My grandmother passed away when I was in my twenties. She was the best kind of human: funny and loving but, most important, a character. She'd come to dinner dressed in every piece of jewelry she owned or cook you an entire chicken dinner in the middle of the night. There was photographic evidence that she once was a can-can dancer, although every time we asked about it, we were given vague answers that usually involved a wink.

Although she was blessed with a long life full of adventures and friends, she also had her share of heartache. Toward the end of her life, I found her in her living room with hundreds of pictures splayed out in front of her that went back as far as girlhood. She picked up one of a man and handed it to me. He was maybe sixteen or seventeen and unfamiliar. She told me his name was

Karl, and she had been in love with him, but he was from a poor immigrant family (just as she was from a poor immigrant family), and her parents wanted her to marry "up." She followed their wishes, but she always thought about Karl. That love still held a place in her heart, and I think she always wondered how her life would have been different if she'd ignored her family and followed it.

Fast-forward to a few years later. I am at a party with friends and family, and I find myself sitting next to a woman in her nineties. Her body may have been elderly and frail, but her mind was in that glorious place where she had seen some shit go down in her lifetime and had long ago stopped caring what people thought about her. Within minutes of our meeting, I was given a history of everyone in the room, how she knew them and her opinions on them. When she got to my boyfriend, she spared listing his beige flags and instead asked, "Does he take you dancing?" I answered yes (although it was less foxtrot than she was probably thinking). Either way, it seemed to earn her approval, and she told me her own love story. She married an incredibly wealthy stockbroker when she was very young because everyone told her she would be silly not to—her life would be comfortable and easy. And to some extent, it was. She was widowed and extremely wealthy, but like my grandmother, she regretted her choice. "Listen to an old woman and marry for love," she told me.

Those words stuck with me, and I thought of her often, especially as Kitty began to form in my head. As I was starting to write this book, I came across a Buzzfeed article that asked senior citizens about the one piece of advice they'd give a young person. Of all the women interviewed, almost all of them said something along the lines of "get an education." It made me think of my grandmother and this woman from the party, neither of whom had more than a high school education (as was the norm in their time). Their stars were very much linked to who their fathers were and who they married; they made choices that weren't always for love but instead to give themselves and their future families more than what they had.

So Kitty isn't a reflection of one, but of the many women in my life who have wanted more. The dedication in this book, "For You," is a nod to how my grandmother would label all her Christmas cards. She'd hand them out to each of her grandchildren, and the identical message inside would read, "You are my favorite. Don't tell the others." But I like to think it works on another level, too. This book is for all of the women whose choices have enabled me to grow up with the privilege to set my own path, marry for love, and spend my time writing about happily ever afters.

Keep reading for a sneak peek
of Kate's next book,

A Solar Eclipse of the Heart

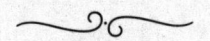

Chapter 1

I CAN HEAR the music pumping from the store's speakers as soon as I round the corner onto Queen Street. It's some obscure song by some obscure band I don't even attempt to pretend I've heard of. The store's front door is propped open by a tiny stone garden gnome painted to loosely resemble Snoop Dogg, allowing the tiny blue-haired woman to wheel out a rack of carefully curated secondhand treasures onto the storefront sidewalk.

I freeze, not entirely sure if I feel up to the inevitable lengthy conversation that is bound to happen should Koko Hayashida, the owner and sole proprietor of Thrift Me Baby (One More Time), look up and spot me.

For a moment I consider ducking into the alcove of the Indian restaurant and waiting until Koko heads back inside, but just as I inch my loafer toward the concrete step, she locks the metal latch of the clothing rack with her foot and looks up.

"Oh, hey, Lise." Koko waves a white crocheted vest in my direction. "Happy Friday."

Within twenty-eight seconds of our first encounter on this exact same spot three months ago, she gave me a nickname, immediately dropping the dowdy "Anna" half of my name for the much cooler and shorter "Lise."

"Hey." I brush my dark, fringed bangs from my forehead and loop my right hand under the strap of my backpack, letting it slip from my shoulder in an effort to look more cool and Lise-like.

"Looks like you've been doing some shopping?" I incline my head and peer into her already crowded vintage shop, wondering where this rack of clothing even fit before she pulled it out onto the sidewalk.

"Yeah. That place over on Dufferin had another pop-up." Koko pulls a bright yellow beaded gown from the rack and holds it up. "I think most of the stuff came from that *Law & Order* spin-off they were filming downtown all last year, but they had some cute dresses." She turns the gown so the light makes the beading shimmer. "Fifteen bucks for this. I couldn't resist." She hooks the hanger back onto the rack.

"Are you just getting home from work?" She glances at the gold vintage Cartier on her left hand. It's another one of her second-hand finds. As per last week's sidewalk conversation, she thrifted the watch for forty dollars from an impromptu garage sale she happened across on her walk to work last month. Even from the upside-down angle, I can see that the time reads almost six.

I nod. "Yes. Long day. Looking forward to being home." I slowly inch my way past her, toward the painted yellow door next to her store that leads up to my second-floor apartment. But as I shift my weight, she claps her hands, startling me and again freezing my deer instincts in place.

"You look like you could use a drink or three," she says. "I'm closing up in an hour or so. What are you up to later? You should come out." She says it more like a statement than a question. "My friend Lucien knows this guy who is bartending at this great new place in Ossington. He says the cocktails are a little gaudy, but that's kind of the norm these days."

I smile like I know what that means. "That sounds really great;

I'm just not much of a drinker." Or a stay out past nine-thirty-er or a socialize with strangers unless I absolutely have to-er.

She continues to smile at me.

"And I actually have a thing tonight."

In my awkward haste, I'd almost forgotten I actually do have somewhere to be this evening. "It's a dinner at that big Polish church over on Roncey," I explain. "They awarded me this scholarship for my PhD. It's not all that much—just two grand—but they're having this awards ceremony tonight for all the recipients. You know, stand on stage, get a big cardboard check kinda thing. But they are giving me money, so I should be there. Thank you for the offer, though."

Koko looks surprisingly disappointed, and that puzzles me. We've only known each other for three months or so. Since she opened her thrift store below my apartment, replacing the dry cleaner, who I highly suspect was using the place as a front for money laundering, seeing as he only seemed to be open on Tuesdays and every other Sunday. But since the first time we met, I've gotten the impression that she wants to be friends, which I find very weird.

Humans, as a species, typically prefer forming close bonds with similar people. It's a biological instinct driven by our mammalian brains. Our personal safety is dependent on flocking with herds that are as akin to us as possible, and I cannot imagine anyone describing Koko and me as birds of the same feather.

Koko likes dive bars and concerts with blaring music and indie bands I've never heard of. She's effortlessly cool in her two-sizes-too-big carpenter pants and a tiny cropped top that looks like it once lived a double life as an elderly man's necktie. She has glossy blue hair. I have practical penny loafers and the same button-down blouse bought in three colors because it fits my short torso and disproportionately long arms.

We simply don't match.

Putting all that aside, there's also the fact that I have less than three months until I'm heading off across the pond to Liverpool to pursue my PhD degree in neuroscience. It doesn't seem like the best use of our time to invest in a relationship that will eventually dwindle to an obligatory sporadic text message every few months.

And yet here we are.

"What are you wearing?" Koko's question catches me so off guard that I stare down at my blouse, wondering if I accidentally said that last part out loud.

I pull at the hem. "It's one hundred percent cotton. The store had a BOGO."

Koko laughs. "No, not right now. I meant tonight. It sounds like it's a big deal. Do you have something special that you are planning to wear?"

Again, my eyes fall to my sweater, preferring the previous question to this one. "Uh . . . I don't know. Maybe like black slacks and a shirt?" My voice inflects upward as if I'm asking her the question.

She shakes her head in a way that I immediately know I've said the wrong thing. It's confirmed as she grabs my wrist and tugs me inside the store with a roll of her eyes and a "Come on."

As soon as I'm inside, Koko begins pulling clothes from three different racks, all within arm's reach.

"I have a few ideas," she says, tossing me a brightly patterned dress. "Those stuffy church halls get hot this time of year. Everyone's turned their air off. You'll want something that breathes and a jacket for when it gets cold later."

She's right about both things. I find a room full of people stifling on a good day, let alone the mid-September heat waves we seem to be having. But there is a nice breeze once the sun goes down. It blows right off Lake Ontario, keeping the south end of Toronto a few degrees cooler than the north and thus making a commuting jacket a necessity.

Koko drops another dress into my hands along with a tube of fabric I'm not entirely certain is a skirt or a top. "Pop these on." She nods toward a tiny dressing room separated from the rest of the store by a pink velvet curtain.

I obey, slipping inside and pulling the curtain closed behind me. I take a second to breathe before I slip out of my blouse and jeans. The dress slides on easily, but there is no mirror inside, so I am forced to pull back the curtain and step back into the store and Koko's assessing gaze.

"Cute," she says, addressing the dress and not my socked feet, which I've only now realized are two black trousers socks that are noticeably different lengths.

"But maybe try the blue one next." She shoos me back behind the curtain. "It will bring out those beautiful ocean eyes."

I do as she says, grateful that, unlike the fabric tube, the blue one is a scooped-neck sundress with puff sleeves, tiny buttons, and, more important, a zipper, which makes it very clear to tell the back from the front.

When I step out again, I can immediately see from the lift of Koko's eyebrows that she approves.

"What do you think?" She turns me toward the three-way mirror and watches me appraise my reflection. The dress's cinched waist gives the illusion of curves where they otherwise don't exist, and the periwinkle does seem to bring the blue out in my eyes. I lift my arm to glance at the price tag. It's eighty dollars. I wince, knowing I would think twice about buying a dress like this new, let alone used.

"It's vintage," Koko says as if reading my thoughts. "And it's my treat." She turns my shoulders and steers me back toward the dressing room. "It's my way of saying thank you for not calling the cops last weekend. We went way later than I said we would."

I am fairly certain she's referring to the party she held last Saturday in the store. It was her friend Ramone's birthday. The music thumped up through my floorboards until after three. My only other neighbor was away at a yoga retreat, so I put in my earplugs, knowing it was fully in my right to complain but lacking the heart to do it, especially since Koko had once again invited me.

"That's really nice of you to offer, but I totally don't mind paying," I tell her, pulling the velvet curtain closed behind me.

"No, no," she calls from what sounds like the opposite side of the store. "That dress was meant for you. I insist."

There is a zip then a ding from what I'm certain is the cash register opening and closing. It's followed by footsteps and the high-pitched squeak of metal rubbing on metal, as if she's sifting through one of her clothing racks. The bell above the door tinkles as if it's been opened. I hear Koko say, "Okay, thanks," presumably to the person who walked in. The bell chimes again and the store grows quiet until Koko asks, "Any plans for the weekend?"

I freeze, unsure if the person actually left or this question is directed at me. After a long pause, I feel certain I'm the other half of this conversation and mortified it took me so long to answer.

"Um, yeah . . . I guess. My new roommate moves in tomorrow. Her bus gets in sometime in the morning, so I need to stick around to give her a key."

"New roommate. That's kind of exciting. What's her deal?" Koko's voice is noticeably louder than a moment ago, placing her on the other side of the curtain.

I shrug, even though she can't actually see me. "I don't know too much about her other than her name is Mackensie Smith and she's a musician from some small town up north. I guess she got a job down here. She plays the tuba, so maybe the Toronto Symphony? We've only really emailed, but she seems quiet. And nice."

"I'm sure she is." Koko's arm juts through the crack of the dressing room. "Here, try this on too."

A wooden hanger dangles from her fingertips. On it is a black leather biker jacket, cracked but soft, as if made from quality leather but aged with years of use.

"What size is this?" I take the hanger from her hands. The jacket looks like it would fit a large man.

"It's meant to be big," Koko says, her voice getting farther away with each word. "Oversized is in right now."

I know the moment I slip it off the hanger, the jacket will be a hard no. It's too big. Too edgy. Too far from the nerdy wannabe neuroscientist who actually enjoys the shapeless institutional cut of her lab coat. Still, I zip up the dress I was only a moment ago taking off and slide the jacket on. I've opened my mouth to tell Koko thanks for the offer but I don't think it's going to work, when the world around me suddenly goes dark.

KATE ROBB is the author of *This Spells Love* and *Prime Time Romance*. She dated a lot of duds in her twenties (among a few gems), all of whom provided excellent fodder to write weird and wild romantic comedies. She lives just outside Toronto, Canada, where she spends her free time pretending she's not a hockey mom while whispering "Hustle" under her breath from the stands, a Pinot Grigio concealed in her YETI mug. She hates owls, the word *whilst*, and wearing shorts, and she aspires to one day be able to wear four-inch heels again.

katerobbwrites.com

About the Type

This book was set in Baskerville, a typeface designed by John Baskerville (1706–75), an amateur printer and typefounder, and cut for him by John Handy in 1750. The type became popular again when the Lanston Monotype Corporation of London revived the classic roman face in 1923. The Mergenthaler Linotype Company in England and the United States cut a version of Baskerville in 1931, making it one of the most widely used typefaces today.

DIAL DELIGHTS

Love Stories for the Open-Hearted

Discover more joyful romances that celebrate all kinds of happily-ever-afters:

dialdelights.com

@THEDIALPRESS

@THEDIALPRESS

Penguin Random House collects and processes your personal information. See our Notice at Collection and Privacy Policy at prh.com/notice.